Honorable Lies

The Honor Series
By Robert N. Macomber

At the Edge of Honor
Point of Honor
Honorable Mention
A Dishonorable Few
An Affair of Honor
A Different Kind of Honor
The Honored Dead
The Darkest Shade of Honor
Honor Bound

Honorable Lies

Commander Peter Wake,
Office of Naval Intelligence, United States Navy,
and
His Five Perilous Days Inside Spanish Cuba
1888

Tenth Novel in the Honor Series

Robert N. Macomber

Pineapple Press, Inc.
Sarasota, Florida

Inquiries should be addressed to:

Pineapple Press, Inc.
P.O. Box 3889
Sarasota, Florida 34230

www.pineapplepress.com

Library of Congress Cataloging-in-Publication Data

Macomber, Robert N., 1953–
  Honorable lies : Commander Peter Wake, Office of Naval Intelligence, United States Navy, and his five perilous days inside Spanish Cuba 1888 / Robert N. Macomber.
     p. cm.
  ISBN 978-1-56164-802-3
  1. Wake, Peter (Fictitious character)--Fiction. 2. United States. Navy--Officers--Fiction. 3. Cuba--Fiction. I. Title.
  PS3613.A28H657 2012
  813'.6--dc23
                        2012014579

Design by Shé Hicks

This novel is respectfully dedicated to two of Cuba's most
legendary sons:

José Martí

and

Antonio Maceo

One was a white poet;
the other, a black warrior.
Together,
they were the soul of Cuba.

I believe some background on the fictional hero of the Honor Series, Peter Wake, might be helpful for both new and longtime readers. Wake was born just east of Mattapoisett, Massachusetts, on 26 June, 1839, to a family in the coastal schooner trade, and he went to sea full-time at age sixteen. He volunteered for the U.S. Navy in 1863, at the height of the Civil War, and his career lasted until 1908. He married Linda Donahue at Key West in 1864; the couple's daughter, Useppa, was born at Useppa Island, Florida, in 1865; son Sean, at Pensacola in 1867.

After serving as a deck officer for sixteen years, Wake began his intelligence work while observing the War of the Pacific on South America's west coast from 1879 to 1881. He then joined the newly formed Office of Naval Intelligence (ONI) in 1882. As one of the few officers who was not a graduate of the U.S. Naval Academy, his career path was without major ship commands, and he remained in ONI for the next twenty-six years. Most of his efforts were for the clandestine Special Assignments Section (SAS), which worked directly for the Chief of the Bureau of Navigation (parent command of ONI) until 1889, and subsequently for the Assistant Secretary of the Navy himself. There has never been any record of the SAS's existence.

The first six novels in the Honor Series were told in the third person, but in the 2009 novel, *The Honored Dead*, a fascinating discovery was described: Wake's collection of memoirs were purportedly found in the spring of 2007 inside a 124-year-old, ornately engraved, Imperial Vietnamese trunk, hidden away in the attic of a bungalow on Peacon Lane in Key West. It was owned by Agnes Whitehead, who had recently died at age ninety-seven. There has been much speculation among Honor Series fans about Agnes Whitehead, her relationship to the Wake family, and how she came to possess that special trunk. With each novel after *The Honored Dead*, another facet of that puzzle is revealed.

The individual accounts in the trunk (more than a dozen were found) were typed by Wake himself in the 1890s and early 1900s, usually a few years after the events within occurred. Each contained an explanatory letter to his son (who became a naval officer) or daughter. Wake did all this because he wanted his children and their descendants to understand what he endured and accomplished in his career, since the official records of most of it were sequestered in the ONI vault in the State, War, and Navy Building, now known as the Eisenhower Executive Office Building. A note in the trunk requested that none of the material be made public by the family until fifty years after the death of his children. Sean died in 1942; Useppa, in 1947.

Sean Rork, an Irish-born boatswain in the U.S. Navy and best friend of Wake, served with him in the naval service until 1908 and shared ownership of Patricio Island, on the lower gulf coast of Florida. He was eight years older than Peter, and Sean Wake was his namesake.

This volume of Wake's memoirs was written in 1896, eight years after the events in the account. It must be explained here that Wake was a product of his times, and his descriptions of people and events may not be considered "politically correct" in a modern context. He was, however, also remarkably tolerant and culturally astute, and his political observations were usually proven accurate. Much of his rather arcane academic knowledge was gained through an international network of intriguing individuals met during his assignments, with whom he kept a lasting correspondence. Few military men of the period had as diverse a selection of intelligence sources as Peter Wake.

I have corrected only the most egregious mistakes in Wake's grammar and have kept his spellings of foreign words, though they may be debated by twenty-first-century scholars.

An important note about this novel: After finishing a chapter, I strongly suggest that readers peruse that chapter's endnotes at the back of the book, where they will find interesting background details I've discovered while researching this project. My goal is to educate as well as entertain.

Thus, with the Honor Series, we have the unique opportunity to see inside the events, places, and personalities of a critical period of American and world history, through the eyes of a man who was there and secretly helped make much of it happen.

Onward and upward…
Robert N. Macomber
Twin Palm Cottage
Matlacha Island
Florida

1

A Matter of Naval Honor

Palace of His Excellency
Don Sabas Marin y Gonzalez
The Captain-General of Cuba
Plaza de Armas, Havana
Tuesday, 25 September 1888

The man was there to kill me.

I knew it the instant he turned those smoldering black eyes toward me. Two minutes later, when his name was announced, I saw the resemblance and understood exactly why he was going to kill me. Two years earlier, I'd faced another enemy with those same eyes.

Then, seeing the satisfied sneer on the face of another man at the back of the crowd, I realized how my "accidental" death had been orchestrated.

It was the perfect trap.

None of this was in my hastily conceived plan, of course. The affair was supposed to be a "friendly" fencing competition between professional naval officers of equal age and rank, representing their respective navies.

Following my request, on the preceding afternoon, Rear Admiral Stephen B. Luce, commander of the North Atlantic Squadron, had planted the idea of an internaval competition with his Spanish counterpart, the senior admiral of the Spanish West Indies. Steering the conversation toward the difference between American and European fencing, he artfully managed to get the Spaniard to challenge the U.S. Navy to a match.

Luce then dutifully accepted, as if it was entirely the Spanish admiral's idea in the first place, and volunteered me on the spot as the American participant. In similar fashion, a middle-aged officer from the staff of the naval arsenal in Havana was volunteered by his admiral to be my competitor. It would be a ritualized demonstration of archaic martial skills performed in front of an appreciative audience: the gathered social elite of Havana and the senior Spanish and American naval officers in the West Indies.

The thing would be over in fifteen minutes. No matter which of us won more fencing points, national honor would be preserved and perhaps even a little international camaraderie could be gained. God knows we needed something to calm the tension that had been building in Havana, Madrid, and Washington in recent years.

The important thing was that no matter who won, there would be, *de rigueur*, several days' worth of social events afterward to celebrate the occasion, as the culture of Spanish hospitality demands. Those legitimate entrées into Havana would allow me— *persona non grata* with Spanish counterintelligence—enough time to accomplish my mission while staying ashore at Hotel Inglaterra.

Their intelligence could try to watch me, but they dared not do much else, since I was there quite overtly representing my country, as the honored guest of their country's navy.

This was much better, and far more comfortable, than the original plan hatched in Washington: surreptitiously make my way ashore in a small boat through the harbor, accomplish my mission, and flee quietly back to the ship with several fugitives. This way, I would be the personal guest of the senior Spanish leadership and therefore have greater protection and freedom, not to mention some very decent food and drink.

But now that strategy, *ad hoc* though it was, had been superseded by the very enemy I sought to avoid, an enemy who had grasped my intentions from the outset and introduced an element designed to end one of their thornier problems—me. My options were limited: Violate the fencing conventions and fight for my life at the outset, killing the man before me, or hope I was wrong and follow the rules, to be killed myself in what would be ruled a random twist of fate in the sport of gentlemen. I fleetingly wondered how many in the Spanish leadership outside of Spanish counterintelligence knew of the trap set for me. Probably few, if any, I decided. If the plan to *intentionally* kill a U.S. naval officer ever got out to the American press, there would be war within days.

Or was that part of their scheme? One never knew for sure with foreign secret services, especially the Spanish. Machiavelli had nothing on them.

Whatever the extent of the conspiracy to kill me, I was certain that, after the fact, the Spanish would arrange a magnificent display of military respects for my casket as it was rowed out to the ship, right after they expressed their profound condolences to my admiral. The officer who killed me, ostensibly through an accidental sword thrust, probably through my throat, would be called away on a distant assignment, probably to a colony on the other side of the globe, in Africa or the Philippines. He would regrettably be unable to appear before an American inquiry. My demise would not be a stain on his career, merely an official embarrassment. After all, it wasn't as if it was a *murder*, right?

I was trying to come up with a suitable counter to all this when I suddenly realized that everyone was looking at me.

"Commander Peter Wake, of the United States Navy, if you are ready to begin the formalities of the combat, we will commence in five minutes' time. Your opponent is ready. Are you ready, sir?" inquired a Spanish naval lieutenant in fluent British English, complete even to his condescending tone.

The fellow had the gold, braided shoulder loop of a staff officer and was serving as the official translator. I could tell by his pale, unlined face that he'd never spent any time at sea, and his smug scorn told me he didn't think much of my chances in the upcoming contest.

"Yes, Lieutenant. I am ready," I replied, glancing at Admiral Luce. Beside him stood none other than the exulted Captain-General of Cuba, Don Sabas Marin y Gonzalez, personal representative of the king of Spain. Luce looked apprehensive. Don Sabas looked faintly amused.

We were in the central courtyard of the captain-general's palace, a centuries-old citadel in the heart of the ancient quarter of Havana. Around us were dozens of finely dressed ladies and gentlemen, the social elite of the city, not a single one of whom considered himself or herself Cuban. They were Spaniards—or *peninsulares* in the local jargon—protectors of the ancient global empire of Castile and Leon, and damned proud of it. Invited by their friend the captain-general to watch the event that morning, they'd already shared a sumptuous breakfast in his private apartments. For my part, I'd endured some sort of egg and pork souse aboard the ship. That may have been a mistake, for it was now congealed into a disagreeable lump that seemed to be getting larger by the second.

The staff lieutenant acknowledged my reply with a curt nod.

He then paused long enough to make sure he had everyone's attention and proclaimed melodramatically, first to the crowd in Spanish, afterward to me in English: "Then you may take this time to compose yourself, Commander, as we bring out the weapons, a pair of beautifully matched foils—personally provided by His Excellency, Don Sabas Marin y Gonzalez, Captain-General of His Majesty's Most Faithful Isle of Cuba and personal representative of His Majesty Alfonso León Fernando Maria Jaime Isidro Pascual Antonio de Borbón y Austria-Lorena, King of Spain and all her dominions across the Ocean Seas."

Predictably, a huge cheer went up from the assembly, eagerly awaiting the chance to see the Yankee ruffians get a shellacking from the home team in the fine art of sword fighting. Fencing was the art of gentlemen, and, as every true son of Spain knew, *norteamericanos* were mere barbarians without an iota of gentility among the lot of them. Gonzalez bowed in appreciation for the mass adulation and raised an imperial hand to wave at his minions.

And what of the king who was named in such flamboyant fashion? Alfonso was a two-year-old toddler. The real royal power was his Austrian-born mother, Queen Maria Christiana, widow of the king's father and regent over the king until he turned twenty-one. It all was a ridiculous indication of the true state of the Spanish empire.

I glanced over at Boatswain Sean Rork, my petty officer assistant, who stood behind the American naval officers. His face was grim—he'd seen the look in my opponent's eyes too.

Standing the regulation four yards away from me, my newly arrived adversary continued glowering in my direction, muttering something under his breath about *sangre*—blood. He wasn't the man I'd been told the evening before would be my opponent. It seemed that fellow had mysteriously contracted a sudden illness at the last moment and couldn't attend the match. Not to worry, the staff lieutenant had informed me fifteen minutes before, for another officer had been found as a replacement. I remembered the staff lieutenant smiling as he said that.

The substitute fencer, a lieutenant commander, was junior to me in rank and age and possessed an intimidating physique. I bowed politely to him. His expression changed, the eyes losing the hatred, becoming animal-like and devoid of emotion. He was evaluating me…noting my weaknesses…savoring what was coming.

It was at that moment that the reason behind the trap was revealed to me. The staff lieutenant gestured to us and spoke softly so only we could hear. "Commander Wake, please meet your opponent, Lieutenant Commander Julio Cesar Boreau y Morales."

Boreau?

Could it be? There weren't many in Havana with the name of that family, French planter refugees from the Haitian slave revolt who'd settled in Oriente, the province in the eastern end of Cuba, in 1803.

Yes, it must be. I'd heard that the Boreau I had the misfortune to know had a son in the navy. And there was no mistaking the eerie similarity of those close-set, coal-black eyes and the thin-lipped mouth, which showed that same curl of disgust on its left side. It was true. Lieutenant Commander Julio Cesar Boreau was the son of the Spanish agent sent to assassinate me and my family in Florida in 1886—the man I strangled to death six months later in New York harbor.

Lieutenant Commander Boreau proceeded to exhibit his prowess with a foil, slicing it through the air in various patterns with lightning-quick speed, the whole time gauging my reaction. It was obvious he was good, very good, with a foil, the lightest of fencing weapons. Nevertheless, observing him, something registered in my mind. His movements were classical but flamboyant—not the stuff of one who has actually used a blade to kill an armed man.

That gave me an idea.

The staff lieutenant was positively beaming now, taking

pleasure in his own performance as he strutted back and forth before his superiors like an actor on a stage. I could see him mentally planning his promotion party.

Raising my hand to get the little weasel's attention, I quietly said, "By the way, Lieutenant, as the party who was initially challenged by the Spanish navy, is it not my right to choose which *type* of weapon we will use in the combat?"

The reader of this account will think me a bit disingenuous with that comment, but technically, I was correct. The Spanish admiral *had* challenged us—after Admiral Luce skillfully germinated the idea.

My query literally took the wind right out of the staff lieutenant. Poor lad's chest deflated. My question wasn't in the script for his big show. "Ah...Commander...," he stammered, "the agreement between the admirals of our respective navies was to engage in a demonstration of combat by fencing." He shrugged his shoulders slightly. "So, obviously, it must be with foils. They are the fencing tools of gentlemen."

Boreau scowled. He didn't exactly understand my words in English, but he got the idea something was afoot. Something devious. *Yanquis* were infamous for that.

It was now my turn to be condescending, so I smiled and said with not-so-sincere sympathy to the nonplussed translator, "No, my dear Lieutenant, I regret to say that you are mistaken. In the world of fencing, there are *three* weapons of choice: the foil; the rapier, or épée, as it is sometimes known; and the saber. The foil and rapier are excellent for training and demonstrating the art of fencing for sport among *civilians*. But we are not civilians, are we?"

He looked confused. I continued.

"The saber, however, is the weapon of *warriors*. It is closely related to the naval cutlass. And since my opponent and I are both professional naval warriors, I therefore state that it is a matter of naval honor to conduct this combat with sabers."

Then, ignoring the lieutenant, I executed a perfect parade-ground right-face and addressed His Excellency, Don Sabas, myself. "*Tu Excelencia...Debo que insistir en usar los sables para la demonstración del combate entres guerreros navales, en la tradición más alta del honor de nuestra profesión.*"

Including the words *warrior* and *honor* in my demand hit the figurative target dead center. The Spanish aren't the only ones who can turn a flowery phrase. A gasp rose from the crowd when they heard my demand, spoken in their own lingo. I don't pretend to be completely articulate in the language, but the expressions on their faces proved I got my gist across. Especially to the military men, who knew that the saber is heavier and more difficult to use, potentially more dangerous, and far more demonstrative of *machismo*. And, alas, I fear they got no joy at hearing honor being invoked by a lowly, uncultured *norteamericano*.

The lieutenant went a bit wide-eyed at all this and passed along my entire earlier statement in Spanish to his admiral also. That worthy and the captain-general had a quick conference, after which they publicly pronounced their decision to the audience. Another unfriendly buzz rose from the crowd. I caught enough Spanish from one grandee to know he was opining to his mates that the perfidious Anglo used a minor procedural point in order to delay the inevitable—probably out of abject fear.

The lieutenant then explained in English the captain-general's official reply to my request: "It will be our pleasure to provide a matched pair of sabers, Commander Wake, from my personal collection. Unfortunately, this request necessitates a slight delay in order to procure the weapons, and we beg your indulgence. Perhaps ten minutes, sir."

I bowed to the captain-general and said to the translator, "Lieutenant, please present my greatest respects and profound appreciation to His Excellency, for his gallant approval of my simple appeal. Now we will have a true test of combat skills between naval men."

After shooting me a questioning glance, Admiral Luce smiled

in gratitude to the Spanish admiral and captain-general. Rork had lost his smile, however. He was the only American present who knew about Boreau's father and had been right beside me in Havana, Florida, and New York back in '86.

His face tightened and he shifted his eyes from me to the far corner of the courtyard, behind the well-dressed throng. Following his gaze, I scanned the faces and stopped, understanding immediately. Standing slightly apart from the others was a man I knew, the commanding officer of my opponent's father, Colonel Isidro Marrón, head of the Spanish counterintelligence service in Cuba, a shadowy unit loosely affiliated with the well-known Military Corps of Public Order, or Orden Publico, which had detachments everywhere.

Marrón's outfit concentrated on island-based Cuban patriots fighting for independence, their off-island colleagues, and their American supporters in the United States. It was notorious for its efficiency and cruelty, a reflection of the commander's personality. I could testify to both those traits. It was Marrón who had captured Rork and me. It was Marrón who had conducted the subsequent interrogation in the Audiencia dungeon. After we escaped, it was Marrón who had sent Agent Boreau to kill me. Our eyes met. A faint smile washed across Marrón's hawk-nosed face.

Rork coughed loudly, getting my attention. Then he briefly held up his left hand. Actually, Rork has no left hand anymore. The arm ends in a stump below his elbow, the result of a sniper five years earlier in French Indochina. It'd nearly been his death, for gangrene had set in. Fortunately, surgeons from the French navy saved his life.

What people see now is in reality a finely detailed India-rubber forearm and hand, complete with wrinkles and fingernails carved in. Its fingers somewhat opened, the hand is in the shape of a slightly opened fist and can grip a bottle of rum, an oar, or a belaying pin. One must be very close, indeed, to spot its counterfeit nature. Rork gets its realistic flesh tones repainted once a year by a longtime lady friend who plies her evening trade near the Washington Navy Yard. Rork says she does it *gratis*, as her patriotic effort for the navy.

More important than the aforementioned capabilities, the rubber hand part can be removed in a split-second to expose a very wicked-looking, five-inch-long marlinespike. This is securely anchored to a prosthetic appliance underneath, making it an extension of his still-strong upper left arm. Rork's spike is extremely useful in our field of work: concealed, lethal, and quiet. And during dialogues with the lower sorts of humanity, it's an excellent motivator for cooperation. My friend is inordinately proud of it.

His upheld left hand suddenly dropped—a long-standing signal between us. It meant I was to hold nothing back. This wasn't a friendly match anymore.

His Excellency, Don Sabas, was true to his word, and ten minutes later a breathless servant arrived at a run down the five flights of marble steps from the captain-general's second-floor personal apartments, carrying a long leather case. Glistening inside were two steel sabers, polished to mirror brightness and beautifully engraved, elegant tools of death, which Don Sabas then personally presented to each of us.

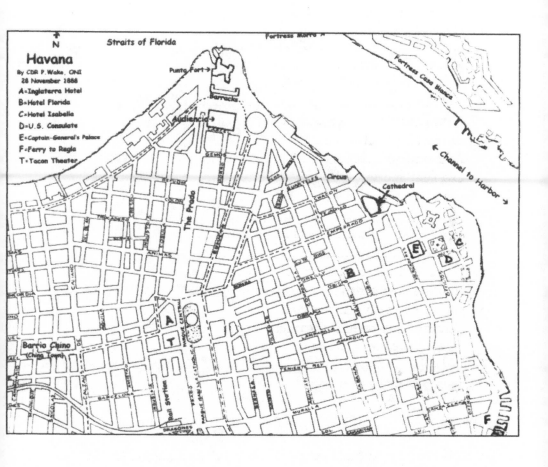

N

Straits of Florida

Havana
By CDR P. Wake, ONI
28 November 1888
A=Inglaterra Hotel
B=Hotel Florida
C=Hotel Isabella
D=U.S. Consulate
E=Captain-General's Palace
F=Ferry to Regla
T=Tacon Theater

Fortress Morro

Punta Fort

Barracks

Audiencia

Fortress Casa Blanca

Channel to Harbor

The Prado

Circus

Cathedral

Barrio Chino
(China Town)

Rail Station

2

Anticipation

Palace of His Excellency
Don Sabas Marin y Gonzalez
Captain-General of Cuba
Plaza de Armas, Havana
10 a.m., Tuesday
25 September 1888

The palace of the Captain-General of Cuba is more than three hundred years old and commands the Plaza de Armas, the government square close by the entrance channel to Havana Bay. Around this plaza stand equally ancient edifices, most of which are occupied in the civil and military administration of the island. The porous coral stone of the palace, faded to a dirty tan or gray, makes it look even older, reminding me of Roman antiquities— moldy, crumbling, evoking past glories and better days long gone by.

The palace is magnificently colonnaded with massive stone pillars across its entire front. Behind the pillars is a high portico, where visitors disembark from vehicles before a small entryway in the center of the palace's eastern wall. That very morning, a line of fancy lacquered and gilded carriages took the American naval officers from the boat landing to the portico, where we disembarked and were greeted by a great falderal of trumpets, drums, stamped feet, and shouted commands.

The Spanish are the very best in the world at presenting a gracious welcome. In this case, it was accomplished by a platoon of Spanish soldiers on guard duty. Fabulously attired in sixteenth-century uniforms of red and gold blouses and pantaloons, with shining brass breastplates and peaked helmets, they stood like statues in the sweltering, humid air. In addition to their tropically inappropriate uniforms, the soldiers carried heavy broadswords and pikes, the weapons apparently as old as the building. Their formation and drill in our honor were impeccable.

The interior of the building is typical of Spanish palaces—a magnificent courtyard, or garden patio, with elaborately decorated balconies overlooking it from two floors. The center of the garden featured a gleaming white, alabaster statue of Christopher Columbus, backed by graceful palms and a panorama of meticulously tended tropical flowers in every color imaginable. Fountains provided the cooling sound of falling water as peacocks and blue herons strolled among the garden, like beautiful moving pieces of art. Frangipani and jasmine scented the motionless, damp air, and from somewhere on the upper floor came the faint echoes of a gentle guitar melody. I recognized it as classical Andalusian, the Moorish laments coming through clearly.

The whole thing was a fairy-tale scene of graceful, imperial beauty. "A forlorn fantasy of benign feudalism on a global scale, and an obscene justification for slavery," as one Cuban, dark-skinned friend explained his Spanish overlords' attitude to me. "After all, they needed slaves to build their pretty palaces."

I must admit, the Spanish had certainly done it up right that morning. The demonstration of martial skills was to be carried out on a regulation fencing *piste*, the French word meaning "path." The *piste* delineates a seven-meter-long-by-one-meter-wide rectangular strip, within which adversaries must remain. The opponents initially face each other from two meters on either side of the center line, which runs athwart the *piste*.

If a man retreats along his half of the *piste* as far back as the one-meter-long warning box near the end, it constitutes a serious setback. If he retreats through the warning box to the final one meter at the end of the *piste*, it is a sign of cowardice. The entire *piste* that morning was constructed of wide planks of heavy mahogany, elevated by its thickness to perhaps three inches above the stone floor of the patio.

There were three members of the jury, or judges, to administer the match. Two members of the jury took their places close around the *piste*, beside and slightly behind their fencer, in order to see the results of the attacks and defenses. The president of the jury took his position in front of the center of the *piste*. His subordinates would report their observations to him. His decision on whether a point should be awarded would be final.

The staff lieutenant indicated that my foe and I should take our positions. Both of us wore black jackets padded with several layers of tightly woven, heavy material. The right sleeve was padded out to the wrist. A thick, white gauntlet glove protected the right hand. The left arm and hand, usually held behind the fencer, were unprotected. Under the jacket, I wore standard-issue working-dress trousers and a shirt. A leather helmet with meshed metal mask was held under my left armpit, the saber in my right hand, pointing downward.

We stood there, facing each other, but had yet to be formally introduced to the audience. The lieutenant now took care of that detail, doing so first in Spanish. Then he repeated it in English.

"Your Excellency, Don Sabas Marin y Gonzalez, Captain-General of His Majesty's Most Faithful Isle of Cuba. Your Excellencies, the distinguished Admiral of the West Indies, the Lieutenant-General of all Armies of the Spanish Americas, your Eminence the Archbishop of our Most Catholic Church of Cuba, the Rear Admiral of the North Atlantic Squadron of the U.S. Navy, and our other distinguished guests, fellow officers, and visitors from the United States. I have the distinct honor to introduce our combatants this morning."

His hand swept around toward me. "Representing the navy of the United States, we have Commander Peter Wake, a veteran of twenty-five years of service, and recipient of the Legion of Honor of France, the Lion of the Atlas of Morocco, the Order of the Sun of Peru, and the Royal Order of Cambodia. Commander Wake is a staff officer, currently assigned as the officer in charge of procedural protocol for the admiral aboard the warship *Richmond*, flagship of the North Atlantic Squadron."

Polite applause fluttered.

"And now, representing the honor of the magnificent navy of His Most Catholic Majesty, Alfonso León Fernando Maria Jaime Isidro Pascual Antonio de Borbón y Austria-Lorena, King of Spain and all her dominions across the Ocean Seas, we have Lieutenant Commander Julio Cesar Boreau y Morales, a veteran of fourteen years of service to His Majesty, and the recipient of the Cross of the Order of Military Merit, Second Class. Lieutenant Commander Boreau is currently assigned to the cruiser *Reina Regente*, the newest of our mighty fleet, as the senior gunnery officer, a position of great martial ardor and responsibility. He also has the considerable merit of being the eighteen-eighty-seven foil fencing champion for both the Mediterranean Squadron and the West Indies Squadron!"

Cheers and thunderous applause reverberated in the patio. Surrounded by faces distinctly unsympathetic toward me, I was beginning to understand what the animal feels at a bullfight or what Christians felt at the Roman Coliseum. I caught sight of Marrón, standing there, arms folded, calmly taking it all in from his perch on the corner staircase. His revenge seemed about to be realized.

At this juncture in the narrative, I would think the reader has grown suspicious of the true nature of my work and exactly why I came to be aboard *Richmond* in Havana in September of 1888. Well, nothing is ever as it first appears in Havana.

Not even me.

3

Naval Intelligence

In the past at
Cuba, Florida, New York City
1886 and 1888

As was announced to the onlookers in the palace, I had twenty-five years of naval service by 1888, but they weren't all aboard ships or at shore stations, or even in uniform. For the previous seven years, I'd worked in a field far different than that usually associated with the navy. I was an operative in the Special Assignments Section of the Office of Naval Intelligence.

Since 1882, the Office of Naval Intelligence has been the sole organization in the United States government charged with discovering the political, military, naval, and industrial capabilities of other countries. We use naval attachés, squadron intelligence officers, and special operatives to gather, analyze, and disseminate this information. When American presidents (few of whom speak a foreign language, have traveled abroad, or possess a detailed understanding of other cultures) need to know what is transpiring in various parts of the world, they call on our expertise, so they may make better-informed decisions. Well, that is our hope, anyway.

My area of operations is the Caribbean, more specifically, the turbulent island of Cuba. I am expected to be familiar with the facts, flavor, and nuances of the Spanish government's domination of Cuba through its military and civil organs, as well as Spanish military and naval capabilities against the United States. I am also expected to be well versed in the personalities and activities of the Cuban revolutionaries who have been fighting for independence since 1868. I keep my professional assessments objective, but my personal sentiments are well known to be pro-Cuban. I have no doubt the Cuban patriots will prevail, and I count several in the independence movement as personal friends.

Back in 1886, I was sent to Havana to follow through on a secret message that had been delivered to a young New York politician named Roosevelt, presumably from a revolutionary group. The message warned of great bloodshed about to be unleashed in Cuba and of a Spanish spy in the American government, possibly at Key West, a place already well known as a nest of Cuban revolutionary intrigue. The message called for a clandestine meeting in Havana with Roosevelt. My impression was that the meeting would seek formal recognition of the Cuban rebels by the United States, in the hope that it would hasten the fall of the Spanish and avert the impending slaughter.

My assignment was to attend the meeting in lieu of Roosevelt, to determine the validity of the threat of massive violence and the extent of Cuban revolutionary activity between Havana and Key West, and to try to uncover the Spanish spy in Key West. But things quickly unraveled. The message was from the Cubans, but Marrón had intercepted and deciphered it, then sent it on. When the trap was sprung, he got me and Rork instead of Roosevelt. We were taken to the infamous Audiencia dungeon.

It was quite a catch for him and potentially disastrous for the United States. But before he could publicly flaunt our capture, Rork and I were whisked out of his custody and escaped the island through the good offices of a senior friend in the Catholic Church and the wily skills of a noxious Cuban bandit.

Marrón then sent Agent Boreau on my trail. He followed me to Key West, then Tampa. We finally ended up in a confrontation at Patricio Island, my home on the lower Gulf coast of Florida. Before dawn one morning, Boreau and some of his cohorts invaded the island and attempted to kill me, my daughter, Useppa, and Sean Rork. They very nearly succeeded.

Only Boreau survived among the Spanish attackers, a result of my daughter's moralistic Christian plea not to complete my business and execute him after his capture. With misgivings, I sent his wounded body—Rork put that spike through his shoulder and I'd shot him—back to his colonel in Havana with the warning that should I ever see Boreau again in America, I would finish the job properly. Six months later, I saw him in New York City and fulfilled that promise.

In June of '88, I again had a mission involving Havana. Tensions between the United States and Spain were rising over private American citizens' support for the rebels on the island. Money, guns, supplies, and manpower came from Cubans and Anglo-Americans alike living in the eastern United States, especially in Florida and New York City.

In Spain, there were calls for a naval blockade against the United States in the Straits of Florida, and some even wanted war. In Washington, President Grover Cleveland's administration wanted no part of Cuba or the revolutionaries, much less war with Spain, but neither could it abide the humility of a Spanish blockade off Florida. The true character of the Spanish navy's ability to conduct a sustained naval blockade—and its lethality against the American navy should war break out—needed to be taken into account before U.S. national policy was decided.

Since Cuba was my bailiwick, I drew the assignment and oversaw an espionage mission that used extortion to make a man named Paloma, the number-two Spanish official at the naval repair and supply base in Havana, one of our informants. In exchange for our not letting the captain-general know of his violent and grossly unnatural proclivities concerning adolescent boys—he was a horrifying fiend—Paloma gave us a whole store of inside knowledge, along with his word that the depravity would stop. Thus, I held his life in my hands.

Yes, I know that this effort was not high moral ground, but intelligence work seldom reaches those heights. It did yield crucial information, however, for we learned that the Spanish navy looked ominous only on paper. In reality, their ships were low on fuel supplies, in desperate need of repair, behind on gunnery training, and short of trained seaman and gunners. Only one warship in Cuban waters, the armored cruiser *Reina Regente*, newly built and recently arrived from Spain, was of any real intimidating value. The Spanish repair facilities were obsolete and under-equipped. They couldn't maintain any type of blockade, mobilize for war on a global scale, or do any major naval damage against the U.S. at that time.

This good news allowed our executive leadership to dampen the zealots in Washington and let tensions ease during the summer. To prolong this state of affairs, I intended to keep control by maintaining the extortion over my Spanish informant to continue our access to such good intelligence.

Then, in July, I became involved in another, unrelated series of incidents in the Bahamas and Haiti that claimed my attention. I was incommunicado in those countries until my return to Washington in early September. My reception upon returning to headquarters was frosty, for in my absence disaster had struck the Paloma mission. I was summoned to the office of my superior, Commodore John Grimes Walker, chief of the Bureau of Navigation.

It was in Commodore Walker's office that I learned what was known. There were three men in the room—Walker, myself, and a portly older man with a New York City accent. I'd never met or heard of the man, who was introduced only as Mr. Smith from executive branch. Walker explained that our sadist informant,

Paloma, had disappeared from Havana in August while I was in Haiti. So did one of my Cuban operatives who helped us on the project, a man I called by his alias: Casas. Neither man was known to have left the island, so both were assumed to be under arrest and in the dungeon under the Audiencia in Havana. Several other operatives in Havana had not replied to communications sent them. Mr. Smith was particularly worried and wanted to know how badly our intelligence operations in Cuba were compromised.

Without waiting for replies, Mr. Smith rattled off rhetorical questions to me: Was Paloma in fact under arrest? Had he been executed? Was Casas in the Audiencia with Paloma, or had he been executed also? Had they both told all they knew of that operation and our other efforts to Colonel Marrón and his henchmen? Or was the opposite true? Was Paloma in actuality a double agent run by Marrón, feeding us false information while the entire time gaining knowledge for the Spanish crown about *our* intelligence operations? Was Casas his accomplice? Had we—make that *you*, Commander Wake—been completely duped? Were the Spanish making us complacent with false intelligence while actually building up their own abilities against us, perhaps contemplating a first attack?

Walker was clearly uncomfortable with Mr. Smith's arrogant and accusatory attitude, a sentiment with which I was in increasing agreement as our little conference continued. With a level tone and furrowed brow, Walker gruffly interrupted Smith's monologue and resumed command of the meeting by informing me that, since I was "responsible for the whole Paloma thing from the beginning," it was I who was going to Cuba to solve the problem.

I would join *Richmond* that very day as a supernumerary on Admiral Luce's staff with the ridiculously pompous title of "protocol officer," a topic I know little of and care about even less. *Richmond* was making a five-day courtesy call in Havana, part of the de-escalation of tensions between Spain and the U.S.—a result of Paloma's information on the Spanish fleet—before heading around the Caribbean to show the flag at other places of turmoil, such as Panama and Haiti. Walker further informed me that as of that exact minute, I had eleven days in total to accomplish the mission. But, he warned, that included transit time to and from Cuba, so only five of the days would be in Havana.

Mr. Smith, whose soft hands and suave manner indicated a lack of familiarity with the more tumultuous regions of the world, then chimed in by announcing that the mission had three objectives. The first was to quietly determine what had happened to the two missing men and the potential for other losses in our network of informants. Second, to rescue the two men if they had been captured and put in the Audiencia dungeon, as I thought probable. This was to be a false flag mission, he emphasized, with us portraying ourselves as something other than Americans. He suggested Cuban patriots. The third objective was to be undertaken while rescuing the men in the dungeon—I was to take that unique opportunity to remove documents of intelligence value in Colonel Marrón's office in the dungeon.

After all this had been done, we were to make our way back to the anchored *Richmond* under cover of darkness and depart Cuba immediately, hopefully with none in Havana the wiser, or at least without possessing *proof* as to how the prisoners had escaped the Audiencia. I was to cable a report in cipher from Key West to Commodore Walker in Washington no later than Monday, October first, relating what I had discovered and subsequently achieved.

Following that, I was to return to Washington, where I would personally present an account of the mission to Commodore Walker, Admiral David Dixon Porter, commanding admiral of the navy, and the enigmatic Mr. Smith. That would occur no later than eight o'clock on the morning of Thursday, October fourth. All this meant I needed to be out of Havana by the first day of the month, send the telegraph message, and board the first north-bound steamer in order to travel all the way back to headquarters in time. And even then, it would be a very close-run thing.

"Why the time limit, sir?" I asked Commodore Walker

in perplexity, since something like this needed far more time to plan and execute. My unstated opinion was that only a fool in Washington with no experience in the real world—which undoubtedly was Mr. Smith—could have concocted this fantasy of a plan.

My question was answered with a nebulous reply by Mr. Smith, whom I was beginning to truly despise. "Commander, the time parameters are due to upcoming decisions in Washington that might be influenced by events in Cuba."

An hour later, I learned from an idler in the staff offices, one of those who paid attention to such things for the advancement of his own career, that there was to be a political campaign rally for the president in Washington at high noon on the day I was to brief my superiors at eight in the morn, the fourth of October. A Texas congressman—and former Confederate colonel—who was in favor of the president's policy of reducing tariffs on imports, including sugar from Cuba, was to be primary speaker at the event.

Aha, thought I, *that explains it all.* Cuba, tariffs, and the upcoming presidential election—it all coalesced in my mind. The navy leadership, like everyone in Washington, thought President Cleveland would have an easy reelection. The leadership didn't want any bad news out of Cuba that would incur the wrath of the Democrat-controlled executive branch or Congress, for the navy was trying to modernize and desperately needed political help for the budget. The Republican candidate, Benjamin Harrison, a former Union general, was crisscrossing the country and publicly espousing his support for a modern navy and high tariffs to protect American industry and agriculture—but no one really thought he would win. It was a delicate balancing act for the navy, but wily old Admiral Porter had been doing just that for the eighteen years he'd been the senior admiral of the U.S. Navy.

As I took in my present situation in the patio of the palace, that meeting in Washington seemed ages earlier. I bitterly wondered what brilliant advice Mr. Smith would give if he could see my predicament now.

It was no use to dwell on all that. Before I could do anything else to accomplish my mission in Havana, I had to fight—of all the men in the world—the son of a man I'd killed two years earlier, in what some would describe as the very darkest shade of honor.

I have used a blade in combat, but my limited knowledge in the art of fencing was of recent origin. Fortunately, the quality of my instruction outweighed the quantity, for in the previous year of 1887, I'd had occasion to study briefly under two of the best *sabreurs* (masters of the saber) in the world.

It started with an athletically enthusiastic friend in New York City, the very same man who received that message in '86, Theodore Roosevelt. He'd been constantly haranguing me to try various manly martial arts like boxing and sword fighting. To get my young friend to stop, I finally said yes to fencing. He arranged five saber lessons from one of the top instructors in the city, the famous Captain Hyppolyte Nicolas, formerly of the Hungarian hussar guards. Accordingly, I spent five long and strenuous nights in a row at the captain's fencing club on Twenty-Fourth Street, with Roosevelt shouting a steady stream of inane encouragements from the side.

At the end of the week, Captain Nicolas pronounced me a natural at the saber, with the observation that I obviously had Hungarian blood somewhere in my family lineage. More importantly, he taught me several moves that are designed to be of use in a real sword fight, as opposed to a sporting match.

Then, a few months later in the fall of 1887, I was in Europe on a courier assignment and had the occasion to be in Great Britain for a month. With my interest in fencing having been sparked by

Captain Nicolas, I took the opportunity to attend classes taught by the legendary Captain Alfred Hutton, late of the 1st King's Guards Regiment of the British Army in India. Hutton, an expert in various edged weapons, has a particular affinity for the saber and instructs his students how to use it in combat against various other weapons. His training is even more strenuous than the Hungarian's, and, after several weeks of sore muscles, contusions, and a few lacerations, I had learned quite a lot the hard way.

And so, it may now become apparent that my reason for requesting sabers over foils was to gain some small advantage over Boreau, who I predicted would allow his rage to overcome his judgment and thus degrade his skill, especially with a heavier blade than he was used to handling. In addition, though he was a champion in the art of fencing, I had some life experience, which I guessed my foe did not. You see, unlike many naval officers in this advanced day and age, I've actually killed a man with a naval cutlass.

There is nothing artistic about it.

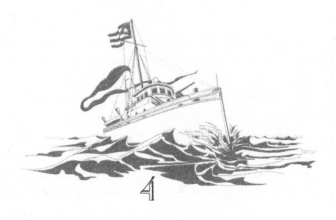

4

Passata Sotto!

Palace of His Excellency
Captain-General Sabas Marin y Gonzalez
Plaza de Armas, Havana
10:20 a.m., Tuesday
25 September 1888

Boreau and I stared at each other as the sour-faced president of the jury was introduced. He was a veteran fencing master named Gondolfo, who looked old enough to have fought under Napoleon. The president got right down to business, introducing the jury members and announcing the rules of combat. They were simple. The match would continue without time limit until the first man scored five "touches" of his saber on the other. The areas of the body open for attack, by slashing or thrusting, would be everything above the hips, including the head and hands.

One of the jury members took a piece of white chalk and ran it up and down our blades. That was to mark the hits on our black jackets. He then examined the very tips of the blades, making sure they were bent back and blunted. The other man inspected our masks, then the *piste*. When they were finished, the jurymen took their positions and bobbed their heads to Gondolfo, who stood ramrod straight and clapped his hands for quiet.

"The combatants will now execute their salutes!"

Boreau went first. Facing the captain-general, he whipped his saber up and across his front in a dramatic demonstration of control and speed, coming to attention with a click of his heels and ending up with the bell guard at his face and the blade absolutely vertical. He then swept it down to his right front, the rippled swish clearly audible. Don Sabas acknowledged the salute with a leisurely nod.

In similar beautiful fashion, Boreau saluted the president of the jury and the other members of the jury, each of whom reacted by bowing slightly. His final salute was to me, which he managed to accomplish with a gross sense of disdain, barely lifting his bell guard to his face and refusing to look me in the eye.

Not to be outdone in the theatrical department, I stamped to attention—I've seen enough Brits do it to get the hang of the maneuver—and faced Don Sabas, flourishing my blade in a wide S-shaped arc from the floor to the present-arms position in front of my face. I then did the same for each member of the jury. Finally, I made my salute to Boreau, with the added touch of pressing the *forte* section of the blade, the strongest part just above the guard, to my lips while smiling at him. The kiss of death, delivered with haughty pleasure, as it were.

This impertinence elicited just what I'd hoped for, a low growl of fury from Boreau. Oh, yes, he was aching to kill me, all right. It was all he could do not to run me through right then and there, which would be an exceedingly bad breech of manners since old Gondolfo hadn't given the word to start yet.

Ten seconds later the president of the jury ordered, "Masks!" We both put on our masks and stood in the prescribed stance: right foot advanced and pointed precisely forward, the left foot one length astern and pointed an exact ninety degrees to port, with both knees slightly flexed and the saber pointing downward at forty-five degrees.

The assembly grew hushed. Behind Boreau, I noticed a mature woman in the audience flutter a fan for air, her bejeweled bosom heaving in very apparent anticipation.

Gondolfo shouted, "*En garde!*"

Boreau lifted his saber. I could hear his breathing, deep and rhythmic, exhaling like a steam engine. He chose the classic position of foil fencers. His hand was extended and raised to just below the level of his shoulder and slightly to the left of his line of body, the upper arm and forearm in the traditional right angle. His blade slowly elevated to a forty-five-degree upward angle. I noticed the tip didn't shake at all.

I chose the same opening position. Not as a preference but as a feint, as if I was an experienced foil fencer too. Waiting for the word from Gondolfo, I studied Boreau's perfect body position through the mesh of my mask and willed my hand to do what Nicolas had drilled into me, remain loose but in control. Stand your ground, let the fingers direct the saber, and make the other man expend the energy.

The Hungarian's words came back to me: "Ach, Peter, you are so very American. Your movements are too clumsy and easy to discern in advance. Kindly remember to relax your saber hand, so that it is more supple and therefore more difficult to predict or counter. Allow your hand to do the work. And above all, *enjoy* the combat…"

"Commence!" Gondolfo ordered.

I was still registering the order as Boreau raced toward me, his blade leveled at my chest. I parried it up and immediately knew I'd made a mistake. He wanted me to do that, taking my movement and turning it into his real attack. His saber lifted up and then instantly slashed down.

Thwack! Boreau's blade came down hard, cleaving into the top of my mask's helmet. The classic cavalryman's move. Without that protection, I would have been dead right then. As it was, I stood there stunned at the speed and weight of the attack, wondering far too late if my helmet had the regulation amount of leather padding. But, of course, there was no time to ponder such things, and one is not supposed to remove the helmet and contemplate the size of the dent he has just endured.

"*Touché*," I said, belatedly, in the traditional admission of a hit upon me.

"*Un touché à Boreau!*" announced Gondolfo. The Spanish audience applauded. Laughter came from somewhere.

I heard, "*En garde!*" and seconds later, "Commence!"

This time I was a bit quicker on the draw, getting my blade over and down to the left into the number one position of parry, where it descends from the hand held at chest level. That was enough to block Boreau's slashing *molinello* attack on my chest, but before I could *riposte* effectively, Boreau had jumped away. The man was all over the narrow *piste*, lunging and backing, while I remained pretty much in my original position. There was no way I could match his footwork.

Boreau began a rapid advance, his saber cutting through the air, reaching out for me. With no time for fancy moves, I feinted to the left, then slashed upward and across my front, parrying his saber. Since I didn't move, he ended up running into me, a *corps-à-corps* situation where our bodies came into contact. Before Gondolfo could call for us to separate, I tapped Boreau on the arm with my blade, leaving a nice white chalk mark. Point for me.

This sort of back and forth thing went on for the next ten minutes—an eternity when you're faced with a homicidal maniac. His attacks on me were hard, slashing hits. I felt a trickle on my abdomen after Boreau had done another lower *molinello* attack, ripping hard into my guts. I hoped the padding had held and that it was sweat. That point got him an ovation from the Spanish and a groan from the Americans. Another of Boreau's hits was a slash exactly on the bone of my right forearm, the pain seriously degrading my strength and saber control.

My own clumsy hits were lightweight, without powerful follow-through, but I managed, using Nicolas's and Hutton's techniques, to land four touches to Boreau's three. If the match had been on style or *machismo*, he would have already won, but it wasn't. And unlike me, I could see that the bastard—I was long past the point of niceties—wasn't hurting or tired at all. But I did have him infuriated by my score, plainly ready to cast all caution aside.

Breathing heavily now, I willed myself to silent exhales, trying to slow my heart as it pounded in my chest. My clothes were soaked from the incredible humidity in the courtyard. I was beyond caring what I looked like. The mask had turned into a slimy, claustrophobic tomb for my face, but there was no way to remove it and wipe away the sweat before we would begin again. The scent of frangipani and jasmine was just a memory. All I smelled now was fear.

"Commence!" shouted Gondolfo.

Boreau advanced steadily, then did a *ballestra,* the Italian jumping lunge attack that changes tempo and catches the opponent off guard. He feinted to my right, then again to my right. That and the *ballestra* were enough to confuse me, and I left my vulnerable left side open. It took only the fraction of a second for him to take advantage of my lapse. Before I knew it, his saber was making a wide swinging arc, the blade flying toward the left side of my neck. It was obvious what he was doing. Boreau was going to slash through my mask and open my carotid artery.

The accidental *coup de grâce.*

I turned my body quickly to face the threat, but my left hand remained where it had been, now next to the left side of my head instead of behind it. That was a basic error—you *always* keep your unprotected left hand and arm behind you. I realized my mistake as the tip of his saber sliced through it.

The hand slowed and deflected the blow enough to allow me to instinctively duck as the blade went over my head. Pain was instantaneous and severe, like the hand was on fire. I shook it and blood splattered everywhere. Several women screamed.

Boreau's attack had such force to it that he spun almost all the way around, but he quickly corrected and used his momentum to advance for another attack. I was stumbling backward, into the warning area near the end of the *piste*, when Gondolfo pointed to Boreau and yelled, "*Basta!*"—"Enough!" Boreau shook his head in disgust and took up the standing position on his half of the *piste*, chest heaving with fury.

The president of the jury came to me. "Commander Wake, blood has been drawn, and the match will now end. With this new touch by Lieutenant Commander Boreau, you both now have a tie at four points each. An honorable end. Congratulations. And now we will attend to your wound."

I examined my bleeding hand. Because it was blunted, the tip of Boreau's saber had opened a very ragged, three-inch cut along the bottom edge of the hand, perhaps half an inch deep. It hurt like hell, but the pain cleared my head and filled it with anger.

Rork dashed over with a cloth and bound up the hand tightly. Glancing at Boreau, he grumbled, "That bloody friggin' Spic bastard's—" then stopped, seeing my reaction and abruptly remembering our mutual agreement of a month earlier. We had both agreed to lessen our cursing and diminish derogatory ethnic slurs.

Rork had no illusion that the pact was mainly aimed at him, for he, like all bosuns, could swear a blue streak. What I never could understand, though, was how he, who suffered like so many Irish immigrants from derogatory myths about his people and faith, could be such a xenophobe regarding other cultures. So "we" decided to change that. From then on, no more Dagos, Spics, Krauts, Frogs, Rag Heads, Camel Jockies, Chinks, Limeys, Poufs, Micks, Wops, Cheesers, or Polacks would emerge from that Irish mouth, or a penny would be forfeited each time. I am pleased to report that the cursing had diminished by that day in Havana but must admit the efforts against ethnic epithets weren't going as well. Back in Washington, a jar was already filled with penance.

With great consternation he changed his verbiage to "Sorry, sir. What I meant to say was that Spaniardo Boreau fella thinks yer done for." With typical lower-deck wit, he added, "So now that ye've got that bugger fooled nice an' good, go ahead an' kill 'im.'"

"Spaniardo" was Rork's substitute for previous untoward descriptors of Hispanic people. His opinion of Boreau echoed my thoughts—the man was gloating at that very moment. Gondolfo had offered the perfect way out for me, and logically I should have taken it. My goal was accomplished, and I could stay in nice quarters ashore in Havana. But I wasn't thinking logically by that point. The mission was completely gone from my mind. There was only Boreau, and I'd be damned if I would quit now while he was standing there, arrogantly planning his final move to ensure my death.

"Precisely, Rork," I wheezed, trying not to double over in pain. "Glad you recognized my plan. He's completely overconfident."

I turned to Gondolfo. "Mr. President, I am fine. It is a minor cut and my own fault for having my left hand in the way. We can go on and finish the match."

Gondolfo didn't like that. He'd seen Boreau's attacks and knew there was something personal going on. This wasn't an exhibition of skill and sportsmanship.

"I *insist*, sir," I told him, probably a little too strongly through my gritted teeth. He scowled, then looked at the now red cloth around my hand.

"Commander…" he began, but I interrupted.

"Mr. President, I am sure my adversary did not intentionally target my left hand, but it was a legitimate hit and a minor wound. I don't need that hand to continue the fencing match. This is a matter of personal honor, so I am now *demanding* we continue."

Gondolfo shook his head. "Very well, Commander."

I turned to the audience and announced, "*Touché. Soy listo que continuar.* I am ready to continue."

Admiral Luce had been walking toward me but stopped and went pale when I made my statement. Rork grinned at Luce and pointed to his rubber left hand. "No worries, Admiral. He'll be right as rain on a Derry mornin'—hand wounds're me specialty!"

Boreau wiped his saber on his white trouser leg, my blood

making a long smear like a trophy. He looked at it, then me, snickering quietly.

Enjoy it now, you son of a demented son of a lunatic, I thought, *for my turn is coming.*

"The match will continue," announced Gondolfo, sadly. "The score is now even, *la belle,* with four touches for each of our honored opponents. The next touch will be the winning point."

It is customary when a match becomes tied, known as *la belle,* that the fencers salute each other before resuming. It must have been obvious by that time to the onlookers that Boreau and I were anything but "honored opponents," but we dutifully executed our flourishes when Gondolfo ordered, "Salute!"

Seconds later, he commanded, "*En garde,*" then, "Commence!"

And with that, Boreau and I went at it for the final time.

I had gone into the *terce,* or third, position. It was a slightly higher stance, and the one Hutton taught me for serious saber fighting. Boreau didn't seem to notice the change and proceeded to attack violently without even feinting. It was what I thought he'd do—another accelerating advance with a beautifully done *ballestra,* which didn't confuse me in the least, for in that split second I saw his leveled saber in position for a high *molinello* slash to my chest.

His mistake.

Because I'd started in the terce stance, I already had my blade up and executed a *coulé,* sliding my blade along his saber, turning it into a circular envelopment that loosened Boreau's positive control of his saber. Forcing his blade up and away, I dropped my body down with the left hand on the *piste* in a very low *passata sotto* position, denying him a target as he ineffectually swung the saber over my head. Before he could recover, I lunged onward and upward.

A good fencer would probably have done a *molinello* slash to Boreau's undefended midsection to score the point, but I was far beyond fencing by that point. With a growl and the last of my strength, I rammed my saber's tip directly into Boreau's solar plexus and bulled him backward along the *piste* until he stumbled and fell. It wasn't a pretty move, but it worked.

My blade never left him, following Boreau down, the tip ripping the outer layer of padding and traveling up his chest and under the lower edge of his mask toward the throat until, at the last moment, I forced myself to lift it away, putting his mask askew. He tried to stand but was too wobbly and fell rearward again—off the very end of the *piste*.

The crowd gasped in horror. The despised *yanqui* had won. The beloved Spanish hero had not only lost but was humiliated. Dead silence. I quickly saluted Boreau and Gondolfo, then the captain-general. Heart pounding and ears ringing, I executed an about-face and walked away.

Thank you, Captain Hutton, for teaching me the *passata sotto*.

5

Instinct

Palace of His Excellency
Captain-General Don Sabas Marin y Gonzalez
Plaza de Armas, Havana
10:30 a.m., Tuesday
25 September 1888

After the grandees recovered from their shock, they quickly headed for the entrance and their carriages. The Spanish civil and military leadership curtly bowed to Admiral Luce, then retired up the steps to the captain-general's offices, I presume to discuss how the Americans had pulled off this latest trick. Boreau, still stunned, was taken off to a room somewhere near the stables by Lieutenant What's-his-name, the staff translator, whose magnificent show had evaporated in front of him.

Indeed, the ambiance of the place had changed from haughty to funereal in the space of seconds. I was left standing alone by a peacock in the corner of the patio, rather stunned myself and still trying to catch my breath.

Rork and Luce came over to me, satisfaction and worry

competing in their expressions. "How are you, Peter?" asked the admiral.

"Tired, sir."

"What happened there? That was no fencing match—he was out to kill you."

"It was a trap, sir—set up by an old enemy of mine in the government here, but it failed."

"Can you still carry out your mission? Does this negate it?"

Hmm. Well, it hadn't really helped it. Admiral Luce hadn't been told the *exact* nature of my mission in Havana. Only Rork knew that. I simply said, "Yes, sir, I can still carry it out."

To my relief, the admiral, one of the sharpest minds in the navy, didn't ask for further clarification. Telling an admiral he's not important enough to be let in on a secret assignment is definitely not good for one's career. Especially when the admiral knows the *enlisted petty officer* with you is privy to the entire plan.

Rork diverted the dialogue by producing another handkerchief and wrapping my hand anew. The old one was sopping red, and he tsk-tsked me. "Aye, ye've gone an' opened up the bloody damned thing, Commander. Needs a wee bit o' sewin', by the looks o' it."

Another tsk-tsk, accompanied by a disapproving shaking of his head—as if my wound was *my* fault. Well, actually, I suppose it was.

I ignored Rork's verbal transgression, for by then I was ready for some foul language myself. A palace servant stared at me from the balcony while talking to someone out of my view. Embarrassed by all the attention over my hand, I told my friend, "Oh, stop clucking like an old lady about it, Rork. It's a small cut."

"Aye, 'tis smaller than some. An' wee cuts're still serious on a hand, what with infection an' all." He raised the index finger of his real hand. "Take me word on *that* subject! But nary's the worry, sir. Me an' that ol' sailmaker'll get ye sewed up an' squared away inside o' three snaps o' a bishop's garter."

Rork glanced warily around us. The few remaining people

in the courtyard were giving us distinctly unfriendly looks. "Aye, sir, 'tis time to get under way an' outta here. Let's get onboard o' *Richmond*. We'll come back ashore later."

"Take my carriage straight away, Rork," ordered Luce. "I'll board another one later. I want to have a word with the Spanish admiral anyway, if I can find the man. They all seem to have disappeared on me."

With a less-than-amused tone, he added, "And for God's sake, Bosun Rork, get Commander Wake to the ship's *surgeon* immediately, not the blasted sailmaker."

I appreciated his kind offer of quick transport, for though the cut was small in comparison to others I've had, that ragged gash was beginning to throb considerably.

Rork wasted no time in piping up, "Aye, aye, sir," and propelled me through the line of guests in the entryway. We rushed toward the fancy carriage reserved for the American admiral.

Ahead of our vehicle was an even more ornate coach, the amount of its gold gilt obviously denoting royal rank. Several sour-faced, mature ladies were boarding. A young gentleman with them, perhaps sixteen years of age and dressed to the hilt, was rattling off in a thick Castilian accent details of a soiree that evening.

Rork jumped up to the driver's bench of our carriage—only officers ride inside—as a footman opened the door for me. I was about to board when a movement to my right, beyond the royal coach, caught my attention.

It was a figure in a plain black suit at the edge of the park that covered the plaza. Standing there by himself on the empty street, he looked like a merchant's clerk and harmless enough, but he had a large object clutched in both hands. And he was openly staring at the line of coaches under the portico.

No, it was more than that. *Glaring* is a better description. There was clear hostility in his face. Suddenly he began sprinting across the intervening street, shouting in a Cuban accent, "*Abajo con los gusanos reales!*" ("Down with the royal worms!") Calling someone a "worm" in Cuba is a serious insult. Two costumed soldiers farther down the street, armed with three-hundred-year-old pikes, began heading his way.

The man in black had more than insults for the royals, though, for he suddenly hurled the large object, which I now saw was a satchel, toward the young nobleman by the royal carriage. The boy stopped and watched as the satchel flew in a shallow arc right at him.

Having divested himself of his burden, the intruder now produced a revolver from his pocket and screamed, "*Muerte a los tiranos!*" ("Death to tyrants!") He raised it in the boy's direction. The soldiers were running flat out now but were still too far away. The pistol clicked—a misfire—but the Cuban kept it aimed and was trying again. The satchel had landed at the boy's feet, hissing and smoking ominously.

It was one of those tableau moments, frozen in time. Rork yelled, "Bomb!" An officer in the entryway shouted an order to his men, one of the women in the coach screamed, and everyone else just stood there.

Why and how I did what came next, I cannot explain. Instinct, probably.

It took me three strides—and perhaps half as many seconds—to reach the boy and shove him back into the crowd at the palace's entry. I then kicked the satchel as I would a ball, launching it in a trajectory away from the carriage and confines of the portico, toward the open street.

By this point, the bomber had arrived at my location and did not take kindly to my interruption of his work. He switched targets from the boy to me but failed to notice that I had targeted *him*. My right hand moved faster than his trigger finger, executing a passable sweeping parry from below. It knocked that weapon out of his hand. Captain Hutton would have been proud to see my adaptation of his lesson on singled-handed defense against an armed adversary.

There was no time for self-congratulation, though, for several things occurred simultaneously: The royal youngster sprawled on the floor behind a massive potted plant by the enormous mahogany palace door, felling several people in line; one of the arriving soldiers slammed his pike into the bomber's stomach; and Rork used his navy-issued Colt to shoot the bomber in the face from fifteen yards range, which I thought an impressive shot.

And out on the street, the bomb detonated.

The thing had been packed with small nails. The makeshift grapeshot blasted out in all directions, lacerating everything in its path. Four other costumed soldiers, running across the street from the park to reinforce their comrades, were flung sideways, their bodies contorting in unnatural poses as they collapsed on the street. The nails thudded into the street side of the carriages lined up for the passengers. Horses shrieked from their wounds and bolted with the vehicles. Several windows along the front wall of the palace disintegrated. A dozen people were wounded.

The concussion was thunderous in the portico. I was thrown sideways, my head impacting that decorative stone planter the royal youngster was behind. Several nails penetrated my left arm and leg, but thankfully I escaped the fate of those soldiers on the street. It could have been worse. The bomb was homemade and not of military-grade explosive, or there would've been more dead and maimed.

After firing his shot, Rork jumped down to assist me. Thus, he was behind the bulk of our carriage when the bomb went off. Untouched, he ran over and knelt beside me, running his hand over my head and looking quite anxious while speaking to me. I could see his lips moving, but heard only a constant ringing. "What?" I asked.

His lips moved again. I tried to stand but lost my sense of balance and keeled forward face-first toward the floor. Rork caught my right arm in mid-fall and gently lowered me to the ground. Every time I tried to lift my head, my vision swam in circles and nausea rebelled in my stomach.

Beside me the boy was shouting frantically, but it just sounded like muffled babbling to me. Women with blood-stained gowns stared at each other before bursting into shrieking hysteria. Two officers were dragging a wounded comrade away to the interior of the palace while modern-clad soldiers with real armaments started arriving from the nearby fortress, their faces tense as they formed a protective perimeter, waiting for another attack.

I grew angry at Rork's mumbling and yelled, "What is it you're saying?"

He pointed to my sleeve and trouser, where little blotches of blood were blossoming, then pointed at my head, saying something. Curiously, I had no pain—yet.

"They're just minor, Rork. Now why the hell don't you speak up?"

Admiral Luce, who had been safe inside the palace, rushed over. He also said something unintelligible to me, gesturing for me to stay on the ground. All sound was overwhelmed by that damned, high-pitched noise buzzing inside my skull. I made another attempt to stand, but it was my last. *Head wound, probably a concussion and maybe blown-out ear drums,* I realized as I went down again. Then all went dark.

6

Hotel Florida

Hotel Florida
252 Obispo Street
Havana, Cuba
7 p.m., Tuesday
25 September 1888

It was Rork's voice I heard first: "Aye, ye'll be the death o' me yet, Peter Wake, but I'll be damned if yer luck didn't hold out, an' we didn't land on our feet one more time. The Spaniardos put the hero o' the hour up in some pretty decent quarters. Fit for a cardinal, they are."

I slowly took in my surroundings. They were unfamiliar, but I had no inclination to complain. The room was spacious in length, breadth, and height, with opened floor-to-ceiling doors along one wall. Light filtered through gauzy muslin curtains, swaying in a gentle wind that mitigated the heat a bit. The bed was huge and incredibly soft. I'd never been in a bed that large or comfortable.

I was naked, with only a light cotton sheet over me. On a chair beside the bed was one of my regular duty uniforms, cleaned and pressed. Rork was in a white linen suit and shirt with a blue tie, looking like one of the many businessmen who inhabited the city. I'd never seen him in that suit or appearing that prosperous. He looked positively dapper.

Assessing my physical state was the next effort, beginning with wiggling my fingers and toes, then lifting arms and legs. Limbs were working. Bandages covered my left hand, arm, and leg, where pain throbbed but was manageable—I'd had far worse in the past. I tentatively raised my head, then lowered it to the pillow. No problems so far. And I could hear, so my eardrums weren't destroyed.

"Where are we?" I croaked from an impossibly dry mouth.

His face reflected amazement as he looked around the room. "Ooh, me boyo, we've fetched up at none o'er than Havana's finest digs—Hotel Florida. Suite number twelve on the upper floor, to be exact, with a lovely balcony over Obispo."

Hotel Florida, on the famous Obispo Street, was one of the grandest hotels in Havana. Diplomats, aristocrats, and tycoons stayed at the Florida. It was even swankier than the Inglaterra. The upper floor had the nicest accommodations.

"How?"

"The head man o' the island, Don Sabas himself, arranged it. Ye've made a friend, there. Saved his sainted nephew's life, ye did."

Nephew? It must've been that young nobleman. "The boy? Is he all right?"

Another voice answered me in precise English from another corner by a door.

"Yes, Commander Wake, the boy you saved is unhurt. He is the nephew and godson of Captain-General Don Sabas Marin y Gonzalez. The captain-general is very appreciative and has ordered you to have the finest attentions for your recovery. Please allow me to introduce myself. I am Ricardo Manuel Acera de Sevilla y Idel, the personal secretary to the principal deputy of the foreign affairs ministry, Don Pedro Rodriguez de Aragon."

Acera was standing at attention in a formal gray pin-striped suit, the very picture of a diplomatist. He bowed from the waist with a grand gesture of the hand, his handlebar moustache twitching as he spoke. "I am at your service for anything you may desire, sir. And you as well, Mr. Rork."

Yet another voice sounded in the room. "And I am Doctor Jorge Cobre, Commander Wake. I am a military surgeon and the personal physician to the Captain-General of Cuba, who has sent me to be your attending physician."

The doctor was dressed in white linen like Rork. Young, maybe thirty, with serious eyes behind rimless spectacles, he advanced to my bed and proceeded to examine my pulse, respiration, eyes, and left arm and leg. I noticed he used a new Cammann stethoscope, the expensive kind made by Wocher & Son in Cincinnati. I use the same device but for clandestine purposes of a less noble nature.

Cobre straightened, announcing in a monotone, "You are progressing well, Commander. The wounds of the arm, hand, and leg are superficial lacerations. I have seen far worse on the field of battle from the machetes of the enemy insurgents. Some suturing was required, but nothing of consequence. However, I have been far more concerned about your concussive head injury, fearing a subdural hematoma within the cranium."

That sounded bad. "A what?"

"A gathering of blood within the outermost meningeal layer, between the dura mater, which adheres to the skull, and the arachnoid mater. But I see no indications of such a development. You are extremely fortunate that did not occur. It would've killed you by filling the cranial space with blood, putting excruciating pressure on the brain. A most painful death for you."

"Oh..." was the only thing I could say to that.

Cobre continued, never deviating from his professorial lecture. "And you are most fortunate the concussion did not rupture the tympanic membranes." He saw my confusion and added, "Your eardrums...as it did some others who were wounded by the blast."

Cobre rubbed his hands absentmindedly. "Now I insist that you must totally relax. I do not approve of any aggravation of your cranium or movement of your left limbs at all. Everything must be allowed to heal properly. Do you require medication for pain before I leave you to your rest?"

Rest? I had no time for rest, but naturally I couldn't tell the good doctor that.

"No, I can handle the pain—I've had worse. Thank you very much for your attention, Doctor."

He nodded and turned to leave but stopped. "I must further say, Commander, that I have no doubt you have had worse pain in your life. You have some very intriguing scars. It appears that several people have tried to kill you over the space of several years by various methods. Gunshot punctures, bladed weapon lacerations, blunt-force contusions—you have scars from your head to your legs. In fact, I have never seen so many wounds on a body that was still alive."

Rork had been there for all of them and possessed more than a few himself. By the silly grin on his face and the faint aroma of rum in the air, I belatedly realized that Rork must have imbibed a bit. The doctor saw Rork's expression and frowned, then began a short sermon. "It is my duty as a physician to strongly advise you to discontinue such a lifestyle. At your advanced age, these previous traumas will most probably have engendered an unknown deleterious cumulative effect upon your health, one that any new injury or distress to your body could trigger with disastrous results. And now that I have fulfilled that duty, I bid you a good day, sir."

His bedside manner was sorely lacking, but damned if the man wasn't right. I do have many aches, pains, and scars— no doubt each already reported in detail by the good doctor to Spanish intelligence. And I'd just added several more. Cobre's admonition made me feel even more exhausted. Forty-nine years of age is far too old to be engaging in saber matches, deflecting bombs, or disarming lunatics.

"Is Admiral Luce around?" I asked Rork after Cobre departed.

"Nay, sir, he's gone to sea. Got some hurry-up orders from Washington that came in this afternoon by telegraph, an hour after we got here to the hotel. *Richmond* weighed anchor right after that. She's joinin' *Galena* over there in Haiti. Them revolutionaries're threatenin' foreigners' lives again, so Uncle Sam's got Luce goin' there to keep the peace. The flag lieutenant told me we'd get a telegram from either Haiti or Jamaica if *Richmond* or *Galena* can be here afore Saturday. Otherwise, we're to get passage by steamer to Panama an' join the flagship there." His eyes strayed briefly to Acera, a warning for me to be prudent with my words. "So, all in all, methinks we're…alone here…while ye're recuperatin' from all o' this."

"I see." I raised a hand toward Acera, standing beside Rork. "Thank you for your assistance, sir. Please convey my sincerest appreciation to the captain-general."

"It is our honor and pleasure, Commander. And His Excellency sends his personal wishes for a quick recovery. He also hopes you will agree to be his honored guest at a special private dinner in His Excellency's apartment at the palace and at several soirees we have planned this week."

I was impressed—he actually made it sound sincere—so I responded in kind. "Thank you, Señor Acera. The people of Spain are justly famous around the world for their hospitality, sir. I would be delighted to attend the private dinner and the soirees. Perhaps tomorrow we can speak of them in more detail. But now I must ask that you please excuse me from further discourse, for I am very tired and about to fall asleep. My visit to Havana has been less than tranquil and I am old, as the good doctor reminded us."

"But of course, Commander. Please take your rest. Should you or Mr. Rork need anything, I am constantly in the room beside you and at your service."

After Acera exited the room, Rork whispered, "We can talk now. There's no one else here."

"Very well, Rork. We need to get to work." I tried propping up on an elbow, but my back ached, so I lay back down.

Rork chuckled. "Yep, yer old scars really impressed that young sawbones, ya' mutilated ol' beast."

"Hell, your scars are more exciting, Rork. I'm surprised the doctor never asked about your fake hand."

"Kept me sleeve pulled down, so that young medico never even noticed, much less figured it out. No need for these buggers ta' know about me special attributes, is there? Besides, all eyes're on *you*, me heroical friend. So, is yer brains workin' all right o' are they scrambled more'n usual?"

"Yes, I'm fine. Minor concussion. Just a little tired, is all. I played it up a bit for our hosts. How long have I been out?"

"About eight hours. They gave ye a bit o' laudanum an' that did the trick. 'Tis Tuesday still but almost seven o'clock in the evenin'. So, is it time to work yet? When do we commence doin' what it 'tis we're here for—"

I stopped him with an upheld finger, for I had noticed something odd on the dresser at the far wall. Doctor Cobre had been smoking a cigar and had left the nearly extinguished stub in an ashtray atop the dresser. A thin trail of smoke rose from the stub, but instead of dissipating in the room, its course bent like a stream toward the wall behind the dresser, where a decorative piece of vertical trim molding ran from floor to ceiling. The smoke unnaturally disappeared into the molding. It is the classic sign of a false door—and eavesdropping.

I spoke a bit louder. "You mean the social events, Rork? Yes, I suppose we'll have to go. I'm old and tired and sore from these wounds, but it's expected of us by our Spanish hosts."

Rork—like most Irishmen, a born conspirator—immediately comprehended and played his role. "Aye, them social duties're the worst part o' goin' ashore. The sooner we get 'em done, the sooner we can go home. Yer lookin' a bit worn, sir. Need that pillow plumped up a bit?"

He leaned over close to me and made a fuss of fluffing the pillow as he whispered, "Time to take a gander at that moldin', ain't it?"

I nodded in reply and, for the benefit of the hidden audience, offered in my stage voice, "Thanks, Rork. I must say, these are some quarters, aren't they? The fine craftsmanship in this wood is impressive. Just look at that molding. Beautiful workmanship. Perfectly aligned. We don't see that at home."

He was at the molding, examining the seam. A faint sound of scuffling shoes came from the wall. Rork put his hand on the wall and pointed to a corner of the ornamental trim, mouthing the word *hole,* then said, "Aye, these Spanish fellas're damned good carpenters, that's fer sure. Built strong as a frigate!" He then proceeded to pound the wall hard, which produced more scuffling beyond.

"Strong, indeed, Rork. I think I need some fresh air. Let me get some clothes on and we'll go out on the balcony."

He grinned back at me. "Capital idea, sir. An' we'll bring me bottle too."

7

Aficionados de Ron

Hotel Florida
252 Obispo Street
Havana, Cuba
7:15 p.m., Tuesday
25 September 1888

Once we were out on the narrow balcony overlooking busy Obispo Street, Rork's tone tensed. Shadows and potted palms provided a bit of privacy as we looked down on the lane below, which was jammed with people shopping in the many stores or heading home after work. Negro street vendors lyrically called out their wares. Carts clattered by. Music emanated from a barroom down the street. I glanced up at the narrow strip of sky visible between the buildings. It was covering over quickly with blue-black banks of cloud. Rain was coming. It came almost every evening in September in Havana.

Rork nodded his head at me in admiration. "Clever o' ye to follow that smoke an' find the hidden door an' peephole. Aye, ain't no doubt on it, that bastard Marrón's clearly out to do ye in—an' me as well, thank ye very much. An' we'd better keep a weather eye out for Boreau junior too. Ye should'a skewered his throat an' done 'im in, like he damned near did to yer own self."

"Yeah, it wasn't much of a friendly exhibition, was it?"

"Nay, an' things're bound to get worse, now that we're without *Richmond* nearby. Methinks we're better off quartered together, where we can watch each other's back, so that cot in there is for me. An' by the by, both me horses an' me gutbuster, along with your skullcrusher an' scattergun, were brought here from the ship for us afore she got under way. Me horses're on me person an' the gutbuster's in me seabag. Yer lot's in yer seabag by the bed."

Good news. Rork was referring to our personal weapons: his pair of Navy Colt Model 1861 .36-caliber revolvers and his amputated Winchester 1887 12-gauge, five-round, pump-action shotgun. Mine were a 44/40-caliber Merlin-Hewlitt revolver with the fighting grip that gave it its nickname and a Spencer 12-gauge repeating shotgun. We always carry them, ever since that mission in '86 when we found ourselves without protection at one point and nearly died because of it.

"Good thinking, Rork," I said. "You're going to have to go out and contact our people while I hold down Marrón's surveillance here. They have a guard near the door, don't they?"

"Aye, that they do. They're callin' 'im a 'royal servant.' The bugger's in plain clothes with a big bulge under his coat on the right side. An' mean as a snake, by the look o' his eyes."

"With probably another one down in the lobby, I expect. That means you're going to have to get away quietly." I glanced down. It was twenty-five feet at least to the street, too far to jump. He could shinny down bedsheets, but there were too many people in the street who would notice. Obispo Street is always busy, fairly late into the night. "Any ideas?"

He thought a minute. When Rork ponders a problem, his face is an animated study of cogitation, as if you can actually see the effort of those mental wheels turning inside. "Aye, sir, that me do. Our chambermaid's a comely lass but maybe a wee bit less than a smart one. Methinks she's bit lonely. Could let her know how lonely me own bones are right about now an' suggest she take me out o' here in the linen cart for some sippers o' rum an' some dancin' somewhere. Maybe flash some coin while I'm about it an' tell 'er me escape's from the likes o' that veritable ogre o' an officer that's me boss man. She look's to be right willin' to fall for that tale. Probably works fer an ogre herself." He paused, looking at me doubtfully. "O' course, ye'd have to do yer own part in convincin' the lass."

Somehow I knew a girl would end up part of his idea. "All right, Rork. Pray tell, how do I accomplish my part?"

He laughed. "By doin' what comes natural-like for a wounded heroical ogre type—bleedin' all over the pretty bed linens an' then yellin' fer new ones, demandin' 'em right now, dammit all, an' actin' nasty that it's takin' so friggin' long. Simple enough stuff for a highfalutin officer. She'll have to change the whole lot o' it—an' there's the reason for the cart—an' all the while gainin' plenty o' sympathy fer this ol' Irish sailorman's puttin' up with a jackass such as ye."

It was my turn to nod my head in admiration. "You never cease to amaze me with your devious mind, Rork. Not to mention that lusty heart. For the life of me, I do not know how you come up with these things, but it sounds better than any notion I have. So, yes, Bosun Rork, I duly promise to do my part and bleed profusely, then act unpleasantly, like a good arrogant officer should. Now, are you ready for your assignment? To be done after you finish the romp with your new wench, naturally."

"Aye, aye on that, sir. First things always done first. Then what's me duties?"

"Contact as many Aficionados de Ron as you can. Ask them if they've heard anything about Paloma's disappearance—or maybe something about a high-ranking official getting arrested. Of course, they don't even know about Casas. Then tell each of them, except for Rogelio, to meet me at the number three house Thursday morning at four a.m. I want Rogelio to meet us at the number five house at dawn on Thursday."

The Aficionados were my network of informants and operatives inside Havana. Rork digested his orders and said, "Aye, aye, sir—information about Paloma, meet at number three at four a.m. Rogelio at number five at dawn. If we can get me under way by nine o'clock, then ye'll have me back by midnight, one o'clock at the latest." He snapped his fingers. "Ooh, what o' the other lads we brought in from the north? Want me to get to them?"

Before embarking on *Richmond*, I'd hastily arranged for three more operatives—civilians with potentially useful skills for the mission—to independently arrive in Havana from Washington and New York City and await instructions. They were supposed to be staying at different hotels. I hoped they'd arrived but had no confirmation. They would have to wait.

"No, not tonight, Rork. Tomorrow morn we'll send a message to each of them at his hotel."

He rubbed his chin. "Things've changed mightily since we planned this up in Washington, ain't they? 'Twas gonna be in an' out o' Havana inside o' twenty-four hours, if Paloma was outside o' prison. Three days if the slimy bastard was inside the dungeon. Jus' break 'im out an' get 'im to *Richmond* at the anchorage, nice an' quick like. But now we're stuck right here, smack-dab in the midst of the Spaniardos, with nary so much as a friendly blue jacket or one o' Uncle Sam's gun-tubs anywhere's in sight." He sighed. "*Richmond* was our ticket out o' here, an' ol' Luce didn't even know it. Gonna have to improvise, ain't we?"

He was right. Luce hadn't known it. Neither had whoever ordered *Richmond*'s departure. "I've been thinking about that, Rork. True, we've lost the use of *Richmond*, but there're other ships we can use to escape."

"Ooh, now, Commander, we can't be buyin' steamer passage for Paloma or Casas, nor sneakin' 'em aboard a liner, nor charterin' a small boat neither. Once we're on the run, the Havana docks'll be crawlin' with Marrón's men, lookin' fer just that move." His brow furrowed in worry. "So just how're we to get aboard a ship to get away from this island?"

I shook my head in mock disappointment. "I'm very surprised at you, Sean Rork. For once in your considerably convoluted and morally degraded life, you're thinking like a law-abiding citizen, not at all like a veteran navy bosun and true Irishman. You must be getting old and dotty on me."

His face transformed into a giant smile.

"Why, pardon me all to hell an' back, sir. 'Tis as easy as a Dublin harpie on a Friday night—we jus' *steal* a ship!"

"Precisely, Rork."

Another frown. "But, nay, they'll be lookin' out for that too."

"Then we'd better steal a ship they're not worried about, because they'd never dream of us stealing her. It's time to be creative, my friend."

"But what about doin' all this quiet-like? That's what the commodore said back in Washington."

"Quiet as far as us being Americans, my friend. But if the Spanish don't know Americans stole the ship, they can't blame the United States, can they? So we won't be Americans. False flag operation, a *ruse de guerre*. Don't worry—I've been pondering the matter and have an idea."

He didn't look that confident in me but said, "Aye, aye, sir."

I heard one of the hawkers in the street calling out a headline from the newspaper, and it reminded me of something. "Oh, say Rork, before she changes the sheets, would you please have the new object of your affections bring me a copy of the *El Pais* newspaper. I need to find something in it tonight, while I'm occupying the attention of our hosts."

"Find what, sir?"

"Not quite sure yet, but I'll know it when I see it." Another thought suddenly imposed itself on my increasingly crowded mind. "By the way, Saint Christopher is the patron saint of Havana, isn't he? What's the feast day for him?"

As a lifelong Catholic who only occasionally attends services, Rork is a somewhat dubious source for detailed knowledge on the

Roman Church. He sometimes surprises me, though.

"Aye, that he is, sir. The cathedral here is named for him. An' his day is sometime in late July. Methinks the twenty-fifth, but 'tis been awhile since me schoolin', ye know."

"July, eh? Then he won't do at all. Now listen, Rork, I need a Catholic saint for this week. There must be hundreds of them, so don't you have one for this Thursday? Remember, we've got a time limit here to work within. Five days, at the most. And this first day was practically wasted."

His mind began cogitating again while he muttered, "Oh, yer heretical Methodist soul's tryin' me somethin' fierce here. Me memory's fadin'...but ah...wait." The leathery face twisted with the effort. "Aye, there's one I surely do know—me dear ol' Saint Michael. His feast is always the twenty-ninth o' September, each an' every year."

"Damn, that's not 'til Saturday. A bit late for our purposes, but I suppose he's all we've got to work with. There'll be a celebration among Catholics, right?"

"O' course! He's one o' the very biggest saints o' all. Nothin' less than an archangel, ol' Michael is. An' a patron o' sailors too, not that ye heathen Protestants would even know or care."

"Well, this heathen Protestant does care. So the sailors in the harbor will be observing the feast day too? Let me think about that. Yes, Saint Michael just might work out quite well, actually."

Rork raised an eyebrow in that devilish look I've seen before. Rubbing his hands together, he grinned and said, "Methinks a plan's afoot in that bounced-up brain o' yers, Peter Wake. Aye, action's comin' soon—I can feel it in me right foot, I can. Startin' ta ache like the devil."

I'm not superstitious like my Irish friend, but I *always* pay attention when Rork's bones hurt, especially when that right foot starts aching. Unfortunately, it usually means mortal danger lies ahead.

"Thanks for the warning, my friend. Yes, this'll require some action, all right. We've got to be smart about this, Rork, but one way or another we're leaving Cuba together on Saturday—with Paloma and Casas, if they're still alive."

That said, I began squeezing my arm to make it bleed. Obliging my efforts, several red blooms appeared. I returned inside the room, lay on the bed, and smeared it liberally around the sheets, then bellowed for the maid to "get in here and change the friggin' linens!" When little Cornelia finally arrived, a suitably exasperated Sean Rork greeted her at the door. He asked for the day's newspaper and, pointing to my blood-stained bed, a full change of sheets. She returned a few minutes later.

Endeavoring to appear as grumpy as I could—actually not that difficult given the situation we faced and the pain I felt—I sat in a chair and read the paper while Rork helped her change the linens. As I had hoped, on page three I found something useful for my fledgling plan, all the while listening covertly to my friend ply his Gaelic charm. Using broken Spanish in whispers to gain Cornelia's sympathy, he soon had her giggling softly as they both glanced furtively at the ogre reading the paper. When they were done with the bed, Rork helped me to it, where I collapsed. Trying not to overdramatize my role, I growled to him, "Now, turn out the damned gas lights and let me rest, you stupid brute."

In the ensuing darkness, I heard more giggles as the linen cart rolled away, straining under far more weight than when it first arrived. Good. It meant Rork was well along in accomplishing the initial stage of his dangerous assignment—escaping our "hosts" and finding the Aficionados. It was almost ten o'clock in the evening. I waited a few minutes, then lit the bedside lamp and examined the newspaper again, making sure I understood the information I'd found earlier. It would be a crucial component to our mission.

The Aficionados de Ron—loosely translated as the Fans of Rum— is by all outward appearances the name of a social club devoted to the appreciation of fine sipping rums, of which Cuba has the best in the world. In reality, it's a collection of people who have been supplying me information about conditions inside Havana for several years. Those conditions include commercial, agricultural, mineral, industrial, transportation, and communication viability; popular attitudes toward the civil government; Spanish military and naval activities; Cuban revolutionary activities; and any anti-American trends among the people.

The Aficionados also provide information about the darker peccadilloes of those in positions of authority, thus making them susceptible to blackmail. Extortion is the ancient method for one country to obtain valuable information about another, from persons in authority who would know such things.

The Aficionados consisted of four island-born Cuban operatives who despised the Spanish colonial government and its repression of the people within the colony. Beyond Rork and me, just two men at naval headquarters knew of the Aficionados, Commodore Walker and Admiral Porter, and then only by their aliases.

"Leo" was a layman administrator at the Jesuit monastery; "Rogelio," a rum broker; "Marco," a beef and commissary broker to the Spanish army and navy; and "Casas," a ship repair and supply agent. All of them professionally knew of Paloma through his position at the Spanish naval yard, but only Casas knew of his personal transgressions and my operation against him. None of the Aficionados knew each other, either by alias or true identity. They'd never physically met, and their only connection was through me.

The charity for the elderly at Leo's monastery received donations from a sham company in exchange for his information. The others received payments for false contracts from another dummy company. The rum club was merely a convenient ruse. I was the only person who knew their real names, which will not be revealed here.

Casas was the sole Aficionado who'd dealt directly with Paloma during the man's journey out of Cuba to carry Spanish naval secrets to me in Saint Augustine. After delivering those secrets and learning just how much evidence I had of his depravity to ensure his continued cooperation, Paloma returned to Havana two weeks later, in mid-July. He was to be contacted by Casas again so we could continue to use him as an informant, but Casas reported on the twenty-fifth of July that Paloma had disappeared. By mid-August, two attempts to communicate with Casas went unanswered.

My man in Nassau then tried to contact Rogelio, Leo, and Marco and received enigmatic replies, leading to speculation they were under Spanish surveillance or possibly had been turned into double-agents. And now, on a rainy night in the heart of "enemy" territory, Sean Rork was about to discover if the Aficionados still existed. To say I was nervous as I waited is a gross understatement.

8

For the Honor of a Lady

Havana, Cuba
Midnight, Tuesday
25 September 1888

Rork's journey was purposely circuitous. First he had to make sure none of Marrón's men were following him, for I was sure our "servants" were in the colonel's pay. Then he had to fulfill his promise to Cornelia, who, providentially, was just completing her work shift. After that, he was to vary his routes to the four separate locations of the Aficionados, all of which were in the ancient original quarter of Havana, near the waterfront. I estimated perhaps two miles of walking in total and a few minutes at each place to ask the questions and give the message—easy enough to accomplish in a little more than two hours, barring complications. Finally, he had to somehow reenter Hotel Florida and report to me.

It started out well. Upon emerging from the rear of the hotel into a narrow alley, Cornelia took him by the hand and led him through the downpour to Aquiar Street. Alleys between buildings in Havana are unusual in that they have nondescript doorways that open to the streets. From thence, they walked southerly to the taverns along Desamparados Street, across from the San Jose docks. Not the most impressive neighborhood of Havana by a long shot but close enough to three of the Aficionados for Rork's purposes. Soaked to the skin by this point, they ended up huddled at the corner table inside the misnamed El Refugio de Los Santos. It is a dismal place Rork and I patronized once by mistake back in '73. Once was sufficient for me.

There, courtesy of a gold dollar from Rork's pocket, they proceeded to imbibe an entire bottle of *aguardiente viejo*, Cuban "firewater" that is eighty-five or more percent pure cane alcohol and aged for a grand total of two weeks, if you're lucky. Soon, little Cornelia felt absolutely no inhibition in word or deed. It was at this point that Rork deviated from the plan.

Now, I know what the reader is thinking at this point. I was imagining the same thing, sitting there in the hotel room waiting well after the agreed-upon time for his return. But my imagination, as fertile as it is after twenty-five years with Rork, wasn't anywhere near the equal of what really happened.

Sean Rork is a naval bosun and frequently reminds me that since the navy does not consider him a commissioned officer and he is therefore not a "gentleman," he is under none of the constraints by which commissioned officers feel bound when on liberty ashore. Such an attitude sometimes leads to consequences that are unfortunate, to say the least, and usually require my intervention after the fact. However, whilst I was busy bloodying my bed, I anticipated that potential problem and thought to preempt it by reminding him, "Kindly remember that tonight you're *not* on a real liberty with this young lady, Rork. You're working, so stay sharp and don't dally long with her."

I remembered his words as he cast a mildly perturbed look in my direction. "Ooh, not to worry, sir. Nay one wee little bit. Me mind's sharp as a sailmaker's needle, whether me body's drinkin' or lovin'—an' that's no empty boast, not at all. Jus' a drink o' two with the lass an' some friendly dancin' to make her feel good about helpin' me. Methinks nay more'n twenty minutes with the lass. An' then it's off to do me duty an' find our wayward Aficionado lads. Back here by midnight or so, fit as a fiddle an' still rarin' fer more."

That glib reply put me even further ill at ease.

For dear, little, shy Cornelia ended up dancing one of the sultry local tunes known infamously as a *danza criolla* with a big, one-eared longshoreman thug, who sported a livid purple scar running from where his right ear used to be down to the corner of his rotten-toothed mouth. Known around the docks by the quaint moniker of "El Strangulador," this cretin's favorite form of sport was strangling anyone who physically opposed him. Rork was the only *gringo* in the joint and also the only one there who didn't know the thug or his nickname. Worse, Rork had also lost all common sense by that time and mistakenly thought he would defend the young lady's honor when the longshoreman began pawing Cornelia and she shrieked in horror.

Had my friend been sober, or only half-soused, he would have realized it was all a setup by his demurely affectionate lass, the newest love of his life, with whom he was planning further amorous adventures later that evening. But alas, the rum-induced haze, similar to the well-known fog of war for commanders, was just a little too thick for Rork to recognize a trap.

By Cornelia's second shriek, Rork was facing the thug and prying one of the paws off the girl. In a perfectly choreographed maneuver, she retreated out of range as El Strangulador roundhoused my friend with a left, expertly targeted to the point of the chin. Rork, his head snapped backward, was propelled astern into a table of other ne'er-do-wells, one of whom promptly bashed him over the skull with a bottle. Any normal man would have been dead, unconscious, or, at the very least, in severe pain. Not so, my friend Rork. He is certainly not superhuman, but he is Irish and uncommonly lucky.

From what I can determine, the *aguardiente* inside him

provided sufficient anesthetic to mask the pain; that thick skull of his, barrier to so many of my entreaties over the years, thwarted unconsciousness; and God's well-known fondness for drunken Irish idiots prevented death from ending it right there and then. Rork was stunned, though, as he lay sprawled on the rough plank floor while the patrons laughed at his comeuppance at the hands of the local bully. Feeling small hands going through his pockets, he turned his head to see Cornelia smirking as she counted out her newly acquired wealth.

Suddenly the truth intruded into Rork's rattled brain like a hot poker. His blood boiled instantaneously, to the quick regret of pretty Cornelia and her partner in crime, El Strangulador. The other patrons and the owner of El Refugio de Los Santos, ignorant of whom they were dealing with, were already clamoring to Cornelia for their cut of the *yanqui*'s loot.

Because she was female, Rork used only his real fist on her and avoided her face, putting it right into her stomach. Eyes wide and mouth gasping for air, Cornelia loosened her grip on the money. Rork grabbed the gold coins and shoved them back in his pocket where they belonged. Then he jumped to his feet and looked for his large nemesis. The monster had apparently departed, and, for a fleeting second, Rork thought the episode over.

But El Strangulador was behind Rork and gave away his position with one of those malevolent, guttural chuckles that anticipates the pleasure of killing a man. What the giant didn't anticipate was that wonderfully concealed marlinespike.

As the American in the now-bloody linen suit rose, seemingly from the dead, he deftly deposited that false India-rubber left hand in his trouser pocket and left it in there, extracting the arm with the marlinespike, ready for action. By the time he felt El Strangulador's sausage-sized fingers come from behind and dig into his throat, Rork was already spinning to the right, spike held at the approximate latitude of the creature's face.

It is axiomatic that no matter how huge or strong one's opponent is, if you can reach his brain and shut off his system of nerves, like one of Edison's new electrical switches, then the fight is immediately ended. Your foe is dead. The fastest route to the brain from the front is through the orbital cavity, otherwise known as the eye socket. Approximately two inches to the rear of the eye—three inches for a mammoth like El Strangulador—the cavity narrows to a passageway, enabling the optic nerve to reach the brain. A small target, but well worth it. At five inches, Rork's spike is more than long enough for the job, and once it pierced that passage, the monster fell in a heap before the stunned crowd.

The immediate mortal threat having been eliminated, my friend now surveyed his surroundings for any others. However, the crowd's enthusiasm for blood and/or money had vanished by then. So had Cornelia.

Rork wiped off the spike, reinstalled his rubber hand over it, pulled a Colt revolver from inside his jacket, and leveled it at the face of a man at the doorway who was defiantly holding a machete. Wisdom prevailed, and the man dropped his weapon as Rork calmly walked out, leaving the audience with a final comment in Spanish regarding their establishment, a translation of which would be unsuitable for these pages.

It was now eleven o'clock and he still had much to do, so Rork darted down a side alley to stop and assess the situation and figure out what should come next. That decision turned out to be fortunate, for the bar mob could be heard calling for the police, shouting the word "*Asesinato!*" ("Murder!") and "*El asesino es un norteamericano!*" ("The murderer is an American!") Locals were filling the street, demanding the *policia* find and shoot the American.

The first police arrived quickly and began blowing whistles to summon more of their number. It didn't take long for them to be everywhere, searching for the drunken *gringo* who carried a strange weapon in his left hand. The witnesses had given varying descriptions since everything had happened so fast. Some said it was a knife, some an ice pick, others a muffled derringer.

In the performance of our intelligence duties over the years,

Rork and I have had occasion to observe the municipal police of Havana, who patrol in groups of three. Each is armed with a short, broad sword and a truncheon, with the senior member of the trio carrying an 1880 model Obrea Hermanos .44 caliber five-shot revolver. The police are not known to be overly aggressive toward foreigners and are usually open to pecuniary negotiation should there be an infraction of one of the city's myriad laws, since the colonial government is frequently six months in arrears for their meager pay.

However, when the crime is violent, such negotiations are moot, and the police have a reputation for making a quick arrest—of somebody. These prisoners have the unfortunate habit of being killed while trying to escape or, evidently, even thinking about escape. From the point of view of the police, this solves several problems: The streets appear to have been made safer; the courts are less clogged; and the well-to-do feel more at ease to patronize the city's various establishments. The result is that there is very little violent crime in Havana.

Rork knows this. Hearing the clamor, he therefore thought it prudent not to go to the police and explain his side of the equation. He also realized that the streets were no longer safe for him, so instead he went aloft to the rooftops, three stories above the police, to escape unnoticed and make his way to the nearest Aficionado. It was a good idea, except that he was in Havana, where everything is different—and usually more difficult.

The rooftops of Cuba are generally without peaks and ridges, but instead are flat. Most are subdivided by short walls into small patios, where many families have gardens of fruit and flowers. It is a brilliant concept and well suited for the tropics. It also means that, unlike in northern climes, there are a lot of people up there, sleeping in hammocks, since the heat, humidity, and bugs are less oppressive on the roofs. On rainy nights, awnings are spread over the sleepers to shed the water away.

This being Havana, it was too early for them to be asleep when Rork reached the roofs. At eleven o'clock on a Tuesday night, most of the residents were sitting and talking quietly about their day's events. None expected a tall, frighteningly bloody *gringo* to suddenly appear, dashing through their private space into the dark of the next-door rooftop.

It didn't take long for a trail of alarming shouts to erupt along the path of Rork's flight. They were heard down below, and soon the pursuers on ground level were following the sound of Rork's progress above. I imagine that when he ended up at the end of the last roof in the line, those chasing him thought they had the murderer cornered. But, of course, they didn't know that a sailorman, especially a bosun, possesses unique skills alien to most landsmen.

Rork stood at the edge of a roof overlooking San Isidro Street. Fifty feet behind him was a small band of irate fathers and husbands, all armed with whatever sharp tools they could grab and heading for the *yanqui* criminal who had just run through their patios and terrified their families. By this time, the rumor being yelled out was that the American had killed two nuns and their carriage driver, and no one was stopping to consider such niceties as the truth.

Forty feet below him was a patrol of police, the senior of which had his revolver pointed at where Rork stood. For most men on the run, the gig would be up, but that's when Rork did what bosuns do every day at sea. He strode to the corner and flung himself off, looping his hands and feet around what on a ship would be a stay—in this case it was a telephone wire—and using his false appliance and spike as a running sheave, he slid rapidly down the line and across to the top of the two-story building on the other side of the street. Two shots boomed out, but the shooter, as Rork surmised, hadn't had target practice in several years and misgauged the speed of his target in the dark. Both rounds missed.

Once at his destination, my friend headed for the end of the roof on that block of buildings but deviated course to the starboard at the last minute, riding another telephone line down to the ground at Damas and Paula Streets. His return to earth took only seconds, but it was enough to elude his foes. Rork now ran east on Paula Street and ducked inside a dark shadow at the Church of the Merced, where he watched the police and vigilantes continue north on Damas Street in fruitless pursuit. After five minutes of seeing no one searching his immediate position, he shed his fearsome coat and rolled the pair of Colt revolvers up inside it, which he then stowed under his left arm.

Calmly walking two blocks east to Paula Park on the waterfront, he tacked to port and went three more blocks north to Acosta and Inquisidor Streets. Checking the building on the northwest side, he looked up at the second-floor, corner apartment window, where a lamp was lit and a shadow was moving about inside. It was the home of Casas, our missing operative, the first Aficionado on his list to contact.

By now, Rork was stone-cold sober and his senses were acute. He sat in a nearby shadow and watched the apartment awhile. He saw no one enter or leave the building and no signs of police presence. At midnight, he went inside the front door.

9

Mobilization

Havana, Cuba
Before dawn, Wednesday
26 September 1888

After creeping slowly up the creaking stairs in the darkness, Rork paused at the apartment door and listened. No sound emanated from within, but a dim light shone under the door from inside, presumably from the lamp. The door was locked. The building was unusual for Havana, since most had a central patio with mezzanines above, onto which opened the surrounding apartments. This particular one had no central patio and mezzanines and was instead built in the North American fashion, with a hallway spanning each floor, along which opened the apartments. Either end of the hallway had a window.

Pondering the situation, Rork had a premonition not to knock on the door. Instead of a frontal approach, he decided to flank the position, going out the second-floor hall window to a narrow, open-air balcony that wrapped around the exterior of the building.

Sidling along the ledge, he came to the window of Casas' apartment and looked inside. It was in extreme disarray, with furniture cushions ripped open, cupboards emptied onto the floor, and clothing strewn—obviously the result of a detailed search. A man's form darted through the far side of the apartment, slamming the entry door behind him as he exited. Rork decided against breaking the window open and doing his own search, not knowing whether the apparent burglar, who he assumed was one of Marrón's agents, would return or might have an accomplice remaining inside. In any case, it was clear that Casas was not residing there, so he determined to visit the second Aficionado on his list.

Rogelio, a forty-four-year-old bachelor *bon vivant*, lived over his rum brokerage office in a building at Officios and Santa Clara Streets, two blocks north of Casas and close to Plaza Luz. The richly appointed apartment, in an ornate French-styled building, was a symbol of his success in selling raw molasses and rum to the U.S. Sugar Trust, run by the famous Henry Havermeyer, a man of considerable political influence in the United States. Rogelio didn't know Havermeyer personally—I'd checked—but he was the type to enjoy dropping the man's name in conversations. Fully cognizant of his shallow nature, I used him for minor information on the social and political scene in Havana, thinking that someday he might provide something significant.

Having attended the theater that evening and consumed a fair amount of brandy, Rogelio was none too happy to be suddenly disturbed at such an early hour of the morning, especially by one of the American agents to whom he sometimes gave his minor information. In fact, his hostility was barely concealed when Rork asked why he had not replied to our inquiries by telegraph. "I have been very busy with my *real* work, Mr. Rork, and had no time for your silly questions."

Rork, as the reader can well imagine, was by this point in the evening no longer interested in the long-winded civility expected within the Latin culture. He bluntly asked Rogelio if he knew what happened to a Señor Paloma from the naval yard, who seemed to be missing lately. Rogelio, who had always been the most mercurial and marginal of my Havana operatives, declared he neither knew nor cared about Paloma's whereabouts.

He added that he would be quite thankful to be left alone by the *yanquis* in the future, since times were politically difficult in Havana and perceived traitors were not being treated lightly. In normal times, I would have agreed to his request and severed our relationship. But I'd had my suspicions about Rogelio. Was he an informant for the Spanish? I wanted to see him face to face, to gauge his eyes, hear his voice, watch his hands. If I judged him to be indeed a double agent, that was fine, for he could be useful to me in unwittingly disseminating false information back to the Spanish.

Rogelio was truly incensed by Rork's next comment, which came in the nature of a command: Be at house number five at dawn Thursday morning for a meeting with Commander Wake. This was, it should be remembered, two hours later and half a mile east of where the other Aficionados would be gathering—for the meeting with Rogelio was to be far different in nature and required there be no witnesses. And I should explain here that there were no rendezvous points numbered one, two, or four. Nor was house number five a real house. The numbering designation and house descriptor were simple subterfuges to confuse and divert any counterintelligence.

Rogelio proceeded to curse in Spanish, loud enough for the neighbors to hear. Then he announced with a defiant tone that he wasn't going to meet Commander Wake at all. That was a mistake, for Rork decided that a stronger argument was needed.

Like most navy bosuns, he can be quite persuasive with recalcitrant subordinates, especially those who have forgotten they *are* subordinates. Accordingly, he leaned over the diminutive businessman and growled, "Lookee here, ye uppity little slacker. Paloma was jus' the first to disappear. Them Spaniardo dons probably've already got a suspicion o' ye ownself by now, an' the bastards're jus' waitin' fer their own good time to come an' arrest yer fat little arse."

Rork leaned even closer. "Aye, an' won't that be cute, when they drag you out o' here by yer pencil neck, blubberin' like a baby for yer mummy. Mark me words, yer only hope for *survival* is with me an' Commander Wake. So now's the time when you say, nice an' quiet-like, 'Aye, Mr. Rork'—an' then shut yer damned hatch an' get the friggin' job done. Remember, dawn—that means sunrise—on Thursday morn at house number five. Don't be late."

Rogelio mumbled an acknowledgment, but its genuineness wasn't convincing, so Rork included an addendum while putting that heavy left hand of his on Rogelio's shoulder. "An' if ye're thinkin' o' doin' us wrong an' turnin' stoolie for Marrón, then know this, Señor Rogelio..." The rubber hand came off, unveiling the still-bloody spike, only inches from Rogelio's face. "Ye do *that*, an' by the end o' the week, ye'll be lashed to a plank in some Havana cellar, dyin' real slow an' real painful—with me enjoyin' every friggin' hour o' it."

The man's next assent had far more sincerity to it. Concluding that his efforts had been successful, Rork departed seconds later, leaving a still-shaken Rogelio sitting on his embroidered satin sofa, staring at the parquet floor.

The next Aficionado had the most unusual address. For thirty years, Leo had been a clerk at the ancient monastery on Luz Street, where it intersects Compostela. Now, at age fifty-one and in worsening health, he was the senior administrator, a lay position of some authority, at the Iglesia de Nuestra Señora de Belén. Home of the Jesuits since 1842, this monastery was the residence and office of my friend Father Viñes and his astronomical observatory.

Benito Viñes was the Jesuit leader in Havana, president of the Cátholic college, and world-renowned for his work in tropical cyclone meteorology. In '86, at the request of influential Jesuit friends of mine in Italy, he was the one who arranged for me to be rescued from Marrón's clutches. Most improbably, he used a notorious bandit to accomplish the mission. In the years since, we'd maintained a correspondence and friendship. But at present, he wasn't available to me, for Benito was at a scientific exhibition in Barcelona.

Here I believe an explanation is due about the religious situation in Cuba, which is assumed by many in North America to be devoutly Catholic. It used to be, but times are changing, and not in the Church's—or the Madrid government's—favor.

The Spanish colonial government, whose institutional paranoia knows no limits, allows very few island-born priests to serve in Cuba. And they allow no native-born people to ascend to a rank above a clerk within the colonial administration. The joke is that "the one thing a Spaniard cannot do in Cuba is raise a Spanish son," for once they are born there, they are no longer eligible to hold Spanish office on the island.

There is no separation between church and state. Priests serving in Cuba are paid by—and for the most part are politically loyal to—the government in Madrid. Some, like Father Viñes, have friends on both sides of the independence issue, but then the Jesuits are known for their liberal tolerance, sometimes thereby incurring the wrath of the senior establishment of the Church.

Many Cuban Catholics have joined the burgeoning Protestant churches, particularly the Episcopal and Methodist. This trend—there are now some 8,000 Protestants in Havana and Matanzas alone—is very alarming to the regime. There are rumors the government may try to harass the Protestant churches off the island, especially since so many of the independence supporters attend them.

These colonial policies—and many others about taxes, tariffs, and individual liberties—have infuriated many Cubans. That anger led them to support the independence movement and any other efforts that might act against what they see as their foreign Spanish occupiers. Leo is very much a loyal and devout Catholic, but he is a Cuban and disgusted by what he sees. As long as it does not violate the Church, he quietly does what he can to help independence. One of his efforts is to assist me with bits and pieces

of what he hears, something his employer and my friend, Father
Viñes, does not know.

The vigilante commotion about the murder in the streets
apparently over, Rork made his way through the still-rainy night
along Luz Street to the monastery. Slipping the night watchman
ten pesos and explaining with a cocked eye and sly smile that he
was delivering a note from a lady, Rork made his way through the
dark central patio to the stairs leading to the upper mezzanine.

He'd never been to Leo's quarters but remembered the man's
general description of their location once. The problem was that
it was pitch black and there were six doorways in that area, each
opening to a sparsely decorated room containing several snoring
bodies. He couldn't tell which was Leo's. Proceeding to check them
one by one, in the fourth room he saw a form that resembled the
Aficionado and reached down to wake him, but stopped at the last
moment. Wrong man. Too thin.

The sixth room held only one man, a very big one, whose face
was buried in the pillow. Rork surmised that Leo's seniority would
give him that privacy and the form was the correct size, for though
dear Leo had few possessions, he loved good food and wine, as
anyone could deduce upon sight of him.

Fervently hoping it was the right person, Rork jostled a
shoulder and was rewarded with a surprised Leo, who, unlike
Rogelio, was not hostile but bemused by the clandestine visit. In
the subsequent whispered conversation by lamplight, Leo reported
he had heard a rumor that Paloma was missing from his office but
had no further information on where he might be. However, he
did have a bit of news Rork found interesting.

The young man who'd exploded the bomb at the palace
had been identified. He wasn't from one of the main Cuban
independence groups but was part of the anarchist faction in
Havana, led by a Spanish anarchist who'd come to Cuba a few
years earlier, Roig San Martin. Martin published a broadsheet
called *El Productor* and was a confederate in the socialist workers'
organization, *Circulo de Trabajadores*.

Leo explained that the *Circulo de Trabajadores*, which had donated money to the defense fund of the Haymarket anarchist bombers in Chicago two years earlier, was currently supporting a tobacco workers strike against several factories in Havana and soliciting funds for their behalf. Demonstrations were planned around the city for that very week. So far, the anarchists had not been violent. Leo thought the bomber's actions were probably not sanctioned by the group but said that frustrations among workers were building to a level where similar *ad hoc* attacks might occur. Giving Rork a questioning glance, he said that there were rumors that a *yanqui* naval officer had thwarted the bomber at the palace, saving many lives. Rork admitted it was me. Leo promised to try to have more information for us at the meeting the next night.

Rork's last contact was Marco, who lived near the main cathedral, at Chacon and Cuba Streets. Marco was the thirty-nine-year-old son of a Protestant German mother and Catholic Cuban father who had met in Paris during the revolutionary days leading to the French Second Republic, an intriguing story he'd promised to tell me some day. A supplier of food provisions and dry goods supplies to both the Spanish army and navy, Marco lived in an unpretentious but quite comfortable apartment very close to his clients at the colonial government offices. He was one of my most valuable assets in Havana, with contacts everywhere in the military. Rork and I had been there once before.

The house servant, roused out of his bed, was reluctant to do the same to his employer for some disheveled and blood-stained American who smelled like rum and sweat and whom he only recognized as one of his boss's many business acquaintances. His concern was understandable, for by then it was almost one o'clock in the morning.

Rork, displaying his disarming Gaelic charm, prevailed over the man's wariness by explaining that yes, he'd been drinking all night but had won at gambling and was honoring the promise he'd made to immediately repay a loan the man's squire had given him six months earlier. All of that was total nonsense, of course, but Rork can conjure such blarney and let it roll off his lips as if it were the holy gospel. The next moment, he had the servant laughing with him about the whole thing for, after all, his boss would love the gesture and also the money.

Rork and Marco quickly got down to the business at hand.

"Paloma, the administrator?" he replied to Rork's question. "Last month there was a rumor he is a prisoner in the cells below the Audiencia, arrested for diversion of treasury funds, and would be sent home in disgrace as an example to the others. I thought that a very unusual situation for a man of Paloma's status. Of course, everyone in authority takes a little, but he probably did not include his superiors in the diversion. I will discreetly ask around tomorrow and see if I can learn more for our meeting Thursday morning."

It was after two a.m. and still raining when Rork, soaked, soiled, and very sore from his ordeal, avoided any of Marrón's men in the lobby and returned to our room the hard way—by scaling, mostly one-handed, the outside of the building onto the balcony, for Obispo Street was finally deserted. In the dark, he collapsed in the chair close beside my bed and whispered a report of what all had happened to him. He ended it with a "Damned sorry to the hilt, sir, about muckin' up our plans with that damned fight." He added sheepishly, "Truly thought the lass was bein' molested an' did what came natural-like ta defend her, but now me knows it was bloody friggin' stupid o' me. One o' the oldest traps in a harbor town."

Rork clearly needed bucking up. "Well, my friend, I'd wager you're not the first foreigner she's pulled that stunt on. I'd also wager she got you to drink most of that *aguardiente*. But it's done and over, so we'll adapt and move on."

He nodded. "Aye, an' me's thinkin' she'll not come back 'round here to work in the morn."

"Yes, I agree on that. But the word's out about a *gringo* who killed a local, so we need to take that into account with our plans. Get some sleep, and come morning, deep-six those clothes someplace so they won't be found. We've a lot to get done and only four more days to do it."

I heard snoring moments later—Rork can fall asleep in a gale—and spent the next few minutes analyzing his episode with Cornelia and her acquaintances. Was she in the employ of Marrón? No, probably not—Rork had initiated the contact with her. But the incident had considerably complicated our freedom of movement. Rork could no longer go out in the daylight, lest he be recognized as the suspected murderer by the crowd and the police.

That led me to a solution Rork wouldn't like at all, but his preferences weren't important anymore, for we had no other alternative. I needed him to accomplish several other things in the four days remaining to us in Havana, for I would be occupied with my own duties. Thus far, I had been on the defensive, reacting to the adverse events affecting us in Havana, never a comfortable scenario for me. Now it was time to go on the offense, to *make* things happen in our favor.

10

Distinguished Visitors

Hotel Florida
Obispo Street
Havana, Cuba
10 a.m., Wednesday
26 September 1888

That morning, our second in Havana, was enlivened by two unique visitors, both of whom I had expected. It was ten o'clock when the first arrived.

Mr. Ramon Oscar Williams was a distinguished older gentleman with gentle eyes, white beard and moustache, and thinning hair. The man possessed an air of quiet confidence, along with a huge amount of responsibility. The long-time consul-general for the United States in Cuba, with authority over subordinate consulates in Matanzas and Santiago de Cuba, Williams and I had occasionally met in our official capacities over the years. All visiting or transiting naval officers were required to check in at the consulate—a formality that was usually handled by a junior consular clerk, but sometimes a middle-grade or senior officer would have the opportunity to meet the consul-general himself.

A resident of the island since childhood, Williams had an outstanding reputation as our country's representative on the Spanish island. He was a diplomat who understood Cuba better than any other American in the State Department, and he wasn't afraid to clash with the colonial authorities while defending American interests.

Knowing me only as another naval officer passing through, he had never been privy to my work in Cuba for ONI. Our general rule was to keep diplomats at a polite distance, for their sake of deniability as well as for our own flexibility. The two professions have divergent responsibilities and requirements, and ways of viewing a country's assets and actions.

Although Rork had registered us with the chargé d'affaires at the U.S. consulate on our visit in '86, Consul-General Williams wasn't aware of our clandestine mission, the subsequent capture by Marrón and incarceration in the Audiencia, or our escape from the island. In fact, the last time I'd seen him was in '84, when attending some excruciatingly boring reception at the consulate while passing through the island on my way north.

With concern evident on his face—I was still in bed, continuing my charade—he shook hands with me and said, "Commander Wake, good to see you again. Been years, hasn't it? I'm very sorry I missed your fencing exhibition yesterday morning, but I was off at Cienfuegos and couldn't make it. Very sorry for your injuries from the bomb. Is there anything I can do?"

"No, sir. It's all pretty minor stuff, really."

Williams paused briefly, then added, "I understand that saber match was quite the show." He regarded my bandaged left hand. "Very heated, almost *personal*, according to my friends who were there. The Spanish navy's embarrassed, to say the least."

I could just imagine how William' friends in the Spanish elite would've described it. I decided to downplay the whole thing.

"Personal, sir? No, not at all. Certainly not on my part. Just a fencing match that got rather strenuous. The cut to the hand was an accident and my own fault. Let it get in the way."

It was clear my version didn't impress him one bit. "Hmm. Well, I also heard that the lunatic who threw the bomb had as his target the captain-general's young nephew. And apparently, *you* saved the boy's life. I must say, you do seem to lead an exciting life, Commander. I think you're possibly the most exciting man in Havana right now."

I didn't want or need *that* title. "Just coincidence, sir. I happened to be near the young man, so I just kicked the damned thing away from him. Nothing special, believe me."

That smile again. One of those knowing smiles that says *I know something's going on.* "Nothing special, eh? Well, I may believe you on that, Commander. But don't expect anyone else in Havana to agree with your modesty, particularly His Excellency, Don Sabas. In fact, I believe the captain-general himself should be here at any moment now, to express his personal appreciation for your heroism and your wounds. Do you mind if I remain and watch? This will be very good for our relations with the Spanish authorities in Cuba. We haven't had much goodwill with them lately."

Yes, I did mind very much, for I was about to send Rork out on a courier assignment, but what could I say? Consul-generals have a lot of influence in Washington. And I didn't need the waters stirred up any further in Havana.

"Of course not, sir. Please do stay. And the wounds are very minor cuts and a concussion. Nothing even remotely heroic."

Minutes later there was a commotion down on the street: shouted commands, the clatter of hooves, jingling of spurs, and squealing of wheels. The Captain-General of Cuba had arrived in all of his splendor. Rork, peering out the doorway of the balcony, whistled softly in amazement and observed, "Ooh, jus' look at 'em all bowin' an' scrapin', like it was Jesus him ownself who's pulled in. Like me fellow Gaels, actin' the fool ta' curry a wee bit o' favor with the arrogant English bastards when they'd finally visit their estates in Ireland."

Williams was clearly displeased at that comment and probably worried what Rork might say in front of the captain-general. I learned long ago to never get Rork started on the subject of the English overlords in Ireland, so I switched subjects and asked Williams, "Do you know anything about a social event that I may be obliged to attend, sir?"

"Obliged to attend? Why, Commander, you're the guest of honor! It's tonight at eight o'clock at the palace. Didn't they tell you?"

"Mr. Acera mentioned something about it yesterday, sir, but I was a bit groggy, and since then I've received no confirmation."

A pandemonium of noise erupted in the passageway, and the door was suddenly flung open by our "servant" guarding the room. Williams shook his head at me and grinned. "I think you're about to receive a very personal invitation, Commander."

Señor Acera was first through the door, announcing loudly: "Attention, everyone! His Excellency, the Captain-General of His Majesty's Most Faithful Isle of Cuba, Don Sabas Marín Gonzalez, has arrived!"

Appointed by the king, Don Sabas Marín Gonzalez had been in charge of Cuba for fourteen months. During that time, he had struggled to subdue the growing independence movement that had endured off and on for twenty years. He also tried to deal with the general discontent of the Cuban intellectual and business classes, the emancipation and assimilation of the black slaves, the large segment of mill owners who wanted annexation to the United States, the growing paranoia of the Spanish elite, and the never-ending animosities between Spain and the American colossus to the north.

Somewhere in his mid-fifties, he was the son of a famous colonel of the Royal Artillery and had already built an impressive career since joining the army at an early age. While fighting the Cuban insurgents during the initial years of the insurrection in the late sixties, Don Sabas had been awarded the illustrious Cruz de San Fernando medal. In 1882, he was appointed as governor of the province of Santa Clara. There he distinguished himself by tackling government corruption—a rare endeavor by Spanish administrators—and by marrying Matilde León y Gregario, a native-born lady of the city of Trinidad. Matilde was the beautiful daughter of another famous Spanish soldier, Colonel Carlos de León y Navarrete, who was the colonial official in charge of the island's postal service and roads.

As Acera deftly backed out of the way, Gonzalez, wearing a less formal uniform than he wore at the palace for the fencing exhibition, strode into the room, trailed by Doctor Cobre and a dozen staff officers. He greeted Williams warmly, nodded to Rork, and turned to me, his face radiating pleasure. I made a show of bravely trying to raise my wounded body in bed, but his hand went up quickly.

"No, no, please remain at rest in the bed. I ask you to forgive me my bad English, Commander Peter Wake. I do not wish to disturb you, but I came here in person to express in your language my thank you for your demonstration of skill and honor at the fencing match, and for your brilliant heroism...in defense of my..." He looked at Acera, who murmured something to him. "My...*nephew*...and his family from that fanatic who attacked us yesterday. I wish that your wounds will heal rapidly. You have the appreciation of myself and my family and the crown and people of Spain."

With clicked heels, he then bowed to me and held out his hand. The man had a firm grip, without the arrogant show of strength some insecure European military men feel obliged to show when shaking hands with an American.

Realizing I was expected to reply to his kind words with some of my own, I glanced at Consul-General Williams for a hint of what to say. His eyes were positively alight with joy at this turn of events, his mind no doubt composing a triumphant telegraphic report to the state department in Washington. Beyond that, he uttered no comment but instead watched me like the rest of the audience in the room.

Rork, standing behind him, back in the far corner, was no help either. He wore the steady gaze of a veteran petty officer in the presence of senior officers. Then his face broke its mask and he winked at me, with a nod to go ahead.

Summoning up my Spanish, I spoke with as much flair as one can while in bed, surrounded by a be-medaled crowd of military swells staring down at you expectantly.

"Su Excelencia, fue mi gran honor que participar a la exhibicion ayer. Señor Boreau fue un advesario muy capacitado, y mi victoria fue solomente porque un momento de buen suerte. Mis acciónes con el lunatico fueran solomente instinto y mis heridas son pequeño. Gracias para la hospitalidad muy bien y las palabras muy agradable. Soy solomente un marinero del mar, no soy un héroe."

My attempt at modesty yielded the hoped-for reaction from both Don Sabas and Williams. The captain-general beamed with happiness and spun around to face his staff, saying in Spanish, "Here is a true gentleman and officer of the highest class. Take note and remember this moment." To Williams, he said in English, "My friend, your country has a very good man in Commander Wake. I wish that all of your compatriots were like him."

Acera gently cleared his throat, an apparent signal to the captain-general, for that worthy now held out a hand, in which Acera promptly put a gold-embossed envelope. With another click of his heels, Don Sabas smiled and handed me the envelope, saying, "Usually this is sent by a senior messenger, but today, Commander, you will receive it by the most senior messenger in all of Cuba—me. Please accept this invitation to be the guest of honor at a small private dinner in my personal apartments at the palace, to be followed by a musical soiree with some of my closest friends in this city. I wish to show them how the military gentlemen of our two great nations can be friends and allies. Of course, this event would have been held last night, after the exhibition of yesterday morning. But the attack at the palace, and your gallant wounds, forced us to postpone it until tonight."

His brow tightened with anxiety as he continued. "Doctor

Cobre assures me that you will be able to participate in the dinner and will be able to, at the very least, watch the dancing afterward, but I have been warned not to impose too much upon you or allow you to strain yourself. Will you please make me happy and accept my invitation?"

It was exceedingly well done on his part—I got the impression he actually meant every word. I did a slight bow of my head as graciously as I could and replied, "*Por supuesto, Su Excelencia. Es mi honor y placer que aceptar su invitacion. Muchas gracias.*"

And so it was that Rork and I ended up in Havana as the official guests of the Spanish crown's captain-general, and finally back on course with my original plan to complete our mission in Cuba.

11

Imported Talent

Hotel Florida
Obispo Street
Havana, Cuba
11:30 a.m., Wednesday
26 September 1888

I could come up with only two methods to sufficiently disguise Rork for his upcoming stroll about the city. One was to dress him as a woman, admittedly a rather large and ugly woman. The large, ugly part would actually be useful to his task, since that would generate far less attraction from the male inhabitants of the place, who are known for their overtly thorough observation of the fairer sex. But at three inches over six feet, his frame dictated female apparel not readily available in Cuba, where most of the ladies are petite and very pretty.

The other scheme was for him to still be a man, the kind of man with whom no one wanted to be in immediate proximity—a leper. The attire could easily be accomplished by what we had at hand: dirty trousers under filthy bedsheets, some of which would be wound around his head for additional camouflage. Furthermore, I decided he would be a speechless leper, the better to hide his badly accented Spanish and *norteamericano* identity.

The leper colony at San Lazaro, next to the ancient Espada Cemetery, where Colonel Marrón captured Rork and me two years earlier, was out on the west side of the city, several miles from our present location. Lepers did not generally move about inside the city, so that would be a problem Rork would have to overcome on the spot, should he incite the attention of an inquisitive policeman. I thought his muteness might help in that regard.

Two other things were necessary before Rork could set out on his assignment. First, he had to have the appropriate symptoms of the initial stage of the dreaded disease, which features red skin lesions and senselessness in the limbs. His false left hand provided a truly senseless limb and some of my blood, rubbed onto his face and hands, did an approximation of lesions. By necessity, Rork's transformation was achieved in the corner by the door, out of sight of the spy-hole in the wall.

The second requirement was the most significant, at least from Rork's point of view. It took him almost fifteen minutes of procrastination and complaining under his breath to shave off his signature walrus moustache. Tired of it, I quietly reminded him, "Quit the bellyaching, Rork. Your unfortunate need for disguise is entirely due to your lack of discipline last night regarding women and rotgut rum while working."

Rork didn't appreciate my opinion, which he categorized as, "Naggin' like an ol' woman."

In the end, by half past eleven that morning, an hour after our distinguished visitors had departed the room, Rork was ready, looking nothing like his usual self. Now came the challenge of an exit, for the balcony was far too visible from the street in the busy daytime. That left the hallway, which meant a distraction had to be manufactured for the armed "servant" standing outside the door. Fortunately, Rork and I knew the layout of the hotel, having stayed there in '85, in the days before I became *persona non grata* with Marrón.

Therefore, I simply went to the door and tersely ordered the servant/guard to fetch me a jug of orange juice from the table on the other side of the mezzanine, about seventy feet away. The man, having witnessed that I was the honored personal friend of the captain-general, wasted no time in complying. While he was thus preoccupied, Rork slipped off to the service stairs, where he descended to the ground and his egress out the back alley.

His assignment was to deliver messages to the three men with unique skills whom I'd hastily arranged to come down from the United States and meet me in Havana. The time had come for them to learn their duties. They already knew a vague outline of their parts from my telegrams to them from Washington, but my newly hatched final version of the plan required each to perform a crucial function in the operation ahead.

The narrow streets were already baking in Havana's windless midday heat as Rork made his way toward Hotel Inglaterra, our haunt of old at the city's central square in the theater district. The square is usually known by its namesake statue dominating the scene: Queen Isabella Park. This is the upper-class section of the city, approximately corresponding to Madison's Square in New York or Lafayette Square in Washington.

Inglaterra—the Spanish word for England—is a favorite hotel for foreign tourists and businessmen, as well as the location where Cuban revolutionaries gathered at the beginning of their struggle back in '68. Now owned by a retired Spanish army captain, it has a reputation for excellent food and drink, and the liveliest café overlooking the smartest promenade in all of Cuba, called the Prado. This magnificent, tree-lined boulevard, along which the beautifully adorned ladies and dandies of Havana stroll, runs north from the park to the Audiencia.

Leonard Pots, a fifty-one-year-old locksmith from Washington's brothel neighborhood near the Capitol building, who possesses suitably adjustable morals and has done other work for me, was, I hoped, lodging at the Inglaterra, having arrived in Havana two days earlier. Rork arrived at the rear of the hotel and found a bellboy to take a scrawled note to Pots' room.

Ten minutes later, Rork saw him two blocks away, at the corner of San Rafael and Industria Streets. Following the note's instructions, Pots was apparently looking for one of the two-wheeled, single-horse Havana cabriolets, known there as a victoria and named for some reason after the British queen.

Rork shambled near him and stooped over as if he'd dropped something, murmuring, "Mornin', Pots, me boyo. Welcome to sunny Havana. Meetin's tomorrow evenin' so listen well. Get tickets at yer hotel desk fer the Tacon Theater's first show on Thursday night. Tacon Theater is right alongside yer hotel. We'll meet ye at the intermission in the men's cloakroom an' give yer orders at that time. Stay low 'til then."

Rork's next stop, via a circuitous route along the Prado and the harbor channel shoreline, was Hotel Isabella, right across the Plaza de Armas square from the captain-general's grand palace itself. Repeating his effort at Inglaterra, Rork got a hotel boy to deliver a note and subsequently met Carlos Mena, the second of our American operatives, at the walkway along the waterfront, overlooking Carpineti Wharf.

Mena was born in the United States to Cuban parents in 1846 and was an actor and writer in New York. He had ties to the Cuban revolutionary movement in New York and was an annual visitor to Havana, knowing the city well and occasionally performing there. I recruited him for his fluency in the Cuban style of Spanish and his ability in role-playing and disguises—two essential skills for our present purposes.

Mena had that rare ability to look extraordinarily memorable, as in portraying a famous historical figure while speaking English, French, German, or Italian; or he could be so nondescript as to blend in with his environs to the point of being almost invisible, such as a servant. There had been rumors he'd been involved in some confidence schemes, though I'd never confirmed it.

Rork positioned himself ahead of Mena. As the man approached, Rork limped out in front of him and held up a twisted right hand for alms. While Mena dropped a coin into his palm, Rork whispered the same instructions he gave Pots regarding the theater on Thursday evening, with an addition: Mena was to go immediately to the city post and telegraph office, check for a letter addressed to Señor Piedra, then get to the Convent of Santa Catalina on O'Reilly Street and place it under the areca palm planter at the southeast corner.

Rork had a second assignment for him. Right after receiving the letter, he was to stop at a livery he trusted and arrange for a silage dray to be at the corner of the park at San Juan de Dios and Habana Streets at three o'clock on Thursday morning. It was to be full of hay, like the many others that came into the city before dawn each day, and be ready for a slight detour from its usual route. Confirmation of the dray arrangement would be a twig laid atop the letter under the planter.

After Mena walked on, Rork stayed at his site, begging from others who came close. None of them donated, but it gave him time to discern any surveillance. Spotting none, he then headed west, away from the government area, along the channel front, en route to his position a block away from the convent.

At one o'clock in the afternoon, Rork observed Mena wander into the exterior garden of the convent and stop for only a few seconds to admire a flowering bougainvillea bush near the planter. Then he walked back to Obispo Street and returned to his hotel.

Rork waited fifteen minutes, watching the pedestrian movements along O'Reilly and Compostela Streets. By then it was the height of the sun's glaring, white heat and the beginning of the daily siesta period, during which shops and offices close, little work is done, and few people walk the city's streets.

Seeing no one else watching the locale, Rork shuffled over and retrieved the envelope. A dried hibiscus twig lay over it. Exiting the garden on Compostela Street, he again made a circumnavigation of the neighborhood before meandering back to our Hotel Florida, where the third specialist was coincidently residing. Rork's route of earlier egress from the hotel building was now deep in shadow, good for his present purposes of reentry. He used the servants' back stairs to gain the third floor and knocked on the door of our man's room, one of the cheaper ones in the rear.

The youngest of my entourage at only twenty-five years of age, Stephen Folger was an expert in electricity from New Jersey and, more recently, Washington, where he worked for Western Union. He knew telegraphy well, having done some scientific tinkering for my friend Tom Edison, and was also an amateur practitioner of chemistry—all skills I believed might come in handy in Havana. He looked like a fellow who spent his life in laboratories, reedy and pale and bespectacled, with a nervous demeanor that made him fidgety, probably from that mind of his churning at all times. But the appearance concealed a sense of adventure, for little Folger loved a challenge and was seldom at a loss for a solution.

Rork went into his orders about the Thursday night meeting at the theater. Then he presented Folger with a more urgent challenge: create a diversion to remove the afternoon guard at our room door so Rork could return.

"Simple," said Folger as he rubbed his hands together in excitement. "Just use a variation on the old standby of yelling 'fire.' But let's give the guard some added incentive. It'll be more fun."

Rork embraced the idea wholeheartedly, and soon our boy genius was teaching the grizzled, old salt how to concoct a simple smoke-generating device. His main ingredients were potassium chlorate and sodium bicarbonate, which Folger carried in a special, sealed container in his "goody box," a repository of various powders and liquids that outwardly appeared to be a common piece of luggage. To this concoction was added an appropriately local touch, several spoonfuls of Cuban sugar from the bowl next to the coffee pot on the dresser. Everything was mixed together and afterward installed inside a glass jar with a perforated tin lid and a long string attached. Folger then dropped a lit match into the jar, igniting the mixture, and handed it to Rork.

Thusly prepared, the pseudo-leper made his way to the northwest corner of the third-floor mezzanine, where a large potted plant provided cover with a view of our room in the southwest corner. Folger, unable to resist participating further in this adventure, stood in plain sight on the east side of the third-floor mezzanine balcony, ready to add his voice to the shouted confusion of the scene once the action began.

Rolling the jar slowly out to the edge of the floor by the railing, Rork carefully let it go off the edge and descend into a large banana tree in the garden patio below, by which time it had a prodigious amount of smoke erupting from the holes in the top. Then he yelled, "*Incendio! Incendio!*"

Folger gleefully echoed the alarm, which was quickly repeated by others, including some hotel guests and the guard, who called out for somebody to get the *bomberos*—the firemen—to the hotel. Word spread into the street. Bells began to ring around the neighborhood.

Hearing the tumult beyond my door, I instantly guessed the culprit and emerged from my room to confront the perplexed man stationed there, just as a woman near Folger screamed for someone to rescue her. Torn between his orders to stay at my door and the obvious duty to help the lady, I helped him along in his decision-making by hitting him on the shoulder, pointing to the mezzanine opposite us, and shouting, "*Dios mio! Que pasa contigo, hombre? Vaya a la asistancia de la dama. Ahora!*"

That did it. Ten seconds of being lectured by a *gringo* on how he should help a lady was enough. He ran off to be a hero just about the time the smoke began to wane, but it had served its purpose well, for my tall leprous-looking friend dashed into the room and I closed the door.

"I think you rather enjoyed that entrance, Rork," I commented quietly, remembering our wall's eyes and ears.

"Aye, sir. Nothin' like a wee bit o' fun while gettin' the job done! Our young boyo knows his stuff," was Rork's whispered answer, while he quickly disrobed out of the line of sight of the peephole. "An' jus' wait 'til ye reads the letter in me pocket from you-know-who up in New York. Me thick head don't get the meanin' o' it at all, but yer mind'll make it out."

12

Ruses de Guerre

Hotel Florida
Obispo Street
Havana, Cuba
1:30 p.m., Wednesday
26 September 1888

I have several acquaintances around the world with whom I maintain a regular, friendly correspondence. I keep them abreast of various social and political developments in the United States, and they provide me information about their locales or their special interests, some of which are rather arcane. Usually we employ *noms de ruse* since they prefer not to have it known they are in contact with an American naval intelligence officer. That sort of thing could prove embarrassing to them. For some, it would be distinctly unhealthy.

In addition to this sensible precaution, we change our aliases every two months, so any compromise of the *noms de ruse* would be of limited duration. We also employ simple substitution codes that on first glance give the message a mercantile or religious appearance. These practices add time and effort but are a layer of protection that prevents our various foes from learning the true nature of our communications.

Instant memorization is a key talent in intelligence work. This includes everything from aliases to message codes to foreign military characteristics to maps. I have learned that simplicity is of similar importance with message codes. One can remember only so much, particularly when on the run in the heart of enemy territory. And mental acuity begins to degrade when you get older like me, approaching the fifth decade of life.

The letter Rork brought me is an illustrative case in point. It was addressed to Señor Juan Piedra, my pseudonym, due to expire in four weeks. It was from Señor Carlos Aponte, the alias of a Cuban revolutionary acquaintance in New York City who was becoming quite well known: José Julián Martí. In the previous two years of his association with me, my aliases for Martí had included Mondongo, Arena, Palma, Cadiz, and his personal favorite, Bordeaux, for he loved French wine. Martí and Carlos Mena were social acquaintances in New York, but, like the Aficionados, neither knew of the other's relationship with me.

Martí was arrested and put in the Audiencia at the age of sixteen by the Spanish for the terrible crime of writing anti-government tracts and then the temerity to proclaim them aloud in public at the Hotel Inglaterra's café. Sentenced to six years hard labor, he had that draconian penalty reduced to exile from Cuba to Spain. He didn't stay there long, heading over the border to France, where he grew to love the cuisine.

My friend then made his way back to the New World, living in various Latin American countries before eventually ending up in New York City. An accomplished newspaper writer, philosopher, and linguist, he was slowly becoming the intellectual stimulus of a broad array of organizations fighting for Cuban independence. Ironically, he was not a devotee of his native island's rum, the only Cuban I ever met who wasn't, but favored gin and tonic water instead, gaining his nickname *Ginebrito*, or "little gin drinker."

Martí said the quinine in it kept the fevers away, which the British had been proving for years in their tropical colonies.

Back in '86, when I'd first met him, he'd helped me with information and contacts in Cuba and Florida, and we had kept up our friendship with dinners whenever I was passing through New York. I found that we shared many hopes and fears for Cuba's future.

Martí was totally in favor of an independent Cuba with a democratically elected government and complete individual freedoms for all citizens, all guaranteed in a constitution. He worried that the revolutionary generals would take over the government once the island won independence, as they had elsewhere in Latin America, and that Cuba would degenerate into the cyclical chaos seen throughout the region.

He was particularly apprehensive about any American domination of the new country, either political or economic, saying Cuba would be swallowed up and lose her cultural identity. Martí admired American ingenuity and energy and democracy, but he despised the corrupt politicians and industrial barons and the blatant racism of the United States. He was adamantly against that culture taking over in Cuba. I agreed with all of these views.

I am sure the questions arise in the reader's mind—it certainly did in mine—of why such a purist Cuban philosopher would befriend a man like me, the servant of the *yanqui* government he despised? Well, the answer is simple: I was useful to Martí and his cause. He used me as a conduit for information he wanted to quietly send to Washington and as a reliable barometer of Washington's attitudes and policies toward his island. It was, however, a symbiotic relationship, for he gave me nuances of revolutionary personalities and policies, as well as contacts inside Cuba. He got to understand Washington better. I understood Cuba better.

Before my hurried departure from Washington, I'd telegraphed Martí, alias Aponte, asking if he had any dependable contacts in Havana I could use should I find myself in trouble. I requested he reply by sending a coded letter to me in Havana by special priority mail on the soonest steamer.

Now I had his answer, and it wasn't what—or in the form—I expected. Usually Martí used a double-substitution code based on a vest-pocket Spanish-English dictionary, copies of which we both carried. Within the United States, we used the telegraph or mail as a mode of communication, but outside the country we used trusted couriers and dead-drop exchanges—small hiding places—for Martí fully understood the need for security. The Spanish counterintelligence apparatus had agents everywhere.

I examined the envelope Rork had pressed into my hand. It appeared secure, though there are various ways to make one look so after surreptitiously opening it. Next, I studied the note. In Martí's typical business-like script was written a simple message:

Tio Juan,

> *Recibé su letra telegráfico hoy y pesar que no puedo ayudarle, sino que estoy seguro que usted tendrá éxito en la transacción del tobacco. La Habana tiene muchos companies el vender dela hoja más fina. Estoy en la montaña Ampersand en Nuevo York noreste para tress semanas próximas, despues iré a casa.*

> *Con Afecion,*
> *Carlos Aponte*

This was not Martí's usual code of late, using the pocket dictionaries. No, this was an earlier one, based on a sole double-entendre, the double-meaning of a single word in the entire text. My translation into English yielded this:

Uncle John,

I received your telegraphic letter today and regret I cannot help you, but I am sure you will have success in the tobacco transaction. Havana has many companies selling the finest leaf. I am at Ampersand Mountain in northeastern New York for the next three weeks, and then I will go home.

With affection,
Carlos Aponte

Of that entire letter, there was only one operative word: Ampersand. Though the letter's text appeared legitimate, it was meaningless. Yes, there is a mountain named Ampersand in the northeast portion of New York State, named after the creek of the same appellation, because the winding stream is shaped like an ampersand, a grammatical hieroglyph representing the conjunctive word *"and."* But the mountain had nothing to do with the message.

Having shed his disguise, Rork was staring at me impatiently and finally couldn't stand it any longer. Glancing at the hole in the wall, he let out his frustration with a muted, "Well, what's the damned thing really say?"

"My dear old friend, I think your recent infusion of rotgut has dimmed your ancient brain. You've forgotten the code word 'ampersand,' now haven't you?"

Hot and sweaty from his jaunt about the town, Rork wasn't in the mood for humor. Rubbing his face where the moustache used to be, he became even more perturbed and muttered, "Amper-what? Oh, just get on with the bloody message...*sir.*"

Having to constantly deal with Rork's Irish humor, I couldn't refrain from subjecting him to a little wit of my own. "Very well, Rork. I realize that you're much older than I and it's only to be expected that these things will happen, but there's no reason to be testy about it. We've a lot to remember and sometimes a word slips by. Ampersand is the only code word here. Martí last used it in eighty-six—December, I believe. Well, perhaps a little reeducation for you is in order, to jog your memory."

He was exasperated, but I made him wait a bit longer while I explained, "An ampersand, as you may now distantly recall, is the ancient Latin symbol for '*et*,' the source of the French '*et*,' which in English means 'and.' An ampersand is written out this way."

I removed a pencil from the desk and walked back to Rork in the corner, out of sight of our minders. On the letter's envelope, I drew the ancient symbol for an ampersand, using the French style:

&

That elicited an, "Ah, o' course me knows that one. Just couldn't recall what the devil it was called." Rork allowed an embarrassed smile. "An', aye, yer right, sir. Me brain's overheated somethin' fierce, an' damned if it can remember the code meanin'."

"It's the code word for two things. The first is: *Read between the lines*."

He perked up. "Invisible ink!"

"Yes. Please fetch me that oil lamp and light it, if you would. The second meaning of this code word is that the hidden message is in original American Morse code, instead of European international telegraph code, for there is no ampersand in European-based international code."

I will digress here to provide my reader with some recent history of our modern system of worldwide telegraph cable communications. The Europeans started their own code system for telegraphy in the 1840s. In 1865, they adopted it as the standard for their empires throughout the globe. Only American railroads still use original Morse code anymore. If Spanish counterintelligence agents had read the letter and managed to discover the hidden ink message, they would be trying to decipher it with the wrong telegraph code system.

Martí was rather good at this sort of crypto-communication. In this case, the ampersand code word would get me to the hidden message, which would get me to the original Morse code, which would probably translate into a riddle—three layers of protection for the message.

I wrapped the notepaper around the heated glass bell of the oil lamp Rork was holding by its handle, and we waited. It took almost a minute, much longer than an oven would have taken, but one must do with what one has at the time.

"Fruit juice?" Rork asked as I held the letter up to the light to scrutinize it. There were many rows of small brown marks beginning to appear between the lines of words. It was a lengthy message. The brown marks extended down the page, well past Martí's farewell and signature as Aponte.

"Very good, Rork. Yes, it appears to be citric juice rather than apple. Came out darker than lemon or orange usually does, so it must be from a lime. Limes must cost dearly in New York this time of year." I sighed at seeing the number of brown marks. "It looks like a long one—this is going to take a while."

It did. I must admit, it was the longest Morse decoding I'd ever done, and it taxed my brain and patience severely. Meanwhile, Rork occupied the attention of anyone at the peephole by standing there, combing his hair and singing Gaelic ballads off-key while admiring himself in the mirror. I think he did it just to aggravate me.

At last I finished, and, sure enough, it was one of Martí's damned riddles. He loved riddles—it was the poet in him. The third layer of security. I motioned for Rork to come over and have a look at it.

No puedo ayudar en la transacción, mi amigo. Pero recuerde por favor, tengo hermanos por todas partes en el mundo y hay siempre ayuda de una paloma francesa por debajo la cruz de ocho.

He shook his head. "Nay, me Spanish ain't near good enough for the likes o' that, sir. You have any idea o' the meanin' o' the riddle?"

"Not yet, but I'll put it in English and we'll look at it again."

I cannot help on the transaction, my friend. But please remember, I have brothers everywhere in the world and there is always help from a French dove underneath the cross of eight.

I looked at Rork again, but he shrugged. "Dunno fer sure, sir. But me's thinkin' the 'brothers' bit is referrin' to Cuban rebels."

"No, I think not, Rork. They're in New York and Florida and some other American cities, but certainly not *'everywhere in the world.'* Got to be a bigger organization, but who? Damn...now what the hell does that mean?"

"A brotherhood o' some sort, eh? What brotherhood is everywhere? The Jesuits? We've friends there."

"Good idea, but the Cuban revolutionaries aren't that close at all to the Jesuits."

Rork exhaled loudly in irritation, then quieted his words. "Ye know, Martí gets a wee bit too full o' himself on these messages sometimes. What's this malarkey mean?"

"Well, my friend, I'll own up that he's certainly made it a *secure* communiqué—even *we* can't figure it out. I suppose that just shows that it must be important somehow. All right, any ideas on the French dove and cross of eight bit?"

"Nary a damned one, 'cept that the Spanish word for dove is *paloma,* an' that's the name o' our informant that got nabbed by the Spaniardos. Connection?"

I shook my head. "Don't think so. Context is completely different, so I think that's a coincidence. Besides, Martí doesn't know exactly why we're here, much less our informant's name. He never knew about that operation."

"Cross o' eight...Eight arms on the cross? O' maybe eight points stickin' out?"

"Depends on which way you look at it, I think. A cross can

have two arms or four, depending on how you describe it. Or some of them have a small bar athwart the main upright, below the main crosspiece, so that'd be two more arms. No, it must be points of the cross, not arms."

"Brotherhood is connected to the cross, maybe? Me's still thinkin' o the Jesuits."

I was mightily tired of *ruses de guerre* right about then. "Rork, I'm thinking we should just forget Martí's message and stay on our plan. I don't have a clue about an eight-pointed cross, or a French dove, or any brotherhood..."

That was when one of those serendipitous things happened that defies later explanation. Annoyed by my inability to comprehend the significance of Martí's words, I was on the verge of burning all three forms of the message in the flame of the lamp, when I glanced away toward our unseen observer behind that hole. Below his viewpoint in the wall was the room's writing desk, and on that was the Havana newspaper.

It suddenly struck me like a hammer—one of the articles I'd perused the night before had the word "brotherhood" in it, but I'd been searching for something else and hadn't read it in detail. I dashed over and flung open the paper, flipping through the pages until I found it on the bottom of page five. The Spanish colonial government was concerned about a brotherhood thought to be involved with the insurrectionists. As a consequence, assorted restrictions were being placed on the activities of the brotherhood, and anyone with knowledge of violations of these regulations was ordered to contact the authorities. It was so simple, so obvious, that I was almost too embarrassed to tell Rork, who stood, warily watching my odd behavior. I returned to the corner and whispered my revelation in his ear.

"It's the Freemasons, Rork! The 'brotherhood' in the message is the Brotherhood of Free and Accepted Masons. They're everywhere in the world. Maceo, Céspedes, Goméz, and many of the revolutionary leadership, including our very own Martí, have been brother Masons for years. Many of the rank and file rebels are too. The paper had an article about how Spanish colonial authorities are cracking down on them. I can't believe I missed that. Should have deduced it right away. My mind must be addled by all that's happened."

"Freemasons? Ye talkin' o' that secret cult o' heretics?"

"Oh, for goodness' sake, they're not *heretics*, Rork. Freemasonry's a fraternal organization that has some confidential rites, that's all. And the Cuban rebels aren't alone in being Masons, not by a long shot. Many of the revolutionary leaders in the North American colonies were Freemasons, George Washington being the most famous. Most of the independence fighters in South America, like Bernardo O'Higgins and Bolivar, were Freemasons."

Rork, bless his soul, is used to my lectures by now, so he stood there patiently waiting while I warmed up to the subject. "In Latin America, and especially in Cuba and Puerto Rico—still under Spanish domination seventy years after everybody else got freedom—they follow the Portuguese model for Freemasonry, which means that in addition to the general precepts of their order, they engage in patriotic political and social activism for the promotion of individual liberty. This is something significant, Rork, and through Martí we've been given an entrée into it."

I could tell he wasn't impressed, even before he said, "Hmm. Not sure about all that, me friend. The Church says the whole lot o' 'em 're heretics...o' worse."

"Yes, it does say that. The Vatican issued another papal proclamation against them just a few years ago. And since the Church and the Spanish colonial government are one and the same here in Cuba, they have considerable power to use against the Masonic brotherhood. In the sixties and seventies, being a Freemason could get you executed by the government. Even now they get arrested. That stance by the Church is why many of the rebels who are Freemasons have also become Protestants. It's all connected in Cuba, Rork—the Protestants, the Freemasons, and the rebel patriots."

He held up a hand in surrender. "Well, since me own blighted soul's probably already under Saint Peter's suspicion for associatin' with the likes o' *you*, methinks associatin' with a few more heretics won't matter none in the long run. Lookee here now, though, this French dove bit, an' the cross—have ye reasoned them out o' the riddle yet?"

"Not yet. But I'd wager they're somehow tied to the Freemasons of Havana. And I'd further bet that Martí has contacted his Cuban Masonic brothers and told them to expect us."

"So's they're to be friends an' not foes, eh?"

I wasn't sure, for I knew some of the Spanish elite in Cuba were also Freemasons as well. Had they infiltrated the rebel movement through the Masonic lodges? My knowledge of the secret world of Masonry was limited to general information. I'd known a few men in Washington who were publicly known to be members but had never spoken to them about their establishment or its principles. I now wished I had done so.

"Time will tell," I said, mostly to myself.

13

The Ever-Faithful Isle

His Excellency's Apartments
Palace of the Captain-General
Havana, Cuba
8 p.m., Wednesday
26 September 1888

Nothing about the room indicated we were in Cuba. Instead, it was a scene straight from central Spain.

Upon the pale yellow walls of the captain-general's small private dining room—the state dining room was next door and well over one hundred feet long—were hung displays of priceless china and tapestries and paintings from Spain. The cherry wood sideboard supported a pair of enormous pink, blown-glass punchbowls full of orange juice, which were surrounded by a vast array of silver serving dishes containing various rices and vegetables and meats. The black and white parquet tiled floor gleamed with reflected lamplight, the servers' shoes clicking as they walked across it.

Completing the regal scene, Don Sabas Marín Gonzalez and Matilde were at one side of the square table, in throne-like chairs that dwarfed everyone else's. They were dressed in elegant attire, he in his formal dark blue uniform with red and white sash, gold-laced sleeves, and three rows of medals dangling from his chest. His white-plumed helmet sat on a table nearby.

Consul-General Williams and his wife, Angela Garcia Williams, sat opposite. The table itself was an ornately carved mahogany affair, with beautifully inlaid Spanish tiles arranged in a green leafy design, all of which was topped by a square of clear glass. It appeared to be a museum piece, at least as old as the palace.

After greeting my hosts and the Williamses, I was introduced to the couple on the fourth side of the table, a visiting viscount from Barcelona and his wife, who possessed a limited English vocabulary. They were inspecting their estates in Pinar del Río, west of Havana, for the first time in ten years. I cannot recall their names, for both of them appeared dull witted and stayed sullen for the evening, their only verbiage being in Spanish and consisting of complaints about the backwardness of the Cuban people. I could well imagine what the Cubans on their estates thought of *them*.

That left one place empty on my side, filled by the late-arriving but pleasant bishop of Havana, Manuel Santander y Frutos, whose English linguistic abilities were well enough developed to convey a lively sense of humor and appreciation for good food and drink.

Rork was not invited to dine at the table with us due to his lowly rank, of course, but as my "aide," he was standing by in the stewards' quarters, ostensibly ready to dash forth and attend to any personal needs of mine. This type of situation commonly occurs in our foreign missions and provides us an excellent opportunity to learn what the lower classes know through Rork's mingling with them. Frequently, we find that the servants know quite a lot, far more than their superiors ever suppose.

Dinner consisted of the usual seven-course banquet of memorable Spanish dishes, dominated by a paella Valenciana and lubricated by some the remarkable red wines from the Rioja region of that country. Spanish cuisine is unequaled in the world, easily addictive, and one of my favorites. To be sure, my only quarrel with Spain is her treatment of the people of Cuba and Puerto Rico, where slavery endured more than twenty years after Lincoln ended that scourge in the United States. Otherwise, I love the music, food, and wine of the great Iberian culture.

The conversation was mostly in English for the benefit of the guest of honor. It was not the equal of the wonderful food and wine, however, being the same tedious drivel I've heard at every diplomatic social function in my career. At one point, my awards became the topic of discussion, courtesy of Señora Williams, who asked, "What are your decorations, Commander. It's rare that I see an American naval officer with so many. Are they American?"

"No, madam, they are foreign. The only American military and naval award is the Congressional Medal of Honor, which I have not received. My medals are from France, Peru, and Cambodia, in appreciation for some of my work over the years."

I then gave a sanitized description of how I received them. A more candid account would have probably offended the political sensibilities of the gentlemen and certainly the digestion of the ladies. When I had first arrived that evening, in full dress uniform and wearing my "trinkets," as navy men call them, I noticed the captain-general recognizing the most famous of my medals, France's Legion of Honor. He'd given me a brief nod of respect, all that was needed between warriors. As I told the story of how I came to receive that award for my work in Africa, I saw him smile faintly, knowing that I was leaving out the more vivid parts.

Finally, as I had anticipated and counted on, for such is the norm at this sort of affair, along about the arrival of the main course, the eventual effects of our many glasses of alcohol set in. Tongues loosened, and things began to get truly interesting, with voices raised and more animated and the laughter more spontaneous.

It was while I was savoring my dessert, a deliciously perfect flan alongside a demitasse of cognac, that the good bishop suddenly inquired of our host, "Your Excellency, may I ask if the man whose attack Commander Wake stopped is a part of the group behind these continuing disturbances in the streets? I saw some of them today. A flagrant disregard of authority, as their name indicates."

Bishop Santander had been in office for just a year but was experienced in political matters. Asking such a question in English in front of an American naval officer was inappropriate, to say the least. Presumably, the conviviality of the evening had something to do with the lowering of the good bishop's guard.

His Excellency's face visibly tightened—whether because of the bishop's question or his coming answer, I know not. But after taking a sip of cognac, he replied in a flat tone, using English for my benefit, "My dear bishop, the short answer is yes. The full answer is that the man who attacked the palace was a member of the anarchists, who are not merely the enemies of Spain but the enemies of all civilized people in the world. And I am ashamed to say that several of them came to Cuba from our beloved mother country to spread their demented cause to the ignorant and disaffected here." He sighed while shaking his head woefully. "As if I did not have enough problems to occupy my time."

Don Sabas' voice grew stronger now as he went on, looking at me. "Allow me to explain, Commander. These anarchists are the ones who are financially supporting the tobacco workers striking against almost all our tobacco factories. The anarchists are the same ones who sent over fifteen hundred dollars to the Haymarket terrorists in your city of Chicago for their legal defense. They are the ones encouraging the gangs of petty criminals to block the streets and..." he searched mentally for the word, "...*bully*... innocent people. They are the same ones who started this so-called Workers' Alliance, union which is trying to cripple the merchants of this island."

He turned back to the bishop. "But worry not, my friend, for we are making great efforts to contain their influence and remove this cancer from our midst before it grows."

The bishop pressed on with his inquiries. "And when precisely will this evil behavior be thwarted, Don Sabas? It's impossible to get through the streets when they take over, even for a priest."

To me, he said, "I understand that you have had this same type of problem, not only in Chicago, but in the other cities of your country. Is that true, Commander?"

To my annoyance, for my curiosity was aroused, the captain-general declined to answer the bishop's question. Instead, he patiently waited for my reply to the bishop.

I said, "Anarchists are a problem for us too, Your Eminence. But it's getting better. The bombing casualties at the Haymarket Riot in eighty-six shocked everyone so much that the public reacted against them. Now the anarchists have calmed down a bit and have confined their protests to demonstrations."

"And you allow such disruptions?"

"As long as they are peaceful, yes. It is our right as Americans, under the protection of our constitution, sir. Actual anarchists are few in the United States and have become only a minor irritation."

The bishop clucked at my portrayal of the labor unrest in America. "A minor irritation? It is said that here the anarchists have five thousand in their Workers' Alliance. It is the largest so-called union on the island of Cuba!"

Five thousand members? That was unheard of in Cuba. I hadn't known the situation was that bad. It must be taking up quite a lot of the government's resources and the captain-general's time. Very interesting information.

Don Sabas registered my digestion of the bishop's comment, for he leveled his eyes at the cleric and said, "Oh, my dear bishop, I am sure our ladies do not wish to spend this evening hearing about such indelicate matters."

Holding up my glass and nodding politely in agreement, I switched the subject to the one I'd hoped to learn more about that evening.

"Quite right, Your Excellency. How can we men speak of such brutish behavior when..." I paused and briefly surveyed the matronly wives at the table, "we are blessed to have such beauty in our midst? I propose we discuss a far more pleasant topic, one that I am curious about and that the esteemed bishop can enlighten me on. Is not Saturday the Feast Day of Saint Michael? Will there be a celebration and parade?"

The ladies smiled in appreciation for my gallantry. For his part, the bishop puffed up and said, "Why, yes, my son. There will be a magnificent procession of devotion that day. Are you of the one true faith?"

"I'm not Catholic, sir. Originally I was Episcopalian, and now I'm Methodist."

"Hmm, I see," he said, his enthusiasm dwindling upon learning I was of the wayward flock. The ladies' expression took on a sad aspect. Williams chuckled softly at the reaction to my statement, then said to me, "Perhaps you can stay in Havana and see it, Commander. Since your admiral was called away, you've no ship here."

"Well, I was planning on getting passage on a steamer in a few days to rejoin my ship, sir. But it really would be a shame to miss the celebration."

To the bishop beside me, I said, "I have great respect and affection for the Church, Your Eminence. And if I am still in Havana on that day, I would like to see that procession. Where does it go, sir?"

That rekindled his attention. "I am glad to hear of your affection for our Church, my son. The procession begins at ten o'clock in the morning, at the park named for our gracious queen of years gone by, Isabella the Second. It moves north along the beautiful Prado to the Audiencia, our seat of justice in Havana, near the Castillo de la Punta. From there, it proceeds along the waterfront and around to the grand cathedral, where I will have the honor of celebrating Mass when the glorious bells toll the median of the day. I think you will enjoy this great demonstration of our love of Jesus and sincere respect and gratitude for the Archangel Michael."

Everyone at the table gave an approving nod to that, and I replied, "I'm sure I will, sir." Then I turned to my host. "But what about the disturbances, Your Excellency? How will you stop the anarchists and strikers from disrupting the procession? They are anti-religious atheists, are they not? I would think it would be a prime target for them, representing all that they scorn."

Don Sabas hadn't lost his hard-edged tone. "Police and soldiers will be put on the streets. There will be *no* disruption of the procession, or the Mass, or any other festivities."

"Really, sir?" I said as guilelessly as I could muster. "I am but a sailor and inexperienced in such matters, but I imagine that's a long route to watch. It would take thousands of men."

His Excellency was no longer the genial host, instead showing his cold military side. "It will, and we have enough. Every infantryman, artilleryman, cavalryman, engineer, and policeman will be called out from their barracks, except for those on direct guard duty. In addition, we will have Orden Publico and Regimento de Voluntarios troops stationed in the parks, the cathedral, and the train station."

His right hand, resting on the table, clenched into a fist as he repeated, "There will be *no* blaspheming disrespect of this sacred day."

I was pleased with his determination to ensure no problems on Saturday by putting all those men on the streets. There would be no immediate reinforcements available inside the Audiencia. That had been a huge worry to me, for there was an engineers' barracks right beside the place. Now I knew it would be empty.

Don Sabas was studying me, waiting for a reply, so I said with open approbation, "Excellent planning, Your Excellency. Good to see that every precaution has been taken and it will be a joyous Christian occasion that no infidel rabble can ruin. Quite a triumph, really, for both the faith and the colonial government."

Don Sabas seemed mollified by my flattery, so I went back to the bishop. "You mentioned other festivities that day. May I ask what they are? Perhaps I could see them as well."

Bishop Don Manuel took over. "Oh, there will be many local gatherings around the city. There is a large one near the cathedral that I think you'll enjoy immensely. It is a circus from one of our colonies in Africa, complete with lions and elephants and zebras and many of God's more exotic creatures. The circus will parade on the same route, a few minutes behind the procession of faith, and will open for the public at the Cortina de Valez just north of the cathedral, directly after the high mass ends. I hope you can stay until then. It will be a day of great joy!"

This information confirmed that which I had gleaned from the newspaper but until then was still unsure of. Saturday would be a very busy day for Havana. It would be busier still for me and my people.

Don Sabas stood and raised his glass toward me. "I, too, hope that you can stay here in Havana and see the celebration, Commander. Please consider our city to be your city. You are, after all, one of our heroes now. Ladies and gentlemen, I toast our guest of honor, Commander Peter Wake, who has demonstrated not only his honor in the field of gentlemanly combat, but his bravery in real combat."

That magnanimous gesture engendered a wide grin on Williams' face and a bit of crimson in mine as I acknowledged it with a slight bow. Once all had dutifully drained their glasses, our host added, "And now I see that it is after eleven o'clock. The other guests await us in the ballroom, so let us proceed there to enjoy the music and dancing."

It was, all in all, an extremely pleasant and, from my point of view, productive evening. In fact, satiated as I was by the sumptuous repast, not to mention the excellent wine and cognac, I even allowed myself a moment of silent congratulation on successfully charming such essential information right out of my adversaries.

My new *buen amigo*, His Excellency Captain-General Don Sabas Martín Gonzalez, ultimate decider of life and death in all of Cuba, walked out next to me. Laughing loudly at some inane joke from the bishop, he made quite a show of camaraderie for our companions as he put a hand on my shoulder. I imagined it was the first time Williams had ever seen His Excellency do *that* with an American naval officer! Things were coming along just fine.

But as we emerged from Don Sabas' private apartments onto the splendid interior balcony surrounding the patio below where I had nearly died the day before, my regal companion leaned over to me, and I saw that a dark veil had descended over his face. The eyes boring into me showed no emotion, were dead-cold black, as he whispered from inches away, "And someday, my heroic *norteamericano* friend, I think we should have a very private discussion of your intelligence activities inside my island."

A chill went through me. I had no chance to reply, for he had already moved up ahead with the American consul-general, suggesting with another chuckle that dancing with their wives that evening would be good exercise for older men like them.

As we circumnavigated the balcony and entered the ballroom at the opposite corner of the palace, the majordomo announced our presence and we were immediately overwhelmed by two hundred bejeweled swells who, even at that late hour, were just getting up steam for a night of revelry. Don Sabas returned to his gregariously self as he circulated through the crowd, greeting everyone by name, periodically calling me over to introduce me to important personages, looking for all the world like an American politician working the crowd during a campaign.

One of the introductions was his sixteen-year-old nephew, he of bomb-blast fame, whom I found to be singularly obnoxious and condescending. While he obediently thanked the loathed *yanqui* for saving his life, I sent a prayer heavenward that this blue-blooded, little despot-in-training wouldn't actually graduate into any position of authority.

Reluctantly fulfilling my function as the hero guest of honor, I danced awkwardly with several ladies. None of the sensuous dances for which Cuba is famous were played that night. No, those are considered licentious by the Spanish elite, so this was stilted and strictly formalized European waltzing, with an ancient minuet added for measure. On my best day I am a minimally talented dancer, and that evening, under the consequences of cognac, wine, a recent concussion, a sore leg and arm, and some very recent intimidation, I was a regrettably poor partner.

One of my consorts on the dance floor was of memorable note, however. She was introduced as Doña Belleza Ortiz y Cardonne, widowed for two years and one of the leading socialites of the city. I remembered her from the upper-class audience at the saber match, where she watched me intently. Belleza was slightly younger than I, had preserved her lovely figure and face well, and most certainly knew it. Fluent in English and French, she was far more confident—I'm putting it nicely—than many of her peers.

In fact, she flirted unabashedly during our tour of the floor, in that manner only the most confident of Spanish ladies can. They have a way of saying more with their eyes than with their lips and leaving no room for doubt in the message. On the second waltz, Belleza gaily offered to be my guide around the various gardens of Havana, hinting by smile and batted eyelash and pressed bosom that she would gladly show me more interesting sights than merely those of the parks and monuments.

Ah, yes, my dear Belleza overplayed her hand.

In my profession, ladies like Belleza are known as "honey traps," a very effective way for the host government's secret service to gain insight, usually over the bed pillow, into any knowledge the targeted gentleman may possess. The French and Russians are the absolute masters of this ploy, but clearly the Spanish are catching up rapidly. I thanked Belleza profusely and promised to consider her kind invitation, but not for the reason she'd hoped. No, the notion entered my mind that she would provide a very pleasant method to get out of the hotel on a seemingly innocent excuse and thereby get some needed reconnaissance done.

By the middle of the ball, I was sorely fatigued and ready to leave, knowing I had much work yet to do that night. But more than that, I was angry beyond words at myself for allowing my mind to be numbed earlier by food and especially that blasted cognac. I was not the master deceiver, but the deceived. And, I ruefully admitted, Rork was not the only one to fall prey to a grog-fueled illusion of security.

Why had I ever theorized that the captain-general would be ignorant of Marrón's work against me and of my espionage operations in the Caribbean? Of course, Don Sabas knew of my work. Of course, he had been briefed about what Spanish intelligence knew of my mission in '86, a year before he became the ruler of Cuba. And of course, he knew about some, if not all, of Marrón's current efforts against me, probably from the colonel himself. Don Sabas' comment was a not-so-subtle reminder and a warning that I was nothing more and nothing less than a spy. And they wanted me to understand that *they* knew it.

14

A Riddle Solved

Havana, Cuba
2 a.m., Thursday
27 September 1888

Our departure from the hotel room was accomplished an hour after we had returned from the soiree, from which I had used my wounded hero status to beg off early. During that hour, we snored heavily for our friends manning the peephole, depicting the very view they expected—two drunks sleeping off a prodigious evening of carousing. Not far off the mark, in my case.

Our egress was made without the advantage of illumination from a lamp, for I wanted the "peepers," as Rork and I had come to humorously call them, to rest easy thinking we were semi-comatose. Once out on the dark balcony, things became far more difficult, even though we had the dim light of a waning moon. Both of us are not as agile as we once were. Plus, my body seemed to be composed mostly of alcohol right then and responded slowly to cerebral commands.

We found a gap in the dwindling pedestrian traffic and lowered the seabag containing our long guns to the street. The pistols were concealed in our waists under our light jackets. Then we carefully climbed down the protrusions on the wall, Rork leading the way. My left arm and leg let me know they weren't healed yet, but once you start down there is no stopping, so I had to endure it. I was not looking forward to the painful challenge of our return ascent.

Upon alighting on terra firma, we darted into the shadows and quickly got ourselves away from Obispo Street. It was dark and mostly deserted by then, but there was no sense in taking chances of being seen by a police patrol walking that main thoroughfare. A stroll of two minutes up nearby Aguiar Street got us to the park in my plan. Sitting low against an alley wall where we could see everything, we searched for anyone else doing the same, but all appeared quiet until the clatter of hooves on paving stone signaled the arrival of our conveyance—the hay wagon. Amazingly for Cuba, it was punctual, which naturally made me suspicious.

The driver sat there, waiting and looking irritated at the whole thing, a good sign in my view. We let him stew for a few more minutes while still checking for any foes watching us in the blackness. At last, he let out a Cuban oath and snapped the crop to get his mule moving, its course heading in our direction.

As it appeared not to be a trap, my suspicions were allayed and Rork sent out a bird whistle—a towhee, I believe—which attracted the driver's attention. My hand extended beyond the shadows and beckoned him to the entrance of our alley. He complied and soon Rork, the seabag, and I were buried in the hay with whispered instructions to our chauffeur to take us into the Chinatown section of Havana.

There are about fifty thousand Chinese, mostly men, in Cuba. The majority live in Havana, mainly in the slum known as Chinatown, or Barrio Chino. Brought in during recent decades to supplement the slave labor force, they are an odd addition to the city. Their impoverished community is understandably wary of non-Orientals. Entry into Chinatown is always noted and sometimes not tolerated.

At the corner of Dragones and Rayo, I handed some coinage up to the driver and we subsequently slipped out the back of the moving wagon. Hastening halfway up the block, we ducked through a double door set into a building, hence into a narrow lane running west between two dilapidated buildings. At the end of this lane, we tacked to port in an even narrower alleyway filled with laundry hanging on lines between the walls and refuse scattered on the ground. Soon we arrived at our proverbial house number three, which was, in fact, not a house at all. It was a room within a jumble of tenements that rose to a height of four stories, one constructed *ad hoc* atop another for the last hundred years by various inhabitants, none of whom evidently had the remotest idea of how to do it correctly. Our lair was on the ground floor of all this.

The resident mongrel spotted us and roused himself into barking, a half-hearted effort that made me sympathetic—he sounded as if he'd had too much to drink also. The dog wasn't *that* drunk, however, for he remembered me and my habit of bringing him something to eat, which he snatched quickly out of my hand. Then he lay back down athwart the path. An old rule of espionage is to always take care of the sentry, by a blade across the throat if you have to, but far more preferably by a bribe. That way you can reuse him.

The sole exterior entry to our rendezvous was a badly hung door at the end of a passageway only the width of a man's shoulders. As we entered, the door creaking frightfully, a quick glance astern assured me the dog was on the job and no one was following.

We sat on the floor in the far corner of the room, backs against the wall, near an interior door that led to the neighbor's place—our emergency exit should things become unpleasant. One always stays low when waiting in a building, for if it turns out to be an ambuscade, your adversary will usually aim too high and illuminate himself with the gun's flash. I was pleased to hear snoring, the raucous kind that can't be faked, from next door, as I kept my Spencer shotgun balanced on my knee and leveled at that interior door. Rork watched the exterior one.

After what seemed at least an hour but was more likely thirty minutes, we heard the dog grunting, then the door squeak open, and the weak light from outside was blocked by a familiar large figure, corpulent, not brawny. Leo, the other man who routinely fed the dog, had arrived. He took his place on the floor next to me, gasping for breath and irritated by the mile-long walk and what he termed "this unnecessary drama."

I took the opportunity to ask Leo if he knew of any auxiliary entrances to the Audiencia. "Supposedly there is a tunnel from the barracks beside it," he replied unsurely. "But that was only a rumor I heard years ago."

I thought that eminently logical. From their earliest days in the New World, the Spanish always built escape tunnels under their churches and forts, for coups and rebellion are not recent inventions.

In another thirty minutes, the dog awakened with a startled snarl, and soon Marco, who never fed the dog—thus the snarling—appeared. Though Leo and Marco had been members of the Aficionados for more than two years, they had, as the reader may recall, never met. While the three of us whispered introductions, Rork circled the outside perimeter again to check the canine sentry and the passageway beyond. Then he made sure our neighbors inside were truly dormant. He reported that all was well. I lit the lamp on the solitary table in the room, around which were three chairs.

There were no windows for anyone to spy inside, and Rork stood near the outside door, shotgun pointed down the alley. We'd gotten started late. My watch said it was precisely 4:14 a.m. We had ten minutes, no more.

Leo and Marco eyed each other warily as I began. "Thank you for coming this morning, gentlemen. I know it wasn't easy for you. We don't have much time, so listen carefully. I have several questions."

They both focused their attention on me, naïve as yet to the subject matter.

"First one is for Leo. What do we know of the anarchists and strikers' plans to disrupt the Saint Michael's Day procession on Saturday?"

"The strikers are loyal Catholics and will not do, or condone, such a thing. As for the anarchists, I have heard no information about their plans, but it is assumed that they will make a demonstration. They are, as you know, atheists and have no respect for the solemnity of the day. They may do something violent, or at least cause a riot."

"Probably in the area of the Martyrs' Place, near the Audiencia, as the procession gets close," opined Marco. "That is where I would do it, if I were an anarchist."

The Martyrs' Place was the location where the infamous executions of 1871 had occurred. The Spanish publicly shot eight Cuban medical students from the university as retribution for desecrating the tomb of a Spanish journalist who had written against independence for the island. The accusations were later confirmed to be false, but that revelation was too late for the dead students. The Martyrs' Place has been a flash point for annual anti-government demonstrations ever since, generating severe responses from the colonial authorities.

Leo concurred, and I had to admit Marco had a good point. "I didn't think of that location. I thought it would be near the queen's statue in the central park. But you're right, Marco. The anarchists would use the martyrs as their rallying point. I have another question: Does either of you know anything about a circus that day?"

Leo did. "The one from Africa?" he said. "Gran Circo Africano comes to Havana once a year. I've met the headmaster of it, an African mulatto named Cesar Melosa from the Rio Muni in Spanish Equatorial Guinea. He brings small animals over to the old people's home at the monastery for their entertainment at no charge. Quite a colorful character. Not enamored of the Spanish, but he takes their money gladly."

"Sounds interesting. Now, two final questions before I give you your orders. What do you know about the Freemasons of Cuba?"

"The heretics?" asked Leo. I glanced at Rork, who smugly smirked toward his co-religionist.

"If that's what you call them, Leo," I said.

"Yes, there are a few in the city. They have several secret meeting places. I think many of the patriots are members, but, of course, as a good Catholic, I am not, nor do I want to be, privy to their activities."

"I know some of them," said Marco. "There are more than a few, Señor Leo. I am told there are more than eight thousand in Cuba right now. And yes, many of the patriot leadership are members, or brothers. There is a group of them—what they call a lodge—somewhere in the old quarter. It has been there for many years. They meet in secret at various places because if they are caught, they will be arrested. During the first war for independence, the Ten Years' Wars, the Spanish government decreed the death penalty for being a Mason in Cuba, since so many revolutionaries were brothers in Freemasonry."

"But you don't know where this lodge meets?"

"No, only their brothers know where they meet. I do know it is called the *Union Iberica*. I am told that is where the Spanish Freemasons, some of whom are in the government and army, meet weekly. You know, there are rumors that Sagasta himself is a Freemason."

I found that very interesting. Práxedes Mateo Sagasta was the prime minister of Spain. He was with the Liberal Party and known to be more progressive in his views toward Cuba. His fellow party member and minister of war, Arsenio Martinez-Campos, was a former Captain-General of Cuba and had negotiated with the rebels in 1878 to end the first war of independence.

"Is Martinez-Campos a Freemason? Or Don Sabas?" I asked Marco.

"I have no idea. I am not even sure about Sagasta. It is just a rumor, but it would make sense, given his views. I am certain that Cánovas is not a Freemason, though. From what little I understand of the order, no Freemason would do what Cánovas has done to Cuba. I fear what he will do when he gets in power again."

I agreed on that. Cánovas was currently the opposition leader in Spain and was remembered for his policy of severe repression in Cuba when he was Spanish prime minister in the seventies. He'd been prime minister again in '86 when I was put briefly in the Audiencia. Colonel Marrón was affiliated with Cánovas' political party. I'd heard that his family was from Málaga in Spain, the birthplace of Cánovas.

Now to the next question. "Very good, gentlemen. Thank you. And what do you know of a dove under an eight-pointed cross? Is that a symbol you are familiar with?"

Marco gestured in the negative, but I could tell Leo recognized it right away. His words contained the same denigrating tone as he used to describe the Freemasons.

"It is the symbol of the French heretics who left the Mother Church a few centuries ago. The renegades styled themselves as Huguenots. Many went over to Protestant England. The cross is a version of the Maltese Cross, with an upside-down dove under it."

Huguenots. So that was the answer to the riddle. I'd heard of them but wasn't knowledgeable in any detail. Another glance at Rork showed he was as ignorant as I.

"Are there any in Havana?"

"No," replied Leo flatly. Too flatly, for my taste. Marco shrugged.

My watch showed we were behind schedule, so I forged ahead. "Very well, now for your orders. Leo, can you find a hiding spot for seven people in the cathedral on Saturday morning, just before the Mass? We'll be there for the length of the Mass and some time afterward."

"Yes. That should not be too difficult. It is an ancient church, with many tiny places to hide. However, it will be crowded."

"We will be there at forty-five minutes after eleven o'clock.

Where should we meet you?"

"The door on the east side."

"No, that's the side facing the Spanish military headquarters. Is there another small door?"

"There is only one other small door, the episcopal entrance at the rear, the one the bishop uses. His procession will arrive there about the same time." Leo paused and thought about that. "Only priests and deacons will be at that door, attired in their finest regalia."

Only clergymen? Hmm. I was about to comment when Leo read my mind and blurted out, "No! I cannot allow you to be dressed as anointed clergy of God. No, I tell you now that I absolutely refuse."

This was when Rork, God bless him, walked over to the table and chimed in with his easygoing manner. "Ooh, Leo, me dear friend. Let me tell ye that me own soul's as Catholic as yers, an' there's nary a doubt in me heart that our divine Lord Jesus him ownself is smilin' down on this wee endeavor. After all, sir, 'tis only a piece o' cloth or two, but the real thing is we're savin' lives here, an' a higher duty isn't known to man. Aye, 'tis our responsibility as Christians o' the true faith—yers an' mine—to help how we can. An' that, me boyo, ain't no blarney nor blather."

Frowning, Leo relented enough to say, "I don't know. It is too irreverent. Blasphemous!"

"No, no. Nothing sacrilegious at all, Leo," I added gently. "No robes or collars of ordained priests, just some plain cassocks. You can get them at the monastery easily. We'll be seminarians, just students, there at the cathedral to assist. Nothing disrespectful or profane. And as Rork said, this is about saving lives."

"Just seminarians? Well, I suppose that wouldn't be blasphemous, would it?"

I was thinking fast now. "No, of course not. Please leave them no later than nine o'clock in the morning in a bag by the...the northeast side of that church, I forget the name, at Monserrate and Chacon. We'll pick them up there."

"It is called the Church of the Holy Angels," Leo said begrudgingly. "And I will leave the bag by the laurel tree no later than nine o'clock." He looked up at the ceiling and added, "Lord, I hope that I am right in doing this and beg you to forgive me for this transgression."

Rork put his right hand on Leo's shoulder. "Leo, God'll be pleased as punch ye helped."

Leo didn't look convinced.

15

Exhaustion

Havana, Cuba
4:30 a.m., Thursday
27 September 1888

Seeing Leo's mood, I changed our focus to the other man at the table.

"All right, Marco, I need you to charter a boat that can carry ten men. Have it left at the seawall alongside Cortina de Valdez, behind the cathedral, at one o'clock Saturday afternoon. No later than *one o'clock*. No crew is needed. Just the boat and three pairs of oars. Create a suitable story to explain it, something connected to the Mass. As usual, you will be reimbursed through the sugar company account at the bank."

"Yes. I can do that."

"Very well, then, gentlemen, here are your final orders. Three subjects for you to inquire about: First, try to discover anything you can about any significant prisoners Marrón has in his custody. Who are they? Where are they? How long have they been there?

"Second, ascertain the latest on Colonel Marrón and his

counterintelligence organization. Are they in a state of heightened activity? Are they concentrating anywhere? What areas, and who are they watching?

"Third, what are the anarchists planning for Saturday and for Sunday? Where and when. As always, inquire subtly, through oblique conversation. Understood?"

They both acknowledged their assignments grimly.

"Very good. Each of you will attend the early performance at the Tacon Theater tonight. I will briefly meet you both in the men's necessary room on the ground floor directly *after* the show. That is why I wanted you to meet here, so you would recognize each other at the theater. In the men's room, I will receive any information you have and pass along any further pertinent instructions.

"You both will be assisting me this weekend. Sunday will be the most dangerous day, but by that afternoon it will be over, and Rork and I and two others will be out of Cuba."

Marco had been quite pensive, or was it apprehensive? Now he spoke up. "Whose lives are you saving? What will Leo and I be doing?"

"You don't need to know details on what you'll be doing. Just follow your orders. Now is the time to earn all the money you've been given these last few years."

Leo stared down at his folded hands on the table. Marco held me in an incredulous gaze, and by the tenor of his next comment, I could tell he thought me a lunatic. "But how? I assume we are rescuing prisoners. Even if we discover where these prisoners are being held, how in God's good name will you ever get them away from Marrón and then escape Cuba? It is impossible. No one has ever done it!"

"It's not impossible, and you'll find out your duties later. After this is over on Sunday, you will both need to lie very low. I can get you off the island, if you want."

"You ask a lot of us," said Marco.

"No, I've *paid* you a lot, Marco. For more than two years."

I waited for a retort, but there was none. Leo still sat there, silently gazing at his hands, and I realized he was probably praying. I found it interesting that in all my dealings with him, Leo was never afraid of the Spanish. His only fear was of offending God. Though he was but a lay bureaucrat for the monastery, he'd always impressed me as a man of God, a holy man, with the attendant serenity and strength of purpose one finds in such persons. I respected him greatly.

"So, for my part," Leo began suddenly, still looking down. "I will help you and then stay in Cuba, and do what I can for my Church and my people."

I was about to end our meeting when Rork quickly stepped over to the table, blew out the lamp, and said, "Movement in the alley."

The dog snarled, deep-throated and menacing—a stranger was in the alley—then gave out a bone-chilling shriek that stopped ominously.

I joined Rork at the door and saw a dark mass in the alley, barely illuminated by the partial moon overhead. The form was bent over the dog. Metal flashed. A big cane knife.

"Go!" I whispered to Leo and Marco, who needed no more encouragement and fled through the interior doorway into the neighboring apartment.

"Shoot 'im?" asked Rork as the man, fifty feet away, slowly came toward our lair with a pistol in his hand. I would've said yes, but another form appeared behind him, then another.

"No. We'll slow them down a bit and run."

I put a chair against the door, and then run we did. There wasn't enough time or distance from our enemies to be stealthy. Through a torrent of startled Chinese cursing, we ran through the neighbor's crowded apartment just as the intruders reached the outer door of the meeting room and tried to burst inside. It wasn't much of a barricade, but the chair served to retard their progress by a few seconds and increase their caution. By the time they rushed it again, smashing their way inside with a crescendo of commotion that further awoke the area, Rork and I were leaving a side door of the adjoining building and hurrying down a narrow lane to the east. It was a route of emergency egress he and I had scouted out before we'd rented the place three years earlier.

By then, Leo and Marco were long gone from sight. They knew Havana well, and I wasn't that concerned about their chances. I was very concerned about ours. As we dashed across Rayo Street, a block north of the passageway our foes had used to approach house number three, the same alley we'd used, I saw a box wagon drawn up to the passageway and several men standing there arguing. One of them appeared in the dark to have the same thin frame as Marrón. The wagon and men negated the one positive scenario that could explain what had happened. Obviously, our uninvited visitors had not been common street ruffians who'd happened upon some lucrative prey in their neighborhood.

No, it was truly the worst scenario. The enemy had known where to find us.

My mind was awhirl as we ran easterly along the buildings, toward the theater district and our hotel beyond. What to do? Obviously, we were compromised, but how? One of the Aficionados? Which one? Leo and Marco appeared to be genuinely terrified. Rogelio, whom we were scheduled to meet next at house number five, knew of house number three's location but not of the rendezvous there. He was the least reliable of the Aficionados, which was why I kept him away from the other two. Or had Casas been tortured enough into giving it away? Had Marrón simply kept a long surveillance at all our places, waiting for the inevitable gathering to happen?

When we reached the large Havana United Railways train depot, Rork asked where to head next—Hotel Florida, house number five, or the waterfront? Sailors have an instinct to head for water when in trouble ashore. A couple of locomotives were pulling their cars into the station, the first of the morning cargo arrivals. Workers were milling about; the city was awakening. To the east, the sky was discernibly lighter.

Ducking into an alcove, I evaluated our situation. We were

four streets away from the dawn meeting spot for Rogelio and ten from our hotel, both on a straight route toward the rising sun. I checked my watch: It was 4:55. The sun would rise in an hour and fifteen minutes, enough time to thoroughly check for any watchers at Rogelio's rendezvous. I needed to meet Rogelio, to look into his eyes and gauge him. If he was an informer for Marrón, there might be signs of a surveillance, though I imagined they wouldn't expect us to show up after what had happened at number three. They'd expect us to run to our room at the hotel.

"Albisu Theater, where we can observe house number five."

Rork smiled. "Ooh, yer getting' pretty risky in yer old age, ain't ye?"

Following a serpentine route, we arrived at the theater fifteen minutes later. Across Monserrate Street was house number five, another *ruse de guerre*, for it was the corner room on the second floor of the Castillo de Farnes, at the intersection of Monserrate and Obrapia Streets. That public moniker was a misnomer too, for it was not a castle but three stories of apartments over a popular restaurant. The whole building was grandiosely named by and for its owners, who were Spaniards from the region of Cataluña.

I explained to Rork what I had in mind. Rogelio, who lived almost a mile to the southeast of house number five, would be approaching the rendezvous from the east along Obrapia or from the south along Monserrate. He would be walking rapidly, because, knowing Rogelio as I did, he would have gotten a late start. Rork suggested that a man like him would not walk but ride a vehicle. No, I countered, he wouldn't find a carriage this early in the morning. He'd be walking.

But in my plan, Rogelio wouldn't arrive. Rork would be in position on Obrapia near Villegas Street. I would be on Monserrate near Teniente Rey Street. Whichever of us spotted Rogelio approaching would get him off the street and into an alleyway—without coercion, if at all possible—and then to the back lane running east and west between Monserrate and Villegas.

If Rork got him, he would employ his favorite birdcall, that of the West Indian goatsucker nighthawk, a flickering screech that he can project quite effectively. If I found Rogelio, I would call out an expletive in Spanish as if cursing a wife. We'd meet in the secluded side alley behind the Taverna Gallego, where we would interrogate Rogelio.

Surveying the area from my perch at the theater, I spied a lone man in a linen suit standing at the corner. He watched both streets intently for several minutes, then wagged his head in the negative toward someone in the building across the street.

Marrón's surveillance was in place.

16

The Bigamist

Off Obrapia Street
Havana, Cuba
6:35 a.m., Thursday
27 September 1888

We waited over an hour. The city had come alive with sound and motion. In the Latin tropical summer, manual labor work begins before the day gets too hot, ending by ten in the morning and not resuming until the afternoon rain has finished. Those workers were now plying their trades—delivering, building, loading, gardening, hauling, etc.—each intent upon his own problems and little noting a rather nervous man waiting in a byway between buildings.

The sky was developing a yellowish cast to it, diffusing the sun's early light through a thin gauze of haze, but still bright enough to begin its daily task of dissipating shadows and illuminating details. The gloomy color reflected the disruption I felt in the pit of my stomach: trepidation that my suspicions of Rogelio would prove correct and anxiety over what then to do. Options were limited to two, neither of them positive.

Rogelio, unusually clad in faded cotton attire more suited to a working man than to one in his station in life, approached Rork's hidden position on Obrapia Street at a brisk pace. The Cuban's head was down, absorbed in some mental process and oblivious to his surroundings.

Somewhat liberally interpreting my orders regarding no use of coercion if possible, Rork waited until the man passed by, then clasped him by the back of the neck and yanked him into a side alcove, belatedly saying, "*Buenos dias, mi amigo. Ven conmigo.*"

Caught completely unaware, Rogelio responded with none of his normal bluster, instead whimpering, "Rork, what has happened?"

"Nary a thing," said Rork flatly. "Why d'ye ask, me boyo? Was something *supposed* to happen? Ach, now shut yer trap an' come with me."

Without waiting for a reply, he took Rogelio by the hand, as one would do with a recalcitrant child, and pulled him along behind the buildings toward our mutual destination behind the *taverna*. He then emitted his birdcall of the West Indian goatsucker. I think he just likes that name. I heard the multiple, high-pitched screeches clearly over the morning city sounds, for goatsuckers—also known as nightjars or nighthawks—do not as a rule live in cities.

When I subsequently arrived, they were squatting side by side behind a rubbish crate, backs against a wall, silently regarding each other, with my friend casting a humorless face toward his companion. The marlinespike was in full display. The Cuban's thin face showed abject terror, while Rork's transformed into innocence itself as he turned and greeted me.

"Lookee what I found, sir. An' dressed out like us common folk too."

Slovenly attired or not, Rogelio the successful businessman wasted no time in filling his words with indignation. "Commander, what is this about? Why am I dragged here like a common criminal?

Why are we not meeting at the number five place?"

It was time for him to take the test I had brewed while waiting. It would have a bitter taste, and his reaction would be the indicator of guilt or blamelessness.

"Because you are a bigamist, Rogelio, and therefore can no longer be trusted."

Rogelio narrowed his eyes. "A what? I do not know that word in English."

"*Un bígamo.*"

"*Bígamo?* There is a mistake, Commander. I have no wife at all, much less two wives. And what does that have to do with our work together, you and I?"

"No mistake, Rogelio. It is a word used in our line of work for a man who goes to bed with two different people, or organizations, at the same time. You are a bigamist."

Tellingly, Rogelio wasn't surprised or angered by my accusation. His eyes flickered wider briefly, then blinked several times before settling into their usual dark mode. Seeing his mind assessing my accusation, I knew he'd use cunning words to handle this little problem, this bump in the road.

"My dear friend, there has been some misunderstanding here. You think I am working *for* the Spanish? Nothing could be further from the truth. Why do you think that?"

It was neatly done. My accusation turned around into his question, to ascertain the extent of my knowledge of his infidelity. Rogelio was nothing if not a smooth operator. It was time for me to use some guile of my own, to sow seeds of doubt in both Rogelio and his masters. Disinformation can be an effective method for disrupting imminent enemy operations.

"Because I have a well-placed spy in the captain-general's office. He told me about you last night at a soiree there. And just a few minutes ago, it was proven to me at house number five when I spotted Marrón's people watching it, which is why you are here in this alley. Poor Colonel Marrón has no proof of any wrongdoing on my part while in Havana, mainly because I haven't done anything wrong while here. Therefore, he cannot arrest me. But what I do have now is proof of *your* duplicity."

He feigned ignorance of that word also, so I said it in Spanish: "*Duplicidad, por Usted…*"

"No, no! You are wrong, my friend. After these years of our amity, how could you take the word of some Spanish lackey at the palace about *me?* Have I not given you important information about the leaders of the Spanish army and navy? Have I not demonstrated by my actions, my patriotism for this island and my people, for the revolutionary cause?"

I gazed into those eyes of his, those usually haughty eyes that now were beginning to change, dilating in fear as he realized his situation had become life-threatening.

"Do not call me your 'friend,' Rogelio. For *that* you are not and never were. And no, you have never given me important information. The information you provided over the last two years was gossip of minor importance, and none of it was new to me. I kept you as an Aficionado because of your potential for more detailed intelligence in the future, should the need arise. And no, you have never demonstrated your patriotism for the Cuban people, only your disdain for the classes you perceive as below you."

His eyes began to fill as his face reddened. "I cannot believe this is happening to me. I swear to God above that I have been loyal. Please tell me what I can do to show you my sincerity to the cause of Cuba."

It was good acting but devoid of the spontaneous passion a Cuban patriot would display if falsely accused. His words were affected, calculated. That was when I knew for certain that Rogelio was guilty.

Rork sensed it also and moved a bit closer to the man, that spiked hand resting on a ledge beside Rogelio.

The Cuban knew he'd failed the test, but he played out his losing hand. Looking at the ground, he mumbled, "Please, tell me what you want me to do, Commander."

What was my next step? Kill the man? Or allow him to live and use him? Eliminating him would be the most expedient option. But if I chose the latter, how best to use him? I'd no time left for prolonged contemplation. When I did not immediately reply, Rogelio locked his eyes on mine, as if he could peer into my mind. There was no arrogance left in his gaze, no semblance of strength at all. He was the condemned looking into the eyes of the judge, about to hand down the sentence.

"First, tell me how Marrón got to you initially. This is your final test. Do not lie, Rogelio, or they will be your last words on this earth."

His shoulders collapsed, the final sign of total submission.

"My gambling. Bolita, roulette, whist, horses, dogs, cocks...I thought myself good at all sorts of gambling. But actually I was not that good at all."

"Go on."

"The debts were very large and widespread to various men. The colonel heard about them. He knew I was about to lose everything—my business export-import license with the government, my home, my reputation, even my family when they found out about it. My father is a very proud man."

"So the colonel made the debts go away. When was that?"

"Eighty-five."

The year before I signed him up. I'd never known of his wagering. A fundamental mistake on my part.

"And since then, what has Marrón had you do in regard to the Aficionados?"

"I never told him about you or the Aficionados! And never the patriots! I only gave him things I heard around the city regarding the anarchists and unionists."

That made some sense. To my uncertain knowledge, our ONI operations in Cuba had shown no signs of compromise until the present situation. And, until a few hours earlier, none of the Aficionados knew the identities of the others. Rogelio still didn't.

"Why not? You could rid yourself of the *gringo* pressure to perform and at the same time gain favor with Marrón, the man who held your life in his hands."

He shook his head, sniffling now. "No, no…I support the cause of independent liberty, as do you. I could not forsake that."

That part about me was true. I'd told each of the Aficionados that though my government was officially neutral in the struggle for Cuban independence—especially the Cleveland administration—I was personally in favor of it. That sweetener had added to my credibility with the Cubans. However, I doubted Rogelio's motives were as altruistic as he proclaimed.

"No. You needed steady money from both sides, Rogelio. The Spanish and the Americans have been funding you for years now. You doubled your income on the side, with more money for wagering. And thus became a bigamist."

That hit the target. The eyes wavered and filled, blinking constantly. His chest no longer moved as he held his breath for fear of my next words.

I pressed on. "But you must've truly dreaded the day when one of us, the Spanish or the Americans or the Cubans, would find out. Especially the Cubans. You've lived in terror about their finding out for years, haven't you?"

Sniffling turned into open sobbing. "Yes."

"When did Marrón find out about you and the United States?"

"Two days ago."

Interesting. That was the day I arrived. "How?"

"Telegram from New York. The colonel said they are checking all communications from New York, since so many Cuban revolutionaries are there."

He shook his head again and moaned. The words then came out in a torrent. "The Spanish intercepted one from a Cuban friend of mine, Franco Garmendia, to me. It was nothing really. Only a response to a question from me asking if he knew when the patriot general Antonio Maceo would come back to Cuba. The people here say that once Maceo returns, the final fight will really begin. I was merely curious, and Franco said he had no idea of when Maceo was planning to return."

Rogelio took a breath. "Of course, you do not put that in plain language, but in other words that sound more innocent. But our code words were stupidly simple enough for the Spanish to decipher. Then I was summoned..." More tears.

"Talk," I ordered.

"I was summoned to Colonel Marrón this last Tuesday. He accused Franco and me of working for the U.S. government and threatened me with the firing squad. I never told him about the Aficionados though—never! And I do not think he knows, for he never spoke of us or used the word Aficionados.

"He did say that a U.S. naval officer was here in the city and assigned me to find out what the officer and any other *norteamericanos* are doing in Havana. I have the impression he has given a similar assignment to other people in the city. Marrón gave me two days to do that, to prove my loyalty to the crown, or... or...I will be shot at sunrise on Friday at Cabañas Fortress."

"So what did you tell him?" I demanded.

"Only that a message was left for me to meet a *gringo* at one of two places early this morning. I gave him the locations for house number three and house number five and said I chose the second one. I told him I was chosen because of my rum export business with the United States. That was all I said. No details, no names."

"So you wrote a fake message to support your story?"

"Yes. I had to give him something."

"With my name signed?"

"No! There was no name signed at all, only a short message in English to meet at one of those locations."

This time I believed him, for his manner said more than his words. Oh, he was desperate, all right, reporting to his Spanish overlords an anonymous tip for an initial meeting, which might yield the big prize of a *yanqui* naval officer, much as in '86, before I'd escaped. But it was a razor's edge he'd been walking.

Rogelio wouldn't want to tell them anything else, for it would prove how involved he had been with us for years. Now it was time to turn this fragile double agent into a triple one with a carrot and a stick.

"Their trap to catch me didn't work, though. Now they will find and kill you. But you don't have the skills or the true friendships to be able to flee Cuba, do you, Rogelio?"

It came out barely audible. "No."

"Were they following you from your apartment to house number five?"

"No. They said they did not want the foreigner to see them on the street, that I would have to go alone, but they would have men around the apartment building when I got there."

That was a slight positive note in an otherwise depressing litany. "Then they don't know where you are now, here with us, do they?"

"No."

I checked my pocket watch. "Hmm. So it appears to them that you are now on the run, and by now Marrón's men have started searching for you. If they succeed, you'll have only twenty-four more hours to live. You've never been in that dungeon, have you?"

He trembled at the thought, unable to speak.

"Have you?"

"No," he whimpered.

"I have. I've seen what they do. Seen the instruments they use. Yes, it will be an excruciatingly long twenty-four hours, and you will be begging for the bullet by the time they are done."

He made a sound like an animal whining.

"And I would imagine your execution won't be at Cabañas. No, it will probably be at La Punta, by the Audiencia. Marrón will want to make a public spectacle out of your death to discourage anyone else from similar behavior. He will probably force your mother and father to watch, won't he?"

"Yes. Colonel Marrón is horrible. That...is...the kind of thing he would do."

It was time. "If you want to live, Rogelio, I have a way."

17

The Carrot and the Stick

Havana, Cuba
Alley off Villegas Street
6:45 a.m., Thursday
27 September 1888

Rogelio's voice struggled. "You know a way out of this for me? Commander, I *do* want to live. Tell me how."

I paused and studied him coldly, the cleric drawing out the sinner's agony before offering absolution, so that it will be more appreciated. "You must do *exactly* what I tell you in order to escape Marrón. It means losing every possession you have, abandoning everything you are, leaving everyone you know—as of this very moment. Will you do that?"

His head dropped as if all the muscles upholding it gave way, tears and mucous flowing down his face. Before me was the wreckage of a man.

"Yes…"

"Look at me." He didn't. "Rogelio, I said, *look at me!*"

Rork reached over and snapped his face up by the chin. Like

Paloma before him, this dismal parasitic specimen disgusted me, but I kept my tone level. "I have a plan for how you can live a real life in the land of freedom. To get there will be dangerous. You may not make it unless you do precisely what I tell you. If you don't, the Spanish will find and execute you—*after* they torture you for information in the dungeons of the Audiencia. Are you ready?"

"Yes." His pathetic expression didn't inspire confidence in his ability to accomplish the important role I had in mind for him, but my options were dwindling. So was my time. The sun was rising higher.

"Listen very carefully. Do not go home—that place is out of your life forever. Contact *no one* you know. Your old life is over, dead. Immediately go to the slaughter yards down by Barrio Christiana. Hide there. Cut your hair, grow your beard, steal different clothes, and speak street language if you must speak. Alter your appearance as much as you can and use a completely different name. Understood?"

"Yes, sir."

"Good. Then, at this same time on Saturday morning—*not before*—go to the central rail station and take the early Western Railroad train out toward Pinar del Rio. It departs at eight o'clock in the morning. Four miles past Dagume, get off at Cañas, which is the first stop in Pinar del Rio Province. Do you know it?"

"Yes. There are two sugar mills there. I've done business with them."

"Correct. There is also a good road in Cañas that goes to the north. Walk that road to Guanajay. It is only a few miles."

His face grew puzzled. "But why not take the United Railways line direct to Guanajay from Havana? It is newer and much faster."

"Precisely because it *is* faster and shorter, and therefore the Spanish will watch it more closely."

"Yes, of course. You are correct, sir."

"Very good. At Guanajay, walk the small road north out of town, seven miles to Mariel. Take no landau or victoria on either of these roads. The for-hire drivers will remember you when they are questioned later by the police. You are to play the part of an average working man, one who must walk, for he has no money to ride. *Comprendes?*"

"The seaport of Mariel! *Dios Mio!* That is the base of the Spanish army's western fortification trench system. Soldiers are everywhere."

"Exactly. It's the northern flank of the cross-island trenches and therefore the one place they won't think to look for you. And it has fishing boats. Hide somewhere outside the village Saturday night. On Sunday morning, during the church hour, go to the fishing docks in Mariel and find a Greek-Cuban captain named Teodorios Piruni. He will take you and sail with the next tide north to Key West. He has already been paid. Understand all that? Repeat it to me."

Now that he had hope, in the unlikely form of me, Rogelio had regained some of his wits, an essential factor for my plan to work. His words emerging stronger, he repeated the instructions.

"Very good, Rogelio. You will also use this opportunity to observe the Spanish army's defenses around Mariel: fortifications, barracks, batteries, telegraph lines, trench works. Do not write anything down—memorize it. When you reach Key West, go to the San Carlos Institute and tell them you are my friend. They will take care of you. On the fifteenth of October I will come there, debrief you, and give you some money to start life over again. Is that last part about the Mariel army installations clear?"

"Yes, sir. And thank you so much for giving me this chance."

"One last thing, Rogelio. I know your real name, your father's home, and other things about you. If you have not reached Key West by one week, at the latest, after this Saturday, I will give your identity to my Cuban patriot friends and let them deal with you. They are far more efficient at hunting down men than the Spanish."

I leaned toward him. "Rogelio, you *do not* want the Cuban patriots to consider you a traitor."

Rork couldn't resist adding his opinion. "Ooh, an' them *mambises*'ve got a right special way o' dealin' with traitors. Ye've heard what that is, haven't ye, boyo?"

Rogelio couldn't even speak, but gulped out what resembled "Yes."

Mambises, the African-Hispanic farm peasants from the interior of Cuba, were the most feared warriors of the revolutionary army, experts at wielding a machete. The Spanish government's army conscripts, draftees from Spain sent overseas to fight and die in an unwinnable tropical guerilla war, were completely terrified of falling into the hands of the Cuban *mambises*. Horrific rumors circulated in the Spanish army about what happened when you got captured.

"Go," I commanded. "I will see you in Key West."

He stumbled away, the carrot and the stick entirely understood.

My instructions to Rogelio finished, Rork and I still had the seemingly impossible task of getting back into our hotel room. I had no doubt Marrón had already checked the room and confirmed our absence. Why then return? Maintaining our public status as honored friends and guests of the Captain-General of Cuba was our only viable option to stay out of the clutches of Marrón. That meant returning to the hotel and continuing the pretense, for alone in the streets we could be seized without notice, to disappear forever.

So we had to get back into the hotel. All entrances would be closely watched. Whether the police were on the lookout for Rork was another factor. Marrón almost certainly had been advised of the murder suspect's description and had connected it to Rork or me, giving him a nice pretext for a showy arrest of his favorite enemy. Climbing up the outside of that damned wall was simply beyond my physical powers, even if it hadn't been negated by the daylight crowd in the streets. I had a notion, far-fetched to be sure. It formed when I recalled how Rork escaped the posse on the rooftop previously.

We set out quickly, with me in the lead, traversing the various back alleys. We finally reached the narrow back lane along the rear of the line of buildings along the north side of Obispo Street, where Hotel Florida stood.

Choosing an apartment building west of the hotel, I led the way up the stairs to the roof garden. The sun had risen over the Cabañas fortress on the east side of the harbor channel. We hurried over, through, and around the various patios, garden walls, chimneys, gables, and clotheslines of the intervening roofs. When we arrived at the top of our hotel, we peeked over the edge to our balcony, fifteen feet below.

I realize that a drop of only fifteen feet would seem a relatively minor inconvenience to the reader of this account. But deuced if it didn't look ten feet too far to me. My partner flashed me a perturbed frown.

This was one of those times when the officer has to lead—a duty that Rork has the distressing habit of quietly reminding me of at the most difficult of moments—so I growled a sailor's curse, gathered my courage, and nodded to my friend. He grinned and lightly offered the old adage, "Aye, no guts shown, then no glory gained."

"Quite right, Rork," said I, while waiting a few seconds until it appeared no one in the street was looking up. Then I jumped for it.

My leap of faith resulted in a landing that was not graceful in the least, nor was it noiseless, for I managed to knock over a chair and table, inviting the attention of several pedestrians below. After determining my limbs were functioning, I stood and waved sheepishly at them. Their reactions indicated they thought me just another drunk tourist.

Rork dropped our seabag of weaponry down to me but remained aloft himself for five more long minutes, gauging his descent for another lull in the walking traffic below. I was pleased to see his landing was ungainly too.

Our room was as we had left it. I appreciated Colonel Marrón's thugs being neat in returning it to its pristine condition after ransacking our belongings. That they had done so was verified by the absence of one of my hairs, which I had wetted and pressed down across the latch of the drawer where my clothes were stowed—an old but effective trick to determine thievery or interference.

For the benefit of our friends in the wall, Rork and I conversed about the glorious morning we'd spent on the balcony, enjoying the breakfast we'd obtained two hours before from the bakery down the street. Sure enough, a few minutes later, our door guardian entered and inquired in rather good English where we had been and how we'd gotten out. Rork and I exchanged baffled glances—who, us?—then looked at our questioner as if we didn't understand.

He was a new man to us, a bit older than the others, and possessed an air of authority they hadn't had. I assumed he was a sergeant in Marrón's secret service, and registered that the man had omitted his name. Indignantly announcing that a messenger had arrived at five in the morning but we were gone, he cast me a challenging glare.

Judging by the aggressive manner of our new "servant"-turned-overseer, I imagined his predecessors had been sacked after our disappearance had been reported to the colonel. Those poor souls were probably en route to some dismal place in the jungle to fight the *mambises,* and the new man appeared as if he was next on the list, for while the earlier guards had allowed the hated *gringos* to mysteriously escape, *he* had managed to let the *gringos* mysteriously reenter.

I have discovered over the years that it is always better to allow a person with clout to salvage some semblance of pride, some way out of an affront to his authority, by presenting him a convenient alibi to explain an unpleasant outcome. To do this, one often needs to be completely pleasant, almost naïve.

Well, let the record reflect that Rork isn't the only one who can act as innocent as a newborn lamb. I smiled at our smoldering adversary and said, "Why, I have no idea what you mean, my good man. We went for a short stroll before sunrise to that wonderful bakery three streets down. Do you know the one? Then we returned here to enjoy our repast on the balcony and watch one of your glorious Cuban sunrises. Been back here for hours. Didn't your nightman tell you we went out for pastries? Oh, that's right, I'm not sure he noticed us. He looked pretty tired, didn't he, Rork?"

"Ooh, the poor lad was sleepin' the sleep o' a baby, he was. Workin' too hard fer too long, methinks. Wonderful fellow, though. Very friendly, he was."

It's been my experience that every organization has its least energetic and skilled members. Often they are employed on, and prefer, night work, for its distance away from the judgmental eyes of their seniors, the fewer mental challenges, and more opportunities for relaxation. Those in the group who do work diligently and endure the hardships despise those who just idle their way through life.

The Spanish counterintelligence crew in Havana was no exception to this rule. It hadn't been difficult to detect the lethargy, bordering on dozing off, of our late-night door servant/guardian. He was the weak link in Marrón's chain, as it were. Conversation with him had also shown that he wasn't the sharpest knife in the drawer either. Therefore, he was my nomination as the scapegoat for his superiors not knowing where we were when they'd entered the room at five o'clock in the dark of the morning.

Our accuser stood there nonplussed, then departed in silence, growling bitterly. Obviously, he shared my evaluation of his predecessor, whose incompetence I had now elevated from mere neglect to gross misconduct.

I didn't worry about how the new man would explain all this to his superiors, for I had another priority right then. That most comfortable of beds was beckoning me, like an oasis to a parched Arab, and it was with the greatest sigh of relief that I collapsed into it, my ligaments tingling with released tension. I was blissfully unconscious within seconds. There are times when you just don't care anymore.

18

Irish Suspicions

Hotel Florida
Obispo Street
Havana, Cuba
8 p.m., Thursday
27 September 1888

I have an intense aversion to wearing full dress uniforms. And I am not alone in that regard. Military men who are required to wear dress uniforms universally despise them, no matter their nationality.

No, it is the ladies of society who love to see dress uniforms, to be in a room full of them, and to own, or pretend to own, the man who wears one. The more baubles and bangles and gongs displayed—commonly called medals, the masculine version of jewelry—the better. There are two kinds of medals: those worn by men who *earned* them, and those worn by men who were *given* them.

The former class is composed of warriors, of which I am a member, though sometimes reluctantly. They despise the politicos who start wars, for it is the warriors who pay the price. The latter class is composed of diplomats and dilettantes, who know neither defeat nor victory, nor the sacrifice involved in both, but oh-so-bravely dress up and play the part in order to bask in reflected glory.

Both classes attract the attention of the feminine half of humankind. Perhaps it's the power, wealth, and fame that dress uniforms represent that appeals to our disenfranchised females, who possess no organic political power of their own. Or perhaps the cynical view is more accurate: that since ladies must endure their own physical ordeals in the form of corsets and shoes and hoops and hairpins, they therefore vicariously delight in knowing the pain their opposites must also bear when wearing full dress.

Whatever the true reason for female admiration of full military garb, in my not-so-humble opinion, it is bulky, itchy, and suffocatingly hot, even that made of serge, which is somewhat better than wool. All this reaches its zenith of discomfort in Havana in the month of September.

Time was a-wasting, for the sun had sunk, the city was darkening, and the carriage was due to arrive at any time. The theater awaited and I had to go, though I knew not the type or name of the performance. I planned to show up with the crowd, seek a suitably remote seat, stay as unremarkable as possible, and, as quickly as feasible, get the job done—meet with my American team of specialists during the intermission and with Leo and Marco after the show.

Sensing my foul mood while adjusting my collar, Rork tried to lighten the moment by pronouncing, "Ooh, yer'll be the belle o' the theater, sir. Prettiest officer there, or me name's not Sean Rork o' the Sainted Isle o' Gael."

I didn't share his satiric mirth. "Please just stow it, Rork. I hate this thing."

He, of course, wasn't required to be in any such get-up but was allowed to wear simply his number-two rig, since he would not be sitting with me but would await my pleasure in the lobby with the other minions. I fervently hoped there wouldn't be any pretty *chicas* in that area. Rork sometimes gets distracted, and his memory of lessons learned in that field can be distressingly dim and short.

I suppose my lack of levity was understandable, my nerves frayed by the uncertainty of our situation. What I had anticipated happening during our rest earlier that day—the door bursting open and Marrón triumphantly sneering as his men shackled the *yanqui* murder suspects and marched them out of the hotel— never transpired. Instead, Rork and I lay like logs on our respective beds all morning and into the afternoon. I think the wall's peepers might have thought us dead.

Why Marrón *didn't* arrest us was the primary issue in my mind once I awoke. Agitated by the inexplicable emergence of this good fortune, I eventually worked out several explanations. The first was that the witnesses to El Strangulador's death, being mostly criminals themselves, had either disappeared or refused to cooperate. A distant alternative was that the case was determined to be self-defense. Far more likely was that Marrón had informed the civil police that he would handle the matter and was waiting for a better moment to effect the arrest, a time and place more opportune to his motives, whatever they might be in that disturbed mind. Perhaps the theater?

A double thud sounded on the door, and one of the captain-general's couriers entered with a yellow and red envelope, the red sealing wax of which was embossed with the arms of Spain in gold. It was an official invitation by the captain-general to sit with him and Doña Matilde in the gubernatorial box at the Tacon Theater that evening, with dinner afterward at the Inglaterra Hotel next door. I signed the RSVP, and the courier departed, leaving me with the question, How did Don Sabas know I would be at the theater that night? Probably by the people inside the wall or outside the door, I guessed.

Holding the invitation up, I quietly said to my friend, "Well, Rork, it appears the performance tonight is to be Victorien

Sardou's *La Tosca*, with the lead role played by none other than the French *femme fatale* of the world, Sarah Bernhardt."

He wasn't impressed by the evening's illustrious program. Instead, he commented, "Hmm, stuck up aloft in a box with His High an' Mighty, an' only one way in an' out? Don't sound good to me. Any way to get out o' it?"

"No, none I can think of. An invitation like this is essentially a command—as if Admiral Porter had invited me to Ford's Theater. And I can't afford to create an affront to the Captain-General of Cuba. He's the only thing between Marrón and us right now."

"Aye, but me bones don't like it, not a wee bit. Restricts yer freedom o' movement too much."

"Yes, but it won't restrict yours. You'll meet with our specialists at intermission and then after the show with the Aficionados."

He raised an eyebrow. "An' ye think the merry widow'll be there?"

"Yes, Belleza will be there. Probably sitting somewhere close to the royal box. Marrón's the kind who uses multiple avenues of attack, so I think she'll approach me. At least, that's what I'm counting on."

"Aye, methinks yer right as rain, sir. But you take care with that ol' honey trap, me friend. She's more than she shows."

He wagged his head thoughtfully at me, and I knew a speech was coming. He loves to make speeches.

"Now listen to me, boyo. Yer jus' not as wise to feminine wiles as me ownself. Don't let her get ye off into the shadows alone. Keep clear o' her wig, fer many tarts stow a razor 'neath it. An' keep a weather eye fer her garters, fer they usually stow a dagger or derringer down below there. The bigger the woman, the bigger the weapon—an' that Belleza's got some tonnage on her."

"Good Lord, Rork," I growled in a low voice. "Razors in a wig? Derringers in a garter? I do declare that at times your Gaelic suspicions get the best of you. Doña Belleza Ortiz y Cardonne is a widowed lady of the Cuban elite, nothing more and nothing less. Of course, I assume that she provides occasional hearsay to

Marrón. But she's certainly not one of your poxied Water Street hookers from New York, out to roll a drunken sailor ashore on liberty. And by the way, the very thought of *you* lecturing *me* on being careful with a woman is ludicrous. I'll use her for our purposes. She should prove quite handy."

He huffed in exasperation. "See? There ye go, provin' me right. An' afore ye brings up little Cornelia aginst me, let me say that tart's more proof o' me own point. Aye, when even the sinful likes o' me can't judge a woman by the paint o' her topsides, then a decent lad such as yer ownself don't stand a chance in hell o' knowin' what's hidin' down below decks. Nay, mark me words here an' now: Dear Belleza's no lady from the elite o' Havana or any-damned-where else. She's a dressed-up trollop who wears a wig an' stows a blade, an' ye'd best be careful 'round her, 'cause she looks shrewd as hell an' scares me."

There is absolutely no arguing logically with Rork once he gets his mind made up. It is an exercise in futility. But I always allow him his say and listen closely to his opinions, because sometimes those old suspicions end up coming true.

All that having been discussed, I then whispered the instructions regarding his meeting that night with our men and the Aficionados. Seven minutes later, we departed the room on the half-mile journey to the Gran Teatro Tacon. Rork clutched a black, cotton laundry bag into which we had deposited our two long guns, it being slightly less conspicuous than a U.S. Navy seabag. Should someone inquire, the explanation would be that it contained "necessities" for his master, insinuating they were bottles of brandy.

19

Remembering Marengo

Gran Teatro Tacon
Havana, Cuba
9 p.m., Thursday
27 September 1888

Havana's Grand Tacon Theater is the third largest in the world, a fact that is constantly pointed out to foreign visitors by its proud Spanish patrons. The greatest theatrical productions of Europe, the United States, and Latin America include the Tacon in their itineraries. It is truly Havana's window to the world and draws the island's privileged class of Spaniards, along with the Criollo Cuban upper crust, like moths to a flame when the famous appear there.

Such was the case the evening I attended, my first in this imposing monument to the fine arts. Fronting the alabaster statue of Queen Isabella Segunda in the central park, the theater presents an imposing image, dominating the other structures in the area. Inside, you are even more impressed. The word spacious does not accurately describe its interior proportions; the place is simply enormous, lit by the largest array of gasoliers I've ever seen.

The male gentry reposes in comfortable seating in the main arena near the stage, and from this crowd rises a cloud of cigar smoke. Lessers sit behind them, farther removed from the performance but no less pungent. The highest strata of Spaniards sit nearer to heaven in more than one hundred separate balcony boxes set in five layers along the side walls, well above the merely wealthy. Ladies, dressed to the hilt and with fans aflutter, are included in this rarified altitude.

The royal box, decorated in crimson damask and gold satin and trimmed with gold-leafed railings and cherry woodwork, is the closest of the elite to the performance. It is guarded at its entry by the sixteenth-century costumed soldiers of the palace and serviced by eighteenth-century costumed butlers from the captain-general's private apartments.

The view from the altitude of the box is remarkable. Beyond the thousand attendees in their private boxes, fully two thousand spectators are jammed into the room below you under the largest chandelier in the Americas. It is a seething mass of glittering jewels, colorful attire, and buzzing conversation, with the periodic billows of cigar puffers everywhere, like so many volcanoes. At any one time, at least a quarter of them were staring up at me in the royal perch, a disconcerting thing when I first experienced it.

The captain-general and his lady were fashionably late, so I was initially the sole occupant and target of conjecture for those below. The audience was obviously discussing that *yanqui* naval officer, about whom so much had already been said in the city's salons and social circles since my Havana fencing debut. Was that really only two days before?

Feeling like a bird in a cage, I sat down and waited for Don Sabas to arrive and the production to begin, as did everyone else in the place, from the servants to the actors to the snobs below me. *How odd,* thought I, *to be in this extravagant and envied place, where normally I would not even be in the cheapest seats at the rear of the main floor.* And all because I'd reacted instinctively and shoved a spoiled brat out of the way of a homemade bomb.

A commotion in the hallway behind the booth alerted me to stand. Just as a barrage of trumpetry sounded from the orchestra pit, the guards stamped to attention, and all the uniformed men in the room stood, faced my box, and executed the hand salute. The captain-general, ruler of this last great remnant of the glory of Spain, had arrived with due pomp and circumstance.

Waving a hand to the masses, he emerged alone from the curtained entry to thunderous applause, all eyes on his patented smile, which reminded me of Theodore Roosevelt's irrepressible grin. It was then that I realized there were only two chairs, green velour wingbacks with a pattern of gold embroidered crowns of Castile and Leon, set out in the box. Evidently, it would only be Don Sabas and me. We would have privacy, and I recalled his comment about that the previous evening.

"This will be quite enjoyable," he said to me while taking his seat. "Though it has an anti-monarchial air to it, I personally asked for this drama to be played here. Did you know that Victorien Sardou wrote it just for Madam Sarah Bernhardt. She is my favorite actress. Is she not yours, Commander?"

I sat down, trying to act comfortable. Flutes of champagne miraculously appeared in our hands from silent attendants.

"I've never seen her perform, Your Excellency. I look forward to this play."

"I have just talked with her behind the stage." He paused, then raised a finger for emphasis. "She is the most beautiful woman in history—other than my wife, of course. Sometimes a little too self-confident, as are so many of the French, but still, very beautiful. I have heard that England's Prince of Wales is one of her lovers."

I'd heard the same thing while in England a year earlier but had discounted it as idle rumor. "I do believe the lady is recently married, sir."

He laughed. "How very American of you to bring that up, Commander. Yes, Sarah has been married to some Greek actor in London—I forget his name—for six years. I am told he is addicted to morphine. So perhaps there is a shade of gray there in her marriage. Besides, how can a husband like that possibly provide the same attraction to a woman like her as a future king of England? There is a—how do you say it in English?—an...*allure*, yes? There is an irresistible allure to men with political power and wealth and confidence, a magnetism that gathers women like Sarah Bernhardt to them. It is human nature, I think, this attraction of the most beautiful of women to the most manly of men."

He was warming rapidly to the issue, so much so that I began to wonder which man was the subject of his hypothesis regarding Bernhardt—the Prince of Wales or himself? I found his fascination quite interesting, particularly in light of the March 1887 *New York Times* article I'd read. In it, Bernhardt described the audience during her first performance at the Tacon in Havana as "odious people" who smoked and expectorated a lot but hadn't grasped her presentation in the least.

I decided not to bring that up, instead asking, "Are we to be deprived of Doña Matilde's lovely company this evening, Your Excellency?"

"Sadly, yes, my friend. My dear wife Matilde begs your forgiveness, but less than an hour ago she informed me that her head was aching and she did not feel strong enough for an evening at the theater. She was very much anticipating seeing you again and hopes that she will have another chance in the future." He chuckled. "I have the impression she is an admirer of yours, Commander."

She'd bowed out less than an hour earlier? That would have been right before I got to the theater. Then why were there only two chairs set out when I'd arrived? No, our privacy was premeditated, which meant the captain-general wanted to say, or ask, things he hadn't been able to in front of the others at the dinner in his apartment.

I bowed slightly and said, "I offer my best wishes for her recovery, sir, and would be delighted and honored for another chance to spend time in her company."

As the orchestra tuned up and the house manager prattled on from the stage about upcoming concerts, Don Sabas and I spoke polite nothings about the hot weather, the recent hurricanes that summer, and the design of the theater, during which I happened to spot out of the corner of my eye a familiar face studying me from two boxes away.

Doña Belleza Ortiz y Cardonne winked and smiled demurely at me, the invitation fleeting but obvious. Then the ceiling and wall gasoliers dimmed simultaneously across the cavernous room, the stage lights brightened, and we were plunged into Sardou's story about Italian love and treachery just after the battle of Marengo in northwest Italy in 1800. The French victory over the Hapsburg Austrians was where Bonaparte cemented his military reputation and subsequently catapulted his political ambitions.

"Do you know of Marengo, Commander?" inquired Don Sabas pleasantly, as an actor appeared onstage and delivered his lines in French, which I thought odd: A play about Italians was delivered in French to Spaniards in Cuba. Something of the story was bound to be lost in translation.

"Only the basic information about it, Your Excellency. I am not as well versed in European military history as you are."

"Ah, yes, military history is a specialty of mine. I find it better to learn from those who came before me than to provide bitter lessons for those who come after me. Marengo was the crucial turning point for Napoleon, a victory that propelled him as first consul of France after his *coup d'etat* the previous year, and the battle that the French have rewritten ever since to proclaim his greatness as a general."

He leaned over and with a sly expression said, "But there is a little-known component of Marengo that many people do not know. It has nothing to do with the glory of French soldiery or Napoleon's skills. Instead, it involves the dark arts of espionage. I believe the word you use in English is 'skulduggery.'"

He noted my facial reaction. "Yes, indeed, Commander, I am

speaking of the nefarious work of spies." Don Sabas' head slowly shook in disapproval. "That lower province of human endeavor that gentlemen of authority do not care to enter themselves, of course, but are always compelled to use."

Some sort of dramatic action was taking place onstage, but I could not tear myself away from the man in front of me, intensity radiating from his eyes as he described what had happened eighty-eight years before. "You see, Commander, there was a double agent for the Austrians who deceived Napoleon into splitting his forces and sending them to the northern and the southern flanks. A huge mistake. That deception worked well at first, but just then the cunning Corsican—and in my opinion, *all* Corsicans are cunning—understood his error. He began reinforcing his center just as the Austrians attacked. The outcome was in doubt for a long time, but the French army eventually beat them. The rest, as it is said, is but history, written by the victors. I have always had one question that has remained without an answer. Can you guess what it is?"

I had a strong inkling, but I said, "No, sir. With your knowledge of military campaigns, I can't imagine any important detail you don't know."

The intensity faded from his face and he looked saddened, as if he was about to pass along bad news about an old mutual friend. "Oh, it is not an important factor, Commander, just a personal interest in the human side of the affair. I have always speculated on what happened to that spy when Napoleon found out about him? We do not even know the man's name, or how he perished. Such is the way with spies, is it not? They are doomed to live a lonely, fearful life in the shadows, never receiving their due for any success, paying the ultimate price for failure by dying far from their friends and family, not even in the company of comrades, as would a soldier. And in the end, even their masters forsake and forget them as mere disposable pawns in the great game of nations."

I digested all this as the Captain-General of Cuba sat back in his chair and drained his glass, eyes still on me, with the ghost of a smile crossing his face. A noncommittal response was my choice, though it came across as rather moronic, given the circumstances.

"A very interesting point about Marengo and the role of military intelligence, Your Excellency. It is something I did not know. You are quite the historical scholar, sir."

Don Sabas made no comment. Only that knowing smile indicated his thoughts. I was rescued from further embarrassment when the house exploded in applause, for Act One had ended and the curtain was closing. Unknown to me, while I'd sat there completely mesmerized by my companion's monologue, Sarah Bernhardt had made her appearance onstage and the place had loved it.

As if he'd been watching her the whole time, my companion said, "What a great actress she is!" Then he stood, swept his hand around the room, pointed down to the stage, and cried out, "*Bravo!*" Soon everyone, including the *yanqui* spy, was on his feet, echoing the captain-general's sentiment.

20

Façades and Candor

Gran Teatro Tacon
Havana, Cuba
10 p.m., Thursday
27 September 1888

The curtain rose. Act Two, set at the gambling tables of the Renaissance Farnese Palace in Rome, began with French actors portraying monarchy-loyalist Italians babbling on about the Napoleonic French army at Marengo. For me the rapid French was impossible to follow, so too for the crowd below me, judging by their blank expressions.

"Ah, yes, the Palazzo Farnese of Rome," said Don Sabas wistfully. "A beautiful building, from the same period as the founding of Havana. Michelangelo was involved in the design by request of his friend, a cardinal who would later become pope. And now, by a delicious stroke of fate, for the last sixteen years that magnificent three-hundred-fifty-year-old papal palace has been the French Republic's embassy. Have you seen that palace in Rome, Commander?"

"No, Your Excellency. I have not been to Rome yet. But we do have a new public building in Washington, and I have heard that the Farnese Palace was the model for its design by General Meigs. It's called the Pension Building and houses the staff that oversees the government's care of our veterans from the War of the Rebellion. A very large staff, for we have millions of those veterans."

"Ah, yes. Like we Spaniards here in Cuba, you Americans had your own insurgency, didn't you? And crushed it by military might. You were part of that, were you not?"

Memories came to mind. Unpleasant memories of an ugly guerilla war along the coast of Florida. My older brother was killed during operations among the coastal islands in South Carolina. No glory in that war. In any war.

"Yes, Your Excellency. It took years. More than six hundred thirty thousand men died. A terrible waste, begun by politicians who knew not the price of war—unlike warriors such as you and I. We are the ones who pay the price of their folly and bombast."

"So true, my friend. As it has been for centuries."

My attention was drawn back to the stage by the arrival of Sarah Bernhardt. Swathed in an elegant, gold-embroidered yellow gown, she played the role of the Italian opera star La Tosca and swept onto the scene, as other actors paused in their discussions and turned their gaze toward her, the *prima diva* of the play. The audience hushed in rapt awe.

With dramatic flourishes, the actor playing the evil Baron Scarpia took Tosca aside. They were conversing about some sort of third party's love affair when the messengers from the battle arrived with the devastating report that the French had won the fight at Marengo. The announcement caused immediate chaos. One actress—I think she was an Italian queen or princess—collapsed with outstretched arms to the floor. The gentlemen gamblers exchanged frightened glances and hysterical words. Tosca threw something into the air, rushing offstage to find her lover, an Italian hero hiding out from Scarpia. That villainous soul, head of the

Italian secret police who apparently worked for the French, then ordered his men to follow Tosca to the lover, whom he wanted dead. Tension now palpable, the curtain closed.

Translating the French, taking in the stage action, and dealing with the incessant scrutiny of the man beside me—not to mention worrying about various impediments in our soon-to-come action—had all combined to give me a colossal headache. The constantly refilled champagne didn't help. I glanced around the room, now becoming even more stuffy and smoky. Belleza was in her same spot and glanced at me coyly. I waved back and even made so bold as to wink at her. Intermission was coming soon, at which time I would get her to make good on her offer. Well, her *stated* offer.

My host chose this moment to casually observe, "That was a very good depiction by the actors, was it not? Bad news is seldom received well, especially by those of us who belong to the Latin cultures. We are not able to be stoic in times of adversity, like you of the Anglo and Teutonic nations. I fear we tend to become emotional, and our rage makes us sometimes *overreact*." He lingered on that word, then continued. "It has always been our way, especially when we feel betrayed by those we consider friends."

Our glasses were again refilled by a servant who padded in and away in seconds. Another came in with a whispered message for the captain-general, who acknowledged it curtly.

Not liking the way things were going, I changed the subject to something lighter and complimentary. "I think Latin emotion is a great asset, Your Excellency. It creates beautiful art and architecture and music. There is a lot to be said for a culture that accomplishes that. And I greatly admire Spain, as does all the civilized world."

"How very kind of you to say that, Commander. Your own country has affected the world as well by its remarkable mercantile strength and considerable political influence in recent years. You Americans seem to be everywhere and involved in everything. Speaking of which, I have just received word that my dear friend,

Consul-General Williams, will not be joining us tonight. He was to arrive here at the intermission, after returning from Santa Clara, but has been delayed by a torn railroad track. What a pity. The insurgents' work, most probably. They have decreased their banditry but occasionally still annoy us."

I hadn't even known Williams was expected. And the sudden banditry problem seemed a bit too convenient. "I regret his absence, sir. Consul-General Williams is a very good man."

"Yes, he is a very good man, one who uniquely understands both our worlds. He does his duty for the United States quite effectively. However, I find it intriguing that the consul-general does not know of the true nature of your work in Havana, Commander. Entirely understandable, of course. Military men and diplomats seldom mix well, do they?"

His mouth was curved in a smile for the audience, but those eyes had gone deadly serious again, gauging my reaction, not my words.

"I am just a staff protocol officer, Your Excellency, so there is no reason for Mr. Williams to be concerned with my lowly work. I am far below him in importance."

"Below in rank, perhaps. But in importance to your government, I think not, Commander." He gave me a reproachful fatherly look. "Your modesty might impress some of our ladies, but it does not serve you well with me. I know what you do and whom you work for in your navy. I have been told of the scars on your body, though your country has not been officially at war for a quarter of the century. Your career has been active, dangerous, and successful. You have been inducted into the French Legion of Honor and have medals from Peru and Cambodia. No one in authority here believes your pretense of protocol officer."

Well, what could I say to that? The "protocol officer" idea wasn't mine; it was Commodore Walker's. If I got out of this alive, I would certainly let him know the captain-general's opinion of his idea.

The curtain rose for the third act, but neither of us turned toward it. The captain-general leaned closer to me, his jaw now tightened, all pretense at appearing jovial dropped. "You should know that there are some in Havana who want you arrested for what you have done here in the past, Commander Wake. One has suggested you and your man be arrested for a brawl that occurred in a sailor tavern this week. There are even some who suggested— just today, in fact—that you should have an accident. A mortal one. None of them have provided me actual *evidence* of crimes, however, and so—though I doubt you are here as a protocol officer and do not doubt you are here as an intelligence agent—I have not authorized your arrest or something more permanent. Yet."

He shook his head slowly, as if amazed at his own charity. "In fact, the only reason you are alive is because you are under *my* protection. That is because I respect you. You earned that respect at the saber match and the bomb attack. In disregarding your own safety, you conducted yourself with great honor that day."

He gazed up at the giant ceiling for a few seconds, then intoned a phrase in Latin: "*Summum crede nefas animam praeferre pudori, et propter vitam vivendi perdere causas.*"

Teignmouth Classical School and Mr. Stonehead's Latin lectures from forty years earlier filled my memory as I translated aloud: "I believe that the greatest abomination is to prefer life over honor, and on account of life to lose the reason for living."

"Very good, Commander. It is the eighth satire from Juvenal, who lived in second-century Rome. He was a soldier before he was a poet and therefore understood honor—a concept that spies lose sight of in their shadowy world, for shadows tend to blur solid lines and forms, do they not?"

I was trying to formulate a reply to all this, but he had more to say. "I am being candid with you, Commander, as one gentleman to another. We are adversaries, yes, and may very well one day soon be enemies, required to kill each other, but I see no reason that we cannot be friends now.

"So, as your true friend, I am telling you to leave Havana as soon as possible. The next steamer north departs Sunday for New

York via Charleston. And while waiting for your passage, take great care to remain innocent of even any *appearance* of espionage. This is not an idle warning, Commander. Do not mistake my kindness for weakness. Do you understand my candor and the consequences of disregarding it?"

There are times to continue bluffing to the end. This was not one of them. Besides, I got the distinct impression that the Captain-General of Cuba *didn't want* me to get arrested, for then he would be compelled to execute me as a foreign military spy, and he knew that even if done quietly, with my murder faked as an accident, the word would get out. And once the press in the United States published it, there was no telling what would happen in Washington, Madrid, and Havana.

No, even though there were hotheads in the island's colonial government—I knew Marrón was among them—and in Madrid who wanted to force the issue and take on the Americans while their navy was not yet modernized, my impression was that Don Sabas was not of that ilk. He and Prime Minister Sagasta were trying to keep things under control. And he had quite enough to handle in Cuba without having a confrontation with a *yanqui* naval officer escalate into a deadly international conflagration, ultimately killing thousands.

He needed assurance, so I gave him some. "I understand your meaning completely, Your Excellency. And appreciate your candor. I do not wish to intrude upon our friendship and will be on that steamer Sunday."

Don Sabas' face perked up, and he said pleasantly, "Ah, very good, then! Let us enjoy the rest of the lady's performance, shall we? I think some dramatic action is about to happen."

He returned his attention to the play, looking damned satisfied with himself, while I tried my best not to show my trepidation, which had grown to monumental size. It's not every day one is threatened with death by a man who has but to literally snap his fingers to make it happen.

Don Sabas' prediction was correct, for soon screaming filled the air from offstage, as Scarpia described in vivid detail to Tosca how her lover was being tortured in an adjoining cell within the castle. The screams were extremely realistic, making women in the audience gasp and cry out. I glimpsed Belleza turning away in horror.

Seconds later, Tosca's lover took a suicide potion. Tosca refused to confess whatever it was that she knew—I never did get that part. And as the curtain descended for intermission, her lover was dragged away for execution at dawn.

The Captain-General of Cuba turned and fixed his eyes upon me for several long seconds before rising to meet his friends in the lobby.

I understood his message completely.

21

Le Croix Huguenot

Gran Teatro Tacon
Havana, Cuba
10:39 p.m., Thursday
27 September 1888

During intermission, the first-class lobby was stifling hot, choked with cigar smoke and the pungent odor of well-clad but closely-packed patrons. Waiters edged their way around, balancing trays of chilled flutes of champagne. Each glass was downed in one unabashed gulp by the men, the ladies doing the same, but more daintily. Men stood near the bar and women near the canapés, the room abuzz with jabbering and posturing. The ladies chattered away with sharp judgments about the quality and appropriateness of the actors' costumes. The gentlemen had another subject in mind and proceeded—quietly, so their wives wouldn't hear—to exchange ungentlemanly opinions of Miss Bernhardt's personal abilities offstage.

I found Belleza standing with an elderly man dressed in a suit of blue with ruffled white collar and cuffs, a fashion throwback to an earlier age. She was listening, and he was mumbling while feasting his eyes on her nicely displayed bosom.

I interrupted them. "Doña Belleza, how beautiful you are tonight. The most stunning rose of this magnificent bouquet of Spanish ladies."

The old man possessed no English and looked at me, clearly perturbed. I didn't care, and neither did Belleza. After patting the gent on the arm, she turned away from him and said, "You Americans are so very forward. It would take a Spaniard at least twice as long to say something like that to me. An Englishman would take three times as long."

"Well, you know we are still young as a country, and not as polished as the great cultures of Europe. Do you remember your kind offer for the tour of the city? Is it still available? I can pick you up tomorrow, if you don't mind flaunting Spanish tradition and riding alone with me."

She tossed her head back with a laugh. "My goodness, Commander Wake. You are *beyond* forward. You could be considered by some in this room to be entirely obnoxious."

"Perhaps they might. But do *you* consider me obnoxious—or just hopelessly smitten and eager?"

The flash of her eyes was impressive. It took a fraction of a second and said far more than an hour of words. "I think I will flatter myself and choose to describe you as smitten. As for riding alone in public without an armed, male family guardian or servant to protect me from the rapacious advances of Havana's most famous *yanqui* barbarian, I will take my chances." She laughed. "I do not pretend to be a young innocent anymore, Commander. I do not need a guardian, and I do not care what people say. Let them wag their tongues."

I took two flutes off a passing tray and gave her one. "How refreshingly modern of you, my dear. Perhaps you can be the one who changes Havana's more antiquated customs."

"They need changing. We ladies hate being locked up behind the barred windows of our houses, or paraded around in uncomfortable *volantes* without permission to even walk the streets of our own city, lest we be molested by leering, brutish men who stink of rum and cigars."

Belleza was right—the males of Havana were infamous for their lack of civility to ladies, local or foreign, seen out on the streets without an escort. Frequently these louts make boorish comments and occasionally even venture to touch a woman riding in a carriage or strolling on the street alone.

Volantes are the strange-looking carriages of Cuba, more akin to American surreys than anything else. They hold a single bench seat, on which two or sometimes three ladies are arrayed. The wheels are fully six feet high, and the braces sixteen feet or longer. Two horses with silver-studded harnesses and severely braided tails are arranged fore-and-aft within the braces, with a splendidly uniformed postilion—the family coachman—in shiny black boots, red tunic, and black top hat, sitting atop the forward horse.

Ladies enter the *volante* at their home and never alight from it until their return. It is a mobile prison for the ladies of Havana. They are to see and be seen and nothing else. When they go shopping, the shopkeeper brings his wares out to the *volante*. Foreign ladies visiting Havana are frequently aghast but quickly conform to convention, for they too are targets if they behave as they would back home and dare to tread the sidewalks. This practice is quite similar to those in the Muslim world, where the fairer sex is treated almost as property. My daughter Useppa, liberal Methodist Christian that she is, would no doubt end up in police jail should she venture to Cuba.

Martí told me he planned to end such chauvinistic tribal practices by enacting laws against crude male behavior when his new Cuban nation came into being. His dream country is a place where civility and equality reign supreme. I suggested to him that perhaps some well-armed ladies would be a more effective and rapid agent of change against the lechers of the city. He frowned and said I sounded like Rork.

I raised my glass in genuine salute to the lady. "You have me intrigued by your strength of character, madam, and I am even more eager to spend time with you. Tomorrow I will hire a vehicle, and we will have a pleasurable tour of this ancient city. I want to see all the sights through your lovely eyes. What time and place should I call for you?"

"I am staying at Hotel Isabella at the Plaza de Armas. Let us meet at a civilized hour, say five o'clock in the afternoon, after the worst of the heat has finished for the day."

I quickly tried to figure out that timing and if it would interfere with my plans. I'd wanted the morning. "What about the afternoon rains? Won't they dampen our tour? Would not the morning be cooler, my dear?"

I received a shy flutter of her fan. "I do very little in the morning, Commander, and consider it a time of repose. Yes, the afternoon rain might be a problem. But if we are forced into fleeing from the storm, I know of a very comfortable place where we can take refuge."

Sometimes I know when to fold. "Five o'clock it is, then."

The bell sounded, alerting everyone that there were only ten minutes left in the intermission. We bid each other *au revoir*, each anticipating the coming day for different reasons.

As I concluded my initiation of an *affair d'amour* with Doña Belleza Ortiz y Cardonne, Rork was busy in the general-class lobby bar below us, meeting with the American specialists: Pots the locksmith, Mena the actor, and Folger the chemist. With wine in hand, they stood at the crowded bar individually, for all outward appearances unlinked. Rork issued the final instructions to them one at a time as he moved through the crowd, carrying a tray of wine, presumably for his superior.

While passing each man, he devoted sixteen seconds to quietly deliver his orders: "Saturday mornin' at exactly ten minutes to ten under the laurel tree by the Isabella statue at the central park. Wear a linen suit an' a *jipijapa* straw hat. Carry only a small bag o' yer tools. We're walkin' in a religious parade an' not comin' back."

That having been done, my men went their own ways as Rork delivered the tray to a puzzled waiter and returned to his station at the base of the stairs leading up to the first-class area, there to wait upon his master's wishes with the rest of the retainers.

Whilst Rork was extracting hearsay among the plebeian class, I returned to my luxurious roost and was awaiting Miss Bernhardt's fourth act and my esteemed host. Both arrived simultaneously in a thunder of approbation, the acoustics of the place increasing normal applause to an astonishing magnitude.

Shortly afterward, a serious-looking, dark-haired young man in formal black appeared at the entry of the box. The man offered profuse apologies in fluent Spanish to the captain-general for the intrusion, then presented equally profuse apologies for Consul-General Williams' absence. To my surprise, he then said he had an additional communication to pass along to me.

Bending over my chair, he said in the Low Country drawl of South Carolina, "I do humbly beg your forgiveness, Commander Wake, but I am Jacques Lafleur, aide to Consul-General Williams. The consul-general has telegraphed me from Santa Clara with the wish that I convey to the captain-general and you his regrets for not makin' the performance tonight. He told me to also pass along an invitation to you, sir, to be his guest for a private luncheon with him tomorrow at two o'clock at the Café del Mar at Plaza de Luz. Is that luncheon feasible within your schedule, sir?"

That wasn't in my plan, but there was time for it. I didn't have to meet Belleza until five. And, of course, one does not snub a consul-general, particularly when in his own city, so I told Lafleur, "I'd be delighted to have lunch with Consul Williams."

"Very good, sir. I shall telegraphically reply to the consul-general to that effect." Then, with a furtive flicker of his left eyebrow, he added quietly, "And should y'all need my *services* while in Havana, please let me know."

By that inflection, something clearly was afoot about his services, but what they were and what they consisted of was beyond me at that moment. Though Don Sabas had his eyes on Sarah Bernhardt dealing with the evil Scarpia, I could tell he was listening to us as well. So, in true sycophantic fashion, I replied somewhat loudly, "Thank you, but I'm fine. The captain-general's gracious hospitality has supplied me with everything I could possibly want."

Lafleur bent over again, this time facing away from the captain-general, and reached into his coat pocket to extract a business card. As he pressed it into my hand, he said, "Here is my personal card, sir. Should y'all find that you do need assistance, I would be honored to help." Then, in a muted aside, he added, "I am a brother of your friend."

His insistence on helping me would have smacked of immoral pleasures regarding certain women of the port had it come from someone in a lower station. But I was reasonably sure we had no procurers working at our Havana consulate and that this man was no blood relation to any of my friends, despite his statement. The scene was getting curiouser and curiouser—and I, more uncomfortable—by the second. Overwhelmed by my worries and full of champagne, I wasn't in a mind to unravel some minor diplomatist's conundrums and desired some good old American plain talk.

"Thank you, Mr. Lafleur. I'm leaving on the Sunday steamer, so I won't be here long enough to need anything from the consulate," said I in polite return, again loud enough for my host to hear.

At first, the "brother" reference was lost on me. But then my attention went to his lapel, which he had nonchalantly lifted to reveal an intricately enameled cloisonné pin underneath. Encircled by a gold ring was an eight-pointed, golden cross. The arms were equal in length, like that of the Maltese version, each of the four arms having two points on its end. Below the cross hung an upside-down dove with wings outstretched. Suddenly, my brain made the connection.

Le Croix Huguenot.

Lafleur winced imperceptibly while holding me in his gaze. Glancing at the servant in the corner, I raised my glass for more champagne to cover a whispered question to Lafleur, "And where does your brother live?"

"The old name for the city was New Amsterdam," he replied.

His brother was in New York—where Martí lived.

Standing erect, Lafleur bowed his respects to Don Sabas and me and departed. My host missed my private exchange with Lafleur, for he was now absolutely riveted by Miss Bernhardt's heaving bosom, a direct result of Scarpia's indecent proposal that she bestow her charms upon him in lieu of her lover being executed at dawn. It was a most fortuitous diversion of the captain-general's eavesdropping—and absolute proof that heaving bosoms certainly do have their place in espionage. Someday I may tell Miss Bernhardt of her role in all this.

While putting Lafleur's card in my pocket, I noticed its contents. No name, just an address. Not printed by a stationer, as is a regular visiting card. No, this one was carefully handwritten in elaborate, French-styled script. And the address was not that of the consulate, located at the Plaza de Armas. It was another location: 30 Empedrado, corner of San Ignacio. That resonated somewhere within my memory, which conjured up the map of the original section of Havana. Yes, I knew that intersection. It was at the northwest corner of one of the most ancient squares of Havana, La Plaza de la Catedral, right across the street from the cathedral.

What was at that address? What did it have to do with the French Huguenots? I grasped that the "brothers" reference meant the Freemasons and now assumed Lafleur to be one of them, alerted by Martí to assist me. Not wanting to alert Don Sabas by my pensiveness, I returned my attention to the stage.

Evidently, a lot had been happening there. The captain-general was standing and clapping heartily, for Act Four had ended. The massive curtain was descending over a dead Scarpia, a dagger protruding from his chest. To the side, a horror-stricken Tosca, her satin gown stained red, was slipping off the stage.

"You see, my friend, the most beautiful women are also some of the most dangerous!" Don Sabas exclaimed with a chortle as the house lights came up. The entire place was standing, reverberating with admiration. Belleza caught my eye. On her feet like the rest, her hands were held high in applause for Bernhardt's work. Turning back, I registered that my host was regarding me most quizzically. It would seem he was expecting a reply to his witty comment.

"Quite right, Your Excellency. Men like us must always beware of beautiful women, lest they lead to our premature death."

That jest got a proper belly laugh from him, in which I dutifully joined.

For Act Five, I was properly attentive. The action and tension built as Tosca's lover was executed by Scarpia's equally evil aide, and she admitted killing Scarpia. The audience grew hushed, waiting for what would happen next. In that final moment, Sarah Bernhardt climbed to the stage's castle parapet and, hand drawn across her beautiful eyes, flung herself off in a suicide so spectacular that the Captain-General of Cuba dropped his head in sorrow.

Once the show ended and the repeated ovations had faded, the three thousand attendees began filing toward the doors. It was a surveillance nightmare for Marrón, but I kept myself nicely visible for his men to occupy their interest. Rork, the main protagonist in our mission that evening, went about his function of meandering through the bustle to the gentlemen's room, where Marco and Leo had been fretfully waiting for him.

None of the other men gathered there appeared to be agents of the government, so the three had a casual conversation about the play, as strangers might, interspersed with quiet bursts of information regarding any new developments regarding Marrón, significant prisoners, or the anarchists' plans for Saturday.

Marco passed along a rumor that Marrón's men were arresting

known leaders in the socialist, anarchist, and tobacco worker union movements, but it was unknown where they were being kept. Leo said he'd heard the anarchists would try to disrupt the procession somewhere along the Prado. Rork advised them of the Saturday morning meeting place and time, implying it was to go over further information and gather supplies preparatory for the real mission on Sunday. Then they dispersed.

Ten minutes later, after begging off from a late-night dinner with Don Sabas, I met Rork and we headed back to Hotel Florida. It was one 1:00 a.m. on Friday. Everything was ready, except one final detail: the reconnaissance.

22

Nom de Combat

Café del Mar
Plaza de Luz
Havana, Cuba
2:12 p.m., Friday
28 September 1888

It was a pleasant afternoon for late September, the first we'd had since I'd arrived in Havana on Tuesday. A fresh sea breeze from the north was the instigator of this climatic change. It funneled through the entrance channel to the harbor, between the moldering buildings of the old quarter on the western side and the scrub-covered hills and faded walls of the Morro and Cabañas fortresses sprawled across the other. Flying ramrod straight from half a dozen tall masts, Spain's crimson and gold flags proclaimed the dignity, if no longer the might, of the empire's dwindling place in the world.

As we relaxed in the shade of the café overlooking Havana's harbor, I could see that Consul-General Williams was in an equally good state of mind. From what I could tell from his brief conversation with my new acquaintance, Lafleur, who sat opposite me, the chief diplomat's day so far had been uniquely positive. His trip the previous day to the sugar mill called Soledad, owned by Bostonian Edwin Atkins, and thence to Santa Clara had been successful. The track had been repaired, and the train had returned him to Havana early that morning.

One of the major concerns of Williams' position was to look after the considerable New York and New England investment in the Cuban sugar industry. I'd always found it sadly hypocritical that the same Northern men who decried slavery in the South made enormous money from its labor in the Cuban plantations for twenty years after our Civil War, until it was finally ended in 1886. It was more than a monetary investment, however, on the part of the American sugar barons. No fewer than two hundred engineers and managers from New England lived in Cuba, overseeing operations in the mills belonging to the newly formed U.S. Sugar Trust. Their boss, Henry Havermeyer, had serious political influence in the state department. The profits were enormous and reached everywhere; it was money from brokering sugar to Americans that had funded wayward Rogelio's gambling lifestyle. That money also lobbied for a reduction of tariffs against the importation of Cuban sugar.

Lafleur was delighted to report to his superior that the latest communiqué from Washington contained—wonder of wonders—an approval of some of his ideas on American-Cuban trade, including lowering those tariffs. Williams smiled contentedly but admitted it was Congress that would have the final say on that policy.

Ever the busy aide, Lafleur, having received his directions for the rest of the day, offered a polite *hasta luego* to us and rose to go about his duties, getting things done from behind the scenes. Interestingly, there were no muted riddles, no nonchalant signals, no winks or nods toward me from the Huguenot Freemason, just the usual courtesy to one more naval officer in transit. Yes, I decided, Lafleur played his game very well, which indicated he had been doing it for a while.

I returned my concentration to the consul-general, who had my respect. I solicited and received his views on the various aspects of the political situation in Cuba. Williams dismissed the anarchists as rabble. He felt Cuban-American relations were exacerbated by American tariffs and Spanish taxes. The future of Cuba he foresaw was unsettled. Violently unsettled.

I asked, "Sir, of the four possible outcomes—continuing the crown colony status under Spain; autonomy for the island but remaining a part of Spain; becoming part of the United States; or full independence—which has the most adherents on the island?"

"Hard to tell, Commander. Many in the U.S. think the whole island is seething for full independence, but that isn't true. There are a number of Spanish-born *peninsulares*, Loyalists to the crown who want to retain the status quo. Most are in the sugar areas and are very well organized. They consist of the merchant and planter classes and a lot of the old slaveholders, who are afraid of Cuba's turning into a disaster like Haiti upon independence from Spain. Thirty thousand of the Loyalists formed special volunteer regiments in the eighteen-seventies and did some ruthless but effective work in combating the independence rebels. They don't have a numerical majority, but they do have political and military muscle. They hate the rebel insurgents far more than the average conscript soldier sent here from Spain."

"And the Autonomists?"

"Probably more numerous than the Loyalists, but without the same clout. The pro-American faction, the Annexationists, is relatively small and mainly businessmen centered in Havana and Matanzas."

Those concise summaries echoed what I knew of the situation. I inquired about those Cubans who'd fought for twenty years already with some success but without real victory. "So what's your opinion of the pro-independence revolutionaries' chances, sir? They seem to be sputtering along but not making any decisive progress."

"The idea of independence will not disappear, Commander,

and it has spread across color and class lines. It's no longer an Oriente-based movement—it's everywhere on the island. And yes, I agree with most that they are sputtering now, but I think that someday the Cuban independence patriots will win. They have but to consolidate under one leader, one organization. The primary question is not *if* Cuba becomes independent, but when? The secondary question will then be how the United States treats the winners."

"And how should we, sir?"

"If the Cuban people vote for annexation, then so be it, let them in—it's simply a small extension of our continental borders. But I think they won't, so treat them as an independent nation but a favored friend. Lower the barriers. Keep our trade ties close, as we do with Canada."

"And what is your opinion of Captain-General González, sir?"

"The man is a relatively honest and decent administrator and an honorable man. He has to walk carefully among the various factions here, particularly the Loyalists, who some people consider vigilantes. I don't envy his position, Commander."

"Hmm. An unstable situation, indeed. Is he in complete control of the colonial government and its armed forces?"

Williams' eyes narrowed for a moment—I'd asked a question few did—then tented his hands in a pensive posture before answering carefully. "Most of it but probably not all. Some of the army and police commanders are known to be..." he paused, regarding me closely, knowing what he said would be repeated to my superiors in Washington. "...*zealots*...when it comes to dealing with those Cubans who favor independence. Most of those commanders are members of Cánovas' conservative movement in Spain, and many have ties to Rear Admiral Beranger of the Spanish navy, neither of whom has any love for those they consider weak for tolerating Cuban dissent."

"I've heard of a man named Marrón who might fall into that category, sir. You know him?"

"Met him but don't know him well. Secret police official who stays out of the public scene. How do you know him?"

"I don't, sir. Just heard he was important. I wonder if he's one of the colonial government's vigilante types."

"I do believe he is, Commander. But few foreign people know about him."

Williams was openly staring at me by this point, so I changed the subject.

"Say, have you heard of a man named Martí, a Cuban writer up in New York?"

"The newspaperman and poet who got exiled from Cuba at sixteen? Yes. He's a young philosopher who writes about his hopes for Cuba's independent destiny. Widely read in Latin America. Also does some consular work in New York for some of the South American countries."

"A thorn in the Spanish side?"

"Not at this time, but I keep hearing about him and think he might be the one to unify the Cubans in New York. Maybe elsewhere. And how do you know of that young man?"

"Heard someone speak of him while in New York awhile back."

I maintained the attitude of a naval officer listening to a diplomatic superior but could see my queries had ignited some curiosity. Williams, being a skilled veteran of the art of the tête-à-tête, gradually steered the course of our conversation until it centered upon my visit and the subsequent public events.

My opinion of the city, of the culture, of the Spanish navy, and of the Cuban people were all asked and answered in a positive light. Adroitly maneuvering the inquiries closer to his objective, he asked about my work as staff protocol officer for Admiral Luce's squadron and the professional assignments of my career.

Well, that was getting into dangerous waters—after all, the man knew far more about protocol than I did—so I recited my customary boring explanation of staff work at naval headquarters in Washington. Experience has taught me that if you provide a monotone depiction of writing paperwork, bookkeeping, and analyzing reports in a windowless back room, within seconds your questioner's eyes will begin to glaze over in abject tedium or sometimes dulled pity. In my meager defense, I will say it's not total perjury, since there are times when I have to do those things, but thankfully it's not my main function or I would end up at the District of Columbia's asylum for the insane. My ploy did the trick, however, and in what seemed desperation to stay awake, Williams changed tack.

"No, sir," I replied to his inquiry of whether I would stay until October tenth, the twentieth anniversary of the declaration of independence by the Cuban revolutionists. "I would imagine the Spanish will have their hands more than full on that day and agree it would make an interesting show to be around for, but I'll be leaving aboard the Sunday steamer for the States. I'll disembark at Charleston, then book separate passage to Panama, where I can meet up with Admiral Luce and the squadron. Got to get back to my work."

"And until Sunday?"

"As you know from our dinner the other night, I'll watch the Saint Michael feast day procession and attend the cathedral Mass tomorrow. In the afternoon, I'm visiting the south coast by train."

"Really? Where?"

"The parks at Batabanó, then dinner at a famous restaurant—I can't remember the name right now—and perhaps return that evening, or maybe spend the night and return the next morning in time to catch the steamer in the mid-afternoon." I paused just long enough to make it significant, and added, "This afternoon I'm touring the sights of the city with a certain lovely lady."

"Ah, yes. Doña Belleza, I believe. A woman of beauty and intellect and a recent addition to the social circles of Havana. I understand her husband died a few years ago. Was a *peninsulare* sugar planter from somewhere out in the Oriente province, at the eastern end of the island. Word is out that you two have been seen talking closely and sharing no little amount of gaiety. The perception is the two of you are quite an item."

"*Really*, sir? *Me?*" I replied innocently. "We've only met at a couple of social functions."

"Havana is a nest of intrigue, Commander. Society vipers' gossip has long been elevated to the level of predatory slander here. Lafleur, who, it seems, has spies in every *boudoir* and *salon* of the city, tells me the matrons of Havana have been cackling about your behavior since your arrival. Half of them are proud of Belleza for ensnaring you, and the other half are jealous. My wife appears to be one of the latter. All of them expect a detailed report from Belleza about you—the mild-mannered *yanqui* who became a tiger and vanquished his foe in combat, only to save the life of a potential future duke of Spain an hour later. Do you know what some of Havana's more romantically inclined females call you?"

"No, sir. Had no idea anyone was saying anything about me."

"*El Conquistador Suave.* The Suave Conqueror. I presume I don't have to explain the nature of the impending conquest to which they refer. Rather an unusual *nom de combat* for an American naval staff officer visiting a foreign country, don't you think, Commander? Especially a place as tense as this…"

El Conquistador Suave, eh? Well, that was a bit more than I'd set out for, but, still, it was essentially what I wanted: gossip spreading about Belleza and me, clever observations and sage opinions that I had fallen under her spell—or she under mine—with mutual infatuation. If it had reached Williams, it was all over town. Excellent. Let them spread the word that I was an idiot in love or in lust. Just another *gringo* fool, with no time for anything else than Doña Belleza, the beautiful, lonely widow.

What did Marrón think when he heard it, I wondered? Whether Belleza was in his employ or not, if he believed I was preoccupied by her, he might underestimate me, thereby lowering his guard a little. My fictitious obsession with Belleza was one more tiny chink in his armor. The chinks would add up eventually. And with a bit of luck, Marrón's misunderstanding of the situation would be just enough for me, the matador, to sidestep him, the charging bull, and accomplish what I'd come to do. To be sure, it was a convoluted route to that goal, but those are often the pathways of my work.

Espionage is a poker match in which both sides use disinformation, decoys, feints, and false appearances. In this contest, relative overt strength means little in the end. Intimate knowledge of your enemy's psyche means everything, enabling you to turn his own strengths against him. The strategies employed include making the opponent spread out his resources, inducing him to lower his estimate of your abilities, leading him in false directions, frustrating his morale with failure after failure, and disrupting his communications, all of which discredits his authority. In the end, if you have done these things cleverly enough so he doesn't realize he's being duped, the enemy will inevitably make that one crucial mistake in judgment, allowing you the victory, though your nominal strength is far less than his.

Having informed me of my new nickname, my lunch companion sat there regarding me with lips pressed and eyes hardened. I was getting the very distinct impression that the U.S. consul-general for Cuba was not amused by all this tittle-tattle about my being a conquistador, quiet or not. No, Williams' apparently lighthearted narration had a sharp edge to it, a very nicely veiled warning that I had better straighten up my image.

It was time to continue my performance as the staffer suddenly in an unwanted spotlight, one who hastens to retreat before a superior's displeasure. "Conquistador? Not sure I follow that. I have done nothing improper, no matter what the gossipmongers say. Why...well, I'm just flabbergasted by this," I stuttered in ostensible embarrassment, before blurting out my ultimate defense, "Sir, I'm a *Methodist!*"

Williams sipped his coffee and slowly lifted his patrician head to look at me. He was a man who had seen and heard it all over the years—including a lot of denials from Anglo gentlemen tourists who had immensely enjoyed discovering the delights of the ladies of Spain, then were caught with the consequences. He removed the gloves in his next comment.

"Yes, of course, you are, Commander Wake. However, a man with your length of naval experience can see how these things can get out of hand. You are more than a naval officer and gentleman here. You are the most visible, uniformed representative of the United States of America in Havana today. The protocol officer of your squadron. Your reputation is synonymous with our country's reputation. And it is being sullied."

Timing on these things can be delicate, but I judged it the right moment to get upset. I huffed and pursed my lips, glaring at him. "What *exactly* are you saying, sir? That I am sullying America's reputation?"

William's tone leveled. "Yes, I am, Commander. And yes, you are. And I want you to stop this flirting and drooling immediately. Good Lord, a man of your age acting like this? You are making a fool of yourself, carrying on with this woman like some young ensign. And you're making *my* life and job far more difficult, because some of these local gentlemen are jealous of your attentions to one of their women. It's not easy dealing with the Spanish authorities, who distrust our every statement and action and think us crass barbarians. Your behavior is undermining all the goodwill we gained by your gallantry at the palace on Tuesday."

Drooling? Where did he hear that? The rumor mill must have been in high gear, manufacturing what it wasn't given, like some cheap French novelist. God knows what would have been said if I had actually *done* something in public with Belleza.

Very well, now would come my surrender, the chastised sailor repenting. "Well, I suppose I did get a bit carried away by it all. It's just that she's beautiful and charming, so very different from our American ladies, and I want to spend time in her company. Thank you for the cautionary advice, sir. It is well taken," I said as contritely as I could muster.

The consul-general exhaled a visible sigh of relief. Another of his problems solved. National dignity and diplomatic equilibrium had been restored in Havana. Levity returned to the table as he raised his coffee cup.

"Commander, I'm glad that is behind us. I knew a word to the wise would be sufficient. Now, I propose a toast. To our country and our navy."

Thus, I deceived both the Spanish captain-general and the American consul-general, leaving them blissfully ignorant in their impression that Peter Wake was not doing anything he shouldn't while in Havana.

23

Eyeball Reconnaissance

Havana, Cuba
5:10 p.m., Friday
28 September 1888

I returned to Hotel Florida to take a short rest and to check on Rork. Now that I had made the chief American diplomat and the chief Spanish administrator my friends, my second performance of the day would be to deceive the chief Cuban paramour of the city. I intended to enjoy this next phase of the mission. Yes, it would be totally at odds with Consul-General Williams' admonition, but all the better to camouflage my true intentions from the Spanish.

Yet some additional camouflage was needed. My status as a suspected *provocateur* had by now been elevated by Colonel Marrón to the point where his surveillance was doubled or tripled. There were always two men at the hotel room door, as well as two more on the street below our balcony. No telling how many new peepholes had been drilled in the walls. Unchaperoned departures from our luxurious abode were no longer possible.

The new watchers, as well as the ubiquitous Señor Acera, were always proactively engaging us in conversation, offering to do any errand, fetch any item, help Rork and me in any way, inquiring into our likes and dislikes, and repeatedly letting us know that we were honored guests in Havana. In fact, so obliging were they that they arranged the carriage for my tour with the lovely Belleza.

I had requested a single-horse victoria for just the two of us, but such was not available. Fine, then we would have a paired-horse phaeton, a sporting vehicle offering greater speed and geographic flexibility. I would handle the reins myself. It was also the sort of thing a man out to impress a lady would do, though it would cost dearly.

Rork, having shouldered much of the action the night before at the theater, was relaxing in the room and, once the shade increased, out on the balcony. A glass of rum-infused orange juice in one hand, a weighty tome on the history of Cuba in the other, and two cigars in his shirt pocket for enjoyment later, he presented the very picture of a man of leisure. His repose had the added professional value of tying down a portion of the considerable complement assigned to our surveillance.

I noticed Rork was moving a bit slower than normal and upon my asking the cause, he said the exertions of late had tired him a bit. An understatement, if ever there was one. He had eight years beyond my forty-nine and had earned those aches and pains the hard way, as an ocean seaman for well over thirty years and an intelligence operative for the last seven. The former had given him arthritis in his hands and feet, common to veteran sailors. The latter had taken that left hand and part of the forearm and given him serious wounds all over the rest of his body. Not for the first time, I worried about Rork and wondered if I had put too much on him lately.

Warriors use humor to mask pain, both physical and otherwise, so I bade him to rest and admonished him against female companionship in my absence. That got the hoped-for chuckle and the quip, "Yer the one what's bound fer trouble with a lady today. Me ownself'll be takin' it easy as a lordship in his castle. Feelin' rather fancy right now."

Standing close to the wall and our peepers, I reminded him, "Very good, Rork. Don't forget that tomorrow will be a busy day, as we'll be walking in the Saint Michael's procession, then attending services at church, and afterward both of us are having lunch with Belleza."

I put in a special postscript for our listeners, "Oh, and remember to lay out a second set of clothes, because tomorrow afternoon we're taking the train with Belleza to the city of Batabanó for dinner—it's about an hour's ride down to the south coast. She said there's a good restaurant and garden there she wants to show us."

"Aye, sound's like the morrow's gonna be a right good day then. Have fun tonight."

"I intend to. Don't wait up," I said with a wink.

At the appointed time, I descended to the lobby front, accompanied by one of our door Spaniards, ready to hop into my phaeton and head off. But to my disappointment, there was no small, fast vehicle waiting for me. I found, instead, nothing less than a fully appointed landau in front of the hotel. Capable of seating six, it had a white driver in a red tunic with shiny black boots perched up on the box in front, unusual in a city where most drivers were African. His presence became clear when I perceived his close observation of me, of a manner more in keeping with a detective than a chauffeur.

The harried concierge explained the landau with profuse apologies and much wringing of hands, the justification being that he had found all the city's phaetons hired for the day, a most curious occurrence. He was providing the larger replacement and its driver at no extra cost, since I was, of course, an honored guest. He begged that I would understand.

After assuring him that I certainly did understand, we started off—me a happy American sailor with thoughts of romance showing on his face. Such a display wasn't difficult for me, for Doña Belleza was a very enticing woman.

Trotting by the U.S. consulate, where I waved to a surprised Mr. Lafleur at the front door, we rounded the corner and arrived at Hotel Isabella, across the Plaza de Armas from the captain-general's palace. I was three minutes late due to the vehicular confusion at the hotel. Madam Belleza was another fifteen minutes late due to her preparations and probably a premeditated attempt to impress on me who was to wait on whom.

Her arrival at the hotel's entryway was inspiring, a performance Sarah Bernhardt would've applauded. The crowd literally backed away and opened a passage for her as she swept out of the lobby onto the portico. As I have said before, Spanish ladies do not travel on public streets with strange men in the same carriage without familial guardians, and the onlookers' expressions were a mix of admiration for Belleza's appearance and shock at her brazen disregard for social norms. She ignored the gasps and appreciated the ogles and smiled ever so sweetly at me.

I have no skill at describing these things, but Belleza's efforts deserve at least an attempt. She was resplendently attired in a light pink, lacy satin dress that nicely flattered her figure, chiefly her *décolletage*. The dress was trimmed in miniature, red fabric roses and some sort of black doodads around them. Down over it all streamed an exquisite, black lace mantilla—the famous Spanish veil—dotted with real red roses. The mantilla framed her face perfectly and completed the whole image, a uniquely Spanish blend of bashful innocence and knowing calculation. It was an unusual adornment, however, for Spanish ladies wear a mantilla only for formal occasions and High Mass. I thought it yet another sign that the lady was a nonconformist and supremely self-confident.

But that was not all. Bending low enough upon embarkation to tease me with visions of future pleasures—with perhaps a little more than she had intended me to see—Belleza arranged herself in the back seat and snapped open an intricately painted fan. Holding it partially over her face, she then flitted it a few times in a flamboyant gesture. As in the mother country, the Spanish ladies of Havana communicate messages through the positions of their fan, a language they enthusiastically learn when very young. I had been taught something of this language while in Sevilla in '74 and now comprehended that Belleza was signaling to one and all that I was taken, off-limits to all other females.

The driver apparently understood fan signals also. He grumbled while adjusting the canvas top. Shooting me a nasty look, he put the top up just enough for some shade but low enough to allow us to see the sights. And, of course, we could be seen by other watchers along the route. He then stowed the matching, pink parasol she'd brought along.

I was outfitted in the same thing I'd worn elsewhere in Havana, other than at the formal occasions at the dinner soiree and the theater, when I wore a full dress uniform. My clothing this particular evening was the standard blue working rig uniform, which had been delivered from *Richmond* to my sick room at the hotel. I was not pleased, for unlike tropical whites, the damned blues are heavy and hot, but I couldn't blame Rork, though he apologized for it. He'd been occupied with getting our personal weaponry ashore in the seabags, a far more important chore. His apology for the oversight included the usual, never-to-be-fulfilled compensation, a round of rum at our next liberty port.

So there Belleza and I were, pink and blue, clattering and swaying our way up the gentle incline of Obispo Street past the palace, where four days earlier I had made my mark. The shrapnel marks were still fresh in the columns and walls, and several windows were not yet repaired. She saw me looking at them and squeezed my hand supportively, a gesture apparently spontaneous and genuine, unlike most of her mannerisms.

Shadows began filling the streets as the glaring, white siesta hours gave way to evening pastels, while the people of Havana emerged from their places of refuge from the sun. The sound of guitars and drums, their staccato rhythm so different than in America, came from a corner *taverna* at Cuba Street, where a girl laughed uproariously at some joke. Kitchens were beginning to cook the evening's dinners, which would be consumed around eight or nine. The roasting pork and fish and chicken scents wafted over me, making me hungry. The city's gentlemen strolled along the street, while *volantes* bearing the fairer sex perused the shop windows and each other. All were dressed in their best and heading toward the boulevard of the Prado, for it was Friday evening and everyone who was anyone would be out and about on that magnificent promenade.

Belleza leaned close and asked, "What do you want to see of Havana?"

I replied dreamily, "Everything, my dear, through your beautiful eyes."

The fan flapped quickly as she cast her eyes downward shyly. "Oh, I see that you are still eager, Commander Wake. So let us start with the city's churches. Perhaps some religion will help cool your ardor."

"Call me Peter, please. Commander Wake is far too formal for us, especially on this lovely tropical evening."

Again the fan flapping, an act that is cute at first but rapidly grows wearisome to me. Her fluency in the custom rapidly outdistanced mine—I no longer had a clue what she was signaling. "Very well, Peter. And I insist that you call me Belleza."

"Belleza, why don't we start with some of your famous Havana churches. How about the pretty one down by the docks? Paula something?"

"La Iglesia de San Fransisco de Paula? Yes, it is a lovely church, very romantic. We will begin there."

We arrived moments later, and she pointed out the stained glass for which the three-hundred-year-old church was well known, then the adjacent hospital, which specialized in female patients. From there we went west to the gates of the Spanish naval yard, which I ignored, having been inside on several occasions. A drive farther west took us to the elevated suburb of El Cerro, where the richest of the rich reside and look out over the city and harbor. Next, we drove to the overgrown ruins of the Bishop's Gardens and the monastic church there, an ancient retreat for the Church's upper crust in Havana.

Returning to the original quarter of the city, we clomped passed the famous Dominica Café, a popular spot for fruit-flavored ices infused with rum. By now I imagined that our wandering itinerary had disguised my intent, so I had her tell the driver to take us to the world-famous Prado. We turned north on Egido Street, a main thoroughfare of Havana, en route to another church near the city center. Though the rainless sky still shed some light over the city, the streets were now lit by the occasional lamp. The air temperature grew perceptively cooler to a wonderful, life-energizing crispness, courtesy of that first autumn wind blowing over the island from North America.

At the main train depot, just south of the central park on the Prado, I had the driver stop. Without any more explanation than, "Back in a minute, my dear," I dashed in and bought three tickets for the three o'clock train to Batabanó the next day. It was encouraging to see that Marrón's men were as efficient as I'd hoped. The cigar-smoking man in the planter hat with the broad black trim, who'd been on horseback behind our carriage two blocks back, now appeared in the giant reception hall, watching me from the entrance. I knew the clerk would give the Spanish agent details of my transaction and my intentions in Batabanó, for I'd taken pains to pass them along to him.

Once back in the landau and under way along the course that the Saint Michael's procession would follow the next morning, my lady sat closer and closer to me, until she was positively melded to my left thigh and arm. I could feel the soft warmth of her bosom pressing against me, but Rork's admonition came to mind, and I found myself in the ridiculous position of attempting to surreptitiously study her dress in an effort to ascertain if she had a derringer in her garter.

Then, with a mischievous flash of her eyes, she spread a thin shawl over our laps, a gesture that effectively precluded my scrutiny. In addition to this incredibly bold—for a gentle lady in Havana—display of friendliness, she insistently queried me about my foray into the depot, which I deflected with a knowing smile while saying, "It's part of a little surprise gift for you for tomorrow. *Muy romantico.*"

That caused her to raise her eyebrows in delight and gained me a breathy, "*Muchas gracias, mi novio.*"

I particularly noted the word *novio*, which is a personal endearment, loosely translated to "lover" and used only when a relationship has progressed to intimacy. Secure in the knowledge she had me hook, line and sinker, my *amor* now set about impressing me with her mind. She began a running commentary about the various edifices and parks we passed, demonstrating a surprisingly detailed knowledge of the city's cultural and architectural past, remarkable for a lady from Oriente who'd been in the city for only two years.

But it wasn't all a dry historical recitation. She giggled like a schoolgirl at my inane attempts at humor and used the cover of the shawl to launch a ticklish expedition up my left thigh with her fingers. All the while, she never let up on her tour guide recitation, an impressive exhibition of mental and physical prowess. The lessons were highlighted when she would lean closer and exclaim about some beautiful thing, allowing delightful glimpses of her cleavage far beyond my initial one. And behind that delicate protective veil, the lady's eyes had lost their coyness, openly conveying a hunger for something more than riding in a carriage.

All these signals I understood completely, and I reacted with the expected male responses, both verbal and otherwise. Soon, the temperature in that back seat escalated to the point that I began to wonder if we would make it through my planned geographic itinerary.

I will admit my mind was beginning to waiver on the decision to use Belleza only as a decoy. For a moment, right about when those fingers arrived at their intended destination, I entertained the thought of allowing some pleasure to coincide with my mission in Havana. What harm could that do, really? An hour, maybe two. Then back to work.

But alas, sanity made an appearance, along with a disconcerting observation. From what I'd seen of Belleza, which was a fair amount by then, not only lust but also a warning had risen in my mind. I decided to dampen my own fires a bit by asking her vaguely about several other churches. She obliged by having the driver take us to them, not knowing they were on or near my planned route of ingress and egress for the next day.

Though I know Havana relatively well, I needed to do a last-minute reconnaissance to see for myself the layout of streets and buildings and if there had been any changes. Cover, concealment, and open, dead ground where we would be vulnerable to fire needed to be understood clearly. I had to plan potential secondary and tertiary avenues of escape. It was my last chance to do so calmly—well, relatively calmly—for once my men and I were committed and the action began, there would be no time for deliberation.

The driver, professional that he was, never turned around to openly spy upon us, but his eavesdropping by way of cocked head was plain, and I made sure he had a lot to hear, mainly of an amorous nature. We joined the heavy traffic and traveled the Prado northbound, waving to the scandalized grandmothers and stern policemen observing our intimacies. On both sides were magnificent apartments, rising three and four stories. On their balconies, couples pointed down at us, while around us girls in *volantes* tittered at our freedom, and the eyes of angry-looking men on strutting Paso Fino horses flared in rage at my impudent invasion of their romantic domain. I thought it great fun, and by her defiantly pleasant expression, so did Belleza.

Reaching the northern end of the Prado, we circled around the Audiencia, I being careful to never look at it directly, instead surveying it peripherally while admiring the ocean beyond. I noted that the routine number of guards were in place and none appeared on alert. Most of them were watching the inmates of the *volantes*. Once beyond that dreaded portal into hell, we traversed the park by the Punta fortress and headed south on Compostela, passing the Church of the Holy Angels and the tree where we would pick up our bag of cassocks.

There are times when one's mind clarifies abruptly, realizing an opportunity has arrived. Such was the case in that landau, for after perusing her intimately for an hour and gaining insight about the lady, I had a new notion regarding Belleza's usefulness to me. She wouldn't be just a temporary veneer for my reconnaissance that evening. No, she could be of far more in-depth and long-lasting use. A gamble on my part, yes. It could go wrong. Dead wrong. But I had a spark inside that told me to seize the moment.

And so it was that I bid the driver to take us to the Plaza de Luz. We needed to take a little trip out of Havana, though Belleza didn't know that yet.

24

A Most Revealing Sight

At the harbor
Havana, Cuba
6:43 p.m., Friday
28 September 1888

We parked near the docks, where a small steam ferry was belching smoke, getting ready to take passengers to Regla, the town on the other side of the harbor. Fifty yards away was the giant derrick, largest in Cuba or Puerto Rico, used by the Spanish navy. A hundred yards farther north was the naval commandant's offices and quarters, overlooking the waterfront. In the harbor nearby, the newly commissioned cruiser *Reina Regente* lay at anchor. Newly built for Spain by the Brits, she was the pride of the Spanish West India Squadron, and I recalled that Lieutenant Commander Julio Boreau was her gunnery officer. Studying her, I saw a ship stronger than anything we had currently in the U.S. Navy, though several of ours currently being built would be better.

The driver was nervous—the *yanqui* was blatantly spying on the Spanish navy—and glared at Belleza. She asked why we had stopped. I pointed toward the town across the harbor and whispered to her, "We're going to Regla to have dinner at a place I've heard about. It's called La Sevilla. Supposed to be very good, very cozy."

She hesitated and glanced at the driver. "Ah, I do not think that is a good idea, Peter. I know a nice little place close by here where we can be alone." I felt a hand in my nether region. "We can eat dinner later. You will be even hungrier then."

I had no doubt she had a place nearby. With a nice big bed. And several peepholes in the wall near the pillows. That was her plan, or rather it was Marrón's, but it wasn't mine.

"No. Time to be spontaneous, my dear. An old American trait."

Instantly, I dragged her by the hand out of the carriage. Displaying my most salacious smirk, I told the driver in Spanish that we were going on a romantic voyage. I then ordered him to wait there for our return in an hour or so. That got him really agitated—the foreign spy was running off with the colonel's spy!

The driver didn't know what to do. His orders didn't cover this contingency. Should he hurt me or ignore me? While he was trying to make that decision, I thrust an arm around Belleza and strode onto the dock platform, shoved a palmful of pesos into the attendant's hand, and hauled her to the boat. We were the last to board, just as the ferry was casting off and backing away.

It was chilly on the water, an excellent excuse to hold my disinclined companion close. Around us a hundred, tired-looking passengers stood jammed together, heading home from their day's work in the city. I quickly surveyed the crowd for signs that any of them were Marrón's people. Several were looking at the naval officer and the lady—we were the best-dressed people there—but none showed any interest in us beyond our appearance. No, the surveillance crew didn't have time to get a man on the ferry boat. We were beyond their sight and reach, at least while aboard the ferry.

Belleza's affection had disappeared by this time. She was

downright angry and surprisingly strong. "How dare you treat me this way and force me away from the city?"

I gripped her hand, squeezing it hard, pressed her to me, and looked into those dangerous eyes. "You've been lying to me since I met you, and you're very good at it, but I know what you do. How long have you worked for Marrón?"

"Who is Marrón? What are you talking about?"

She tried to squirm away from me, but I seized both her hands, crushing them tighter in what others took to be a fond embrace. I expected her to scream for help, but instead she changed her indignation to a plaintive tone. "I am starting to love you. Why do you suddenly hate me, Peter? What have I done to you to make you hate me?"

A good liar never answers the original question, but instead asks her own. She was very good. It was clearly time to shrink Belleza's considerable self-confidence with some harsh reality. I leaned in close, to outward appearances whispering a loving endearment to her.

"You aren't enamored of me. And you aren't a widow or a wealthy lady. The one thing that I know you *are* is a whore from Santiago who's been trained by Marrón to be a courtesan in Havana. Oh, yes, he spent a lot of money turning you into his *femme fatale*, didn't he? I can imagine some of his training sessions. He cleaned up your grammar in Spanish, English, and French. Taught you social etiquette, how to style your hair, and wear fancy clothing. He put you up in a fine room at the Isabella, created a nice history for you, and had you introduced around Havana society as a lonely, refined widow from the plantations of Oriente."

I paused and laughed softly for the crowd's benefit, a lover hearing a naughty jest. Then I pressed against her tightly again and returned to the subject.

"That training enabled you to spy on his enemies, especially the most dangerous ones, the Cuban intellectuals. But there was one tiny thing he couldn't change about you, wasn't there? Marrón took away all the dirt from your life and made you look like a lady, but he couldn't change that one thing, could he?"

She wasn't denying anything, but those eyes revealed more than words. She would have killed me right then if she could. I remembered Rork's warning about concealed weapons.

I stared openly at her chest. "Your tattoo. It's showing, Belleza."

Cascarilla is a fine white powder ground from eggshells that the ladies of Cuba apply liberally to their skin in an effort to appear as white and delicate as possible. The overall effect is pleasant at first, but perspiration can erode the powder, and that's precisely what had happened to Belleza's chest in the carriage.

Gripping both her hands tightly together in my right, I used my left to pull the lacy hem of the pink bodice back two inches, revealing a tattoo on her left breast. It was a blue heart within a pink rose. In the dark of a bedroom at night, the detail would not be discernible, but I had seen it in the landau while the sky was still light. A nearby deck lamp now furnished enough illumination to reveal something most of her lovers wouldn't understand. There was an original tattoo underneath. Among the rose petals, I could make out the original insignia and the final three letters of a word.

"Remember when you spread the cover over our laps in the carriage? You really shouldn't have bent over that far, for you showed me more than your lovely bosom, Belleza—you showed me your past."

The change on her face was amazing, from animal hatred to wide-eyed horror.

I continued. "Spaniards and Cubans don't know what that underlying tattoo is, but I do. It's none other than dear, old U.S.S. *Galena*. Bet you were drunk that night. What was it? Ten, fifteen years ago? Yep, that old tub's been down here in the West Indies for decades, and the boys always liked Santiago for a liberty port. The girls there have a helluva reputation for fun. On behalf of the Unites States Navy, I thank you for your services."

"Peter…"

I put a finger to her lips and deadened my tone for the *coup de grâce*.

"There's nothing you can say. You know what I am capable of, so listen well, Belleza. Very well. If you do not do *exactly* what I tell you to do, I will let the Cuban patriots have you. You have heard what they do to traitors, especially your kind of traitor. Two of them are standing behind me, by that post, waiting for my signal. Your body will be found in the morning, floating at the Regla docks. Water inside the lungs—an apparent drowning. Regretful, but this sort of thing does happen when a lady traipses around the lower-class areas, doesn't it? "

I looked toward two mechanics in greasy overalls conversing ten feet away.

It worked. A graduate *cum laude* of the mean streets of Santiago de Cuba, Belleza knew when to change course and go with the current winner. Her evaluation took maybe five seconds. "So what do you want me to do?"

"Two things. First, tomorrow you will take the three o'clock train to Batabanó. Here is your ticket. I will meet you aboard the train once it is moving. Once at Batabanó, you and I will spend the night in a hotel room, and I will interview you about your work to better understand Cuba and the Spanish colonial government. On Sunday morning, we'll return to Havana, for I'm leaving on the steamer to Charleston and New York.

"Second, you work for me in the future. Continue to serve Marrón, but you will work for *me*. Report about his organization, about his agents, and about whom and where they have penetrated. You will be contacted in two weeks from this Sunday by a clandestine patriot who will use the password *miel*, honey. He will provide you with an account number. The value of five Spanish *onzas* of gold—that's worth about eighty U.S. dollars—will be wired on the tenth of each month into an account at a Spanish bank's branch office in Havana. You can check on that account at any time and withdraw from it once a year, on December tenth. We will communicate by constantly changing methods. The Cuban patriots will be watching you and acting as our intermediaries."

She recoiled from my words. "That scares me. It is too dangerous, Peter. Marrón will kill me if he even *thinks* I am telling you things about his operations."

"And the Cubans will kill you if you don't. Spare me the sympathy bit—you're a whore, a predator, and your life has always been dangerous. You have a choice, Belleza. Die at the hands of those men over there, or cooperate and live to take your chances in the future. Yes or no?"

The boat was about to dock at Regla, and the crew began readying their lines. I moved Belleza aft to get away from the departing crowd and nodded a fake cue to one of the mechanics when he happened to glance at me. Both would have to walk close to us on their way to the forward gangway.

"Time is up."

She eyed the mechanic, who met her gaze like a true Cuban male, without embarrassment or hesitation, running his eyes slowly over her body, appreciating her charms. An interested leer crossed his face.

She made an obscene gesture to him and turned back to me, her voice devoid of affectation and all business. "Yes...I will do what you say, but I want a thousand dollars to begin with."

"Two hundred."

"Six hundred.

"Two fifty, and the information had better be important and verifiable. That's as high as I go. You'll already be getting eighty a month."

She frowned. "Very well, I agree."

Passengers for the return trip were boarding, filling the open decks. I had to assume some were Marrón's men, alerted by the telephone line from Havana city, so I stood facing forward to better study the arrivals.

"Good decision. Now report what the colonel has told you about me."

She lifted her hands in the air and shrugged like a peasant woman. "Peter, he does not tell *me* much. Only that you are dangerous, that you killed some of his men years ago. He wants to know why you are here."

"The colonel has been overwhelmed by his paranoia, Belleza. I came here to do a fencing match and got left behind when my ship departed."

"Marrón does not believe that."

The sun was setting gloriously over the ramparts of the Antares Castle. Back at the Havana dock, the irritated landau driver stormed up to me. Telling him the lady felt ill, I had him drive us to Hotel Isabella, where I informed Belleza that we weren't having dinner together and we weren't going to any "special place" that evening. Our little tour of the city had ended. She seemed surprised and, might I add with a trace of modesty, genuinely disappointed.

Then I kissed the lady unabashedly before she disembarked from the carriage. She suddenly got into the spirit of the moment, and we put on quite the show for the astonished guests and doormen—the Anglo sailor lusting after the Spanish lady. That sort of thing simply isn't done in public, even in New York. And particularly not among the Spanish elite in Havana.

"*Hasta mañana, mi novia—y nuestros viaje romantico a la costa sur,*" the hotel doormen heard me call to her as we trotted away.

My watch said 7:38 p.m. when I returned to the hotel room. Preparations were complete. The operation would begin in thirteen hours and twenty-two minutes. It was time to get some food and rest, for I was certain that my next opportunity for those niceties might be a long time coming.

25

The Final Round

Hotel Florida
Havana, Cuba
10:30 p.m., Friday
28 September 1888

"All's well, me friend?" asked Rork, his face lengthened in mock sadness. "Ye've been quiet since gettin' back to our little home here from yer jaunt with dear old Doña Belleza, the most beloved tart o' Santiago for every man Jack in Uncle Sam's bleedin' navy. Ooh, hope it ain't me company that's stilled yer tongue."

We'd just come up to the room from an excellent dinner in the hotel restaurant, when Rork pronounced it the "finest last supper" he'd ever had and said he needed a nightcap. Normally, I'm against drinking rum the night before action, but I gave in upon Rork's insisting to me, "Ooh, now Peter, me boyo, how about just'a wee dram more o' that Matusalem tonight? That'd do nicely ta cauterize the inside o' any nasty wounds we might be receivin' *mañana*. Think o' it as preventative medicine."

Other than that bit of Rorkian wit, and telling him that my reconnaissance with the lady had shown the route and rendezvous point were as I had expected, and that he'd been correct about Belleza being a whore, I *had* been quiet. I'd too much swirling about in my mind.

We went out onto the narrow balcony, each with a final glass of Matusalem, our very last alcohol, and sat down with our feet up on the railing. I waved to one of our watchers across the street, who instantly looked the other way. Below us was a stream of chattering people on Obispo Street, enjoying the new feeling of relative briskness during their traditional Friday evening stroll. Winter was truly coming, when the temperature would plunge to a balmy seventy-five degrees during the day and the humidity would be down to maybe seventy percent.

Rork tried again. "Still thinkin'? Silly to think too much on the future, boyo."

He got a chuckle out of me. "Yeah, I know." Then my glumness returned. "I was thinking about the past. Being with a woman, even the likes of Belleza, reminded me what I'm missing in life."

"Aye, me thought so. Cynda, is it?"

Rork knows my melancholy moods better than anyone. He was right. I was thinking about the lady I'd fallen in love with that very summer. While on leave from the navy, I'd set off with her and an entourage that included Rork on an unauthorized, private mission, ending with my overstaying my leave and getting into deep trouble at headquarters.

Cynda and I had parted ways at Key West only three weeks earlier—I, heading north to face my superiors' wrath in Washington, and she, heading back to an empty home in Puerto Rico—after she had spurned my offer of marriage. She did it gently, but it hurt. It still did.

For some reason, I'd had bad luck with women after my wife Linda had died seven years before. I suppose, in all honesty, that my job didn't help. Actually, it seemed to be the major hindrance.

A hidden part of my life that consumed more than merely my time, my work at ONI consumed my mind and focus as well, constantly intruding and overwhelming everything and everyone else.

Cynda's rejection was a crushing culmination of that bad luck. She said my work *was* my life and that I wouldn't be the man she loved without it. But she also said that any woman, even a wife, would end up secondary to the work. She spoke of my work as if it was an exotic mistress, providing excitement in an otherwise dull life. Perhaps she was right, but it didn't feel like much of an exotic mistress right then on the balcony in Havana.

Not only had my affair with Cynda ended badly, it had offended my daughter, Useppa, in Key West, who did not approve at all of Cynda or my less-than-moral behavior. The entire affair had rendered me tired and depressed. I was convinced that if I had been available when ONI had tried to find me while on leave, and if I had gotten back to headquarters that summer, the entire situation in Havana wouldn't have come to this disaster. Now it was my mess to clean up.

Rork has always been my sole confidant. He's seen my weak side, knows my frailties. Not even Cynda had seen this side of me during our perilous journey into the darkest dangers of Haiti to search for her missing son.

Cynda. Lovely Cynda.

My mind filled with the last sight of her, standing at the ice cream shop in Key West, beautiful blonde hair waving in the sea breeze. Those sad, dark blue eyes filled with tears as she said good-bye. My heart melted at the memory. I wanted her back in my arms. I wanted softness in my life again. I wanted normalcy, like other men had. This work, this sort of life, was slowly killing me, robbing me of my humanity and decency. She was like a life-saving vest thrown to a drowning sailor, then yanked away.

Rork was regarding me with concern, patiently waiting for my answer, and as always, somehow knowing my thoughts. He ascribed a mystical explanation for his ability, calling it simply "sympathetic Gaelic intuition."

He was still waiting, and I could see him regarding me closely.

"Very well, Rork," I replied at last. "You're right as usual. It's Cynda who's on my mind. You know, sometimes I think I'm doomed to this kind of life forever, devoid of real feminine love, with the only women around me the parasites or predators I use to gain information or who are trying to get it out of me. Maybe I'm just tired."

"Aye, lad. That we both are. But listen to me well. Ye've known the love o' two good ladies in yer life, which is more than most men have. More'n me, that's fer sure. Ooh, me life's had some good romps an' rogers to be sure, but nothin' like the quality o' love, that real love, that ye've had. But all the same, me own spirit's still high, an' the right one'll come along fer me some fine day. Aye, an' she'll be even the more special for the waitin' for it. Jus' hope me bones ain't too old an' tired to enjoy it, that's all."

Some Spanish sailors ambled by, singing a happy-sounding song about a girl in a port. Rork grinned. "Aye, now those young lads ain't tired a wee bit. Liberty ashore!"

"For me it's more than being physically tired, Rork. I'm sick of dealing with the scum of the earth, like Paloma, and Belleza, and Rogelio. Tired of having maniacs like Marrón for enemies. Look at those sailors down there. I miss the days at sea aboard a warship when the enemy was obvious and your duty was clear. Even in peacetime, it's decent, honorable work."

He waved his rubber hand at me. "Methinks that's all bilge water, Peter Wake. Yer damned good at this sort o' thing, an've saved Uncle Sam's bacon more times than that whole lot o' paper-pushin' idlers at ONI put together. There's them that do, like us. An' then there's the staff wallahs, what write reports about us that do. An' the lads afloat these days're bored to their ears. No action, no enemy. Just ship's routine, day after day."

He held up a finger of his right hand and wagged it, his voice deeper. The bosun in him was coming out. "Nay, Commander, yer just feelin' down 'cause yer missin' dear Cynda, an' 'cause we're in a bit o' a tight spot here. But we've been in far tighter ones than this place, ain't we? Aye, remember seventy-four? Them blue-painted devils had us as slaves in a goat box cart in the Sahara, on the way ta get sold to some bugger in Timbooktoo? Ooh, now *that* was a bloody tight friggin' spot, indeed."

I smiled at him. Rork had made the opening move in a game we sometimes played to buck up our spirits.

"No, Sean, your elderly mind has forgotten those catacombs of the dead under Lima. That was rougher than the African desert. Remember the bone dust clogging our lungs? Those Chileans chasing us through the tunnels in the dark? Now *that* was bad. Good God, that was claustrophobic." I shuddered at the memory. "Like being in a coffin."

"Ooh, Peter, me lad, I may be older than you, but me mind recollects that the pirates o' Cambodia, led by that she-devil o' a woman pirate her ownself, take the top o' the cake fer sure. Now *there* was a dicey deal. An' we were alongside the king o' bloody Cambodia, no less. Thought we were goners a couple o' times that day. An' what about starvin' ta death after, while driftin' about in the South China Sea on that friggin' waterlogged derelict o' a hulk. Remember that?" His tone softened. "Ah, but how can we forget those lasses on that island we fetched up at? True lookers, every single one o' 'em. Yers was the best o' the lot. What was her name?"

"Her name was Ahn."

I chose to ignore the battle and starvation memories and concentrate on the lovely ladies of Con Son Island, especially Ahn. "Yes, they were incredibly beautiful. What a cultural mix, French and Vietnamese. Remember how graceful they were when they walked? And those eyes. Captivating."

It was a great memory. Rork knew well the image in my mind right then and offered, "Aye, a good evenin' that. Damned romantic, it was."

I remembered Ahn in that *ao dai* dress. Azure blue with gold lace. No young girl, Ahn was the Vietnamese widow of a French soldier, the first woman I'd kissed since my Linda's death. I thought I'd lost the ability to muster tender feelings until that night.

"Yeah, Rork, it was romantic. Dancing on the verandah in the moonlight, overlooking the South China Sea—until George Dewey showed up and spoiled the whole damned thing."

"Aye, that he did. Took us back into that friggin' war that warn't even ours."

He didn't finish the sentence—*where I lost my left hand.*

I raised my glass. "To your old hand and to the new hand."

He looked at his false hand. "Aye. Indo-friggin'-China. Only decent thing about that place was the lasses. Bad times."

"Yes, Rork, but Indo-China wasn't the worst. The ultimate terror for me was at Patricio Island, when Boreau attacked us in our sleep."

My daughter had been with us and had been one of the targets of that attack.

Rork turned toward me, suddenly grave-faced. "But we bloody well won, didn't we? An' every one o' them friggin' monsters, who would kill a girl like Useppa, lost the fight permanently—though it took a while to end Boreau. An' by mañana, Colonel Isidro Marrón will know just what we're made of. With any luck, me spike'll get the chance to run right through that bastard."

He raised his glass. I tapped it with mine and grinned. "To our best one yet, Rork—tomorrow. We'll steal those boys right from under Marrón's nose."

We drained the last of the rum. I checked my watch. Almost midnight. The melancholia was gone, pushed away by memories of past ordeals and victories, replaced with a quiet confidence.

We had work to do.

26

Parque Reina Isabella

Parque de Reina Isabella
Havana, Cuba
9:45 a.m., Saturday
29 September 1888

My finely honed plan, complete with optional routes of ingress to the Audiencia and egress out of Havana, almost came to a grand stop in the morning shortly before the rendezvous with my colleagues at 9:45. At 8:00, a courier from the captain-general arrived at our room with a personal invitation to meet him at the beginning of the procession at Queen Isabella Park, and later attend Mass with him and his wife at the cathedral at noon.

I decided that meeting Don Sabas in the park was a good idea—it would continue my charade as long as possible. Rork could handle making contact with our people in the crowd and brief them on their expected duties.

Accordingly, we split up at the park at 9:30. Rork carried the black, cloth bag containing our two shotguns. His two pistols and my one were concealed within our clothing. A vast crowd of thousands—far larger than I'd anticipated—was gathering in a joyous mood under sunny skies and a gentle breeze, the second day of that wonderful wind from the north.

Brass bands were tuning up. A mulatto drum troupe was putting on a display of their African-Cuban dance, swirling the drums above their heads. Proud Spanish cavalrymen, professional descendants of the conquistadores, clickety-clacked by, their twelve-foot lances streaming ribbons. Shouting children in colorful costumes dashed about as shy, teenage girls promenaded in their first grown-up dresses. Unsmiling priests in their finest robes supervised harried lay leaders, struggling to hold aloft a giant cross with Jesus, while others carried an enormous Saint Michael statue, complete with sword in hand.

All around me, genteel Spanish ladies in dazzling white and pink and yellow dresses, with matching parasols, strolled alongside their distinguished gentlemen in somber gray and black. Platoons of infantry soldiers in the various colors of their regiments marched by or stood guard. Poor Chinese men looked on from the periphery, their faces a study in careful neutrality as they watched this alien culture's celebration.

To the east, near the rail station, street vendors with braziers in their carts did a brisk business in roasted pork and rice and fish, the heavy scents mingling with the park's flower beds and the ladies' perfumes. Merchants strutted by in white linen suits, sometimes engaging the foreign tourists, who stood there confused and awed by the scene.

It was the most diverse gathering I'd ever seen in Havana. Everyone was singing, dancing, laughing, and talking, reaching across those long-recognized social lines to other classes, all in the name of God's warrior angel. A fascinating phenomenon to observe, had I been a mere tourist. I was quite pleased, for the raucous noise and swirling motion overwhelmed one's senses and would impede any surveillance, which made it perfect for my purpose.

Organizers were forming the parade participants into bigger sectional groups, then herding them into their places and getting everyone ready for the start. Various religious icons of saints from churches all across Havana, set on little wagons or held by sturdy men, were being positioned. With each saint was a group from that church's congregation in their finest attire, holding a wide banner proclaiming their home parish. Incense from the wagons' shrines added its thick, sweet aroma to the air, reminding all of the mystical flavor of the occasion.

At the head of a long line of dignitaries' open carriages was that of the captain-general, who had not yet boarded. Seeing his plumed helmet bobbing as he greeted people, I made my way over and presented myself with a bow and smile. I was rewarded with a hearty handshake and welcome. He was in his element, introducing me to various members of the upper crust around him as the gallant *norteamericano* who had saved his nephew's life. I recognized many of them from previous events that week, where I'd already been introduced.

Now, however, I registered a slight reticence among them in their acknowledgment of me. Evidently, I was old news. My fame was wearing thin. *Well,* I thought, *with any good luck I'll be a distant blur in their memory by tomorrow.* If things went wrong, I would be a blaring headline in Havana, Madrid, and Washington.

Don Sabas engaged in a rapid-fire discussion with one of his assistants and a senior priest, both of whom were trying very politely to get him away from his admirers and into his carriage so the parade could get started. Bishop Santander, our dinner companion from Wednesday evening, was already ensconced in the back seat next to Doña Matilde, both looking perturbed at the delay. Ignoring them, Don Sabas abruptly turned to me again as if he'd just noticed me and asked, "Where is your servant, Commander? I never see the man; he must be invisible."

It was so unexpected that at first I just stood there, trying to gauge the reason behind the query, then recovered enough to say, "He is Irish Catholic, sir, and wanted to see the icons and relics more closely. This is a special day for him, so I gave him permission."

The captain-general waited a few seconds, making my heart skip another beat, then said quietly, "Ah, one of our brothers-in-faith from the Isle of Ireland. Yes, they are among the most devout. That is a very decent thing for you to do. In addition to your personal sense of honor, you are a good leader, Commander. I look forward to having you sit with us at the Mass at our magnificent cathedral. It will be a beautiful experience. And now I will enter my carriage, for I must not be tardy and incur the displeasure of the bishop. Enjoy the procession!"

He boarded, surrounded by his ceremonial guard close by and an outer perimeter of modern soldiers. With a great fanfare of trumpets, the parade got under way at last. Following the royal carriages were those of the social elite, dozens of them in two parallel lines.

One of them was filled by mature ladies dressed to the nines and all aflutter with fans, obviously reliving thrills long gone by as they imagined male eyes focused on them. I spied my companion of the previous evening with them. Belleza, playing her part as the still-glamorous queen of the social set, was holding court among her pseudo ladies-in-waiting.

I wondered what her friends would say and do if they ever discovered what she really did, probably with some of their husbands. When they saw me, a great, high-pitched chattering went up until Doña Belleza herself half stood and waved her fan at me, saying, "Peter! Oh, Peter! Please ride with us! We would love to have a gallant naval gentleman as our escort."

Her fellow passengers were breathlessly silent while she was speaking, with all eyes glued to my reaction as Belleza ended her request with a coquettish wink. The carriage erupted again with female twittering and fan fluttering. Belleza, in full character and enjoying every moment of it, then sat down after telling the driver to pull over and wait.

Though it didn't look like it to Belleza and her friends, I

had other things to do right then, and this second interruption wasn't making my life any easier. But appearances had to be kept up. I doffed my hat, bent at the waist, and proclaimed loudly so all could hear me, "My dearest Belleza, nothing could give a naval gentleman greater pleasure than to ride in a carriage as an escort to the most beautiful daughters of Spain in this lovely city of Havana, but alas, I must find my servant, who seems to have gotten lost. I will see you this afternoon, though, and I am *eager* for our reunion, *ma cherie!*"

There is nothing like a little French endearment to spice up a comment. The ladies got that part instantly. Belleza's translation of the rest produced appreciative nods for my compliment, then knowing sidebars about me behind their fans, followed by giggles that sounded pretty licentious to me. *El Conquistador Suave's* reputation was obviously still secure with some of Havana, at least. Call me a cad if you will, but I'm still rather proud of those giggles.

Having had their fun, my clandestine hooker friend and her unknowing upscale society sisters reentered the parade and resumed their refined deportment. Amused by the episode, I turned to go find Rork and get things moving. Timing was important to the mission, and I was already a bit late. That was when I was confronted with my third unanticipated interruption, the sight of which instantly sent an icy feeling down my spine.

Emerging from the mass of onlookers—not ten feet away and glaring right at me—was Lieutenant Commander Julio Cesar Boreau in his dress tropical whites, with pistol and ceremonial sword on his belt. I hadn't seen him since the match, figuring they'd sent him off somewhere to cool down or at least be out of the limelight and thus spare his considerable pride.

"*Buenos dias, Comandante Wake. Y felicitaciones para su victoria impresionante en el palacio del capitano-general.*"

His congratulations on my "impressive victory" didn't exactly ring with sincerity. No smile or offer of a handshake from Boreau. He appeared instead like he was going to jump me or shoot me. I kept track of that right hand, which was gripping the flap of his holster. He then turned his gaze to my still-bandaged hand, his lips curling into an evil little smirk.

Oh, yes, the apple didn't fall far from the Boreau tree, and I knew in my gut that I would have to kill this maniac eventually, maybe before I could get away from Cuba. Admittedly, for a fleeting second it was a titanic struggle not to pull my pistol, put some lead into that snide face, and end the horrific family lineage right there, probably saving countless future lives in the process. But the timing wasn't right.

His presence there was no coincidence. A provocation by Marrón to push me into an arrestable offense, perhaps? I tried to keep my reply lightly toned and respectful, explaining with a shrug that yes, I'd had luck, but he'd had ability.

"*Si, fue suerte en mi parte, Comandante Boreau. Pero Ustede tienes mucho habilidad.*"

My compliment didn't assuage him in the least. In fact, he unnerved me completely with his next words—in fluent English.

"Commander Wake, we will meet again with blades, but without all the encumbrances of masks and pads and *pistes,* and silly rules designed by old men to keep the combat safe. An oxymoronic phrase, is it not? Safe combat. Would you, the famous *yanqui* warrior, who enjoys invoking his sense of honor in front of an audience, like to do something like that? A real test of combat, man to man, but with no audience to impress by your words. Just you and me, privately. Let us do it before you leave tomorrow at four o'clock on the steamer to your country. Yes, I see that you are surprised by my use of English—how very stupid of you to think we Spanish are all ignorant of our enemy's language."

I tried to defuse the situation, holding my hands out nonthreateningly. "Look, Julio, obviously there is a mistake and somehow we've gotten into some sort of a hatred situation here, but—"

Boreau interrupted me, far too enraged to be calmed. His next statement was simple: "You know precisely how and why this started."

My eye saw the fingers of his hand edge toward the button on the holster's flap. I calculated whether to reach for my own revolver inside my coat or continue holding my hands out in an apparent gesture of nonviolence, but actually readying them to seize his pistol hand. I chose the latter—it would be faster and look better for the witnesses.

Up ahead, military bands were fully engaged now, with great flourishes of trumpets and drums reverberating off the elegant apartment buildings lining the Prado. The crowd was moving en masse northward, parting and closing around Boreau and me, leaving the two naval officers their tiny spot of privacy, one pace apart. Caught up in the excitement, the people around us seemed blissfully unaware of Boreau's hostile stance and words. It was a bizarre scene, surreal and about to get even more fantastic.

Boreau stepped forward, clicked his heels, and slapped a white glove across my face. "No, not here, commander. Noon on Sunday at the seawall at La Punta. Bring any blade you like; it matters not to me. Be warned, though, if you do not appear at that exact time and place, I will shoot you down at my leisure before you can board the steamer and run away."

And with that he executed an about-face and marched away, barging a path across the flow of the revelers. I stood there, taken aback for another ten seconds, then got about my business, woefully late and very disconcerted.

Rork was not amused at my tardiness, as it was now well after ten o'clock and things had started. I didn't have time to explain in detail beyond, "Just ran into Boreau. Seems he really wants to kill me tomorrow. Invited me to a duel at noon at La Punta. By the way, he speaks fluent English—better than you, in fact."

Rork wasn't impressed. "Well, sir, 'tis yer own damned fault for pullin' yer blade back at that last second at the duel. Should'a killed 'im when ya had the chance."

"If I'd killed him, we wouldn't have been invited to stay ashore as guests of the captain-general, Rork. You can't always succumb to desire and kill these fellows when you want to. Anyway, he'll be there all by himself at noon tomorrow. And madder than a hornet."

"Aye, 'twill be a day late an' a dollar short fer that little bastard. Ooh, hey, maybe he'll kill himself in frustration when ye don't show up. He looks the bloody stupid sort."

That quip said, he then tersely briefed me on the scattered locations of our men. Except for Leo, they were keeping a discreet eye on Rork—he stands a head above most men—as a guide for their pace within the crowd. Leo was off ahead of us in the procession, part of the Jesuit contingent near the bishop and the captain-general, but he'd already told Rork the cassocks were in place by the laurel tree at the Church of the Holy Angels.

The pedestrians of the procession were moving along the half-mile-long central median of the Prado, a stone-paved promenade bordered by low walls and laurel trees in planters. On either side of this median were the traffic lanes for vehicles of the parade. On the Prado's outer sidewalks, along the unending cliffs of magnificent apartment buildings, tense soldiers stood at fifty-foot intervals.

In the median, Rork had arranged our men in a loose diamond pattern with him and me in the center. Pots and Folger, the two men who understood very little Spanish, were closer by us, Pots on our right and Folger to the rear. Folger carried his small case of "goodies" with him, and Pots carried his locksmith tools in a little, leather bag.

The Spanish-speaking Mena and Marco were a bit farther away from the center of our diamond—Mena up front, carrying a valise containing disguises, and Marco out on the left flank. Marco, who up until that morning had no idea of his duties, looked a bit nervous, as was to be expected, for I had led him to believe that the action part of the endeavor would be the next day. Now he was suddenly thrust into a perilous effort and had a crucial role to play.

All of our men were praying and singing the hymns like

everyone around them, whether they knew the words or not, blending in as much as possible, and looking like the many other men in their straw hats and white suits. I glanced at Rork and signaled my approval. Everyone was in place and ready.

As one would expect, I was scanning everywhere for Marrón and his men, but it was impossible to tell who was who. They could've been right next to me and I wouldn't have known it. Somewhat eerily, the scene reminded me of that at Bedloe's Island in New York City's harbor, when the elder Boreau had tried to escape me in '86. But now the proverbial shoe was on the other foot. I was in *their* backyard, and I knew that somewhere they were watching and at least one of them wanted to kill *me*.

27

Anarchy

El Prado Boulevard
Havana, Cuba
10:48 a.m., Saturday
29 September 1888

As we approached the intersection where Colon Street crossed our path along the Prado, I gestured slightly to Marco, who meandered through the procession and then east on Colon the three blocks to the Church of the Holy Angels, having been briefed on his task by Rork. I looked for anyone taking notice of his departure and saw none.

Then, as we passed Refugio Street, I heard two things I'd been counting on. From ahead to starboard, about half a block this side of the Audiencia, I heard the sounds of chanting, but not the religious kind. Just the opposite—the *anti-religious* kind. And then, above it all, came the ultimate offense, the shouting of anti-government slogans.

Excellent, thought I, for the anarchists were up ahead at the spot where the Cuban medical students had been martyred by the

Spanish in '71. I hoped there would be chaos in a few minutes as the army and police reacted.

Rork touched my elbow, and to the right I saw Marco in a cassock on the side street, passing a soldier and joining the procession again, carrying a large burlap sack. He resumed his position to our left, next to a priest, loudly singing the praises of Saint Michael's exploits against the wicked warriors of Satan. The faithful were all singing louder now, a collective effort to outdo the anarchists ahead.

A new sound came from behind me—an elephant trumpeting. The circus parade was behind us, having started out from their camp near the central railroad station. In my plan, I had estimated the circus would pass the Audiencia approximately fifteen to twenty minutes after our part of the procession did. Those would be some very busy minutes for us.

We were almost there. I stepped on Rork's foot while raising my hands in praise of Jesus, the sign for him to wave his hands and sing out, "*Viva La Iglesia!*"

In the next sixty seconds, all of us disappeared from the procession. Marco tacked obliquely to port, down Genios Street. Mena began speaking to a soldier on guard along the left side of the boulevard, allowing the procession to pass him by, then followed Marco. Pots stopped to tie his shoe, while Folger, Rork, and I continued on another hundred yards. Pots finally tagged along with some youngsters onto Refugio Street. I went left on Consulado Street; the other two swung right onto Carcel Street, named after the jail down in the dungeon of the Audiencia.

The Audiencia, the most dreaded bastion of Colonel Marrón and his counterrevolutionary thugs, loomed dead ahead of us. Standing with its face toward the city and its back to the sea, the large, squat Audiencia wasn't as imposing or elaborate as Don Sabas' palace. Instead, it looked decidedly functional, the Spanish version of a courthouse above ground. Like everything else in Havana, those dark-gray stone walls and columns had faded to tan with mold and had crumbled by salt air and age. Martí had been judged, sentenced, and imprisoned in that building at the tender age of sixteen, then sent to the prison quarries to break rocks under the hard Cuban sun.

Marco dropped cassocks from the burlap sack in the side alleys off Colon and Refugio Streets as he went around the block and rejoined the masses in front of the Audiencia. Both he and Mena had donned theirs, and as they went to distribute the others to Rork and Folger on the right side of our track, I went the two blocks around to the left and back to Refugio to retrieve mine. Pots arrived to get his as I headed back into the crowd on the Prado.

The reader, I am sure, is wondering about this elaborate choreography and whether it was really necessary, given the general confusion in the streets that morning. The simple answer is that I wasn't sure and therefore had overcompensated for my concerns about a surveillance of our members.

This would be our most vulnerable point prior to entering the dungeon below the Audiencia. Each of the men was to resume his position and be identified by Rork and me. To say I was anxious is a gross understatement. After I returned to my central position, my senses were fully employed, looking everywhere and waiting for the jerk of a uniformed arm on my shoulder at any second. I saw Mena and Marco and Rork in position, wearing their ankle-length cassocks, hoods covering their faces. Pots and Folger, my two least acclimated members, finally showed up in their assigned spots, wearing their new attire.

A pull on my left shoulder spun me around, ready to fight, but instead of a Spanish counterintelligence agent, it was Lafleur, of all people, standing there wide-eyed, his Southern drawl higher pitched in his surprise. "Commander Wake? What in the world are y'all doin' dressed up like *that?*"

I answered in grinning Spanish for the benefit of anyone around us, *"Si, mi hermano, es un dia de alegría para todos los niños de Dios!"*

He stared at me in disbelief. Rork, seeing me in apparent

trouble, slapped Lafleur on the back. "*Viva San Miguel, mi hermano!*"

The consular aide stepped back, glanced at the Audiencia, and shook his head, muttering, "My God, y'all are goin' to try to get inside there, aren't you?"

At that point Folger completed his first task, in the form of a muffled explosion to our right, where most of the anarchists were gathered. It was nothing lethal, just a small pop and some smoke billowing up from behind a tree in the park, but it was enough.

The paradegoers gasped; some dropped their religious banners and screamed. Most picked up their pace to get forward quickly, away from the anarchists, and join the forward half of the procession, which was now rounding the back side of the Audiencia and passing near La Punta Fortress, where Lieutenant Commander Boreau had so kindly scheduled my death for the next day.

As I had hoped would happen, many of the dim-witted anarchists thought the explosion was actually planned by their leaders and doubled their uproar in approval, enhancing the effort by throwing some rocks they found lying around. Their escalation didn't intimidate the police and soldiers one bit, however. They waded into the mob with truncheons and a fair amount of gusto. A cacophonous din rose immediately, a combination of African animals honking and growling behind us and the army bands ahead, resolutely trying to overwhelm the noise of the rioters.

I grabbed Lafleur and yelled in his ear. "You didn't see us here, so keep your mouth shut, even to Williams. Now go!"

Eyes shining in anticipation, he yelled back, "Let me help."

There was no time for this. "You're not part of this, Lafleur, so go."

He looked perturbed, almost angry. "All right, you know where to find me. There's always help for my brother's friend!"

Rork put a hand on my shoulder, turning his head toward Mena, who had Marco by the arm. They were nearly at the side door in the east wall of the Audiencia. I could see Folger coming across Carcel Street. When I turned back to look for Pots, Lafleur was gone.

In a first-time experience for me, Rork and I hitched up our skirts—or whatever one calls the bottom of a monk's cassock—and started running for the east side of the building. We slowed to a walk to get around the flank of an infantry platoon facing a new wave of rioters in the park to the south.

Our disguises were the perfect enablement. No one stopped us. In fact, one officer implored us to seek cover by the building, afraid we seminarians might get caught in a crossfire. Several other platoons arrived and deployed next to the first. The impossibly young-looking second lieutenant—known in the Spanish army as an *alférez*—came running over, shouting to the men to hold fire, not to shoot. His newly sewn single braid and six-pointed star on his cuff gleamed in the sunlight as he repeated the order more adamantly. To our left, half a dozen veteran cavalrymen—the dreaded Hussars, by their gold sleeve insignia—were eyeing the anarchist mob and fingering their sabers, plainly itching to get in among them.

"*Requerda los mártires jovenes de setenta y uno!*"("Remember the young martyrs of seventy-one!") came the throaty roar from the smoke-filled little park. A rock landed with a thud in the grass two feet away from us. It would've seriously wounded or killed me had it connected with my skull. From the range, it was clear they were using slingshots. It wouldn't be long now before the soldiers fired, whether their officer wanted them to wait or not.

I couldn't see Pots. "Rork, we'll have to go in without Pots and try shooting the locks off. Maybe all this noise will cover the shot. Try to time it with that platoon's volleys when they fire. And, remember, we're going to Marrón's office first!"

His "Aye, aye, sir," reply sounded ludicrous coming from within a cassock's hood. Beneath that covering, I could see that Rork's eyes were wild.

"But them Hussars're about to charge, sir. The infantry won't fire if they do."

The Prado was rapidly emptying. Everyone knew what was about to happen and wanted to get out of the way. The religious procession had rounded the Audiencia and was almost running toward the cathedral, half a mile to the east, along the channel front. Four or five blocks to our south, the circus had halted on the Prado, the handlers trying to calm the animals, which smelled danger in the air.

Passing the main entrance in the Audiencia's south wall, Rork and I finally reached the nondescript side door set into a shallow alcove in the east wall, the prisoners' portal to that underground world. Mena was talking animatedly in Cuban with two armed guards in faded, light-blue-and-white-striped *rayadillo* cloth uniforms, as Folger fidgeted with some things in his box a few feet away. The guards were anxious, and I registered the newly issued .43-caliber Remington rolling-block rifles in hand at the ready position, with bayonets fixed.

"Sixth Battalion, Light Infantry, fresh in from Spain, methinks," observed Rork quietly to me, noting the unit number on their crossed hunting horn, brass insignia. "Aye, these boyos're regular lifers, sir. Bad sign—nary a conscript among 'em," he added soberly.

In our whispered discussions while preparing for the operation, we'd counted on disinterested and incompetent draftees to be stationed around the Audiencia. Cuba was full of them, and they frequently were more a hindrance than a help for their leaders. These soldiers were experienced, however, their heads swiveling constantly, fingers near the triggers, searching for threats while trying to be polite and not show their annoyance with these stupidly naïve monks who clustered around them in the middle of a riot.

It may be remembered that the Aficionados had not yet met my American technical experts, though all hands knew Rork and me and knew their fellow comrades would be wearing monks' robes. Marco was warily regarding Mena as we arrived. So I greeted my seminary brothers in Spanish, gesturing around them as a nonverbal introduction. Careful nods were the result, all recognizing they were now irrevocably in each other's hands.

At this same time, Folger approached the guards from behind. In each hand he held a rag, sopping with a special concoction. Both soldiers turned to him, the one with a corporal's red stripes respectfully offering his concern: "*Señor, por favor, ten cuidado. No es seguro aquí.*"

Fortunately, they were oblivious to Folger's intent as he stepped up to them and smiled while raising his hands. Seconds later, each one had a lint cloth covering his face and was falling backwards into the arms of Rork and Mena, Folger and I taking charge of their rifles, courtesy of an extra-heavy version of Billroth's mixture: one part alcohol, two parts ether, and three parts chloroform.

The soldiers were quickly dragged inside the small vestibule, followed by the rest of us. The entry was as I recalled it from two years earlier—a heavy, wooden door that barred further entry. This was where Pots was to have come in. Rork glanced questioningly my way. The Hussars hadn't charged yet and the platoon hadn't fired, but we couldn't wait any longer for noise to cover the shot.

"Shoot it, Rork."

Everyone covered his ears as Rork drew his Navy Colt, cocked the hammer, and aimed.

"Oh, for God's sake, don't ruin that beautiful lock!" Let me pick the damned thing," said a voice from behind. My oldest team member had arrived, out of breath. "Rork, shooting that little darling won't open her anyway. She'd laugh at a bullet!"

Rork stopped and hid his weapon but couldn't help his anger. "An' just where the bloody hell 'ave *you* been? Off idling the day away with some poxy friggin' tart, were ya? Get yer bloody arse in here an' do yer job!"

"Running for my elderly life, you big, dumb Mick. What'd'ya think I was doing? They're about to start shooting out there. Now stand aside and let me get acquainted with this lock."

Producing a pocket lamp, its tiny flame magnified by a small Fresnel lens, which he gave to Marco to hold, Pots shook his cassock's hood down away from his face and leaned close to the lock mechanism. In both hands were small picks, which he inserted into the lock hole and used to feel his way around the interior.

Rork huffed some foul oath and sternly watched our chaotic surroundings as all other eyes watched Pots' lined face, which was a study in concentration as he manipulated the picks. First he studied the keyhole, then put his ear right up against it so he could hear as well as feel the inside of the lock.

"There she goes!" announced Pots as he twisted the knob and the door swung open. "One of Linus Yale's new cylinder types. Easy as pie if you know what to feel for."

We quickly entered and locked the door behind us, Pots not-so-gently reminding Rork that if he'd shot the lock we wouldn't have been able to relock it.

I led the way into the damp passageway that was rough hewn through the coral rock. Dim electrical lamps flickered a yellow glow every fifty feet or so. The floor was covered by a thin layer of sand and rock dust and sloped steeply downward. Rork and Marco deposited the two guards—trussed up like pigs with bandanas blocking the use of their mouths—in a small storeroom on the side and ran to catch up to us.

With each step, the memories came back to me from the sole night I'd been there in '86—the animalistic screams of the victims, the pungent smell of excrement and blood and gore, the terrifying sight of the ancient Spanish instruments of torture arranged neatly on a side table next to the victim's chair.

That night the jailers had pointed out to me that those tools were the originals, three hundred years old, as if from a museum of the Inquisition. Each was incredibly intricate, almost delicate, like Pots' lock picks. I suppose they had a similar function, designed to penetrate specific parts of the body to produce different types of suffering in order to unlock the information stored within the prisoner. But their work wasn't an antiquated skill. No, they were still used every day on the patriots of Cuba to extract all they knew, even as the poor bastards begged for the jailers to kill them and end the agony. How many people over those three hundred years had suffered?

They hadn't used the instruments on me, only threatened their use, displaying a most sinister sneer as they did so. I was an American naval officer, and that made them hesitate, which gained me time and in the end saved me. But I freely admit that the mere threats were enough to nearly destroy my psyche back then, for I'd clearly heard, saw, and smelled the victims during my brief time there. On many nights since, those tortured souls still came into my mind. Rork has told me he gets those nocturnal visits too.

Rork and I escaped that night through the truly divine intervention of a priest and a bandit, both strangers to me before then. I think—no, I am certain—the experience changed my life. My faith in God was renewed and made whole, but my faith in so-called civilized human nature was destroyed forever. For this terror happened not at the hands of some alien pagan culture in a forgotten distant corner of the world, but in the heart of a "civilized Christian" empire.

I stopped and checked my pocket watch. Eleven-forty. We had only fifteen minutes at the very most for the pandemonium to continue topside before somebody noticed the guards at the east doorway missing. During that time, we had to find and breach Marrón's office, then find and extricate Paloma and Casas. After that, we had to escape the dungeon, get away from the area, and meet Leo at the cathedral. It seemed impossible.

I checked my companions. Rork stood grim-faced, his jaw clenched. The others looked like frightened children, ashen-faced and silent, completely reliant on Rork and me. I knew it would get worse. They hadn't seen the dungeon yet. I started down the tunnel again, this time faster.

It was then that we heard the first scream.

28

Descent into Hell

Dungeon of the Audiencia
Havana, Cuba
11:39 a.m., Saturday
29 September 1888

Seconds after the scream, barely discernible as human, we reached an intersection of tunnels. I searched for familiar sights and found them: ancient oil lamps set into sconces along the walls, dripping with condensation. There was no electricity this far inside the lower reaches.

I remembered those lamps and the peculiar oil smoke they gave off, the cheap sort of fish oil, with a sweetish-acrid smell. The next doorway was Marrón's office. No name plate announced it, and no secretarial or other desks for administrative sorts would be found inside, only a safe and a simple writing table. Probably none of Marrón's superiors had ever been down in the dungeon. Certainly not Don Sabas.

This wasn't Colonel Marrón's *official* office. That was somewhere in the ministry of justice at Plaza de Armas. No, this was his *working* office. This was where he kept his secrets secure, be they people or reports.

"Where is everybody? This place looks deserted," asked Folger, nervously holding that special box of his. He'd readied more lint cloths, plus a couple of medical applicators called Allis masks, keeping them in an airtight tin container.

"This is a holiday weekend, remember?" I said. "Most of the nonessential staff types are off, pretending to be pious, or just sucking down rum in a *taverna*. The extra guards who are usually down here are topside, pressed into service against the anarchists."

"At least you hope they are," said Mena with a nervous laugh.

"Oh, there'll be some around here. We'll run into them down in among the cells. They'll be in the special Orden Publico units, with different uniforms than the regular soldiers topside."

I tried the office door. It was locked, but Pots snickered, said it was "a cinch," and, sure enough, had it quickly open using only one pick. Inside, next to the vacant writing table was the safe containing Marrón's files, including those for Rork and me. I'd seen him perusing them while I'd sat there, shackled and waiting for his decision on my fate.

Pots didn't like the look of the thing. He grabbed my hand holding the pocket watch and noted the time, then knelt by the safe. It was a modern Kromer, he explained as he tinkered with it. "One of those German jobs by Theodor Kromer and damned hard to open. Must be something really valuable in there," he guessed aloud.

His comment got me thinking about my orders, both official and unofficial. In addition to those on Rork and me, there would be other files in the safe: some on the Cuban revolutionaries, some on Marrón's own informants, and maybe some on my Aficionados. I was taking them all, an adjunct to the main mission, which wasn't in my orders. As I was departing after receiving my official instructions, Commodore Walker had accompanied me into the passageway, out of the hearing of Mr. Smith, and quietly mentioned he wanted me to take everything I could from Marrón's office while I was inside the Audiencia getting Casas and Paloma.

"Don't take time to sort through the information," he said, trying to sound nonchalant, though his face was furrowed with concern. "You won't have time, so just grab all the dossiers you see and bring them back to me. I'll examine them in detail here."

I was returned to the present by someone speaking to me, for Pots was quietly lecturing us while working the lock. I suppose it was to keep his hands and nerves steady and his mind free of the trepidation gnawing at everyone else.

"Ah, yes, our dear Colonel Marrón clearly has some clout," he opined. "This little gem is one of the newest German styles, no more than a year old, at the most. Yes, I'd say she's a *third*-generation Theodor Kromer; the original was patented back in seventy-four. Yep, this one is new and *very* expensive. State of the art, my friends. You'll probably never get this close to one of these dearies ever again in your life, much less watch somebody seduce her open without the key."

"Can you really get it open?" asked Marco.

Pots paused, his hands remaining exactly as they were while pivoting his head around to give the Cuban a nasty look. Then he returned his focus to his metallic adversary and continued his monologue. "Herr Kromer's design is pure genius. There are eleven tumblers grouped around a turntable cylinder. That little devil is placed inside yet *another* cylinder. It takes a double-bitted key with no fewer than *eleven* notches. Do the mathematics, gentlemen."

He reached for a third pick and inserted it, then a fourth. When no one spoke, for we had no clue what he was getting at, he did the mathematics for us as he barely touched the last pick.

"The mathematics for this lock is simple yet astounding. There are a grand total of eighty-seven *million* possible key variations. Skeleton keys won't even work here. And because of the two tumblers, you only get one—repeat, *one*—fleeting chance to align both cylinders correctly with the eleven tumblers. Ah, yes… Kromer, you kraut-eating mastermind, I salute you!"

Click. The safe door opened and Pots called out, "Time?"

"Six minutes, six seconds," I said with a grin, silently congratulating myself on bringing old Pots along. "Incredible, Leonard. Thank you."

The locksmith smiled and spread his arms, like an actor on stage receiving applause. "Well, it's what I do. What's next?"

"Rork, take them down to the cells. Leave the bag. I'll catch up with you."

As Rork rushed out with our men, I reached inside the safe, not bothering to read anything, just grabbing two large, accordion files full of dossiers and stuffing them into the black bag containing the shotguns. There were some Spanish gold and silver coins on the lower shelf, which I scattered around the office, wanting to show the first Spaniards to discover our operation that robbery wasn't the motive.

Before leaving, I extracted from my pocket a piece of blank notepaper I'd brought along for just this moment. I scribbled on it: *Anarquistas Unidas del Mundo!* I placed the message on the table as part of my fictitious trail leading to the false flag that would be blamed for the rescue, the black flag of the United Anarchists of the World. It was the third piece of the puzzle for the Spanish. The first piece would be the cassocks; the second, Billroth's mixture— the former was anti-religious, and the latter, in wide use in Europe. There would be more pieces before I was through. If I did my job well enough, no evidence pointing to the United States would be found.

I ran and met the rest of them a hundred feet farther in, slowing down as I approached. There was a bend in the tunnel, and they were gathered behind Rork, who was on his belly, peering around it. Beyond the bend was the final door to the cells.

Rork stretched his right hand behind him and held up two fingers—two men up ahead, guarding the door. Then he made his right hand into a pistol shape and flashed it twice—both guards had a pistol. The fingers started walking—the guards were standing, not sitting. The hands turned horizontal, with thumb and forefinger scissoring—the guards were talking. Rork backed up a bit and twisted around to face us, holding his hands apart, as in measuring something, then spread out all ten fingers and flashed them once—the guards were ten yards farther down the tunnel. His joined his hands at the wrist, then opened them slowly—the door to the cells was just beyond the guards.

Another scream came up the tunnel toward us. Drawn out into a long wail, it trailed off into a whimper, like a baby who cries even when he knows no one will come.

Everyone looked at me.

Thirty feet in a tunnel was too far for a stealthy approach to apply Folger's special mixture. We'd never make it five feet past the bend before they spotted us. We could shoot the door guards easily enough—one shotgun blast would take them out—but that was a last resort. I wanted this done quietly, so as to not alert the guards farther inside, whom I estimated from memory to number around five or six. But that was only an estimate, because I'd never been in the farthest reaches of the dungeon. I needed all or most of the prisoners inside to be alive. If the guards in the cells suspected an attack, they would start killing prisoners. Destroying the witnesses to their crimes, as it were.

No, we would have to bluff our way up to the door guards.

My briefing was necessarily mute. I pointed to me, then Mena—I needed his Cuban accent and his acting skills. Next came Rork—I needed his strength and that deadly spike. Then Folger and his potions. In sign language and the barest of whispers, I conveyed how I would be the prisoner of Mena, Rork, and Folger, with my hands to all appearances tied in front. Mena would speak to the guards and get us close. Rork and I would each grab one, covering their mouths to prevent an alarm, and Folger would step in and put them to sleep. Marco and Pots would come up after we had secured the guards. Pots would open the door if it was locked, as I thought it would be.

Everyone gestured his acknowledgment. Mena, Folger, Rork, and I shed our cassocks. Rork's uniform in the dim light of the tunnel would look somewhat official, and Mena and Folger would be plain-clothes agents of Colonel Marrón. I removed my uniform coat and tie, unbuttoned my shirt, spread some slime from the walls on my face and shirt, slumped over, and became a prisoner who'd already been interrogated and was on his last legs.

"*Ay, hombres! Tenemos un otro animal para el zoo!*" Mena called down the passageway before we rounded the bend. I limped around the curve, head down, face seemingly contorted in pain, dragging my right leg as Mena gave me a little push from behind. I noted the guards' had an O and a P on either of their blood-red collar lapels, the emblem of the Military Corps of Public Order, which in Spanish went by the acronym C.M.O.P., or O.P. for short. Marrón's unit was ostensibly attached to the O.P., though in reality he had complete autonomy.

"*Un de los anarquístas! Y por favor, amigos, la habitacion mas fina en las casa para el pobrecito...*" Mena added jovially, asking for the finest room in the house for the poor little anarchist he was bringing in. The guards laughed but looked at Mena quizzically: *Who is this fellow, and how did he get here?*

Mena dismissed their wariness with a wave. "*Teniente Garcia, de la sección especial de la policia del tesoro.*"

His casual description of himself as a lieutenant of the treasury police did the trick. The guards straightened up, for they were facing a lieutenant from a very influential outfit. The older one was still confused, however, and asked, "*Por que aquí, teniente? Porque no en el carcel de tu ministerio?*"

Uh, oh. He'd asked why the lieutenant wasn't taking the prisoner to his own unit's jail. Good question. I wasn't exactly sure where the treasury police took their prisoners and doubted Mena knew either. But the actor had an even better answer. "*¿Por los ordenes de Coronel Marrón. Tiene cualquier otras preguntas?*"

Once they heard that Marrón was involved, they didn't have any other questions. Now they were standing nearly at attention—obviously the colonel scared them far more than the special police at the treasury.

Mena pointed to his minion, Rork, who placed my left bicep

in his right hand and dragged me over to the guards. I kept my head down and started to sob, presenting no threat to the guards. The older one chuckled as he reached out to seize me. Out of the corner of my left eye I saw Rork withdrawing his fake left forearm from his trouser pocket, then saw the glint of metal from the spike. He squeezed my bicep—the signal.

I slipped my hands out of the knot supposedly confining them. The heel of my open right hand shot up as fast as I could make it, catching the older guard right under the chin. His head snapped back and he lost balance, falling backward into the jagged rock wall, my hand never letting go until I heard a dull, squishy thud as his head impacted an outcropping and he dropped like a sack of potatoes. Folger was there immediately, covering his face with the cloth, even though the man was out from the concussion.

I looked to my left. Rork's target was on the floor also, but Folger wasn't needed, for there was an oozing hole in the man's right temple where Rork had roundhoused him. He calmly wiped the blood off his spike onto his sleeve, put the rubber hand back on over it, and looked at me.

"One less o' 'em to fight another day, sir."

29

A Swedish Enigma

Dungeon of the Audiencia
Havana, Cuba
11:49 a.m., Saturday
29 September 1888

Folger and Mena stood there, their eyes going from the pool of blood by the dead body to Rork and back. Pots and Marco ran up, carrying our cassocks, and stopped in their tracks, eyes riveted to the bodies.

"Leonard, attend to that door," I said, getting everyone back to work. "Everyone else, get back into your cassocks. Rork, lash that unconscious man's hands, then post a watch for any counterattack down the tunnel from the front. Folger, get your applicators ready. Marco, search the guards for the key. It's probably not there, but I need you to look, just in case."

I held up a hand for emphasis. "Gentlemen, the moment the door is open, we go in through the first room, get among the cells, neutralize the Spanish guards, and then open every cell we can. We are looking for men named Paloma and Casas. Call out their names. They are our primary concern, but I also want every prisoner who is able to move to come with us. If Casas or Paloma can't walk, he will be carried by the other prisoners who can. I want all of *you* unencumbered. This is it, men. Get ready, because the worst is yet to come. Questions?"

Marco, still staring at the corpse, clearly not a man to rapidly adapt to changing situations, was disturbed with the addendum to the plan. "We are to rescue *everybody* in the prison? I thought it was only two men."

"A large number of escapees will provide greater confusion when we leave the place. Any other questions?"

Only Pots made a sound, whistling softy at the iron-framed, oak-paneled door as he crouched down beside it. The iron lock mechanism was fully a foot across, covered with an elaborate engraving, which showed through the rust. Several layers of metal were apparently below the outer one. I couldn't see the keyhole anywhere and guessed it must've been hidden somewhere under the layers of engraved cover plates.

"My God, she's a classic antique," Pots whispered reverently. "You told me in the telegram she'd be old, Peter, but I didn't really think she would be *this* old. Looks positively medieval. What a gorgeous triple escutcheon, a true work of art."

"Yes," I answered while redonning my cassock. "But I believe it's Renaissance, to be more precise. Probably from about the sixteen hundreds, when this place was first built. I remember the guards on the inside used a massive key to open it when I was here."

Marco stood up and reported to me in a shaky voice, "No key on either of these guards."

"Just as I thought. Up to you to get us inside, Mr. Pots."

Leaving his little picks sitting on the wet floor next to his unrolled bandolier of tiny tools, Pots reached inside his big bag and jumbled things around, searching for something.

"Hmm, this little lady is a bit older than you thought." Still rooting around in his bag, he looked up and added. "And by the way, my friend, she isn't from the country you're thinking of. She's not Spanish. Nope, this little darling is Swedish. They were the very best craftsmen of locks back then. Artists, really. The Spanish crown must've paid a fortune for her. They surely wanted whatever was in here to be very secure."

With a satisfied grunt, he extracted three long, sticklike things. "Knitting needles. Best thing for these dear old bitties. They can get a bit cantankerous, you know, but they're also frail on the inside. Rusty too, after all the years. Have a nasty habit of breaking if you don't have the proper key and start poking around where the maker didn't want you to go."

His hands caressed the outside, fingers tracing the design as he talked. "Just look at this escutcheon. The exterior wards are fascinating. Sometimes we in the business call them *chastity shields*. What an honor this is!"

He leaned closer and murmured to the lock. "Let's see...ah, yes. Just a little peek, my dear. Nothing tawdry...I really do love you..." He rotated a thin, iron facing piece clockwise, revealing another plate below it.

"Ah! Off with the gown and now to the petticoat."

Holding the first escutcheon in place with his right hand, he rotated the next plate counterclockwise and down with his left. "Aha! You see, the keyhole appears, gentlemen." He stroked the lock face and sighed. "Now we're getting somewhere, *ma cherie*."

"Can you accelerate this, Pots?" I asked. "We're running late and don't have much time left."

"I don't think so. These interior wards that protect the keyhole are the most complicated I've ever seen." He glanced up at me. "Could really use a decent drink about now, gents. Anybody holding a flask?"

Rork, who's no slouch in the drinking department himself, frowned at Pots, then cocked an accusatory eyebrow at me—he hadn't been enthusiastic about bringing old Pots on this mission.

To the locksmith, I said, "Forget the drink and just get the damned thing open."

"More's the pity, Peter. These old girls're always more cooperative with a little encouragement and a steady hand. Very well, gents, we'll just have to do this like a Baptist. And now to the real work."

He brought his face to within an inch or two of the keyhole, peering inside. Mena held Pot's little lamp closer as the locksmith felt around the keyhole, which was raised on a lip a quarter inch above the surrounding base plate. "My goodness! What a work of art. Her final ward is nothing like the outer hole would suggest. It's a four-notch circular with a long bottom notch. Barrel notches! How quaint. The key must be wonderfully complex. Peter, did that key you saw look like a barrel inside a shorter outside barrel?"

I glanced at Rork, who was shaking his head in vexation, then replied to Pots. "I was a bit preoccupied at the time to pay much attention to it, Leonard."

I got a lecture in reply, which included a thin reference to the less-than-legal side of his work. "Well, you damned well should have. She's a masterpiece. Good thing I brought my boy Jacques along. Only used him twice in my misled life on unauthorized endeavors, once down in New Orleans and then up in Montreal. Let's see if he wants to help us out here."

He extracted a heavily pitted iron key from his bag. It looked as old as the lock and had a cylindrical attachment underneath the shank. Pots fitted it over the keyhole and pushed, then grimaced. It didn't fit exactly. Too small, with no stud below to fill the bottom notch in the keyhole.

Pots lifted it off and exhaled loudly, swinging his head left and right as he rotated and stretched his neck. I could hear it snap. "Wrong country—Jacques is a French key. I should've known. He gets along well with Belgian and Dutch locks, but she's a big Swede and won't let him play with her. Hmm, we've got ourselves a Swedish enigma, gents, right here in the heart of dear old Havana. What to do? What the hell to do…"

"Ooh, let me just shoot the bleedin' bugger apart, an' we can go about gettin' on with the friggin' mission. We're losin' time, sir," offered Rork to me.

Pots shook his head. "You're a Celtic barbarian, Rork. No sophistication at all. Ah, but wait just a minute. Yes, I've got it! The external wards were the main protection back then, not the internal wards. So, perhaps there is a way I can help. Maybe the Frenchman and the Swedish girl can still be friends."

He took out a bar of milled soap and rubbed it around the French key and the Swedish lock's keyhole. Then he placed the key back atop the raised keyhole and pushed firmly. It went in a tiny bit. He tapped it with a small mallet from his tool set. It went in farther, the rust around the keyhole falling away in flakes.

"Got her attention—and she didn't say no!"

Next he inserted the first knitting needle in the keyhole notch below the key, moving the needle around very slowly, one hand lightly feeling the middle of the needle.

"Yes, darling, I love you. *Je t'aime*," he cooed, then twisted the needle. I heard a tiny click. The second needle went in, below the first. More probing, moving it around. Another click.

The second needle slipped.

"You ungrateful, teasing old bitch!" growled Pots.

"Quiet," I ordered. "They'll hear you on the other side."

He looked about to pound the door in frustration, but instead he straightened up, exhaled deeply, and leaned forward to try again with the second needle. It moved something inside that made a click. He waited for ten seconds. We all stared at the lock. The needle stayed put.

Several quick shrieks, escalating in intensity, erupted from the other side. They sounded close. From the tunnel behind us, something heavy clanged. All eyes turned to me. I checked my pocket watch, barely able to see the hands in the glow from Pots' lamp. It was past time to run. The order had to be given, I knew that, but we were so damned close. More screams from the other side of the door, only feet away, ending with a single word that meant the same in English and Spanish—"*No!*"

We couldn't afford to wait any longer. I made the decision. A death sentence for those inside the door.

"All right, everyone," I announced. "We tried our best. It's nobody's fault that we can't get in, but we can't stay any longer. It's going to be tough to get out of here as it is. Let's go. Get your cassock on, Leonard."

Rork had his shotgun at the ready. He tossed mine to me, and I moved around him to lead us out. I looked back a final time to make sure everyone was ready to run for it.

They were, except for one: our slightly peculiar locksmith, who was still crouched by his Swedish nemesis.

Pots suddenly blew out a breath and backed away, shaking out the tension in his fingers and hands. He looked up at us, oblivious to all I'd just said, and asked, "So how much more time do we have?"

Rork muttered something obscene. I shook my head and said, "None, Leonard. It's over. We're way past the time to leave." I turned to the others. "Follow me!"

They weren't looking at me. They were watching Pots, who held up his hands and said, "Then I suppose I'll just have to be crude and force the issue. Oh, well, so much for romance."

He inserted the third needle and swung its end to the right, producing another click, then hit the French key hard with the mallet. A deep *kerthunk* sounded as a heavy metal object inside the door dropped, striking another solid object. Pots twisted the key and pushed against the door. It moved inward an inch or two.

"Aha! It seems French guile won out, after all. Oh, ye of little faith," he said smugly, looking at Rork.

Mena was the first to move, leaping to put his full weight on the door. Fully six inches thick and incredibly heavy, the hinges squeaking as if they too were in pain, the door opened ponderously, reluctant to the last. Holding one of the guards' pistols, Mena dashed in and around to the right. I was second inside and ducked to the left, lowering my cassock's hood to have full visibility.

Revealed before me was the Dante-esque, torch-lit chamber I'd tried for years to forget. The flickering flames cast shadows around rock walls glistening with humidity. In the middle was the chair, the table beside it holding neat rows of instruments. Every prisoner who went into the cells further inside the dungeon had to pass through this room. The tableau was a warning to cooperate, to tell the Spanish inquisitors anything they wanted to know, and to not waste anyone's time. A quick bullet or the slow chair—the decision was yours.

I stood there transfixed in horror. An older man—what was left of him—was sitting in the chair, the filthy rags around his waist his only remaining shred of privacy. He wasn't even lashed or shackled to the chair. No need—he obviously hadn't been able to move for a while. His head rolled over to its right side as we burst in. Empty eyes gazed toward us, mouth hanging open, strands of gray hair showing through matted blood caked around his mouth. Fresh blood, shiny in the torchlight, leaked out of his ears.

The head turned a bit. He stared directly at me. Face grimacing with the effort, he grunted. I remembered our garb. What must he think of us? Monks with shotguns. Did he think it a hallucination? The eyes were barely alive, their thin, forlorn glimmer leaving even as I watched. Was he wanting for it all to end, for us to put him out of his agony?

It suddenly struck me that he was old enough to be my father, and I wondered why they even bothered to torture him. How long had he been in there? What could he possibly have done to the Spanish to warrant this kind of retribution?

Rork entered behind me and went to the right as I glanced around the chamber again, searching for threats. I heard another sound from the man in the chair, this one only a weak moan. He was nearly dead, but still alive enough for those eyes to follow me. Another gurgling moan—I could hear the frustration in it as he tried to form words.

There was nothing I could do to help him, but there was one last thing he might be able to do to help us. *"Donde estan los guardiános? Estan aqui?"* I asked him.

Then everything exploded into a mass of light and sound.

30

The Dead and the Dying

Dungeon of the Audiencia
Havana, Cuba
Noon, Saturday
29 September 1888

It was a double-barreled shotgun discharging, fired by a Spanish guard hiding in a niche some slave had hacked out of the rock wall three centuries earlier. Mostly blinded and deaf from the flash and thunder of the blast, I saw only a vague shape dart around the corner though the open door. Marco, Folger, and Pots were still outside, expecting one of us to come out, but instead they saw the guard sprint past them down the tunnel to the entrance. It all happened so fast they couldn't stop him.

My vision returned quicker than my hearing. Other than some scratches from ricocheted pellets, I wasn't hit. Mena and Rork didn't even get that. They stood there, stunned beyond words, staring at each other, trying to understand why any of us were still alive. Then Mena pointed at the chair and turned away, vomiting.

The guard's blast hadn't been aimed at us.

His gunshot and escape meant we'd lost the crucial element of surprise and had to get out before the army came in. I still didn't know where the other dungeon guards were. I soon got my answer.

A Spanish uniform showed in the doorway, the man angrily asking, *"Qué pasa? Quiénes Ustedes?"*

Rork swung his shotgun and fired, crumpling the man into a twitching pile on the floor. His hand still clenched a set of keys on a brass circle. It became clear to me. The first guard must have heard the lock get pounded by the mallet, then quickly hid in the niche as we entered, without enough time to warn his comrades about us. The other dungeon guards didn't know what was happening, but they would now, after the shotgun blast.

We had to work fast. "Mena, take Marco, get those keys, and get in that tunnel. Yell for Casas and Paloma. Open every cell you can. Tell all the prisoners to run for their lives up the tunnel!"

Rork stepped over the body, ready to head into the next passageway. I said to him, "Get in there ahead of Mena and Marco and stop any other guards. I'll meet you all back at the first entrance door."

To Pots and Folger, I said, "Follow me! We're going up to that outer entrance door to hold off any counterattack until the others get out."

I pointed to the dead guard. "Take his pistol."

Pots snatched the weapon, saying to Folger, "Age before beauty, son. You can have the next guard's gun."

I was already out the door and called back, "Folger, get one of your smoking jars ready! Both of you, follow me."

We headed up the tunnel toward the entrance, me slinging the bag of files over my left shoulder, Pots helping Folger with his box of accoutrements as we walked quickly. Reaching the last bend before the exterior entry door, I cautiously peeked around. The door was closed tightly. Probably locked.

I heard running from the cell area behind us, but it wasn't the stamping of shoes. It was the softer sounds of bare feet: the freed prisoners, Paloma and Casas among them, I hoped. We needed to get to the entrance ahead of them.

"Folger, do you have anything that can blow that thing open?"

"Nothing strong enough for *that* door."

"Stay here," I said as I crept forward and checked. Yes, it was locked. The fleeing guard had escaped, the alarm was given, and now we were locked inside. Pots could probably pick it again, but the enemy was on the other side, waiting. The Spanish were going to take their time; no need for them to rush.

I went back to the others, my mind racing with a vague alternative plan for escape from the Audiencia that I'd considered back in the hotel room and again on the carriage tour with Belleza. It seemed far-fetched then, and still impossible now.

"All right, it's time for the smoke device."

Folger brought out a jar, bigger than the one he used for the diversion at the hotel.

"I'll have a smoke cloud started in a jiffy, sir. It's ready—just have to add a little potassium chlorate, which I happen to have right here..."

He poured some gray powder in the jar and shook it. Seconds later, it started smoking. "Yep, here we go."

"What's this smoke going to do for us?" asked Pots, his voice higher pitched than usual. He was scared but trying to control it.

"A diversion for the Spanish and a pathfinder for us," I explained. "We're going out a different way, gentlemen, while the Spanish sit outside the door and wait for us to cook."

Folger figured it out first. "Follow the smoke to an air vent?"

"Exactly, son. But we have to convince the Spanish we're dying in here first, burning to death, so they don't rush in through this door. Go ahead and get the smoke going. Then both of you start yelling in Spanish like you're panicking. Remember, in Spanish, not English."

The smoke began to billow from the jar as Folger screeched, "*Ay...yay, yay! El fire-o!*"

Well, that type of Spanish wouldn't work. "It's '*Incendio!*'" I corrected him. He changed to the right word, yelling it over and over while apparently screaming in pain. Pots echoed him, though less passionately.

I screamed toward the door, "*Rendimos!*" ("We give up!") Smoke filled the area quickly, making the electricity lamps give off an eerie, yellowish-amber–colored light. Choking in the pungent haze, we raised our hoods and covered our faces, to no avail—our lungs still filled with the stuff. Our fake cries became more realistic.

The prisoners arrived at our spot in the tunnel right about then, gasping from the smoky air and the exertion of running. They looked like they literally couldn't go another single step: pitiful victims in foul rags, in little better shape than the man in that chair. Collapsing to the floor, they stared at us. *Monks with guns?*

There were only five of them, and they looked like they'd been in the dungeon for years. None of them were Paloma or Casas. Where the hell were the other prisoners? Maybe Paloma and Casas were part of a group that Rork and his men were still helping to come out.

"*Los otros en el carcel? Donde estan los otros?*" I asked the emaciated men, sitting down next to them.

The oldest one, his tone faint and unearthly, answered. "*Todos los otros estan…muerto…o moribundo…*"

All the others were dead or dying.

He leaned toward me and coughed out a question of his own: "*Quiénes Ustedes?*"("Who are you?")

I tried the alibi story I was leaving for the Spanish. "*Anarquistas.*"

No response. Just a curious stare, right through me—and the story.

Outside, somebody among the Spanish suddenly had a bright idea and cut the electricity. The passageway lights went out. Pots lit his little lamp and held it near me.

Rork's face appeared in the gloom. Mena and Marco followed and sat down against the wall, grim-faced, neither of them speaking. No other prisoners were with them. Rork squatted beside me, out of breath, his eyes downcast, despondent. I asked him, "You all right?"

"Aye, but me life's known better times." He surveyed the scene and asked, "This some o' Folger's imitation smoke, o' did we manage to light this bloody forsaken hellhole on fire?"

"Just Folger's smoke. Sean, you got only *five* prisoners out?"

"Grisly in them cells, Peter—*real* friggin' grisly. Dozens, maybe hundreds, o' the poor lads, lyin' about, damned near dead. This lot's the only ones that're strong enough to get up an' move. An', aye, we looked 'round for Paloma an' Casas but seen nary a sign o' 'em. They're dead an' gone already. Take me word on that—nobody'd last long in that death house. 'Tis far worse than where the Spaniardo bastards put us in eighty-six—*far worse…* "

His eyes told me there was more he could say but wouldn't.

"Well, these men won't be able to move much farther. We may have to give them some pistols and leave them behind. What about any guards back there?"

"Shot two farther back in the lower tunnels. That's all me seen down there, but there's probably more hidin'. So what's the plan now, sir? We goin' out the front, o' we goin' with that other wild notion ye had about the air vent?"

"Spanish have the front locked, so that's out. Looks like the alternate plan we discussed: Follow the air current shown by Folger's smoke. There must be a fairly large vent around here."

Rork sounded ancient as he made the age-old acknowledgment, "Aye, aye, sir."

I motioned to everyone. "Let's go. We're going to find an air vent by following Folger's smoke. Mena, explain it to the Cubans and tell them they *have* to keep up with us if they want to escape. You, Marco, and Pots can help them along. Rork, you're our rearguard. Folger, can you get another smoker going and lead the way next to me. I think it'll be down one of those two side tunnels we passed."

Folger quickly answered, "Got it going now, sir. It's my last one."

I saw that Pots was breathing heavily, his face drained of color, left hand trembling. "Leonard, you all right?"

"No, Peter, I'm damned well not all right, but I'll make it. Let's just get the hell out of here."

We all stood and turned to go, each man silent, knowing the odds against our escape. One of the prisoners, the one who had been staring at me oddly, stretched a feeble hand to me in the murk, his thin voice struggling with words. "A...mer...i...cans? He...call...you...*Peter? Peter...Wake?*"

A chill ran through me.

"Pots, give me your lamp."

I leaned close to the Cuban, holding the light near our faces. "*Casas?*"

31

A Thin Tendril of Smoke

Dungeon of the Audiencia
Havana, Cuba
12:15 p.m., Saturday
29 September 1888

He was trying to smile, but tears began streaming down his cheeks.

"*Si, amigo...soy...Casas.*" He squeezed my hand. "Thank... you...for...coming, ...Peter..."

The cadaverous body in front of me didn't look anything like the Casas I'd known. Casas was thirty-five, but he looked eighty now. "Dear God in heaven, when did they put you in here?"

"*Medio...de Julio...*"

Middle of July? He'd been there over two months? He looked like he'd been there for years. How could anyone change that much in ten weeks? Middle of July meant he'd already been captured long before ONI thought. How? The others in the team were staring at Casas as if he were a ghost: the man they'd never met but had come to rescue.

240

"Paloma? What happened to him?" I asked.

He spoke each word with rasping effort. All our lungs were full of the smoke. Then, listening to his voice, I realized the problem was his throat, his vocal cords. I wondered if they've been crushed. Or was it from screaming.

He struggled in English. "Dead...today...you...saw...him."

Another chill went through me.

"The man in the chair?"

Casas nodded.

Rork put a hand on my shoulder. "We best be goin'—no time for this now, sir."

Yes, of course, he was right. My mind was overwhelmed, trying to comprehend what had happened and how. There would be time later, if we lived.

"Right. Mena, help Casas. Pots and Marco, help the other Cubans."

We did not run, couldn't, burdened as we were with the victims, but the smoke wasn't moving fast either. At the tunnel intersection near Marrón's office, I followed the smoke's lazy drift to the right. That wasn't the direction I wanted, for it was toward more danger.

I'd been navigating by speed, time, and direction and estimating where we would be above ground—it's called dead reckoning when done at sea. We'd entered on the Audiencia's east side and had followed the first tunnel more or less westerly for seventy paces until the intersection. The turn to the right meant we were heading north, toward the sea, which was only two or three hundred yards from the Audiencia. Between the dungeon and the sea lay the seaside boulevard named Calzada de San Lazaro, then the army engineers' barracks, and, past that, the fortress at La Punta. The air vent wouldn't be in the boulevard. Would it be in the barracks or, worse yet, the fort?

Another fifty paces northward, the smoke stopped drifting and just hung there. We were still under the structure of the Audiencia, perhaps twenty feet underground by my guess. From somewhere behind us I heard shouts in Spanish.

Folger touched my shoulder. "If the smoke stopped drifting forward, it could mean the vent's somewhere around here, sir. Check the top of the tunnel with the lamp."

Pots' miniscule lamp was the only illumination we had and was almost useless for examining the place. I held it aloft and scanned the rough, serrated roof a foot above my head. Nothing but coral rock.

"Wait! It didn't go forward and it didn't go up, right?" I asked.

"Right," said Folger.

"Then hold the smoker down lower. Maybe the vent's along the bottom of the wall."

I got on my knees and swung the lamp around, peering through the haze. The smoke *was* moving slightly along the floor of the tunnel. I'd been searching for a vent at the top, but I was wrong. It was low, just off the floor, a black gap in the dripping wall, maybe two feet square. I stretched out on the muddy bottom of the passageway and reached inside the hole with the lamp. Twelve inches or so inside, it opened up into a miniature tunnel, cobwebbed and even danker than the main passage. Only three feet high and as many wide, it was less than half the size of what we'd been traversing in the main tunnel. Coffinlike. Terrifying. Except for one thing.

I felt air moving.

A thin tendril of smoke from the tunnel wound its way in and disappeared in the darkness ahead. I crawled forward and held the lamp farther inside. Spiders and roaches scurried around me, making my skin crawl. From the main tunnel, Folger nervously whispered, "Ah, sir? My smoker's gone out. What do we do now?"

Rork called in to me. "Enemy soldiers getting' close, sir. Go straight the way we were, o' go through yer little tunnel there?"

They'd surely catch us in the main passage. This was our last and only resort.

"We go this way, Rork. Put the cassocks on the floor and wrap the Cubans up in them; then we'll drag them through here. It's the only way they'll make it."

Rork put his head in the small burrow. "Then we're not leavin' 'em behind with pistols?"

"No, Sean. We'll try to get them out all the way."

"Aye, aye, sir. Then we need to hurry an' get 'em inside here."

I heard Rork organizing them behind me and felt Folger against my feet. Groans became faint cries as the Cubans were swathed and pushed inside. Folger lit a match for illumination, and I saw Mena helping him pull the first bundle inside.

Turning forward again, I started crawling as fast as I could, ignoring the webs around me and the sticky coating, probably bat guano, on the uneven floor of our subterranean burrow. No one had been through there in a long time. Where was I leading everyone?

I had no idea.

Each Target Gets
One Shot

Dungeon of the Audiencia
Havana, Cuba
12:32 p.m., Saturday
29 September 1888

Twenty feet in, the burrow became horizontally serpentine and vertically undulating, the meandering evidently caused by natural water erosion between more solid rock formations. To continue my navigation, I tried to estimate distance and course but quickly lost my sense of direction.

Behind Folger, I could hear grunting from my men as they dragged the swaddled Cubans, who had gone quiet, not even groaning. I waited for the shotgun blast that would signal Rork's last ditch defense, but it didn't come. Had he gotten them all inside before the Spanish got there? Would the Spanish know to check that opening? Or would they continue along the main passage, wherever that led?

The only positive factor—and the one thing to which I attached all my hope—was that I still felt the air moving. Could it really be getting stronger, or was desperation altering my senses?

My hand touched something long and slimy that slithered quickly away to my rear. For a moment I panicked, cutting my knees open in a struggle to get away from it. I willed myself to calm down, put one hand in front of the other, and keep crawling.

The burrow was getting narrower and the climb steeper, until I estimated it at almost forty-five degrees. My forehead was bleeding from a collision with the rock, the blood running into my eyes, warm and thick, then into my mouth, tasting sweet and metallic. I wiped it away with a grimy hand as I climbed up the slime. The thought of infection for my gashed left hand entered my mind.

"Folger, how're you doing back there?" I asked, hungry for human sound, a connection.

"I hate this," came the young voice back. I could hear the struggle in his tone to stay composed.

No morale-building, "hurrah" speeches from me. Not now. We were well past that stage. He deserved the truth.

"Yeah. So do I, son."

What seemed an hour later—but was most likely only five minutes—I sensed something different about our surroundings. Pots' lamp had gone out by then, but my awareness had grown more acute in the pitch-black darkness. The burrow was getting flatter and wider, and more air was moving. Another fifteen feet on, I discovered why when I fell out into a large passageway, landing painfully on my hands and knees, especially that damned left hand and arm. Instinctively, I swore an oath that would impress even Rork, irate at myself for failing to bring a decent lantern and for getting hurt yet again.

Folger had one match remaining and lit it when he emerged from the burrow. It briefly illuminated a regular walking tunnel, a respite for our cramped muscles and bleeding skin. The question then became, Which way to go?

I examined the flame of the match before it died out. No luck there. It went straight up without a flicker. The others started to arrive, shoving the Cubans out of the hole and into our arms. Laying them down and unwrapping them, Folger and I tried to get them to stand. Four, including Casas, were able to, but one didn't. I got on the floor and felt around his neck for a pulse. Nothing. Such a sad end. The man, name unknown, had died silently before he'd been able to see the sun again, incongruously bound in a monk's cassock and shoved along like cargo by foreigners. We removed the body from the cassock and put it back in the hole.

Mena suddenly said, "Quiet! I hear somebody."

Then we all heard it—Spanish voices. They were searching this tunnel too. I'd been wondering which way to go. That settled it. I started off walking away from the voices, hands out in front of me in the blackness, feeling along the wall. I prayed there was no hole or pit ahead to fall into.

The Cubans began crying out in pain again, every movement agonizing, utterly unable to keep up the pace. I called a halt. It would be faster to just pick them up and carry their slight frames.

"We carry the Cubans. I'll take Casas. I want Rork in front with me and unencumbered."

Mena, Folger, and Pots each picked up a Cuban. Casas was like a child in my arms—he might have weighed eighty pounds. But he was still almost too much for my aching arms and back. None of us were gentle with them. We just weren't strong enough.

Pots wasn't doing well. He put down his Cuban and wheezed, "Need a rest. How much farther, do you reckon?"

"Not much farther, so pick him up and keep going, Leonard."

"I don't think I can carry him anymore."

Rork's voice was ominous in the void. "Just stop yer bloody bellyachin' an' do it, Pots. Them bastards're gettin' closer an' I don't fancy endin' up back there where these poor buggers were."

Grunting and cursing, Pots picked his man up again.

I said, "When we get to a doorway, Rork and I will lead the way through it and force our way out of here. Follow us."

We rounded another bend and saw the faintest loom of light, a barely perceptible leaden shade of black, far ahead.

246

"I feel the air moving," said Folger. "There's air moving *against* us."

The sea breeze, I wondered, *somehow funneled down into the tunnels?*

Now I could see better, and yes, there was definitely gray murk ahead, as opposed to the black void we'd been in. At the same time I heard an odd voice up ahead, the tone modulating up and down, like music. No, it wasn't words, it was a sound, like a flute. The Spanish were up there, knowing we were coming and waiting for us. Taunting us?

In the weak glimmer of light, Rork and I exchanged glances. This would be it. We would emerge from the tunnels but not meekly. A little farther, I'd put down Casas, then we'd charge out of the tunnel and blast whoever and whatever was waiting for us.

I heard the sounds again and whispered to the others, *"Silence!"*

Another curve to the right was coming up. The light was strong now, and I saw a shadow move across the left wall. Holding up my hand for the column to halt, I put Casas down, unslung the Spencer, and took in a deep breath.

"Ready, Rork?"

His grin showed white against the dark background.

"Aye, sir. As ready fer it as a Dublin tart on Friday night!"

God bless him! My friend looked so ridiculous saying something like that in his monk's cassock that I couldn't help but laugh.

To the rest, I said, "This is it. Rork and I go first. Cubans will have to walk. You all have pistols now, so remember that ahead of us every man is a target. Don't waste ammunition. Each target gets one shot. Follow me!"

There was nothing more to say. Rork and I started running, I in front with Spencer leveled and ready to explode lead into the first man I saw.

We made it around the curve and saw the doorway forty feet ahead. A figure stood in it, silhouetted black against the white glare of sunlight. I couldn't tell if he was facing toward or away from us. I raised the barrel and held the butt to my shoulder, slowing to a fast, steady march as the figure turned.

I heard the odd sound again, now recognizing that it was whistling. The man was whistling a tune that didn't sound Spanish. It was familiar but I couldn't quite place it.

No matter—he was in our way and going to die. I focused on the target, eliminating everything else from my mind except the center of that form in the light at the end of the tunnel. The man didn't move. His mistake. I felt my right index finger beginning to press the trigger.

"No!" shouted Rork, reaching out for my weapon.

33

Lost Causes

Engineer Barracks
Havana, Cuba
12:39 p.m., Saturday
29 September 1888

Then I understood. The tune was *Dixie*, the song of the South. The man ahead was an American? He whistled it again, the words to the song of my former enemy coming to me: "Ooh, I wishhhh I wasss in the lanndd of Dixie…"

The man called to us nonchalantly, "Good to finally see y'all. I was starting to wonder if you were ever coming out of there."

I knew that accent and the voice: South Carolina Low Country. I knew only one man in Havana with that accent.

Jacques Lafleur.

"What the hell are *you* doing here?" I exclaimed, lowering the muzzle with a jittery hand.

"Really, Commander, not a very nice greetin' to a fellow American. And y'all were a bit rude to me back on the Prado durin' the procession. In fact, I was sorely tempted to tell Consul-

General Williams what y'all were up to when he asked where you were this mornin'...But, don't worry; I didn't."

Lafleur put out a hand. "Welcome to the barracks of the Corps of Engineers of the Imperial Army of His Most Gracious Majesty, King Alfonso the Thirteenth, not to mention the smartest-lookin' parade-ground lads in town."

He glanced at my grimy bandaged hand, which was bleeding. "You know, you don't look so good, Commander."

"Been a difficult day," I replied as we walked out into blinding sunlight and stood in a stone-paved courtyard, three sides of which were surrounded by a two-story stone building. A short distance away on the fourth side, to the north, sprawled La Punta Fortress. Beyond it, across the entrance channel, stood the huge fortress known as El Morro. It was blazing hot, but I didn't care. A sea breeze flowed across the courtyard.

Rork turned all the way around, searching our surroundings for soldiers. There were none. He called back for the others to come out of the entryway, which was set in a small building in the middle of the courtyard. The magazine entrance, I presumed, as I too scanned for the enemy.

Lafleur casually answered the question filling my mind. "Most of the senior officers are off at the church, and most of the troops are spread out along the Prado. The remainin' reserve platoon's chasin' the few anarchists who are still wanderin' around. Nice touch with the monks' get-ups and the smoke in the park, by the way."

I was too disturbed for humor. "What's going on, Lafleur?"

My entourage appeared, and Lafleur lost his mirth when he saw the Cubans being carried out. They couldn't even stand. His face turned pale.

"Sweet Jesus, what the..." His voice became urgent. "We've got to move fast. The soldiers'll be back any minute. Come this way."

Lafleur closed the door and locked the padlock. We followed him to the east side of the barracks. I told everyone to get his cassock back on.

"What's going on here, Lafleur?" I asked again.

He spoke rapidly. "I suggested to a brother Freemason in the engineers that he take the remainin' men in the barracks to the park and help search for those damned anarchists who tried to ruin the festivities. Of course, the last of the anarchists fled half an hour ago, so I'm afraid it was a fruitless quest, but it did get them away from here. They should be back anytime now, though, and then the deal is most definitely over."

Lafleur looked askance at our attire, which was filthy with mud and slime. "Damn it all, I didn't reckon y'all'd have this many men, Commander. And y'all don't look much like monks anymore."

He was right: Covered with mud and blood, we didn't. But I wanted to know about the soldiers. "You have Masonic brothers in the Spanish army?"

"Everywhere in the whole wide world. But, you know, we in the brotherhood can request only so much of one another. A momentary blind eye, perhaps, but not much more. Follow me around over here." He held up the key to the padlock. "I need to return this."

He turned right, down an alleyway. Behind, Mena, Folger, Marco, and Rork were still carrying the Cubans, Pots limping along alone in the rear.

"Lafleur, I still don't get it. How did you know we'd come out of the tunnels here? How'd you get the key to open the door?"

"By a guess and a prayer, Commander. Everyone knows the Audiencia's dungeon is a maze of tunnels. And I knew there was a sublevel under the barracks for a small magazine, so I figured they might be connected. It would be either here or over there at La Punta Fortress. Glad it wasn't there. I don't know any of those fellas. The key ring was left out in the open in my friend's office, so I borrowed it."

He motioned for us to wait while he entered the barracks' office. Returning seconds later, Lafleur led us out into the open area bounded by the barracks, the Audiencia, and the park to the southeast. No sign of the riot or the religious procession remained, only the last of the circus parade, animals and handlers trudging along toward the channel front to the east.

I glanced quickly over at the Audiencia and saw a group in uniform by the east entry and a larger one assembled near the front entry on the south side. All wore the red collars of the Orden Publico. Several men in plain clothes stood together on the east side. One had the same slight build as Marrón. An unnerving sight. Three hundred feet away were men who would kill us on sight—if they had only known we were there.

We walked rapidly, staying in a tight group to hide the nearly naked bodies we were carrying. Lafleur pointed to a dray cart pulled up by some bushes.

"Put the Cubans under the hay. You monks can ride on top," he ordered. "No driver, I'm afraid. Rork, can you drive?"

"I will," said Mena, adding, "His Spanish is too bad."

"Good. Head for the Cortina de Valdez."

Cortina de Valdez? That was where I'd originally planned on our heading after emerging from the Audiencia, to mix in with the circus as it walked to the cathedral. Rork looked at me and raised his eyebrows as he laid Casas on the cart. *How did Lafleur know our plan?*

As we piled hay over the Cubans, I saw a double file of soldiers marching up Balliarte Street from the south. Wearing the green-trimmed, red-and-yellow hat cockade of the *ingenieros*, the engineers, they executed a column left-oblique and headed for the barracks.

The old, weather-beaten mule clomped along with the tail end of the circus, Lafleur walking nonchalantly near us but not with us. Half a mile ahead, the Gran Circo Africano—the Great African Circus—was setting up camp at Cortina de Valdez on the north side of the cathedral.

The elephants had their own roped paddock, where we stopped the cart. We waited while Lafleur walked over to a light brown–skinned man and shook hands. They spoke for a few minutes before Lafleur returned to us. He said to get the Cubans inside a large box wagon that was parked adjacent to the paddock. Inside we found it crude, hot, and barely big enough for us all, but nobody complained. After laying the Cubans down, we dropped to the floor planks and leaned back against the walls, exhaustion overcoming our limbs. Pots, clearly in bad shape, moaned loudly in relief.

Lafleur entered, carrying a jug of water, and passed it around.

I stood and offered my hand. "First, let me say thank you for saving us, Mr. Lafleur. And now, before we do anything else, please tell me exactly how you knew."

"It was simple. Because of the telegram from our mutual friend, I knew y'all were up to somethin'. So when I saw you with Doña Belleza on the Prado yesterday, I followed along for a while. Wondered if you were doin' some sort of reconnaissance but wasn't sure of what."

He paused and lit up a cigar, one of the fancy, fat Cuban ones that have become the rage. He offered another one to the others but had no takers. We'd already had our fill of smoke.

"So I started ponderin' the question, What was ol' Commander Wake here in Havana for? Couldn't figure it out. Then I saw y'all this morning, the day before you're leaving Havana, and you're dressed up as monks. Very interestin'."

He took a long drag on the cigar, enjoying the attention.

"So I just moseyed along behind y'all this mornin' and waited to see the show. Sure enough, pretty soon I saw y'all disappearin' over by the Audiencia during the hullabaloo with the anarchists. That little smoke diversion was brilliant, by the way. And I don't think Marrón's men ever spotted y'all once the monk suits got put on. I bet somebody's in trouble for *that*."

He chuckled. "Well, like everybody else, my attention got sidetracked to the soldiers and the rioters. When I looked back to where y'all had been by the Audiencia, poof! Y'all were gone. Still don't know how the hell y'all got inside the place. I stuck around and watched the riot, waitin' to see if y'all'd reappear. But you didn't."

He took a swig from the water jug. "A while later, I saw some hubbub at the Audiencia and them bringin' in a bunch of soldiers—real ones, not the O.P. boys. Well, that didn't look good, no, sirree. I figured y'all were trapped or maybe captured. If trapped, there was only one way out that I could think of—that passageway to the barracks. So I just walked over there and suggested to my friend that he get in on the action in the park. I could see he wanted to anyway."

"An' why yer doin' all o' that to help the likes o' us?" asked Rork, his suspicion transparent.

"Because my brother Freemason asked me to. That's the way it works, Mr. Rork. Besides, I'm a Huguenot from Charleston. We know all about lost causes. Been in a bunch of 'em for the last three hundred years."

He stood up and shook hands all around. With Casas, it was a double handshake, Lafleur hesitating before a fleeting spark of recognition showed in his eyes. He quietly asked the Cuban, *"Hirán? De Templarios?"*

Casas barely moved his head in the affirmative, then looked down as he raised both arms as if stretching. All this was done subtly, without the others noticing, but when Lafleur saw me watching the curious exchange, he quickly said, "Y'all need food. I'll go and get some bread and ale."

Who, or what, was Hirán? And the Templarios? After he departed, Rork narrowed his eyes at me. "Got a bad feelin' 'bout that one. Don't trust 'im one wee bit."

"That's just because he's a Freemason, Rork, and you think they're all a bunch of heretics. But so far, the man's done well in my book. He saved our lives, my friend. Besides, I didn't see many choices when we got out of the tunnel."

He wasn't convinced. "Could be he's deliverin' us to Marrón to curry favor with that godless bastard. Aye, an' me bloody damned foot's hurtin' like the very Devil himself's got his fangs sunk into it too."

"Right or left?"

"'Tis me right one."

As explained before in this account, Rork's feet do have some inexplicable Gaelic intuition. I always pay attention to and never discount his podiatric divination, for many times those aching feet have been proven correct. On this occasion, I thought him a bit unrealistic. But I had no strength to debate the issue, so I played along. "Hmm, the damned right one, eh? Well, that's a serious sign, indeed, Rork. I'll take care to double my lookout on Lafleur."

A few minutes later, after sharing the delivered loaf of bread and three bottles of stale beer, my people succumbed to their exhaustion. I told them to rest for ten minutes. Seconds later they were asleep. Only Rork, Lafleur, and I stayed alert.

"How'd we get permission to hide here?" I asked Lafleur. "Another Masonic brother?"

He replied, "Yes. Can't stay long here, but I had to get you out of sight for a bit."

Rork piped up. "An' we gotta get out o' these here mucky-lookin' monks' robes, sir. 'Tisn't a priest alive that'll believe us to be monks."

I checked my watch. "I know, Rork. I was counting on the cassocks to aid our escape out of the city. We've missed the start of Mass, and we're running out of time to get over to the cathedral to make the end. Our clothes underneath are filthy too. My uniform's all ripped up, and I stink like a pig."

"So what'll we wear, sir? Gotta be a disguise o' sorts allowin' us lads to mingle a bit. Got anything 'round here that'll do?"

I explained the conversation to our host. "We've got to get to the cathedral and meet someone, Mr. Lafleur. Then we'll be out of your way."

Lafleur thought for a moment and raised a finger, suggesting, "What about circus jesters? It's Saint Michael's Day and there'll be all kinds of people at the celebration. Jesters're needin' spiritual salvation too."

Rork frowned, but I cogitated on the idea a bit. Jesters…It just might work. Moreover, I couldn't think of anything else at the moment. But how to get jester costumes?

"I don't suppose your fellow brother in the circus has access to some jester outfits?"

Lafleur mused, "Oh, I'm thinkin' that'll be no problem. He owns the circus. One for each of y'all, including your newly liberated Cuban friends?"

Rork let me know his opinion with a disgusted harrumph. "Ooh, me don't fancy lookin' like some poofy jester."

"Rork, two days ago you were a *leper,* so this is a step up. Mr. Lafleur, yes—please get us ten jester costumes."

"Better make that nine," interrupted Folger. He gestured to the Cuban lying next to him. "This man is dead."

Mena looked at the small corpse. "At least he got to see the sun and died *free.*"

No one spoke for a moment, then Lafleur shook my hand and said, "I'll have my friend deal with the body. This is Havana in the sickly season. There're dead bodies every day from disease and such. Listen, after I get the jester costumes, I'm fixin' to leave. Remember the address on the card I gave you, Commander: number thirty Empedrado Street. I rent a room there. That's where I'll be if you need me. Good luck to y'all."

34

La Cámara de Minusválidos

Catedral de San Cristofo
Plaza de la Catedral
Havana, Cuba
12:58 p.m., Saturday
29 September 1888

We all felt stupid. Trust in my judgment was dwindling rapidly among the crew, but the other options were plainly worse, so I made everyone wear the circus clothes and act the part of a jester—as much as a bedraggled troop of clandestine fugitives surrounded by a ruthless enemy could.

Mena and I led the way out of the circus encampment. We entered the rear door of the cathedral during the height of the Mass, where we met a severe-faced Spanish priest with a Barcelonese accent. Mena explained we were with the circus from Africa, had been regrettably delayed by the infidel rioters, and wanted to enter the church and quietly stay in one of the small side alcoves, where we would not disturb anyone but still hear the word of Christ's love and know the tranquility of the great cathedral.

It was well acted, but the priest took in our painted faces, floppy hats, oversized shoes, and garish trousers and shirts and slowly shook his head. No, he replied, you will not violate the sanctity of the house of God with such attire, and *most definitely not* on the feast day of Saint Michael. This is when one of those things happens that is frequently explained as a random, serendipitous event.

I prefer to call them not-so-minor miracles.

None other than dear old Leo walked by, well inside the doorway. He gave us a glance but didn't recognize me. I cried out, *"Leo! Es Pedro, tu amigo! Como esta? Necesitamos asistencia!"*

He stopped and turned around, a grin spreading across his face at my tragi-comical appearance. *"Pedro? De los Aficionados? Es verdad?"*

I tried to gloss over his surprise. *"Si, lo mismo. Por favor, Leo, mis amigos quieran que rezar en la catedral en este dia muy especial. Es possible?"*

The priest still stood there, arms folded, viewing Leo quizzically. Evidently, they'd never had jesters ask to pray in the cathedral, particularly rather disheveled ones who knew a senior church administrator. Plus, I'd inadvertently used my friend's alias instead of his real name.

Leo is a quick thinker. He told the priest that he'd known the jesters for many years, that Leo was their joking name for him since he was the size of a lion, that they were devout and sincere Catholics, and that each time the circus came to Havana from Africa he arranged for them to quietly attend church. Not to worry, he assured the priest, the jesters would be in *la cámara de minusválidos*, the chamber for invalids, and no one's sense of propriety would be offended, least of all God's. And then, without waiting for permission, he beckoned us to come inside.

Our Cuban survivors were barely able to move. Getting them past the unsmiling priest and others within the cathedral was the most dangerous part, for they might appear to be drunk, staggering as they were, thus inviting closer attention and negating our charade. All of us solemnly lowered our heads, pious Christians entering in pairs, with Mena, Marco, Folger, and I walking close beside the Cubans, propping them up.

We followed Leo around the rear of the sacristy through a winding passage to the west side of the building. We entered a small alcove where those afflicted with communicable diseases but who still had wealth and influence could be out of sight, but not of hearing, of the Mass.

I could see that Leo urgently wanted to ask how things had gone at the Audiencia. His sad eyes regarded the pitiful additions to our number with open concern and perhaps with some curiosity about which among them were the principal objects of the mission. He said he would return later, after the faithful had begun to depart the cathedral. Wishing us God's peace, he departed to fulfill his administrative duties.

The harmonious chanting and singing, the sweet smell of the incense, and the magnificent intonations of the ending rituals in the Roman Catholic High Mass honoring Saint Michael energized the air in the massive space overhead—our sole connection with the other congregants, for our alcove had no ceiling but that of the cathedral seventy feet above us. We couldn't see the ceremony, but we could most assuredly *feel* it.

I looked to see how our Cuban friends were reacting to this newest facet of the most bizarre day in their lives. They'd gone from tortured death at the hands of cruel barbarians to the beautiful tranquility of one of God's oldest cathedrals on the island of Cuba, all in the space of forty-three minutes. Casas sank to his knees in prayer. The other two leaned against a votive table, their hands outstretched to their Savior on His cross on the wall in front of us, tears flowing down their faces. No matter what came next, they had made it that far, farther than they had ever dared hope back in those dark dungeons of the Audiencia.

Listening to the ancient rites and sacraments unfolding nearby in honor of the saint many called "God's own warrior," I heard the bishop call out his final blessing, *"Ite, missa est."* And then, after he finished intoning the Last Gospel and the beginning verses of the Gospel of John, the bells rang in joy.

Five minutes later, as a thousand worshippers filled the plaza just outside the cathedral, I gave Marco our cassock that was least damaged. Then I sent him out to check on the boat he'd arranged for us. It was to be at the seawall, close by the cathedral, a four-minute walk at the most. Once he returned with a positive report, we would immediately leave the cathedral, make our way through the crowd to the seawall, get the boat under way, and put some distance between us and the city.

I got everyone up and ready to move upon Marco's return. But while attending to Casas, I was stopped by Rork bellowing out an oath that should never be heard in a house of God. Twisting around to see the reason for such blasphemy, my blood turned to ice. At the entry to our refuge stood Colonel Isidro Marrón.

35

Double-Tap

Catedral de San Cristofo
Plaza de la Catedral
Havana, Cuba
1:19 p.m., Saturday
29 September 1888

Marrón wasn't alone. A dozen O.P. troops rushed in past him, their bayoneted rifles aimed at our torsos. The lieutenant in charge nervously pointed his revolver at my face from two feet away.

Marrón stepped forward into our midst, enjoying the moment, drawing it out until finally speaking to me in British English.

"Good day, sir. It has been far too long since our last encounter, and I am delighted to see you again, Commander Wake. I must admit, you certainly provide me with both a professional challenge and some wonderful opportunities for amusement, like right now. Monks, and then circus *jesters?* How do you ever think these things up? I really *must* remember this scene…"

Regarding his other captives with self-satisfaction, he added, "Humor like this is so regrettably rare in our line of work, is it not? Ah, yes, I will be dining out on this story for a long time."

Marrón's eyes returned to their usual hooded aspect as he narrowed his gaze to Casas and the other Cubans, who visibly wilted. Then he addressed me again. "And, of course, I must thank you for finally supplying the absolute evidence I have long needed to arrest and prosecute you as a *yanqui* spy. Oh, the charges are endless. We will start out with murder, assault, kidnapping, theft, and espionage, of course, and then I will consider appending some of the other crimes you have committed. I so greatly appreciate finding you—as they say in your United States—*red-handed.* This will be of substantial assistance in proving *yanqui* treachery to those in Havana and Madrid who are timid and weak in the defense of the empire."

A thin finger wagged at me. "But, I fear that your new friend, Captain-General Don Sabas Marín Gonzalez, will not share my joy for this occasion, Commander. No, no, His Excellency will be most disappointed in your behavior today. He tried to befriend you and refused to authorize your arrest for killing that thug in the barroom—said I had no conclusive proof it was not self-defense. What a naïve notion. His real reason? He has been scared of war with the *norteamericanos* for some time now. He is a weakling who does nothing to defend our empire from the foreigners who covet it. But now even he cannot refuse to do his duty, for I will present evidence he cannot ignore, evidence that others above his station in Madrid will soon learn.

"You may not know, Commander, that the office of Captain-General of Cuba has long possessed extra-judicial authority to impose quick adjudication and punishment on those charged with treason and espionage against the crown of Spain. While that decision will be swift, I think your *personal* penalty, however, will not be so quick. Oh, no, for the chair awaits you, my friend. Remember the chair? You saw it two years ago, but you did not get to truly savor the experience of it. After a few minutes in the chair,

I will enjoy hearing how you managed to get this far in your plan. If your American comrades are smart and cooperate fully, their ends will be mercifully quick and painless."

He looked back at the Cubans. "As for our fellow subjects of the crown, these worms who turned their backs upon His Most Gracious Majesty, well, I think they will be useful for the first time in their lives. My interrogators need constant practice in the subtleties of anatomical reflexes."

My civilian American friends, having never faced a similar situation or met a man like Marrón, were instantly distraught. Pots had seen a bit of legal trouble over the years but nothing as final as this. Red-faced, with sweat rolling off him and trembling hands, he looked as if his heart would fail at any second. Mena was at a loss for words, probably for the first time in his life. Folger just stood there pie-eyed, gaping at the bayonet leveled at his heart. The Cubans, who knew full well what Marrón was going to do to them, went numb and stood there in abject resignation, staring at the floor, silently mouthing their last prayers.

This state of affairs, however, was *not* new for Rork and me. We'd faced comparable fiends in Africa and Asia and the Caribbean—and survived. We'd emerged bloodied and battered and scarred all over—as the Spanish doctor saw—but most definitely alive. Looking at Marrón relishing our position, I wasn't afraid and knew that Rork wasn't either.

Maybe to those reading this account, our reaction seems an impossible display of bravado, but it is true. Please allow me to digress for a moment and explain.

Rork and I have discussed our reaction to these types of apparently life-ending encounters over the years. We have come to the conclusion that the sort of experiences we have endured lend a sense of perspective to our psyches, giving us the certain knowledge that the fight isn't over—and hope isn't lost—until that very last second of our very last breath. This has provided Rork and me a distinct advantage over adversaries who believe they have established total dominion over our bodies and minds. That, naturally, is precisely what Colonel Marrón believed.

While he was gloating over our capture, I studied Isidro Marrón closely. His hands, face, and mannerisms indicated to me that the most feared man in Havana had never been on the receiving end of the kind of physical cruelty he enjoyed dispensing in the dungeon of the Audiencia. Therefore, Marrón was vulnerable. He didn't know that a man with nothing of apparent value left, but still possessing some strength of muscle and mind, is absolutely the most dangerous kind of opponent there is, for he has reached that final threshold of desperation where he is no longer a human but an animal. The inhibitions of societal rules or spiritual taboos or personal fears no longer apply to him. Rork and I had arrived at that threshold, a place we both knew well, but a place Marrón had never yet visited.

I held my hands out from my sides in a gesture of surrender and said what he expected me to say, a ridiculous alibi. "Colonel, I think you're very mistaken here. We were just visiting the circus, where they allowed us to have the fun of being jesters for a while. Then we came here to attend the church service. Don Sabas himself knew I was going to the circus and the Mass. So please tell your men to lower those rifles, before one of them accidentally goes off and someone gets hurt. That will be difficult to explain to Don Sabas."

We hadn't been searched thus far, for the soldiers hadn't approached close enough to us yet. Marrón listened to my comment with open disdain, then tightened his jaw. He ordered his men to examine us for weapons, then bind us. Half the soldiers stacked their rifles against the wall, several paces out of our reach, and moved in to carry out the colonel's orders. The other half raised their muzzles slightly to allow their mates to pass in front of them and accomplish their task.

This was the precise moment Rork and I instinctively knew would be our opportunity. No communication transpired between us, just a natural understanding of the strengths and liabilities of each other and a situational awareness of how they could be applied to unfolding events.

The astute reader may realize that Rork had twelve rounds in his two Colt revolvers, and I had six in my Merwin-Hewlitt revolver. All three of these pistols were stuffed into the tunics of our bizarre costumes. In addition, we had the two shotguns in the nondescript black bag leaned against the wall six feet away. From the way the soldiers approached us, I could tell they naturally thought us unarmed, jesters' costumes seldom being associated with lethal weapons.

There is a multiple-target pistol-shooting technique known as double-tapping. This is where the shooter rapidly fires twice into a target, puts two rounds into the next target, and then repeats the action a last time. Rork and I knew our present positions—about seven feet apart from each other, with the enemy circled around us—were conducive to such a technique. We'd practiced it before at our island on the Gulf coast, calling it a ring shoot, with me shooting clockwise and Rork counterclockwise, the ultimate effect being the elimination of an enemy ringed around us.

By mutual instinct, based upon two decades of working and fighting alongside each other, we both understood I would initiate the maneuver, the Spanish army lieutenant being the primary threat and my first target. Rork, having the advantage of two pistols, could make even more havoc among the enemy soldiers. Marrón was not an initial target since he did not have his pistol drawn. I would deal with him once the immediate threats were eliminated.

A soldier stepped up to me, careful to stay out of the line of fire from the lieutenant's pistol. As he put out a hand toward me, I smiled weakly and pleaded, "No, please don't hurt me..." He huffed in superiority over the sniveling *gringo* and laughed cynically, just as I thought he would.

Most of all, he lowered his estimation of me—a fatal mistake.

I grabbed that extended hand and yanked it toward me, pulling his body across my front just as the lieutenant instinctively fired. The round hit the soldier's head instead of mine, exploding the back of it into a mist as I ducked and drew my Merlin-Hewlitt, then put two rounds into the officer's face. I heard Rork's Colt discharge as I turned to the right and put two more into the next soldier, then another.

Our rounds were fired so fast they became one massively thundering blast, echoing around the cathedral. Thus, in the space of less than seven seconds, Rork and I dispatched eight of the soldiers. The other four O.P. men fired but missed both of us, one round hitting Folger in his left arm and the remainder ricocheting off the ancient coral stone walls.

My companions, not being privy beforehand to the sudden attack, were caught by surprise and stood there completely catatonic as chaos erupted around them. Marrón was far too slow on the draw for my lunge in his direction. Rork and I had expended all of our ammunition, but, of course, we had other weapons in hand. He had his spike, and I, my pistol's frame, which is not called the skull-crusher for nothing.

Leaving the last four soldiers to Rork, I quickly strode the three paces to Marrón as he struggled to get his pistol out of the holster. Swinging my revolver high in the air, I brought the heel of it down with all my might, resulting in a most satisfying thump right in the center of his forehead. He collapsed where he stood.

With Marrón down for the count and Rork and Mena chasing the last soldier along a side passage, I checked Folger's upper left arm and found the wound had not opened his brachial artery or cephalic vein, missing each by no more than two inches. After assuring young Folger that he would live and ordering him to put pressure on the wound to help staunch the bleeding, I then set about to get our Cuban survivors moving toward the door. Time was most surely of the essence. We had to make a run for the boat, no matter what, for already I could hear screaming inside the main cathedral turning into angry shouts. Spanish reinforcements would be bursting in at any moment.

Rork and Mena, shotguns in hand, returned to report that the soldier had escaped.

"Forget it," said I. "Run for the boat!"

That is when our missing man, Marco, suddenly appeared in the doorway, out of breath and astonished at the ghastly scene around him. Not all the Spanish were dead. Several were convulsing and whimpering, and their blood and gore were everywhere, the whole effect making an incongruous scene in a cathedral. Marco didn't say anything at first, then lifelessly reported the results of his reconnaissance.

"There is no boat…"

36

Help for a Brother's Friend

Catedral de San Cristofo
Havana, Cuba
1:45 p.m., Saturday
29 September 1888

I'd had an alternative plan in case the expected boat didn't materialize. Wearing monks' cassocks or usual civilian clothes, we would blend in with the crowds and make our way to the ferry dock at Plaza del Luz, ride the ferry across the bay to Regla, then board a train heading east. But that option was negated by our present ludicrous attire, for there was no way we could blend in anywhere in Havana dressed like outrageous jesters.

While I fumbled my six reserve rounds into my revolver, Rork opened a heavy wooden door in the south wall and departed to scout out a route of egress. He returned seconds later and reported a squad of regular soldiers jumping over and around pews in the main sanctuary, heading for the sacristy at the north end of the cathedral, the general area of our small room. Marco said he'd seen more coming from the military headquarters next door when he'd entered the back door. Pots asked where we should run. Mena suggested we just run anywhere, and do it fast.

I grabbed Casas, slung him over my shoulder, and led the way out of our room and through another. That place had a similar door, which opened into another, far more ornate space, with the opposite walls composed of delicately carved balustrades from floor to a height of twenty feet, allowing the occupants to see and share in the services yet be segregated from the public in the main sanctuary. It was, ironically, the private chapel of the Captain-General of Cuba. His coat of arms was emblazoned on a plaque.

Fortunately, an exceedingly embarrassing and perilous confrontation was avoided, for my "friend" Don Sabas and his wife had already departed the cathedral, his rank allowing them to exit before everyone else after the Mass. Thus, we had no impediments to our flight into the western side of the huge sanctuary space, which was empty of people except for the soldiers searching for us. But they were on the other side, heading the other way. Mena scooped up a Cuban—I still didn't know the other survivors' names—as did Rork. Pots suddenly became a new man and helped poor Folger along, the lad in great pain from his arm wound but refusing to drop his goodie box.

Our departure wasn't fast enough, however, to evade attention of that posse of soldiers, who had now reached the area of the altar at the north end of the sanctuary. They spotted our escape and reversed course, firing several rounds. The reports of their rifles were magnified by the acoustics of the place, making it seem as if a regiment had volleyed. Providentially, that must have startled them and they missed their marks, but it did have the effect of spurring us to even greater velocity. With a thought for cementing the false-flag scenario and for sowing further confusion, I took the opportunity to shout out, *"Viva los anarquistas! Abajo con el Rey!"*

Meanwhile, level-headed as ever, Rork took more definitive action and used Marrón's pistol to fire a few shots back at our pursuers. That dampened their enthusiasm for the chase and gave us a bit of a lead as I ran full speed ahead for seventy-five feet and found myself near a set of huge oak and mahogany doors in the west wall, which were mercifully still open. There being no time to deliberate what should come next, I relied upon instinct and exited the cathedral, tacking immediately to starboard outside and away from the plaza to the south, where there would be a mass of people. Heading north on San Ignacio Street, my troupe of green-clad, bloodied circus entertainers followed right behind me.

I soon recognized my mistake. We were heading straight into the arms of an infantry battalion massing near the circus to retake the cathedral from whatever villains had caused all this carnage in a house of God. Back to our south, I saw frightened bystanders peeking around the cathedral's southwest corner. Presumably, they were telling others behind them, out of my view in the plaza, our location.

Not good. Out of geographic options, I turned west onto nearby Tejadillo Street, which runs perpendicular to San Ignacio. A hundred feet or so on the left I spotted a narrow door set into the wall of a building. It was the sort of nondescript door that opens onto an alley behind it. I pushed it open and, sure enough, found a narrow side alley, no wider than six feet and cluttered with debris, heading to the south, parallel to San Ignacio Street.

Everyone's chest was heaving as we made our way through the alley to, as our luck would have it, a dead end. The pitiable Cubans were reaching the limit of their stamina, even being carried as they were. Everyone else, even Rork, was not doing much better. Pots' fleeting burst of energy had entirely vanished and he knelt down, muttering his unvarnished opinion of Cuba as he retched in the gutter and clutched his chest.

Rork laid his Cuban down and returned to the alley's entrance door, shotgun ready, as I tried to remember where exactly we were and how to get away. Boots, hundreds of them, could be heard charging south down San Ignacio Street. Rork called down the alley from the doorway, "There's a full company of 'em turnin' into this street!"—meaning Tejadillo.

I quickly appraised our surroundings. There were but a few

doors available. I started pulling on knobs. The first two were locked. Mena and Folger started checking, finding none unlocked. I surveyed the walls. The buildings were two and three stories high, without external moldings to climb up. The sound of the soldiers' boots was thunderous now, reverberating off the cathedral and surrounding buildings.

Rork trotted back to us and reported that the soldiers were about to reach the alley door at any second. My people's frightened eyes were locked on me, waiting for my decision, but damned if I hadn't run completely out of ideas.

That was when I heard…whistling? Yes, it was the same tune, *Dixie*, coming from the doorway at the end of the alley, the one I'd just found locked.

Then I heard the voice that went with the tune.

"Well, I see you found it, Commander. Glad to be of help yet again for my brother's friend. Welcome to number thirty Empedrado Street. Smart to come by way of the alley instead of the front. There's a bunch of folks out there that're pretty displeased. Y'all have stirred up quite a storm 'round here."

Jacques Lafleur held open the door and said, "Y'all want an engraved invitation? Get on in here right quick before those soldiers get in the alleyway."

Lafleur and I shoved everyone inside, closing the door just as I heard troops burst into the alley. An officer shouted for them to search it carefully.

"Dang! A bit too close for my choosin', Commander Wake. I swear, y'all're takin' years off my life," said Lafleur, who leaned back against the wall and drew a deep breath. "I need to get everybody outta sight, 'cause those boys are gonna demand to see inside. Follow me."

Lafleur quickly got us situated in a windowless back room and locked the door behind him, explaining, "I have the only key to this room, but still, y'all need to be very quiet. There's other folks in the house, Spanish folks, and they might not cotton to having folks hiding out here. By the way, how'd you know about the alley?"

"I didn't. Just picked the first door to get away from the street," I replied.

"Lucky guess. And lucky it was me and not somebody else in the house who heard the commotion back here." Lafleur surveyed our apparel and changed the topic. "It seems I'll have to be your tailor and haberdasher yet again, Commander. But this time I'll get you something not so flashy. Didn't have much to work with back at the circus."

"Doesn't have to be fancy, Mr. Lafleur. Just simple street clothes will be fine."

"That's what you'll get." He grumbled to himself, "Martí *really* owes me for all this," then pulled me aside and handed me the key, saying, "Remember, keep your folks quiet and the door locked behind me. I'll be right back."

37

Into the Lion's Den

30 Empedrado Street
Havana, Cuba
2:14 p.m., Saturday
29 September 1888

W e soon heard the soldiers pounding on the house's door to the alley. A man's voice, in an Andalusian Spanish accent, answered them and let them inside. The dialogue was muffled by the intervening walls, but the tramping of boots inside the house lasted only a minute before I heard the unknown man wish the soldiers good-bye and good luck. Then there was silence for what seemed a long time.

As we waited for the Huguenot's return, Rork stood there quietly watching me. His face did not reflect admiration. My plan had decomposed completely, and our escape had become an *ad hoc* litany of disasters. And now, surrounded by enemies, we'd become dependent upon a stranger. I ignored my friend's unspoken dissatisfaction and concentrated on how we could get out of our present predicament. A solution was still eluding me when I heard knocking on the door—three slow thumps, followed by two quick thumps.

"One of the main tenets of Freemasonry is to help others less fortunate," Lafleur explained as he entered the room, carrying a huge bundle of clothes. "Y'all fit that description quite nicely right 'bout now. I got these from our pile of brothers' old clothes for the poor. They're hand-me-downs, but they'll do the job. Some kids' clothes for the Cubans, since they're so emaciated. Mr. Pots and Mr. Rork, being big men, were a challenge, but I think I got close 'nuf.

"By the way," he continued in a somber tone. "The most fantastical rumors are spreading in the city about what has happened at the cathedral. The predominant one is that a group of anarchists attacked the church, several soldiers were killed, and a colonel was wounded, but the lunatics got away." He looked at me expectantly.

"The colonel was wounded, you say? Not killed?" I asked, ignoring the anarchist reference and Lafleur's open curiosity.

"Wounded…is what I heard just now from a policeman on Empedrado Street."

Hmm. I'd hit Marrón hard enough to kill a cow.

Rork sputtered, "Anarchists, eh? We're damned lucky to've gotten outta there alive with that lot o' ruffians runnin' around, shootin' any bloody thing an' anyone in their way. Luck o' the sainted Irish, Mr. Lafleur. Aye, that it surely 'twas, thanks be to God."

Lafleur wasn't deceived in the least but said nothing. My people, still shaken from the ordeal, turned their energies to shedding their disheveled joker outfits and donning the new clothes. All of us got the customary light-colored cotton trousers and shirt. Rork and I got jackets, important for us to conceal our pistols. Lafleur disappeared and returned again, this time bearing shoes and socks. The shoes weren't a perfect fit, but no one complained, since the only other option was our jester slippers. To be sure, none of us would blend in at a society ball, but I felt we could mingle fairly well in the streets of Havana.

Now we were rid of our comedic attire and clad in something normal, I had another favor to ask our benefactor. I started with genuinely felt gratitude.

"Mr. Lafleur, thank you so much for all that you've done for us. Martí may owe you for your brotherly help, but each one of *us* owes you his life."

"You are entirely welcome, my friends. Just please live your lives well once y'all get back home. And think kind thoughts about our brotherhood of Freemasons. We're not the evil cult that some make us out to be, are we, Mr. Rork?"

"Aye, that ye ain't."

I replied to Lafleur. "Kind thoughts are an understatement. For my part, you have my personal assurance of assistance to you or any of your Masonic brothers in the future. And now I must be bold enough to request one last thing."

Lafleur's brow tightened. "Allow me to guess: transport out of here."

"How'd you know?"

He looked at my company sprawled about the room. "Because half your men can't walk, so they'll need to ride."

"You're right," I admitted. "We'll need a wagon to get out of the city. Any ideas?"

Lafleur picked up a jester's slipper and regarded it pensively. "Well, maybe I can get a cart or small wagon from the circus."

Rork, who'd been rubbing his stubbled chin, where his beloved goatee was beginning to reappear, seized upon Lafleur's comment. "Now there's a capital idea, sir! Methinks a large circus wagon'd be the very thing for the job—with something big an' dangerous in it, like a bloody great lion. Them soldiers an' coppers won't be searchin' the likes o' *that* real close."

I thought that an excellent notion, but Lafleur was dismissive. "A lion cage wagon, Mr. Rork? Where do you propose to put your people in it?"

Mena answered for him. "Marco and I can drive it and deal with any roadblocks. The rest can hide inside the frame of the undercarriage and on top, among some supply boxes."

Lafleur wasn't convinced. "The circus owner, Cesar Melosa, is a brother and has already helped me—by the way, I have to pay him for these ruined jesters' costumes—but, gentlemen, he certainly won't give us a wagon with his one and only lion."

I countered, "I'll send you the money for the costumes later, Jacques. We're not asking he give us the lion and its wagon—we'll pay to lease it and then see it's returned to him. We'll need the lion only for a while."

I put two one-hundred-dollar gold pieces in his hand, my last large-denomination currency. Naturally, I had no idea of how much it cost to lease a lion but deduced that this was the time to spend the money and dazzle the circus man with a promise of more.

"Offer him this and tell him it's a down payment for your friends to lease the lion and wagon. He'll get the lion and the wagon back tomorrow and another hundred dollars in gold on October tenth."

Lafleur retorted, "The tenth, eh? The twentieth anniversary of the Cuban patriots' *Grito de Yara* declaration of Cuban Independence. Nice touch, Commander. Melosa despises the Spanish and loves money, so I think this'll get his attention just fine. I'll head over to the circus straight away, and with any luck I'll be right back with an agreement."

"One last thing," I said. "We need the wagon right now. Once you get it from Melosa, take it to Cuba Street, halfway between Tejadillo and Empedrado. There's a small lane between the buildings on the east side of the street. Do you know it?"

"Yes, I've seen that."

"We'll meet you there in half an hour. From then onward, we'll no longer be a burden to you, sir."

Lafleur asked, "And just how are *y'all* gettin' to that alley?"

"The hard way: along the roofs."

"Very good, Commander. The route to our roof is via the stairs in the back hallway outside this door. Please take care not to be seen when you leave this room. For the protection of my friends, I don't want them to see any of you."

His *friends*. A synonym for Masonic brothers. "Jacques, is this a Masonic lodge?"

"No. There are no dedicated Masonic lodge buildings in Cuba. Lodges must operate clandestinely. If the government discovers a man to be a Mason, he'll be arrested."

I'd heard that before. "Why?"

"Quite simple, really. The government is afraid of the brotherhood and our spread across Cuba. Colonel Marrón and his ilk, especially. They consider us heretics and antithetical to the Church, the crown, and the feudal way of life that keeps men in the perpetual darkness of mental slavery. We believe in the light of individual knowledge and in usin' that knowledge to walk the straight path of honor and a life of decency. Despotic rulers cannot abide by individual reasoning; they demand mental slavery by their subjects. Therefore, they consider us their mortal enemies."

"Intriguing, to say the least, Jacques. But I'm curious about why you're doing all this. Obviously Martí and you are friends, as well as Masonic brothers. Did you meet at a lodge in New York, where he lives?"

"We've never met. There are layers within layers within our brotherhood. With each layer higher more knowledge is gained, tighter bonds are forged, and more is expected of a man. You do not ascend to that level unless you're ready to assume the duties that go with it. With knowledge comes the obligation to use that knowledge responsibly. Martí and I are within one of those layers, and we have ways of recognizin' each other, even within correspondence. He requested I help you. That was all that was needed."

Lafleur said all this patiently, as a teacher would.

I was curious about something. "And you have Spanish Masons attending your lodges in Cuba? How do you know they aren't spies?"

With the gravitas of a judge, he said, "Yes, there are brothers here in Cuba who are from Spain. In fact, I have brothers here in Havana who are in the Spanish army, who interact with brothers in the Cuban independence movement. You see, the brotherhood transcends nationality and faith. When among our brothers, rank or position outside Freemasonry counts for nothin'. The true character of a man counts for everythin'. You must understand this also: I will do nothin' that will compromise or discomfort those who are Spanish and have professional responsibilities outside of the Masonic craft that require them to be adversaries. As for their bein' spies and usin' what they know from the lodge against us? Nope. Would not happen. There is much you can't know, Peter—may I call you that now?—for you cannot comprehend it. Just take my word that trust—true trust—exists among Masonic brothers, even ones who must be foes outside the lodge."

He pulled a small sheet of paper from a pocket and said, "The lives of many men—some of whom might surprise you—depend on your not bein' seen by anyone when you leave here. Y'all are gonna have to be careful."

A look at his expression told me not to inquire further. "We'll be careful, Jacques."

He handed me the paper. "And I want you to take this. It's a code message in symbols set inside an artistic emblem, requestin' that the reader of it help you. Present it to any man in Cuba you think might be a Freemason."

I examined the paper. On it was a mosaic design, like the latticework in the windows of Arabic palaces I'd seen in Africa, only with squares instead of curves. Some of the lines within the design were slightly more defined. I never would have noticed them if Lafleur hadn't told me there was a message in it. Alerted to look for them, I saw in the defined lines a set of vaguely Hebraic-looking script, but I knew it wasn't Hebrew. I recognized the lines as a code system the U.S. Army used during the war: pigpen cipher. The message was a series of right-angle and squared symbols, some with a dot inside. Each one was a substitute code for a specific letter of the alphabet.

"This is the old army field code. I didn't know Masons use this."

"Who do you think taught it to the U.S. Army? Freemasons have used this for well over a hundred years. It's our simplest code. We have others, but this one is universal."

It had been twenty-three years, but I did manage to remember the substitutes for the first three symbols in the line: an upside down "U," a squared box, and an "L" with a dot inside—H, E, L. The second word's second letter was "H." The third word's fourth letter was "E." Those were the only ones I recalled. I pictured them in my mind and deduced the meaning of the unknown parts.

$$H E L \_$$
$$\_ H \_ \_$$
$$\_ \_ \_ E \_ \_$$

The message was as Lafleur said: *Help this friend.*

He shook my hand. "Now I'll go arrange your transport. You're a good man, Peter, and I wish you well."

After he left, I told Rork to get our men ready. We were going to be moving immediately, by way of the rooftops.

Pots, however, brought to our attention a new problem. His eyes were glistening, his voice full of grief. "My Cuban fella's dead, Peter. He must've been shot at the cathedral, but he never let on. Now I see there's some blood leaking out of his side. Ah, hell, I never even knew his name..."

I didn't have time for emotion or for a dead body. Damn it all. We couldn't leave an escapee's dead body in the building—that would seal Lafleur's doom. "Clean up the blood from the floor and carry him. We'll leave the body somewhere on another roof away from here. Now let's go."

I guided them out the door and down a passageway, searching for the stairs that would take us to the roof. I could hear voices in boisterous conversation emanating from a door as we passed. It was a dialogue about the cathedral gunfight and who was responsible. One of them said the anarchists.

"Recognize that voice?" asked Rork of me as we crept by.

"No, do you?"

"Aye, 'tis yer very own Doctor Cobre. Suppose he's a Freemason?"

"Who knows?"

At the end of the hall, a door led to a back room containing a stairway. On the second floor, I found a scuttle hatch in the overhead, one of those ingenious affairs with the ladder dropping down from a folded position in the hatch. Ascending the ladder—no easy feat while carrying our wounded and debilitated and trying to remain silent—we finally found dazzling sunlight and ovenlike heat on the roof. It was, as I had hoped, connected to the adjacent roofs, a situation with which Rork and I were now quite familiar. Once everyone was up and the ladder hatch below us was secured, all hands were granted a five-minute rest. We fell where we were, not caring that we were baking ourselves lobster-red in the hundred-degree temperature.

Hating to start the exertion again, I made them rise and head across the roofs, keeping below the surrounding bulwarks so that we were relatively hidden from the streets below or observers atop other buildings. Though the rooftops of Havana are lively at night, they are fortunately devoid of people during the height of the day, and so we made it to the roof overlooking our rendezvous safely.

Going down the stairs alone to check for obstacles such as inquisitive inhabitants, I returned to report there were none—everyone was apparently enjoying the daily siesta. We then all descended—a much easier proposition than the reverse—and found our way to a side door that opened onto the lane. After arranging our companion's body to look as if he had fallen dead while running, my demoralized lot and I situated ourselves behind a mound of rubbish and cast-off orange boxes, and waited.

I heard the main occupant of the wagon even before I saw the vehicle. The sound, rising from a grumbling to a sharp roar, caused me to ponder if the lion had been fed well before beginning his journey. I fervently hoped he had.

When the wagon turned into the lane from Cuba Street, I

noted it was well suited for our journey. The thing was one of the ubiquitous, large-wheeled Cuban wagons used for hauling cargo and people. The grossly oversized wheels were necessitated by the abysmal roads through the countryside, which at that time of year were frequently underwater and deeply rutted. The contraption was pulled by two tandems of skinny mules that appeared older than I and less energetic than Pots. The lion, looking more like a moth-eaten rug than a ferocious example of his species, was stretched out in a rusted iron cage that could've come from the Roman Coliseum. It was difficult to believe that the wretched creature in front of me had made such a fierce sound just a moment before.

Our friend Lafleur wasn't driving. Instead, the fellow atop the driver's box with the reins was a decidedly shifty-looking sort, massive in size, with a pair of deep-set, beady eyes. Upon closer examination, I was amazed to realize that the driver was in fact a large woman of middle age, devoid of any apparent feminine charms. She registered my obvious surprise, and her guttural greeting, using worse Spanish grammar than mine, was devoid of any goodwill as well.

"*Usted consigue mi león, usted me consigue también.*"

"What'd she say?" asked Folger, his scared eyes glued to the woman's stubbled chin, against which Rork's resurrecting goatee was distinctly in second place.

"Well, loosely translated, Stephen, the...ah...lady...says that if we get her lion, then we get her too. Apparently she is the beast's owner, and I presume Lafleur made the deal with her."

"*Y donde esta Señor Lafleur?*" I inquired pleasantly, hoping to gain something of a rapport, since our escape from Havana depended on this surly new addition to our number.

"*No sé. No cuido.*"

She didn't know, and she didn't care. It wasn't said with any drama but as a hard-edged fact to the *gringos* in front of her. Her glare was enough to stop a charging buffalo, but I was determined to melt her attitude with basic human courtesy and kindness.

"*Mi nombre es Pedro, y qué es su nombre?*" I asked with a smile, hoping to get an idea of what happened to Lafleur.

"Culebra," she replied without a smile.

How quaint, I thought sarcastically, *that we've managed to place our fate with a woman named "Snake."*

I tried one last time to discover our Masonic friend's whereabouts. *"Y qué paso con Lafleur?"*

Her reply was a short, flat reiteration of her earlier statement: *"No sé."*

So much for gaining a rapport.

My men were watching this while still hiding behind the pile of refuse. All attempts at pleasantness having evaporated, I wearily ordered, "Very well, men, let's get aboard this friggin' thing."

A Scientific Deception

Near Campo Florido, Cuba
5:24 p.m., Saturday
29 September 1888

It was an excruciating and nerve-racking journey. Rork and I ended up hidden among various crates atop the cage at the forward end. The lion, whose name I learned was Ferdinand, was directly beneath us and covered in flies of various colors and sizes. Occasionally he became interested enough in his new companions to stand up and sniff our bottoms, which rested upon the top of the iron cage. That sensation was manifestly unpleasant, causing immense anxiety to Rork and me, who dared not move or speak at any moment, lest we excite the damned brute into more aggressive curiosity.

Mena and Marco were up front, on either side of a noticeably pungent Culebra, who possessed her own contingent of flies. My men sat beside her not by choice but by my order, because I wanted their linguistic skills up front. It was almost humorous, for the two of them looked as afraid of the woman between them as Rork and I were of the lion.

Our poor Cubans—we were down to just Casas and one other—were also carefully hidden atop a box at the after end of the cage and covered by a pile of hay and bundles. Pots and Folger were below, among the underslung cargo boxes. They had the worst of it, lying supine on planks suspended between the forward and after axle ties and frame reaches, being periodically splattered with mud and sometimes perilously close to being drowned when crossing deep puddles. I'd kept close watch on Folger's arm, fearful of infection, but none had set in yet. Though he was in pain, Folger did have limited use of that limb, which was most fortunate for him and for us. He was to have a crucial role very soon.

When we'd first climbed aboard, I explained to Culebra where to drive us—around the south side of Havana Bay to the Calzada Jesus del Monte, the road that connected Havana to Guanabacoa, a town a short distance inland. That meant driving around the fortress at Antares and certainly through several roadblocks set up to catch the anarchist cathedral attackers.

The first blockade was only a few blocks away on Monserrate Street, as fate would have it, near house number five. Traffic was backed up, and it took several fretful minutes for us to get up to the policemen manning the post. Culebra and Ferdinand proved an intimidating pair. She uttered a secret command—it sounded to me like *comida*, which means food—and the lion obliged by literally rising to the occasion, issuing forth a deep growl, and swiping his paw at one of the constables, who had the audacity to peer into the cage for fugitives.

Mena belatedly warned of the danger: *"Ooh... Ten cuidado con el león, por favor, señor."* The policeman didn't appreciate that small bit of humor and glared up at Culebra and her companions on the box seat. They returned a deadpan stare. The sergeant, seeing the line of vehicles and hearing their drivers' shouted complaints, avoided any further escalation when he told Culebra to take her pet and move on.

The second checkpoint was at the outskirts of the city, near Guanabacoa, this one manned by Guardia Civil militia troops under the command of an older lieutenant, who promptly asked Mena for an "*honorario facilitacion*"—a "facilitation fee," otherwise known as a bribe—to travel further on the road. Mena refused. He had no money; none of us did anymore. The lieutenant threatened them with arrest, with one of his men lazily pointing a rifle toward Culebra.

At that point, our dear lady decided to take command of the situation by explaining in very graphic, rapid-fire Spanish that she and her friends didn't have any money for a bribe to a pig; the little boy's rusty, old rifle didn't have enough bullets to stop her when she got really angry; and if that happened, she would take the rifle away and use it to beat the lieutenant's face into mush for her lion to eat, because Ferdinand liked to eat rotted pig meat.

There was stunned silence for a full thirty seconds, during which Rork and I had our shotguns surreptitiously aimed at the now-nervous squad of soldiers and their astonished lieutenant, waiting for one of them to look like he was about to open fire.

Then—thank you, Lord—the lieutenant, having sized up his female adversary, put his hands on his hips and laughed. It was a nervous little chuckle, soon added to by his minions. It ended with him wishing good luck to Mena and Marco, adding that he hoped they would survive the journey with their nightmare of a woman friend.

After that, he waved us through. A hundred yards down the road, we all let out a collective sigh, except for Culebra, whose foul expression and aroma never changed the whole time I was with her.

Three and a half hours after beginning our zoological escape from the city, we were on the pitted road paralleling the railroad track of the Havana Bay Line, which ran from Regla to Matanzas. I remembered the locale from a train trip from Matanzas to Havana seven years earlier. It was the best location I could recollect for what we needed to do.

At my command, Culebra stopped the wagon a mile and a half past the crude rail station at the village of Campo Florido, fifteen arduous miles east of our starting point in Havana. We disembarked, our muscles paralytic and protesting. Our two Cuban companions were still alive, the older one just barely, with Casas' face a mask of grim determination. To the west, near Havana, a ridge of blue-black clouds was spreading and rising ominously across the horizon, blotting out the sun.

I peremptorily announced to Culebra we were taking the coil of rope from the back of the wagon, that it was included in the original price with Lafleur. Contrary to my expectation, she offered no argument as Rork removed the line. Seconds later, Culebra and Ferdinand, pulled by those four sorry-looking mules, left us and headed back down the road. The woman's farewell was the same as her introduction, without any pleasantry or break in that stolid mien. Conveniently for us, it was also without any questions. What she thought of us and might do or say against us, I could not fathom, but seeing that uncaring face, I worried she might seek to double her money with information to our pursuers.

A hundred yards ahead of us, just around a tight bend, lay a simple, wood-framed shack with a palm thatch roof. Used as a cargo depot by the nearby sugar plantation, it fronted a siding next to the main rail line. The plantation's large cane shed was visible half a mile to the north, above the vast sea of green sugarcane that covered the surrounding terrain. Along the other side of the main track rose a row of pine telegraph poles, stretching east toward Matanzas and west toward Havana.

I motioned for Rork and Folger to follow me while the others rested out of sight in the shade of a nearby royal palm grove.

"You still have the pocket set?" I asked my young scientist.

"Yes, sir. Right here." With his good right arm, he pulled out of his battered box of tricks a six-inch-long redwood case, lifted the top off it, and showed me the sounder and strap key set inside. It looked ridiculously simple, like a toy, but I knew it would do the trick.

"Very well. I'll use it since you've got a bad wing."

"Oh, no, sir!" he protested. "I can do it. Just need a little help up the pole, that's all."

Rork offered his opinion. "The lad can read a fist better'n ye. An' that's important, sir. Besides, getting' him aloft'll be easier than findin' a Guinness in Killarny."

I didn't like it, but Rork had a good point. We needed someone who could mimic the telegraph operator's "fist," or personal sending style, at the Matanzas end of the line. I chose a telegraph pole that was partially hidden by a laurel tree and pointed toward it.

"All right, Folger, you win. Rork'll help you up that pole. I want you to tap into the line. Listen to the traffic for fifteen minutes to study the operator's fist at Matanzas and get the form of the messages. Then cut the line to Matanzas and tap into the line going west, toward Havana. Once you've done that, send this message as if it came from the Matanzas operator. Understood?"

"Yes, sir."

I pulled out a torn piece of Hotel Florida stationery and wrote the following communiqué:

A: CUARTEL GUARDIA CIVIL HABANA
DE: ESTACION MATANZAS

—URGENTE—DE UN CONFIDENTE CONFIDENCIAL EN JIBACOA—ASESINOS ANARCISTAS DE LA CATEDRAL VAN A MARIEL PARA BARCO A CAYO HUESO EN DOMINGO— ESE ES TODO NUESTRA INFORMACION
POR TENIENTE
BASLIDA

The English translation was:

TO: HAVANA CIVIL GUARD HEADQUARTERS
FROM: MATANZAS STATION

—URGENT—FROM A CONFIDENTIAL
INFORMANT IN JIBACOA—ANARCHIST
MURDERERS FROM THE CATHEDRAL ARE
GOING TO MARIEL FOR BOAT TO KEY
WEST ON SUNDAY—THAT IS ALL OUR
INFORMATION

PER LIEUTENANT
BASLIDA

The lieutenant's moniker was a tiny bit of poetic justice on my part that I just couldn't resist. It was the name of the crooked Civil Guard lieutenant who'd tried to force us into a bribe.

The reader of this account will recall that Mariel is the port west of Havana to which I sent Rogelio to find the Greek-Cuban fishing captain named Teodorios Piruni. Of course, the reader may understandably question why I would give the Spanish such valuable information. The short answer is that Rogelio was a traitor to his people and to me. His only remaining value was as an unwitting diversion for Spanish searchers. Piruni was a fictitious person. There was no boat waiting for Rogelio at Mariel.

Belleza was also fulfilling a diversionary role that day, riding toward the south by rail to Batabanó. When I failed to show at the central Havana rail station or on the train itself, I guessed she would continue in the hope I'd come on a later train and she could finger me to her Orden Publico bosses for a hefty reward. I guessed that her offer to provide me future intelligence—and, I expected, other more intimate things—was patently false, a desperate ruse to gain time after I'd seen through her society guise.

Meanwhile, things were proceeding well. Rork went up the pole first, using his spike as a climbing pike. Once at the top, he used Culebra's rope to rig a rudimentary bosun's chair and hauled Folger aloft, lashing him to the crosstree so he could do his work securely. They dropped a length of thin wire, which I then lashed to the railroad track as an earth grounding line. Folger attached another wire to the telegraph cable, which was, in the common manner, uninsulated. He leaned close to the sounder in his pocket set, listening for transmissions.

The cool north wind was but a memory. Cuba's normal summer weather had returned, as the line of thunderstorms to the west proved. In the dank heat of the stagnant, late-afternoon air, far from any cooling sea breeze, the rest of us waited, swatted bugs, and soaked our borrowed clothes with sweat. It was a struggle not to agitate the others by repeatedly consulting my watch, for time was not on our side.

At last, Folger called down to me. "Problem, sir."

"What is it?"

"The line's hot and working. All the message traffic is coming out of Havana. It's in European Morse code. My Spanish is basic, but from what I can tell it's mostly alerts about the attackers at the cathedral today with only general descriptions. Calling them anarchists. And no mention of anything at the Audiencia."

That made sense. The Spanish controlled public information in Cuba tightly. They wouldn't want the Cuban people to know about the rescue of Cuban prisoners at the notorious Audiencia, lest others get similar ideas.

"Nothing from the operator at Matanzas, not even an acknowledgment?"

"Only things out of Matanzas are short acknowledgments of the Havana traffic, but not enough for me to get the sender's style. No long messages. My impression is Havana told all stations on the circuit to hold off on nonemergency traffic."

I'd been counting on Folger being able to listen to the Matanzas operator and impersonate his rhythm of sending. It was critical. If a veteran telegraphist in Havana recognized Folger wasn't the usual operator, my notion to use scientific deception to lead the enemy west would actually end up pointing them east, right toward the place where we were headed.

I decided to gamble.

"Send the message anyway. Do it slowly, as if a junior, inexperienced man was called in to the office to send it."

39

Matanzas

Matanzas, Cuba
8:33 p.m., Saturday
29 September 1888

After Rork and Folger finished their work, we all waited in the cane bushes for the next train to come by. Lightning flashed in the sky over Regla, the storm expanding eastward toward us, which I found hopeful. It would provide more cover for our escape's next phase.

This was the first unhurried moment to speak with Casas. I asked him how he'd been caught. Chewing on a sugarcane stalk to gain strength, his voice was stronger, more like that of the man I'd known before. "At my home in July, Peter. I do not know how they knew of my activities, but they said I was engaged in treason. The interrogator asked me about 'Aficionados.' It was not an accusation against me but a question about the word, put in such a general way that I knew he had heard the name but did not know anything else about us. I think it is important he never said 'Aficionados de Ron.'"

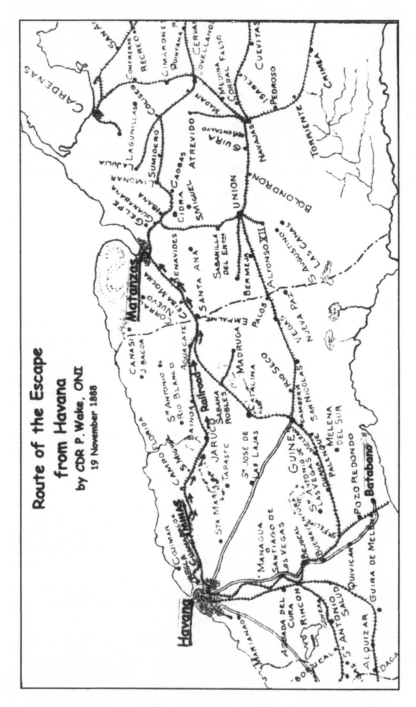

That was disturbing. "Casas, only four men in Cuba knew the name of our group."

"Which means one of us is a traitor, a double spy, working for the Spanish."

Yes, one of them was a spy—Rogelio—but I didn't tell Casas that. Casas, like the others, did not know the others' names. But he was the only Aficionado who knew of my blackmailing Paloma for information, though he didn't know what I was blackmailing him about.

"What happened with Paloma?" I asked.

"He came to the dungeon a couple weeks after me. They treated him far worse. He was dying when you arrived and they shot him."

"Do you know why they arrested him?"

The effort of speaking and thinking was taking its toll on Casas. His breathing became labored, and his words slowed down. "I think corruption originally. Heard rumors…about a contract he had with a foreigner…about something at…the naval yard. He was held in the upper cells at first…with the common criminals. But then, in late August…they put him…down…lower cells… with us."

Casas slumped over, and I put my arm around him. "We'll talk later, my friend. Get some rest now. We'll all need strength tonight."

He teared up. "You came…"

"Of course, I did, my friend. You are one of my men."

He leaned back against a stump and closed his eyes. Sitting in the mud among the cane stalks, bodies around us in various poses of physical collapse, I recalled Commodore Walker giving me my orders in his office at naval headquarters in Washington—so far away, geographically and culturally, from Cuba. Could anyone in Washington really understand this place?

I wanted to go to sleep myself but dared not. We had a long way to go to get out of Cuba, and I had a lot of thinking to do. What contract got Paloma arrested? Who was the foreigner he had it with? And how much did the Spanish really know about Paloma, or the Aficionados de Ron, or about my other contacts in Cuba, including the one I was about to see?

The timetable in the Havana newspaper had indicated a train would pass through Campo Florido around 7:30. I added on another thirty minutes, since Cuban trains were notoriously tardy. I should have added an hour, for that was when the ten freight cars and two passenger carriages finally came into view, pulled by a belching locomotive that slowed to a crawl on the bend. Just then a gust of cool wind leveled the cane stalks, and it started to rain.

I lifted Casas in my arms. Rork took the other Cuban, whose name I discovered to be Andrés and whose anti-government crime was that of being a polemicist and correspondent with the Cuban rebel leaders in New York, José Martí and Estrada Palma. Mena took Folger and Marco took Pots, and we all managed to roughly jump, shove, or stumble aboard the next-to-last freight car, an empty cattle carrier, as it inched along the curve. I cautioned everyone not to sit or lie on the filth-covered deck, since we already were generating enough stench from our exertions and would soon be walking through a city.

We shivered in the rain and wind as the train picked up speed again. Swaying like a boat along the tracks, the rail carriage rushed over narrow streams and through vast cane fields. Here and there were small plots of corn and yucca next to a thatched bohio hut. Occasionally we'd slow for a bend or a rise, but the route was generally level, the track bed solid, and we were able to maintain a good ten knots of speed. There were brief stops at San Miguel, Bainoa, Cieba Mocha, and Benavides, but providentially, no cattle were loaded and our car garnered no attention.

Rork, who I could tell was troubled about something beyond our current local situation, finally nudged me after brooding for some time in the corner.

"What about me ol' friend Leo? By now, Marrón's goons've linked him with the jesters he let into the cathedral. An' what o' Lafleur? Why didn't he come with the lion wagon to see us off?" He lowered his voice for the next question. "One way o' another, methinks we're compromised…"

I'd been dwelling on those same conundrums while waiting for the train. Every obstacle we'd encountered so far had opened up a potential for the enemy to know our getaway plan.

"Yes…it's a real possibility, Rork. Leo couldn't take much interrogation—who could in that dungeon? But at least he's got powerful Jesuit friends, namely Benito Viñes, so maybe that'll help him. As far as Lafleur goes, hell if I know for sure, but my gut tells me he's honest. He had several chances to turn us in but didn't." I added the only positive note I could come up with: "If he got arrested, he's tougher than most, plus he's an American, which might make them go lighter on him. And at the very least, neither Lafleur nor Leo knew where we were heading."

The train came over a small hill, and I saw the city ahead. Behind it was the lead-gray expanse of Matanzas Bay, and on the horizon, below the clouded sky, was the black line of the Straits of Florida.

"Least we're near the sea now," Rork said.

The sun had sunk by the time the train trundled down into Matanzas, slowing to a stop at the central depot on Sebastian Street where it met the Calzada de Tirry, one of the main thoroughfares with a bridge across the San Juan River into the city's three-hundred-year-old original quarter. The rain had stopped, but the sky was still overcast with bulging clouds, meaning more squalls in the offing.

Nonetheless, it was a festival Saturday night. The streets were coming alive with cheerful sounds of the rumba, the Cuban style of music from the docks of Havana and Matanzas with unmistakable African tribal rhythms. The sweet scents of roasting *lechon asado* pork came over us, driving my starved body mad for food, but I dared not even mention it, lest I afflict the others. Instead, I ordered everyone to disembark quickly.

My weary band of fugitives lowered themselves gingerly out of the car and hobbled away from the station yard. In the past I stayed at the Ensor House, a modest but pleasant hotel run by an American exile in Matanzas. Those sunny days were the past, however, for now my status had changed from visitor to escapee.

Holding on to each other carefully, we traversed in furtive fashion the four blocks to a dilapidated section of buildings on the south bank of the river, near the Tirry Bridge. There I had them sit in the dark of a half-filled cane warehouse, the rats scurrying away as they lay back on the bundles. Pulling him aside, I told Rork to keep the men there until my return, for I had to see a man for several items we needed to make good the watery phase of our escape.

Eugenio Galardo, a gentleman of the old school, was the owner of a hardware store on Del Rio Street, just across and up the river. A longtime friend of the independence revolutionary movement, he spoke fluent English because of his business and was one of several people in various locales around Cuba whom I retained annually for a small stipend. These relationships were maintained should I need assistance. Eugenio had last provided me important help in '85, arranging passage out of Matanzas aboard a local fishing boat for some people possessing critical information for me.

Eugenio was at his counter, straightening a display of hammers. As I entered, I realized my appearance was less than reassuring. It had been a very long day. I felt and looked like a haggard old bum, just in from the fields.

Luckily, he was no stranger to adversity and took my unannounced visit and disheveled state in stride. "A great surprise, Peter, but it is good to see you again." He looked me up and down. "I presume you are not staying at Ensor House on this visit."

"No, not this time," I replied. "And I need some immediate help."

A swift glance around was then followed by, "What can I do?"

"I need a revolutionary flag—a big one—and six machetes, like the ones used by *guajiro* cane cutters."

With no more response than a bemused look on his face, he beckoned me to follow him into the back storeroom, where he obtained six new, razor-sharp machetes, each with a hook at the tip for slinging the severed cane stalks. From inside a crate at the bottom of a stack of boxes, he pulled out a flag. He unfolded it reverently and held it up. I'd seen it many times before in the years since the fight against Spanish occupation had begun in 1868: a single white star inside a red triangle, trailed by stripes of white and blue.

These flags are hidden all over Cuba, waiting for the day when they can be displayed without fear of imprisonment or death—the day the island is a free, independent nation. When he handed it to me, my eye caught something I'd not noticed before in my few dealings with him. Eugenio's ring had an odd symbol: stone workers' tools, a compass atop a square, embossed in gold over a dark background.

A refinement to my plan came to me.

"Interesting ring. Are you a Freemason, Eugenio?" I asked.

The hand disappeared in his pocket, emerging seconds later without the ring. "Yes, I am, but I am getting old and forgot I had that ring on in public. A stupid mistake. I can be arrested by the government just for being a member."

"Why wear it at all?"

"It is worn only at private meetings. I always take it off when I leave, but tonight I forgot. I'm glad you saw it and said something, Peter. Someone else might have seen it and reported me. There are Spanish informants on every street."

"Then I'm glad I asked. So how long have you been a Freemason?"

"For thirty years. There are many of us all over Cuba, but especially in Havana and Matanzas. Why do you ask about it?"

"It seems I'm running into a lot of Freemasons these days

who believe strongly in a sovereign Cuba."

He nodded sagely and held up the red triangle part of the flag. "Peter, Freemasonry is not about Cuba or political views; it is about the moral fiber of a man and how he lives his life. But you are correct: There are many of my brother Masons in the movement. In fact, this national independence flag contains symbols that might also seem familiar, for it was designed by a Cuban Freemason patriot, Narciso Lopéz, back in eighteen-fifty."

Intrigued, I pried, "What do the symbols mean?"

"The three blue stripes stand for the three years of apprenticeship in Freemasonry. The five stripes stand for the five years of work in the second level of Freemasonry. The five stripes, plus the triangle and the star, stand for the seven years of work to go from the second level to that of Master Mason. The red triangle symbolizes the Masonic tools, and the three sides stand for equality, fraternity, and liberty."

"And the star?"

"Officially it stands for unity, though, as with many other things, there are secondary meanings that are known only to my brothers in the Craft."

Meanings I would not be privy to, which I understood without complaint. Still, I'd learned quite a lot in the previous two minutes. Though I was the naval intelligence expert about Cuba, Eugenio's explanation reminded me how much more I needed to learn, especially about Cuban Freemasonry.

"Very illuminating, my friend. No wonder the Spanish government hates this flag and your brotherhood so much. You Masons are a huge threat to them, aren't you?"

"Of course. Like this flag, we stand for everything the government seeks to destroy. It is an old struggle, though, for the very first fight for the independence of Cuba was begun back in eighteen-oh-nine by Ramón de la Luz, a well-respected Freemason and lawyer. Why do you ask?"

I took a deep breath. "There was some trouble today in Havana, and a Freemason friend helped get me and my friends out of sight. We need to exit the island tonight, but obviously we can't go openly as passengers. My Masonic friend in Havana gave me this message in case I was in need of any more help while in Cuba."

I handed him Lafleur's mosaic design with the coded message and paused, remembering what Lafleur had told me about Masonic honor—that a Mason would not knowingly commit a crime, much less a serious one. I treaded carefully. "Eugenio, I actually need more than just the flag and the machetes, but I don't want you to violate your Masonic principles." He scrutinized Lafleur's hieroglyphic Pigpen cipher, then looked up at me.

"Do not worry, Peter—I will never violate them. For three years, I have taken your money in exchange for my minor assistance in arranging travel for those who need it. But I will never cross the line that Freemasonry teaches is wrong. Tell me, what more do you need?"

"Four medium-size and one tall-size Orden Publico uniforms, with one of the medium-size uniforms having the insignia for a captain."

Never taking his eyes off mine, he calmly asked, "When?"

"Within the hour."

The obvious deduction that I was planning something very dangerous and very illegal showed on his face as he cleared his throat and glanced at the Pigpen message again. "Ah, ha...so you are *not* going to pose as farm workers and escape on a fishing boat? I was about to warn you not to try that either, for they are stopping all boats on the coast, looking for anarchists trying to escape. Even the fishing boats anchored out in the bay are under close watch."

He noticed my reaction when he mentioned anarchists. "Yes, Peter, the news has traveled from Havana about an attack by anarchists at the cathedral. You now appear here in Matanzas on this night, after such a long absence, and say you were involved in some trouble in Havana. But I am pleased to inform you I hear there is substantial police and military activity to the west of

Havana, around Mariel. Perhaps a distraction from the culprits' real escape route, I think. It is all a curious coincidence, is it not?"

The Spanish were out in force and were searching at Mariel? Excellent—Rogelio's sacrificial role was working. I wondered how my Batabanó ruse with Belleza was unfolding. "Yes, amazing coincidence, Eugenio. But just so you know, the violence in Havana was during a *rescue* of innocent Cubans from Spanish torture cells, not an attack on the Church."

"I see. That would anger some in the Spanish government even more."

"It did. So, the uniforms? They'll enable me to talk our way aboard a vessel without shooting."

His fingers drummed on the shelf he was leaning against. I could see the dilemma being worked out in his mind. Then he announced, "I happen to know the man who supplies the Orden Publico with their uniforms, but the cost of obtaining them from him will not be cheap. Unfortunately, I cannot handle this myself, for I have important obligations this evening. However, my man Segundo will deliver them to you in about an hour. He is a *bozal* I freed many years ago when I bought him, one of my first acts as a Freemason."

A *bozal* was a slave in Cuba who was born in Africa. There weren't many former slaves like that still around in Cuba. Many continued to work for their former masters, or in this case, their emancipators.

"Thank you, my friend. We will be at the old ruined building at Carlos and Comercio Streets, on the river's south bank. Telegraph me the cost later, and I will refund you through our regular payment scheme. It should reach you in December, as usual."

Eugenio put the flag and the machetes in a bundle. "Good luck, Peter, and please try to make your exit without bloodshed. Violence will lead to attention, and certain ones of us in the movement cannot have any attention from the authorities, especially right now. It is a...*delicate*...time."

I revised my estimate of my man on retainer in Matanzas. Not only was he a high-ranking Mason, he was more elevated in the rebel operation than I'd previously thought. My sudden appearance was interfering with both.

"I do not want Segundo involved any further than the delivery. Should you need me in an emergency, my wife and I will be at the concert by José White y Lafitte at the Sauto Theater at the Plaza de Colón."

I thanked him and was about to leave when he grasped my arm and said, "The Spanish are extremely alert, Peter, so please remember the meaning of this city's name."

I acknowledged the warning with a grim nod. Matanzas was the Spanish word for *slaughter*.

40

A Lady Scorned...

Matanzas, Cuba
11 p.m., Saturday
29 September 1888

After my return from Eugenio's store, I sent Rork off on
a reconnaissance mission. An hour later, he reported in.
"Aye, ye were right, sir. The dons've still got a Guardia Costa cutter
usin' the north side o' the main pier, out there at the very end.
But by the looks o' her, this darlin's just built. She's just a wee
thing o' course—only a shallow vessel can lie at that pier. Maybe
eighty feet overall, guessin' a seven-foot draft aft, an' she's sportin'
one o' those new six-pounder quick-firin' Nordenfelt guns on
the foredeck. Crew o' eighteen or twenty, an' all o' 'em, 'cept the
three on the armed quarterdeck watch, just idlin' about topside.
Saw smoke from her pipe, so they've steam up in the boiler, an'
methinks she'll do a good eighteen if the coal's kept comin' an'
the dampers're opened up. Heard a young officer sayin' they'll be
gettin' under way at midnight, bound west to Havana, so that's
got to be our time fer departure." He halted for a second and

added, "An' there's a wee bit o' bad news too. Want it now?"

"Give it to me."

"*Reina Regente*'s lyin' on her hook a quarter mile off the pier, an' there's smoke risin' from one o' her pipes too."

The reader may recall that Lieutenant Commander Julio Boreau was the gunnery officer aboard *Reina Regente*. It now appeared he wasn't going to make our duel the next day in Havana either.

Rork changed the subject and inquired, "So how're we gettin' to that pretty new cutter, sir?"

"Why, Sean Aloysius Rork, I do believe it's time for you to exercise one of those illicit tricks learned in your misspent youth in Wexford."

He caught my drift and flashed a sly grin at his colleagues. "Ooh, methinks a nice big an' strong country wagon'd do nicely! Spotted one o' the devils at a wagonmaker's shop just two streets over an' can have it here in half the time it takes to say it. We usin' the old '*guards an' prisoners*' ploy to get aboard, sir?"

Rork's raillery is infectious and I replied in kind. "Your clairvoyance is absolutely eerie, Rork. Yes, I thought we could use that ruse one last time. Please carry on."

Rork's dishonest skills had not diminished since his boyhood. Ten minutes later, as a gust of cold rain swept through the town, he came clattering up in an outsize wagon normally used to haul sugarcane. Pulled by a brace of three mules, it wasn't a swift or sophisticated vehicle, but it would do.

A dour-faced Mena was playing the toughest role of his acting career: a captain in the Orden Publico. Eugenio's man Segundo had thoughtfully made one of the uniforms a sergeant's, which was worn by Marco. Rork, Folger, and I were outfitted in privates' uniforms. Pots, Casas, and Andrés were our prisoners. The plan was the same as in the dungeon tunnel but with considerably different odds—we'd be faced with five times our number who would see us coming a long way off.

We set off in the rain along Recurso Street and turned north onto the Tirry Bridge to cross the San Juan River into the old city itself. With Mena and Marco on the driver's box and me sitting on a crate directly behind them, we had the "prisoners" in the middle of the wagon bed, guarded by Rork and Folger at the stern. Rork and I had our shotguns and pistols in plain sight. Mena had one of Rork's two Navy Colts, the bosun retaining the other. Each of us had a machete within close reach. None of these weapons was standard issue in any of the colonial armed forces, but I hoped that in the dark their type would remain unnoticed by the Spanish.

We made it past the huddled guards on the bridge, who scarcely cared. At the lantern-lit Plaza de Colon we turned right, rattling alongside the Sauto Theater, heading east across the square toward the Parque Cervantes. Beyond the park lay the city's main pier, protruding like an exclamation point into the inky expanse of Matanzas Bay. Only a quarter mile more for us to go. The shower let up, increasing visibility, and I focused ahead, looking for the cutter, searching for obstacles, willing my senses to warn me of any trouble.

That was when things fell apart—literally.

The hub of the giant starboard forward wheel came completely off the end of the axle, allowing the wheel to undo itself and veer lazily across the plaza. The wagon, robbed of its stability, collapsed into a heap right in front of the first-class entrance to the theater, just as those patrons began to emerge. Our misfortune was multiplying rapidly.

Included in the upper-class assemblage getting a close-up view of our disaster was my man in Matanzas, Eugenio Galardo. Standing with his sour-faced wife hanging on his left arm, he had a magnificently bejeweled lady in yellow satin entwined on his right.

We occupants of the vehicle were thrown to the ground. Temporarily stunned into forgetting their roles, the others instantly looked at me, a private in the Orden Publico, for some sort of brilliant guidance as to what to do next. Having been dashed painfully to the ground myself, I sat there quite astonished at not only our disintegration, but by who Eugenio had on that right arm. It was none other than the redoubtable Sarah Bernhardt. I knew that her engagements in Havana ended Friday evening and that she was heading to Matanzas to board a steamer for Marseille, but I hadn't a clue she was an acquaintance of the ever-more-intriguing Eugenio or would be at the Sauto on Saturday night.

Things were happening fast around me. A squad of police, on guard duty for the theater event, converged on us at a trot. Mena got back in character and called out various orders to everyone in sight. Pots helped Casas and Andrés up, the three of them only just able to move. Marco helped Folger, whose gunshot-wounded arm started bleeding badly again, as Rork began prodding the "prisoners" with his shotgun while covertly surveying our surroundings for threats.

A small measure of good fortune came our way when the bewildered police sergeant acquiesced to one of "Captain" Mena's commands and directed his men to keep bystanders away from the wreckage. The rest of us Orden Publico imposters formed up our captives and moved east for the pier and our target vessel. The remaining quarter mile seemed to be getting longer by the second.

It was too far for our invalids to walk, but at least we were going in the right direction. As soon as we reached the darkness at the edge of the illuminated plaza, one hundred yards away, I was going to order the strong to carry the weak. We'd grit our teeth and march that damned quarter mile.

We were only one hundred yards from the edge of the plaza when another obstacle appeared, in the form of a Spanish swell with epaulettes. The military and naval services of the world are cursed with these pretentious types. They are the ones who seem to disappear when the *incoming* bullets begin buzzing, and all true professional warriors loathe them. Frequently, just before they disappear, these trumped-up idiots in charge issue stupid orders that consign vast numbers of lower ranks to a useless death. And, yes, even my beloved United States Navy has had a few, but I shall refrain from naming them, for some are still in positions of authority.

The particular fool in this instance was part of the upper-class theater crowd, a Spanish colonel with the imperious lisp of an Andalusian accent, a lot of medals, and even more ego. Standing in the midst of mere policemen and militia at a scene of minor disaster, he felt the need to demonstrate to the citizenry his prowess in leadership—an exhibition of a your-tax-dollars-at-work sort of thing that American politicians occasionally display. The colonel stepped forward and began asking detailed questions of "Captain" Mena, who explained that the prisoners were the anarchists from Havana who were to be transported back to that city by the fast Guardia Costa ship at the city's pier.

"A ship!" exclaimed the colonel. "Why a ship, and not by road?"

Mena answered that a ship was a far more secure method than by road, where they might be set at liberty by others of their ilk, who prowled the countryside.

I groaned when Mena said the last part, knowing exactly how that brand of military martinet would take it. The colonel's face darkened, and his coal black eyes took in Mena like a cat looks at a mouse. With the audience hearing the whole thing, he now had the army's reputation to defend from this usurpation of its traditional duty of running all things remotely military on land. He demanded to know why the captain of the Orden Publico, a mere militia group, had defamed the regular professional soldiers of Spain by implying they couldn't securely transport a bunch of bandits just up the road to Havana and needed the Guardia Costa to do it for them.

My friend Mena, not being of a martial background, was caught by surprise. He had no good reply for the colonel, who then sensed his advantage and began to exploit his initial success with orders for all of us to stop immediately and send for a platoon of *real soldiers* to come to the scene and take custody of this tiny gang of peasant scum who had dared attack a defenseless house of God in the heart of the capital of Spain's Ever Faithful Isle. The crowd, predictably, responded to the colonel's manly decisiveness with an ovation and calls of *"Bravo! Viva España!"*

While this ridiculous scene was playing out, I saw that Eugenio recognized Rork and me. The look on his face was anything but amused. Gesturing for his wife to go back inside the theater, he and Miss Bernhardt huddled in conversation for a moment; then she went to follow Mrs. Galardo. Eugenio then made his way to the eastern edge of the onlookers, who had now tripled in number and included common townspeople as well.

I next saw him by the eastern rear corner of the theater. He scratched his left ear, then turned toward adjacent Ayllon Street, where a line of carriages was getting under way to board passengers at the front of the theater. He was looking at the first carriage, a large landau with a red-coated Negro driver, who tipped his hat to Eugenio in return. Then he looked back at me with a quick, questioning look.

Now it should be remembered that I'd never told Eugenio *which* vessel in Matanzas Bay I'd planned on taking over to make good our escape. But it was obvious to me that he, a Cuban conspirator par excellence, had correctly deduced our target to be the government's cutter at the end of the pier. He was offering transport to it. I returned his glance, and the unspoken deal was set.

My watch said 11:45 as I walked up to "Captain" Mena and whispered to him as I passed by. Quick study that he is, Mena then quite smartly saluted the colonel, complete with stamped boot and clicked heels, and announced that he understood the colonel's instructions completely and would await the army's arrival over at the corner of the theater building, out of the way so that the distinguished ladies and gentlemen of Matanzas could go on about their endeavors without further distraction. He culminated the speech with a heartfelt thank you to the colonel for his timely help. The pompous ass fell for it, never knowing he was speaking with the enemy.

His reputation enhanced, the colonel waved a return salute in Mena's direction and strutted off to a waiting carriage, his face shining with the glory of the Spanish army's victory over the local militia rabble they were forced to work with in Cuba.

Mena curtly grunted to me, and we Orden Publico men escorted our prisoners to the dark corner of the park by the Sauto Theater. There was only one vehicle remaining, the driver now missing. But there were two figures beside it in the shadows.

Eugenio introduced me to Miss Bernhardt, who had emerged from the building. Even in the dark she was beautiful, radiating a confidence bordering on arrogance. Her eyes drilled into mine and she declared, "Mr. Wake, my dear friend Eugenio has explained that you and your men need to use my hired carriage for a short journey. Please use it as you wish. I have dismissed the driver and will be taken to my hotel with Señor Galardo and his wife."

I noted that Miss Bernhardt mentioned not a word about my uniform attire, my incongruously non-Hispanic name, or my disheveled companions. What she said next, delivered in a guttural voice devoid of warmth, explained a lot.

"Your face is familiar, Mr. Wake. I believe I saw you during my performance at the Tacón Theater on this last Thursday evening, sitting with His Excellency Don Sabas in the royal box. Despite that, Eugenio insists that you are a true friend of the real Cuba and of liberty everywhere. I am not enamored at all of what the Spanish are doing in Cuba. Several of them in Havana, who have the rank and privilege to know far better, have in fact treated even me quite shabbily on my tour here, confusing my kindness and patience for perceived female weakness. Oh, how wrong these barbarians are—and how much they will regret it. I am a woman of France, the nation of *liberté, fraternité, et égalité.*"

Eugenio had used the same phrase when describing the Masonic triangle within the Cuban flag. I got the strong impression Miss Bernhardt's early years must have been in far different circumstances than her present lifestyle for, as she spoke, her voice became husky, the feminine version of a snarl. It is a tone learned not on the satin sofas of the grand salons of Parisian society but out on the muddy streets at night.

She continued. "I therefore count helping your cause as part of my vengeance upon these arrogant pigs and the oppression they represent. Always remember this, Mr. Wake: A lady scorned never forgets her transgressors, and she always wins in the end."

Then, taking my hand in hers, she softened her tone. "*Bonne chance, mon nouvel ami, avec votre travail pour liberté. Au revoir…*"

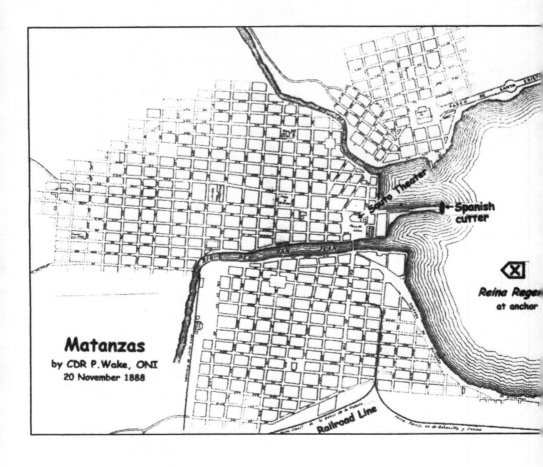

Matanzas
by CDR P. Wake, ONI
20 November 1888

Viva la Bandera de Cuba Libre!

Prisoners do not ride in fancy carriages, so during the final approach to the cutter, "Sergeant" Marco drove Bernhardt's landau, "Captain" Mena rode alone in the rear seat, and the rest of us walked behind, slowly and in pain. The three "prisoners"—Pots, Casas, and Andrés—plodded along, their wrists held together as if handcuffed. Our secondary weapons, the machetes, were in the accoutrement box at the rear of the landau, within close reach. Also in the box was the black bag with Marrón's dossiers, which we had tried to carefully preserve throughout the journey.

There was no guard post at the base of the wharf and none at the end. But even without those impediments, it took several minutes to get to the end of the pier, and we'd cut the timing much too fine. The Guardia Costa cutter was starboard side to the pier, pointed east with a straight run to the center of the bay. She had singled up her moorings and was casting off, with most of the crew on deck handling lines. Smoke streamed from her funnel as the gears engaged.

By the light of a single street lantern, I counted only three of her men—a petty officer and two seamen—armed and then only with standard-issue revolvers. None of the three showed interest in us, being fully occupied with his functions for getting the vessel under way. I doubt if strangers like us would've ever gotten that close to an army or militia post and still been unchallenged. The army knew better, from lessons learned the hard way at the hands of the Cuban *mambises* warriors.

The explanation for this lack of proper security awareness was simple. During twenty years of warfare, the Cuban rebels had never had a naval arm. Neither the Guardia Costa—the Spanish version of our Revenue Cutter Service—nor the Spanish navy had ever been attacked by insurgents. This laxity was what I had been counting on.

The cutter had only her stern spring and a bow line still around the pier bollards. The crew was about to take those aboard when "Sergeant" Marco drove right up to the edge of the pier and called out for them to stop, that his captain with the Orden Publico had urgent orders for the cutter. The cutter's commander, a junior-grade lieutenant, pretended not to hear and looked out over the bow toward the bay. The remaining mooring lines came inboard and a belch of cinders and acrid smoke plumed out of the funnel as the hull moved slowly forward.

Mena sprang up in the landau and pointed at the cutter's captain. Projecting his voice at full stage performance volume, he bellowed through the night in Catalan Spanish: *"In the name of the Captain-General of Cuba, I order you to stop this insubordination immediately and return to this dock!"*

Every man on the cutter's deck swiveled around to see his officer's reaction to this sudden interloper and his stunningly high-handed order. The response was instantaneous. Another cloud of smoke erupted as the cutter lurched to a stop, then gathered sternway and backed alongside the stone facing of the pier.

Meanwhile, during Mena's commanding performance, Rork and I were not inactive. Acting just as high-handed as our Orden Publico captain, we shoved the three "prisoners" into a line and moved them toward the ship. Folger stayed to the rear, his arm in a makeshift sling, and kept a lookout for anyone pursuing from the shore behind us.

The cutter's commander, clearly mystified as to why this thug from the Orden Publico was complicating his life, bounded over to the pier. Seething, he confronted Mena in rapid-fire Spanish with, "You had better have *written* orders from the captain-general."

Just as we'd planned, Mena replied in a highly perturbed fashion of his own, "I have *confidential* orders from the office of the captain-general to any and all officers of the government, which includes even a minor functionary like *you*, to assist us in the transport of these prisoners. They are the notorious anarchists who attacked the cathedral in Havana earlier today. We must get them immediately to the Audiencia in Havana. Your vessel is the fastest and most secure method. Now get us aboard and do not further hinder us or give further insubordination to the captain-general's orders."

Mena stepped down out of the carriage. Rork dutifully leaped to attention and motioned me to walk the prisoners aboard. Tapping his tunic pocket, Mena then turned to the perplexed lieutenant. "I will show you the documents in *private* once we are aboard and steaming to Havana. How long will it take you to get us there at your fastest speed?"

After stammering for a moment, the officer said, "Three hours at most, sir."

At last, I knew we'd made it. Seconds later, we were aboard as the cutter picked up speed and headed out into the black night.

Mena looked questioningly at me—*Is it time?*

It certainly was. I hollered out, *"Viva Cuba Libre!"*

Several things happened at once. Mena put his pistol's muzzle right between the lieutenant's terrified eyes and removed the man's revolver from its holster. In a moment of zeal, Marco forgot his orders and shoved the cutter's young subaltern over the side. Rork punched the armed petty officer, dropping him to the deck like a sack of coal. The other two armed seamen got to see the business end of my shotgun and wisely chose discretion over valor. The Spanish weapons went to Pots, Casas, and Folger. Within thirty seconds we secured the wheelhouse and main deck.

I took the helm while Rork led Mena and Marco below to secure the crew in the engine and boiler rooms. The rest of our number watched over the Spanish prisoners, who sat on the afterdeck with hands on their heads.

I studied *Reina Regente* as we passed her in the dark doing twelve knots. She was anchored in the middle of the harbor, just east of the Bajo del Medio shoal. Her anchor and deck lanterns were lit, her running lights were dark, and a lone figure with a peaked cap stood on the stern watching us. A tendril of gray smoke lifted up from her afterstack, to be blown away astern by the southerly wind. Stars were beginning to emerge through the thinning overcast, lending a tiny bit more light.

The figure walked forward—or was he running?—past the massive stern gun, and I lost him in the darkness around the cruiser's mizzenmast. I decided my imagination was getting the best of me. No alarm had sounded, no shots had been fired, no shouts issued from the city pier. We'd gotten out quietly.

The engine room speaking tube beside me whistled. Rork's disembodied voice emerged. "All's secure below decks, sir. Got four Spaniardos trussed up. Got another one tendin' the boiler, and one tendin' the lubricants an' levers. Mena's doin' the talkin' to the lads an' they thinks we're all Cuban rebels."

"What type of coal do we have?"

"Anthracite, by the luck o' the Irish!"

Good luck, indeed. Anthracite coal from Pennsylvania gives off comparatively little black smoke and is hard to see in the night. Bituminous coal from Europe gives off billows of grayish smoke and is much easier to spot. Most of the coal in Cuba came from the United States. Better to help evade any pursuers.

"Excellent, Rork. We're past the cruiser and all looks good. Increase revolutions for full speed. That'll give us seventeen or eighteen knots. I'm sending Pots and Folger down there to be with Marco and run things. I want you and Mena up here."

The stern squatted down as the screw turned faster. I turned her to port, toward the large hump of land that sheltered Matanzas Bay from the Straits of Florida. Mena arrived and I told him, "Hoist the flag."

As he did so, he shouted, *"Viva la bandera de Cuba Libre!"*

The cutter's lieutenant looked at the flag and turned away. I felt a brief pang of pity for him. He'd lost his ship due to negligence. His career was over.

Doing some calculations regarding the Gulf Stream, I told Rork when he appeared in the wheelhouse, "If the present speed and sea conditions hold, we should be in Key West just after sunrise."

"Aye, that'll do nicely. Right about now, I'd fancy a smoked mullet an' grits an' beer with Kip and the lads at Curry's Saloon on Duval Street!"

Ten seconds later, as I too was imagining a Key West breakfast of mullet and beer, followed by eight hours of sleep in a soft bed, a rude dose of reality interrupted my reverie. A white geyser of water flashed in the darkness two hundred yards ahead of us. In quick succession, four others erupted around the cutter. Five muffled pops sounded right afterward.

I dashed out of the wheelhouse and looked aft. A mile and a half astern, flashes of light winked from the starboard side of *Reina Regente*. Her navigation lamps were lit, and smoke was pouring out of both her stacks, forming a grayish cloud bank against the night sky. European bituminous coal. Another geyser burst on our starboard bow, followed by four others in the same area.

A cheer went up from our prisoners, led by their lieutenant, who seemed to have recovered his morale. A stunned Mena stumbled into the wheelhouse and just stood there, looking aft, muttering a Spanish curse. Rork swore a particularly foul Gaelic oath. Mine was in English.

It appeared that Boreau and I would have our duel after all.

42

The Fastest Bloody
Cruiser in the World!

Matanzas Bay, Cuba
12:25 a.m., Sunday
30 September 1888

I whistled in the speaking tube and yelled to Marco in the engine room, *"Mas velocidad!"*

He explained that they were already doing all they could. He added that Folger, who understood steam mechanics, was keeping an eye on the gauges to make certain the Spanish crew wasn't sabotaging the effort, but the vessel was already at full power.

As Rork went forward to examine our ship's main gun, Mena reported the cruiser's lights appeared to be moving. She was getting under way. I altered course more to port, my plan being to shave the headland as close as I dared in the dark. Fort Sabanilla lay on the point, but I was banking on the artillerymen not having been alerted yet to our escape or being able to see us clearly if they had. Reefs were strewn off the point for some distance. We could make it over them, but I thought they might dissuade *Reina Regente's* captain from taking the same shortcut, thus adding more distance

317

for him in his pursuit. In addition, once we were around the point and out at sea, the intervening high hills would shield us from his view for a while.

Rork came into the wheelhouse, dripping. The bow was plunging into real seas now, and spray was drenching the foredeck and the wheelhouse windows. He informed me the gun was operable and needed a minimum of three men. I told him to take Mena and Casas. I added that he should make sure the prisoners on deck were securely lashed to the stanchions, then get Andrés from the afterdeck and into the wheelhouse with me.

The reader may wonder about the gun. Obviously, fighting it out with a modern, armored cruiser would be suicidal folly. Stealth was our sole defense against *Reina Regente*, but I wanted the gun ready in case other cutters or torpedo boats came after us from nearby Puerto Escondido. The Nordenfelt might be of material use against the likes of them.

Rork and Mena returned with Andrés. More geysers fountained around us. The thump of shrapnel hitting the wheelhouse could be heard above the noise of the engine and seas. One of the side windows cracked into several pieces. A one-inch piece of sizzling shrapnel crossed the wheelhouse and embedded itself in the far bulkhead.

Rork examined it. "Aye, that's them Hontorio twelve-centimeter guns o' hers, so she's still broadside to us. Not bad pieces for Spaniardo-built guns. Takin' their time with it, ain't they, sir? Got the azimuth down pretty good an' should get the range worked out any minute now."

I veered course to starboard for a few seconds, then spun the wheel to bring her hard to port to throw off the Spanish gunners.

I asked Rork, "Characteristics of *Reina Regente*?"

He and I knew more about the Spanish warships in Cuba than anyone else in ONI, having memorized countless reports on the subject over the years, but at that exact moment, damned if I wasn't drawing a blank on the details of our foe.

With a rub of his chin, Rork rattled off the statistics. "Lemme see now. She's a British-built armored cruiser, done up at Clydebank just this last year for the dons. Three hundred thirty feet on deck, five an' a half thousand tons, twenty foot draft, almost five inches o' side armor, hundred fifty-six water-tight compartments, fifty officers an' three hundred fifty men. Main armament is four great big twenty-four-centimeter guns an' six twelve-centimeter guns, along with a bunch o' six-pounder Nordenfelts. Only the main guns can fire forward in the chase, so once she's right behind us they'll use them."

He left out the most important statistic in our present predicament.

"Speed, Rork—what the hell is her speed? It's at least twenty, I know."

"Ooh, that it is, sir. She's the fastest bloody cruiser in the world—*over twenty-two knots!* Helluva ship. Better'n anything *we've* got in poor old Uncle Sam's navy."

"How fast is that on land?" asked Mena, a novice at sea.

"Twenty-six English land miles per hour," I explained. "All right, men. Here's the situation: We can't outrun her or outgun her, but we do have a decent head start and might lose her in the dark. We've got to keep the cinders out of our smoke and all lights extinguished on deck."

The hull slammed down into the trough of a wave, throwing us off our feet. The seas were getting bigger the farther away we got from the lee of the bay's south shore.

"Aye, sir, losin' her's the only way."

As if God was listening and was firmly on the side of the Spanish, a beam of light reached out across the four miles separating us from the cruiser. It swung along the horizon, starting in the east and sweeping west, stopping when it got to us.

Rork pounded the table as the garish light filled the wheelhouse and our prisoners cheered their colleagues again. "Son o' a bitch! Those Limey bastards put one o' them new Edison searchlights on her. The dons must've kept it hidden under canvas. Never saw it when she was at anchor."

The red, white, and blue Cuban flag stood out in the beam of light like an advertisement sign at a saloon. *At least the Spanish will fall for the false flag,* I told myself. Then I realized it also served as an excellent aiming point for the cruiser's main guns. I was about to tell Mena to take it down when everything went dark. The headland at last was interposing itself between us and our pursuer.

I turned the cutter more to port and held the course steady at due west as the seas flattened around us in the lee of the Cuban mainland. On the western horizon ahead of us was a large ship. Obviously a new passenger steamer, ablaze with electric lights, she was traveling westerly at a slow speed. By her profile, I guessed she was the Ward Line passenger steamer expected in Havana on Sunday—the same one Rork and I had told everyone we would leave Cuba aboard. *No use to us now,* I thought, and commenced to surveying the rest of our surroundings.

On our port side, the fifteen-hundred-foot-tall Pan de Matanzas Mountain filled the southern sky. Along the northern horizon spread an eerie void—no stars, no lights, no ships, just the Gulf Stream funneling through the Straits of Florida. Behind us to the east, the cruiser's beam of light searched left and right but couldn't find us, unable to traverse to our present location. No more geysers erupted. We were safe for a little while.

I tried to calculate the ships' relative speeds and, guessing ours to be approximately fifteen knots, came up with an idea, which I shared with my companions. I knew the new Edison searchlights could penetrate the darkness for three miles. It appeared that we'd be near the extreme range of its illumination once the cruiser emerged from the bay. If we could make good speed toward the west, then by the time the cruiser got out to sea and was able to focus its electric beam in our direction, we'd be far enough away to remain concealed in the darkness of the Straits of Florida and run north to the Florida Keys. With a modicum of luck, *Reina Regente*, thinking we were Cuban rebels, would follow our last-known course to the west along the coast toward Havana.

Rork, Casas, and Mena agreed it was the best option available.

I put Mena to work as helmsman and lookout ahead, with Rork keeping his eyes peeled on the sea astern. Casas watched over pitiful Andrés, who could do nothing more than crouch in the corner and stay out of the way, his understanding of English not equal to the conversation, his frailty precluding a more active role.

I decided to use this relatively calm period to see how our cohorts were doing below. I also wanted to inspect the ship and ascertain what assets we had for various contingencies, the particular one in my mind being crippled by gunfire and having to run the cutter ashore and escape overland. We would need food and water and different clothing. First, however, I would check the engine and boiler rooms to see if there was any way to get more speed out of our mechanical beast.

There were two entries to the engine spaces, one from the main deck aft and the other from the wheelhouse. As I descended the ladder in the wheelhouse, I heard a commotion below me. At the same time, Rork pointed to the afterdeck, "Wait, sir—something's amiss back aft!"

At the same time, an agitated Folger struggled one-handed up the ladder, yelling, "Marco aimed a shotgun at me and let the Spanish prisoners go! He's headed up to the main deck. Pots is still down there."

"An' there's that Marco bastard now!" snarled Rork.

On the afterdeck was the shadowy form of Marco, shotgun leveled toward the wheelhouse while behind him the Spanish prisoners from below, now completely unrestrained, were swarming up and out onto the main deck, untying their crewmates and the lieutenant.

As an added punctuation to this disastrous development, from down below I heard the previously steady roar of the boilers and rumble of the pistons promptly diminish and slow to a stop. Marco and the Spanish enginemen had sabotaged our propulsion.

My mind raced as I suddenly understood how *Reina Regente* had been warned. Marco hadn't been overzealous when he'd knocked the officer overboard by the dock: He'd done it to allow the man to warn the Spanish authorities. More evidence became obvious now. Marco had been reluctant on the Prado and inside the Audiencia. He'd departed the cathedral just before Marrón's arrival and returned after we'd been captured, not knowing we'd turned the tables. Until now, I'd never suspected him. Now I wondered what else he'd done.

This wasn't the time to dwell on that. We had to strike before our former prisoners could get organized enough to attack us in the wheelhouse. Marco knew how weak we really were and had probably already conveyed it to the Spanish lieutenant.

I lashed the wheel to hold our course steady and pointed aft, shouting, *"We need to end this friggin' thing right now!"*

Then I went out the portside door and headed toward the stern.

Rork stepped out the wheelhouse's starboard side but quickly ducked back in as Marco fired the shotgun, riddling the spot where Rork was about to step. Seconds later it went off again, shattering the after window and filling the port side of the wheelhouse with lead and glass shards. Mena went out my side and discharged all the rounds in his captured Spanish revolver but failed to hit his target, quite understandable on a rolling deck in the dark. It did result, however, in the enemy hesitating long enough for Rork and me to charge the enemy's position.

By now the reader has no doubt surmised that Rork has more than a mere trace of Gaelic warrior in him, with the extraordinary ability to ignore peril and pain once he gets truly annoyed. Our present trouble became a case in point. With a maniacal growl, he charged aft, methodically working the pump of his Winchester shotgun to spray a hail of lead—a total of forty-one large-caliber buckshot pellets—over the deck where Marco and the Spanish sailors hid behind the cutter's dinghy. That enabled me to gain a position on the port quarter behind our adversaries, thence to get the drop on them, as they say out in the Western states.

Once the lieutenant noticed me about to fire into his men, he shouted for them to jump overboard, promptly leading the way.

With an eagerness they'd probably never shown the lieutenant before, his men obeyed instantly. I let them go. Marco, however, was a bit too slow. When he went overboard, he carried nine lead pellets from my Spencer.

With the main deck cleared, I ordered Mena back to the wheel. Rork followed me down the afterladder to secure the boiler and engine rooms and prevent any counterattack from below. In the boiler room, the boiler stoke ovens were open, showing only scattered lumps of unburned coal. The main steam valves to the engine were closed off, and the relief lines opened. Nothing was getting to the engine pistons. In the engine room itself, the gear lever was disengaged, and the shaft slowly freewheeling. Soon the cutter would be dead in the water.

We found Pots crumpled into a mound by the after-hatchway into the emergency steering room, hand clutching his ailing heart. He grabbed my arm. "Marco's a Spanish spy, Peter. Shoot the sonofabitch."

"Already accomplished, Leonard."

Casas and I did a careful search of the lower deck all the way forward, through the officer's cabins and the galley, into the crew's berthing space and the forepeak. No remaining Spanish were found. Clothes and food were brought up to the wheelhouse. I wanted them instantly available should we have to beach the cutter, which was looking like the only option. Pots and Casas helped each other up to the wheelhouse while I remained below to get the engine working again.

After getting the stoke oven filled and fired, I opened the proper valves to the engine and engaged the clutch to connect the gear that turned the shaft. By the time those exhausting tasks were accomplished, almost twenty minutes had passed. It was with wobbly limbs and a throbbing left hand, again bleeding openly, that I crawled up the ladder into the wheelhouse.

43

A Double-False Flag

Northern coast of Cuba
1:17 a.m., Sunday
30 September 1888

Rork regarded me quizzically upon my return to the wheelhouse. I knew what he was thinking—*Wake looks completely done in*—so I answered before he could ask.

"Just a bit tired, Rork. I'm fine. Got the engine going again, but we'll need some more stoking. Get Mena on that, then spell him in fifteen minutes. What's the situation around us?"

Mena disappeared below as Rork reported, "Cruiser's gone the long way 'round them reefs an' looks about to come out o' the bay, sir. Think we'll have five miles on her, out o' range o' her guns an' that light beam fer now. No other vessels in sight, exceptin' the passenger steamer about two miles or so up ahead. She's doin' maybe ten knots, an' now we're movin' again, we're forereachin' on her quick."

I looked south, toward the jagged coastline silhouetted in the night. We were passing Punta Guano, and the shore had trended

324

south and was a good three miles away. We were doing ten knots and increasing our speed but still had a long way to go. If we ran the cutter ashore and tried to escape overland—a very perilous proposition—we would reach the rocky coast at the same time the cruiser would reach our present position. The gamble that they wouldn't see us was a long shot, indeed.

That passenger steamer was much closer, however, and a dicey scheme chose just that moment to enter my head. I looked aft and saw *Reina Regente*'s navigation lights moving fast as she swung to a westerly course, her search light panning back and forth toward us but still too far away. Doing some fast arithmetic, I reasoned my new scheme would have a better chance of success.

"Rork, I'll take the helm. Get into one of these Spanish sailor's uniforms, then get below. Help Mena stoke the boiler as much as you can before you return topside. I want everyone, including Andrés, in a Guardia Costa sailor uniform as soon as possible and ready for action in five minutes. Mena and I will be in the officers' uniforms. You, of course, will be a bosun."

"Aye! Takin' that steamer, are we? What's yer plan, sir?"

I briefed him, watching his eyes flare when he learned his part. Most men would have winced, but Rork laughed and slapped the chart table. "Ooh, 'tis a capital notion, sir—them Spaniardo bastards'll be madder than hell when they finally figure it out."

With strength born of desperation, everyone went about his tasks and got ready. We soon came along the port side of the steamer, which I saw was the single-funneled *City of Washington*, one of the Ward Line's newer ships. An officer on the steamer's bridge wing leaned out over the railing, examining our unusual flag with great interest.

Mena shouted up to the officer in Cuban-accented English and demanded a Jacob's ladder be put down from the main deck for us to board and inspect, explaining that the cutter belonged to the Guardia Costa of the new and independent Republic of Cuba. Rork reinforced the demand by sighting along the barrel of the Nordenfelt gun, which was aimed squarely at the officer. Right then, the steamer captain appeared on the bridge wing. Visibly perturbed by this latest example of Latin American arrogance, he gruffly ordered his crew to slow the ship and comply with our demand.

Mena and I were the first aboard, followed by our sick and lame colleagues. Once on the main deck, my companions and I assumed the stance—or at least attempted to—of serious maritime revenue men inspecting a potential violator.

Rork was still aboard the cutter, down below in the engine room. Once we disembarked, he engaged the shaft clutch at full speed ahead and then raced topside to securely lash the helm on a course slightly to the south of west. That would take her gradually away from the steamer and eventually onto the rocky coast of Puerto Escondido and the lighthouse at Canasí. There she would lamentably shipwreck with an apparent loss of all life. Having finished those tasks, my friend nimbly stepped off the deck and onto the Jacob's ladder, waving a salute to the now-deserted vessel as she embarked on her final chore for us: to occupy *Reina Regente*'s attention.

Mena and I had reached the bridge by then and were gladdened to see the cutter bounding forward. All of this mayhem was too much for the steamer captain, naturally, who dispensed with the usual niceties extended to revenue officers and demanded, "What the hell is going on here? And just who the hell are you?"

Good questions, both of them, but I couldn't answer immediately, since the captain was surrounded by his officers, all of whom were as displeased as their master. Mena followed our unwritten script and echoed what he'd told the Spanish lieutenant on the cutter. "Captain, my colleague and I must talk to you in private."

This new impudence got even more of a scowl from our host, so Mena upped the ante by appending, "It concerns one of your passengers."

The captain, who had yet to introduce himself, stormed off down the ladder to his cabin just below the bridge deck. Mena and

I followed and were joined by the newly arrived Rork, who looked mighty pleased with himself as he shifted his eyes meaningfully toward the cutter. I noted with pleasure that the cutter had gone ahead of the steamer, moving at a good clip toward Havana, and was now held squarely in a beam of light emanating from the east.

In the confines of the captain's cabin, I shed my Cuban pretense and spoke for the first time since aboard. I was counting on him to be the kind of man we needed.

"Captain, allow me to explain candidly and quickly. I am Commander Peter Wake, an intelligence officer of the United States Navy, and I need to appeal to your patriotism as a fellow American, in command of an American-owned ship, for some assistance."

His jaw gaped open. "So you're not Cuban rebels or the Spanish Guardia Costa?"

I continued. "Neither. It was a double-false flag ploy. Several of the men I just brought aboard are, however, victims of the Spanish regime in Cuba. As master of this ship, you frequent the island and know what the government does in its occupation of Cuba. Our action tonight has been a *ruse de guerre* to escape from that cruiser, for if these men are caught they will suffer a terrible death—and our country will be ensnared in an international embarrassment. You can prevent that."

"What do you want from me?" he asked cautiously.

"Captain, I know you are scheduled to put into Havana tomorrow morning on your regular port call. But I think you should head for Key West instead."

"Oh, really? And, pray tell, why is that?"

Displaying my most sincere face, I explained. "I've detected a disturbing thumping sound coming from your engines, captain. Perhaps a feed water pump is about to overheat and cause considerable damage to your compound condensing engine. Therefore, I would suggest the most prudent thing for you to do is alter course to the north and put in at the nearest American port, where a detailed examination can be done while safely at anchor.

Naturally, that would be Key West."

Before the captain could respond, I waved a hand leisurely, as if the detour would be only a minor inconvenience for him. "Of course, once you've ascertained the pumps are fine, which will be as soon as you reach Key West and we get a boat to shore, you can then steam across to Havana. The stop will cost you only twelve hours at the most, but I can assure you it will gain you several very sincere friendships in our nation's capital—providing all this is kept as quiet as possible."

Admittedly, I'd given the man a lot to take in at almost two o'clock in the morning. The captain, whose name was still unknown to me, uttered, "Well, I'll be a…"

He didn't complete his reply, for out the captain's doorway we saw *Reina Regente* thundering bravely past us, rushing after the distant cutter. At the same time, a far off flash erupted near shore.

I looked at Rork, who woefully wagged his head. "Ooh, lookee there, sir. Them Spanish sailors're careless as a Chinee on opium, always leavin' powder charges lyin' about. Bet one o' 'em just went off accidental-like on that cutter."

"Rork, I thought the plan was for her to run onto the rocks—a shipwreck while escaping ashore."

"Aye, that *was* the plan, sir. But that bloody damned cruiser was gainin' on us a bit too fast—she's as quick as they say—an' they could'a gotten alongside an' seen we wasn't aboard the cutter. Then they'd be addin' two an' two an' comin' up with us boardin' this fine ship. Well, we couldn't have them Spaniardos botherin' the fine American folks here, could we? So me decision was to end it all a bit sooner. An' now the dons'll think we're all deader than hell an' scattered in wee bits across the sea."

After joining us in laughter, the steamer captain made his own decision to improvise. He whistled in a nearby brass speaking tube and called out an order to the officer of the deck.

"Captain to the bridge! Increase revolutions, Mr. Dozier, and lay a course nor'-nor'west to Key West."

The steamer master then went to a side locker and produced a tray containing a large bottle of good, old American bourbon and a set of small glasses.

Pouring a round for all hands, he asked, "As a veteran of the U.S. Navy's Mississippi River Squadron during the war, may I offer a toast, gentlemen? *To the confusion of the enemy!*"

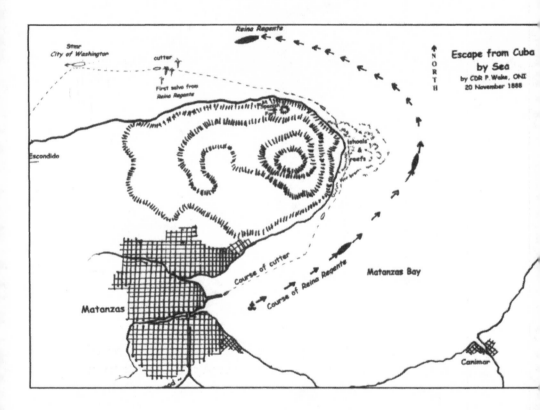

44

Martí

Café Paris
Meyer's Hotel
119 South Street
New York City
Thursday, 20 December 1888

T en weeks after my return to Washington, I journeyed
northward by rail to meet with the man whose long distance
help from New York had proved so critical to my escape from
Cuba.

I was in a positive frame of mind when I entered his fourth
floor office at 120 Front Street in lower Manhattan Island, during
the shadowy, gray hours of a winter evening—quite the opposite
of sultry Havana. It was the first chance I could get to travel to
New York to see my friend and thank him. We had a lot to talk
about over dinner.

With his diminutive frame, protruding ears, thin jaw, delicate
hands, and prematurely receding hair, José Julián Martí didn't look

like a fire-breathing orator of freedom against tyranny. Instead, a stranger could easily dismiss him as just another sickly corporate functionary, no doubt worried about an unresolved deficit in his ledger.

But then you saw those brown eyes watching you. They were set deep in his serious face, above a long nose and prominent moustache. And you'd see them turn as hard and cold as crystal amber, making a chill go down your spine.

Before words were even spoken, you knew this extraordinary man was evaluating *you*, penetrating whatever façade you had erected, deducing your true intent. That leveled gaze let you know he had seen more, done more, and suffered more by the time he was twenty than most men had in their entire lives.

Known for working eighteen hours a day, Martí accomplished such complex duties as being the diplomatic consular official in New York for three Latin American countries, a translator-writer for twenty different Latin American newspapers, and an influential columnist for the *New York Sun* newspaper. These were in addition to his primary commitment—being the intellectual magnet for all the various Cuban organizations which worked for their island's independence from Spain.

Martí was a busy man with no time for ostentatious fools, especially American politicians. He despised the political corruption and racism he saw in New York and around the country, and lamented how it made a mockery of our constitution and national ideal of individual liberty, which he admired greatly. I was hoping that he didn't count me as too close to the American political hacks he so loathed and would welcome me as he had before. He showed me into his modest office and, with those dark eyes twinkling, immediately suggested we head off to dinner. I knew his fondness for good food and of course agreed.

He said he knew a good place to eat, so I followed his lead. We made our way along Front Street to Wall Street, to the teeming wharfs along South Street. Altering course to port and rapidly marching six blocks north—for Martí did not dawdle when walking—we arrived at his choice of restaurants, Café Paris at Meyer's Hotel.

Martí peered at me over his glass of Bordeaux while we started with the steamed mussels, a Café Paris specialty. A true connoisseur of France's cuisine and language, he'd selected the bottle and was savoring the taste as I said, "José, I want to thank you for helping me in Cuba."

"It was my pleasure to be of assistance, Peter. Congratulations on your escape from the clutches of the beast. I understand you extemporaneously used several *ruses de guerre*. You are an innovative fellow, my friend."

I shook my head. "Just desperate ploys on my part. Your Masonic brothers are the real reason we're alive, José. They were crucial to our escape. I hope their identities weren't compromised."

"Thank you for your concern. They are safe. The Masonic brothers of Cuba are noble examples of our worldwide fraternity, and will be a great asset to our new Cuban nation."

A bemused look crossed his face. "By the way, Peter, I think we both have a mutual enemy for life in Colonel Isidro Marrón. I consider it a compliment."

Martí sipped more wine, then tilted his head back slightly for a moment, as if he was studying the ceiling. I knew this expression of his. He was about to say something important.

He swung his gaze back to me. "So, tell me, Peter—did you really *not* know about Marrón's letters when you were sent to Havana?"

Martí, like all good interrogators and raconteurs, waited me out, studying my immediate reaction to his question. I ruminated over his question for a bit. How the hell did Martí know about that letter? And he used the plural: *letters*. I knew of only the one I'd found in Marrón's safe.

I needed to know what Martí knew. "All right, I admit I'm impressed with your knowledge. Just how, and what, do you know about the letters, José?"

His eyes never left mine. "You didn't answer the question,

Peter, so I will assume the answer is yes—you did not know about Marrón's letters when you went to Havana. The answer to your question of how I know about them is uncomplicated. You are aware I have friends at assorted places. When they learn interesting things, they let me know."

He shrugged, a very Cuban gesture far less flamboyant than the French version.

I repeated myself. "Do you actually know any details about the letters?"

He leaned forward and lowered his voice. "There were three identical copies of the letter. You only found the third and final copy in Marrón's office."

"Go on," I urged quietly, while inspecting our fellow diners for signs of Spanish agents. They constantly had Martí under surveillance. I didn't see any obvious candidates.

"The letter was purportedly from a high-ranking Spaniard in the colonial government of Cuba, one Manuel Carlos Ortega y Rioja. This Ortega does not really exist. The letter was addressed to the Spanish envoy extraordinary and minister plenipotentiary to Washington, Don Emilio de Muruaga, who is only too real. It contained a discussion of a fictional secret agreement between the current Spanish Captain-General of Cuba, Don Sabas Marín Gonzalez, and the current administration in Washington. The ostensible purpose of this secret agreement was to lower the U.S. tariffs against Cuban tobacco and sugar molasses for American refining and processing factories, in exchange for some export fees to be paid to administration officials from the Spanish colonial treasury in Havana. This illegal payment was all to begin late last month, right *after* President Cleveland was reelected."

I tried not to react. He was correct on all of it. "What else?"

"Peter, it bears repeating. The letter was completely fake. Don Sabas made no agreement, Señor Ortega does not exist, and Don Emilio never received it. But, all that matters not. Had it been published in the newspapers, it would have been political dynamite in the United States. Quite a clever fellow, our Colonel Marrón."

Martí paused and sampled some of his sautéed filet of cod, which was topped with a sauce of basil-infused *beurre blanc*. After pronouncing it *"très bien"* in a perfect French accent, and enjoying another sip of wine, he continued, his audience of one in rapt attention.

Just a trace of a smile showed under the Cuban's moustache as he said, "Peter, I assume your next question will be: what was the intent of this false document? The answer is simple: to alter the U.S. presidential election. By creating a vociferous animosity among American farmers, who are well-known opponents of lowering the tariffs, the letter would influence other Americans to join the farmers and vote against President Cleveland."

"But that would backfire against the Spanish."

"Yes, exposure of this letter would apparently go against Cuban tobacco and sugar interests, and the many foreign owners on the island as well. It would ensure that President Cleveland would not be reelected, that the Republicans would come into executive power, and the tariff barriers against foreign imports would stay high. Right?"

"Right."

"That is precisely what I thought too, my friend. But we must go beyond the obvious and immediate, for the dark machinations of Marrón are like those of an expert chess player, keeping several moves ahead of his adversary. The colonel wanted to inflame your country's opinion against Spain and ignite the age-old American desire to add Cuba to your flag's constellation of stars—may that *never* happen—thus heating up the political and military animosity between the two nations."

"Do you think Don Sabas was involved with the letter? I can't see him doing that."

"As for your new opera friend, Don Sabas Marín Gonzalez, being involved? No, Peter, I think not. I imagine you know Don Sabas shares Prime Minister Sagasta's conciliatory beliefs toward Cuba. The captain-general is not one of the Spanish warmongers. An increase in military tension would be counter to his position and views."

"But there are others, aren't there? Men who are warmongers . . ."

"Indeed, there are. Heightened tension would certainly assist the agenda of several influential gentlemen in Madrid, and in Havana. They are known to love rattling their verbal sabers, even though they aren't the men who would have to use the real thing in combat. These men include Colonel Marrón's political party colleagues and mentors, the ultra-militant wing of the pro-monarchist party in Spain, who favor keeping Cuba a subservient colony under the Spanish boot at all costs. No autonomy within the empire, no annexation to the United States, and no independence."

It made sense to me, especially within the convoluted world of Spanish politics.

"So let me get this straight, José. The Spanish government, pressured by the militants and the Spanish press, would then tighten the army's screws on Cuba, probably get rid of Don Sabas, and bring America and Spain to the brink of war."

"Exactly, Peter. And now, kindly follow my reasoning to discover Marrón's true objective. By increasing Spanish military forces on the island, they think they can defeat any American invasion threat. Along with that, they would unleash the pro-Spanish *voluntarios* vigilante regiments to counter any Cuban internal threat, just as they did ten years ago. To pay for all this, they will raise the Spanish military and police budgets. This will come through higher taxes for Spanish subjects in Cuba."

"To make the Cubans pay for their own subjugation."

"Correct. The results of the letter becoming public in the United States would lead inevitably to a chain reaction, as in a row of dominoes falling, with the ultimate result being the rise in funding for security. That is Marrón's true objective in all of this. You see, senior commanders traditionally remove a percentage of their unit's funding for their own private purposes, a not so quaint custom I consider embezzlement. Therefore, a considerable rise in Colonel Isidro Marrón's budget means a substantial concomitant elevation of his personal wealth. Yet another demonstration that money is the root of all evil."

"But wait a minute, José. If the United States and Spain went to war over Cuba, it would help your cause. The U.S. might accomplish what the Cuban patriots haven't for twenty years—get Cuba away from Spain. And if the letter made Cleveland lose the election, it would bring the Republicans in, and many of them support Cuban independence. So why didn't you allow the letter go to through?"

"It was a temptation, I assure you. Things are improving for us. The Provisional Executive Commission is consolidating all revolutionary efforts. Generals Gomez and Maceo have indicated they would recognize the commission's authority. However, more needs to be done. Our patriot military forces are not yet ready to resume active large-scale operations. Soon, but not now."

Significant news. A crusty veteran and master strategist, Gomez was Dominican-born and trained in the Spanish army, before he'd converted into a fighter for Cuban freedom. Six years younger than me and a dark-skinned giant, Maceo was a consummate warrior also known for being a cultured gentleman. Wounded two dozen times, he led his Mambises with skill and courage, winning many battles. Spanish troops were terrified of him.

Both men were currently in exile. They'd been wary of Martí, an intellectual who'd never fought in battle. Martí getting them to serve under civilian control was a huge success. But the Cubans still had to get a modern army funded, supplied, and in the field.

Martí cast his eyes down, surveying the tableware. "And, to be candid, my friend, we are not certain at all that your forces, especially your navy, are strong enough to evict the Spanish. Marrón and his political colleagues share that opinion."

Unfortunately, he was correct. The U.S. military had been weakened by lack of funding for twenty years. But things were changing and the navy was finally building proper warships. Another two years and we would be ready.

"Valid point, José. So, back to the letter. What happened to the first two copies?" I asked.

Martí sighed. "I will give Colonel Marrón due credit, for his plot nearly worked. The first letter was mailed in late August to the *New York Times*, where it was assumed to be valid and was about to be published. However, friends of President Cleveland—and there are many here in New York—intervened at the last moment and made sure the letter was never made public."

He went on, "Keeping anything secret in New York is impossible. That is how I knew of it initially—when some other people in New York discovered its existence. I instantly realized Marrón's foul mind was involved in this maliciousness, but had no proof at the time."

"And the second letter?"

"When nothing happened in the U.S. press and there was no resulting political storm against the president, Marrón's second copy was mailed in Havana in late September, just before you arrived there. Fortunately, it never left Cuba. Its intended addressee was the *Washington Star* newspaper, which supports Republicans."

"It never left Havana?"

Martí lifted his glass and watched the blood-red wine swirl around, his right eyebrow lifting ever so slightly. "It is lamentable to admit this, my friend, but the postal service can be very inefficient in Cuba. Somehow, that particular letter became lost in transit."

I continued the logical extension of that information. "And then someone in Washington was alerted about the second letter, so they'd know the *New York Times* letter wasn't the only one. There might be others ready to send to the newspapers."

"How perceptive of you, Peter."

There were some things Martí could not say, but if you knew him, you understood what he meant. *Some other people in New York discovered its existence,* one of whom, I had no doubt, was Charles Anderson Dana, Martí's good friend and owner of the *New York Sun* newspaper. Martí wrote for the *Sun*, and Dana was a staunch supporter of Cuban independence. *The mail can be very inefficient in Cuba*—obviously one of Martí's people in Havana's post office was alerted to watch for any other letters.

"And I took the third copy."

"Yes, indeed you did, Commander. Courtesy of your preemptive actions, Colonel Marrón never got the chance to mail the final copy of his *lettre provocante*, did he? And even better, he is out of action for a while with a severe headache and an impressive scar. Really, Peter—you should have hit him a little harder. It would be so much more satisfying to say Marrón is dead."

It was my turn to shrug. "I tried, but we were a little busy at the time, José."

Reaching for the bottle, he said with a chuckle, "Peter, you are suddenly looking thirsty. Would you like some more of this Bordeaux? I think it is quite good."

He poured the last of the wine as I raised the salient question in my mind, "How exactly did you know I had the third letter? And where I got it? Outside of my small unit, no one knew."

His head bowed slightly. "Oh, I think you know the answer, Peter."

Damn. How stupid of me. It was Casas. He and Andres were in my cabin aboard the *City of Washington* as we steamed to Key West. Rork and I were finally examining the files we'd been lugging around in the black bag, our first chance to assess what I'd purloined from Marrón's safe. I recalled the scene in my mind.

The dossiers were spread out on my bunk, many of them stained and smeared to illegibility during the journey, but some were salvageable. Rork and I studied them as our Cuban *compadres*, their emotions keyed up by the excitement of freedom, drank rum-laced coffee and chatted on with a newfound strength.

Marrón's letter was one of the documents in better condition. It took me a long time to translate its stilted diplomatic Spanish. I assumed it was fraudulent, but instantly understood the repercussions, should it be made public. My anxiety increased as I wondered if the enigmatic Mr. Smith had known of the letter when he specifically ordered me to search Marrón's safe for documents while I was in the dungeons beneath the Audiencia.

Of course he knew. *That's why they sent me inside Cuba,* I realized as I sat on the bunk.

Attracted by my reaction to the letter, Casas must have read it over my shoulder. Then, once he was ashore in Key West and had met with the members of the Instituto San Carlos, the Cuban social club and revolutionary organization on the island, it would've been merely a matter of time before Martí in New York would learn of it.

I remembered Lafleur's flicker of recognition when he and Casas shook hands in the circus wagon, and the odd question he quietly asked Casas—*Hirán, de los Templarios?*

I returned my attention to Martí. "It was Casas. He saw the letter in my cabin on the steamer. He's one of your brother Freemasons, his Masonic name is Hirán. He's with the Templarios, an underground lodge in Havana, like Lafleur's Union Iberica Lodge."

His eyes gave away nothing, which meant I was right. The Masonic labyrinth in Cuba was far more extensive than I'd understood prior to the mission.

"A very interesting and reasonable extrapolation, as I would expect from you, my American naval intelligence friend. Your mind always works on several different levels. You know, with your ability to discern subtle points that shed great light, you would be a good Mason."

"I assume Casas worked for you in Havana. Did you know Casas worked with me?"

Martí hesitated, then answered slowly. "Not from him. I heard from another person he had a *norteamericano* naval officer acquaintance. Logically, it had to be you. After all, Peter, how many U.S. naval officers know Havana like you do?"

"Who told you why I was in Havana?"

"No one did. But I already knew about Marrón's letters and where his office is located, under the Audiencia. Then I got the telegram from you asking for contacts in Havana. I assumed you were there to go after the letters. And yes, I hoped you might rescue my brother Mason, whom you call Casas."

"So you knew more about my mission than I did. And my mission in Havana suited you perfectly, didn't it? You wanted me to get in and out of the dungeon, with your man Casas. That's why you had your people help me. That's how Lafleur knew what I was doing and where I'd be."

"Your real mission for the U.S. government was to save your president's re-election by finding Marrón's letter, Peter—you just didn't know it until afterward. And yes, your efforts in Havana suited us perfectly, for you saved the lives of two of our Cuban patriots, one of whom is our mutual friend. And, in addition, you managed to sow confusion and doubt among the Spanish while showing our flag and spreading our words. The Cuban public will never know what you did for them. But I know—and will never forget it."

"Well, I suppose we all came out ahead, except for Grover Cleveland."

"Yes, ironic, isn't it, Peter? Even though Marrón's final poisonous letter was thwarted by your perilous assignment, President Cleveland still lost the election because of *another* letter. A letter from a person using an alias, addressed to a real foreign diplomat, the reply to which enraged Irish-American voters. What an odd country you have here, Peter."

He was right. Cleveland had lost, and the mysterious Mr. Smith would soon be out of a job. Martí spoke of the reply of Lord Lionel Sackville, British envoy to the U.S., to a letter from a former Briton apparently named Murchison living in California. Murchison had asked Sackville for his opinion in the upcoming presidential election. Should he vote for Republican Harrison or

Democrat Cleveland? Sackville foolishly responded, saying that President Cleveland was pro-British.

It turned out the instigator was not named Murchison, but George Osgoodby, a Republican farmer furious over Cleveland's attempts to lower tariffs on foreign agricultural goods. Osgoodby, ex-editor of the *Pomona Register*, then got his friend Harrison Gray Otis, Republican publisher of the *Los Angeles Times*, to print Sackville's reply in late October, two weeks after I'd returned from Cuba, and just before voting day. The controversy immediately ignited, with no time for the Cleveland administration to effectively refute it.

Newspapers around the country took up the story. The Irish vote, always anti-British, swung to Harrison. Though Cleveland narrowly won the most popular votes, he got fewer electoral votes and thus lost the election, all due to the infamous Murchison letter.

Martí's face lost its grim aspect as he offered, "You know, Peter, lies are a peculiar aspect of human behavior, aren't they? As long as they aren't exposed, they have great strength. They can bring down an elected government, delude an ignorant population, or advance an evil idea. But on the other hand, there are times for another type of lies, legitimate *ruses de guerre*. They can help free the oppressed, save lives, and weaken tyrants."

He smiled and raised his cognac. "A toast then—to honorable lies, rendered by honorable men. And may *our* honorable lies always be successful against the kind of evil we face in Cuba."

I drank to the toast and then said, "José, all this conspiracy and philosophy talk has worn me out. I'm heading to my hotel when I finish this last glass."

Martí routinely stayed up late at night. "But it is still early."

"I know. I'm dog tired, *amigo*, and have to get up early in the morn and board a train for San Francisco. Been assigned to the Pacific Squadron for a couple of years."

I couldn't tell him the whole story. In fact, I was going on a secret ONI mission to Samoa, where war was brewing between

America and Germany. Martí knew there was more to it, but he didn't ask. Instead, he nodded pleasantly and said, "Then I insist we must make our last drink our best drink."

He then grew serious. "Good luck in the Pacific, Peter. Please return alive. Cuba needs friends like you. And remember this: I have brothers everywhere, even there. Get word to me if you need help."

When we parted ways fifteen minutes later, neither of us could have imagined the circumstances surrounding how and when we would meet again several years later—the fateful night when Spanish agents would poison José Martí in Tampa, Florida.

Another story, for another time.

Lt. Sean Wake, U.S.N.
U.S. Naval Station
San Francisco, California
26 June 1896

To My Dear Son,
For years you have heard the rumors circulating about what I did in Havana in the autumn of 1888. Now you know the truth of what happened, but I imagine you wonder what happened to some of my acquaintances afterward.

Regrettably, Colonel Marrón is still alive. He rarely appears in public due to an ugly scar that has disfigured his face. Rogelio disappeared in Mariel. Belleza's role as Havana society dame ended shortly after my departure from the island. The last I heard, she was back working the streets of Santiago. By calling in some old *quid pro quos*, I was able to help Lafleur achieve his dream assignment, *chargé d'affaires* at our embassy in Paris. Casas and Andrés have recovered their health and work for the Cuban cause in New York. Eugenio died from a heart attack in 1892. His Masonic brothers held a funeral service of their own. My dear friend Martí died in battle on May 19th of last year, fighting for his people's freedom on the island he loved so much.

Although I am not a Freemason, I am honored to be known as a friend of their universal fraternity. They are the kind of men who can be counted on when all others turn fainthearted.

Cuba, that island that has haunted and entranced me for so long, has become the political focus of our time. I have no doubt war with Spain is coming soon, and you and I will both be in it. We will face situations we've never experienced or anticipated. When that time comes, always remember that honor is the best guide for what we should do and the best shield for what we have done, as we serve this country.

With unceasing affection and respect from your father,
Peter Wake

A Final Word with My Readers

I am not a Freemason. However, like Peter Wake (and Abraham Lincoln before him), I feel greatly honored to be considered a "friend" of their fraternity. The entire role of Freemasonry in the thirty-year struggle for Cuban independence is a fascinating and largely unknown story, one far too complicated for the limited space of this novel. All of the major Cuban leaders in the revolutionary movement, including the two to whom this book is dedicated, were Freemasons.

But their work didn't end with independence. Throughout the turbulent history of post-1898 Cuba, Freemasons have provided a steady and compassionate hand to their fellow islanders, both Masonic and non-Masonic. Usually these efforts were accomplished without public acknowledgment or acclaim. None was needed, for that is the Masonic way of life.

Freemasonry in Latin America is a serious personal commitment for a man. Following the path is not easy, nor is it intended or expected to be. This is even truer for the twenty-nine thousand Freemasons of Cuba today, who have proven themselves the true heirs of Martí and Maceo. And so, amidst all of our twenty-first-century uncertainty, I am confident of this: Freemasons will always be one of the best parts of Cuba's wonderful culture, quietly doing the right things for the right reasons, to the benefit of their country and their people.

Onward and upward for them all…

Robert N. Macomber

Endnotes

Chapter One—A Matter of Naval Honor

The captain-general's palace today is a museum, one of the finest in the world.

King Alfonso XIII was born after his father died of tuberculosis. He took the throne in 1902 at the age of sixteen. His fourth son was the father of the current king of Spain. Alfonso XIII died in Rome in 1941.

Chapter Three—Naval Intelligence

For more about Wake's ordeal with Marrón and Boreau in 1886, read *The Darkest Shade of Honor*.

For more about Wake's coercion of Paloma into an informant, read *Honor Bound*.

Hutton and Nicolas were some of the foremost saber fencers of their time and are still respected in that field. Hutton literally wrote the book on it: *Cold Steel: The Art of Fencing with the Saber*.

Wake met Roosevelt in 1886 and worked for him in the late

1890s and early 1900s. They stayed friends for life.

Chapter Six—Hotel Florida

Hotel Florida still exists and is a wonderful place to stay in Havana. Visit a great website about it: www.hotelfloridacuba.com.

Chapter Nine—Mobilization

By 1888, Americans were wielding enormous power over the sugar industry in Cuba and owned more than half of the mills.

The old monastery still exists and is today a home for the elderly. For the last several years, the Cuban tourist development office in Havana has been renovating Viñes' observatory and office on the top floor.

In the 1880s, the anarchist movement grew all over the world. Many of the anarchists in Cuba came from Spain and by 1888 were becoming well organized.

Chapter Ten—Distinguished Visitors

Ramon O. Williams was vice consul from 1874 to 1884 and consul-general from 1884 to 1896. He had the reputation as one of our ablest diplomats to ever serve in Cuba and was certainly the one most connected to the Cuban people and culture. He died in 1913.

Don Sabas Marín Gonzalez served as captain-general from July 1887 to March 1889 and again in 1896, just before the notorious Weyler.

Chapter Eleven—Imported Talent

Hotel Inglaterra is the oldest continuously operating hotel in Cuba and is one of my favorites in Havana. The hotel's Café Louvre is where José Martí delivered his famous speech for independence at age sixteen, and its patio still has the best musicians on the Prado. I recommend staying in the corner room of General Antonio Maceo. Visit www.hotelinglaterracuba.com

The very upscale and beautifully restored Hotel Isabella is also still in operation. Visit www.hotelisabella.com

Obispo Street is still the main shopping thoroughfare of Old Havana, though it has lost much of the elegance of the 1880s.

Chapter Thirteen—The Ever-Faithful Isle

Bishop Santander y Frutos served in Havana from 1887 to 1890.

Chapter Fourteen—A Riddle Solved

Barrio Chino still exists, with some good restaurants on Dragones Street.

Today there is a memorial at the wall where the medical students were executed in 1871.

In 1888, the Union Iberica Lodge met clandestinely in Barrio Chino, its members using aliases. Many were, indeed, Spaniards in the government and army, and many others were Cubans, the precepts of Freemasonry allowing them all to meet in peace within the lodge.

Cánovas served as Spanish prime minister six times during his career, frequently alternating terms of office with his political opponent, Sagasta. Cánovas ended up being assassinated by an Italian anarchist in September 1897.

The dove of the Huguenot symbol appears upside down because it is flying down from heaven to earth, bearing peace.

The Cathedral of Havana still conducts services and is open to the public throughout the day. It is well worth a visit.

Chapter Fifteen—Exhaustion

The location of the old Havana United Railways station is now the Capitolio, a slightly smaller replica of the U.S. Capitol, erected at enormous cost in the 1920s. Today, the central rail station of Havana is where the old Naval Arsenal (navy base) was in Wake's time.

Castillo de Farnes is today a very nice restaurant, which I recommend. The paella is quite good and reasonably priced. During his college days, Fidel Castro lived in an apartment over the restaurant, and after he took charge of Cuba in 1959, it was one of his favorite dining places. Just three doors up Monserrate Street is Hemingway's famous haunt, the Floridita Bar, which I don't recommend. The drinks are outrageously overpriced, and it's jammed with tourists. Hemingway would hate it now.

The West Indian goatsucker nighthawk does indeed have a unique call, but I think Rork just likes the name.

Chapter Sixteen—The Bigamist

The sprawling Cabañas Fortress (Fortaleza de San Carlos de la Cabaña) has an infamous history and is located on the eastern shore of the entrance channel, across from Old Havana and just inland from the Morro Fortress. From 1868 to 1898, the Spanish executed many Cuban patriots at what was known as the Laurel Ditch, near a laurel tree inside the walls of Cabañas. It is still a Cuban military installation, but parts are open to the public.

The iconic Morro Fortress (Castillo de los Tres Santos Reyes Magnos del Morro) at the mouth of the harbor entrance is quite impressive and open to the public.

Punta Fortress (Castillo de San Salvador de la Punta) is one of the oldest forts in Havana and has a maritime museum inside.

Chapter Seventeen—The Carrot and the Stick

The trenches Wake referred to were two complex systems of forts and trenches right across (north-south) the width of Cuba. Built by the Spanish army, one was in eastern Cuba, the other at Mariel in the west. Both partitioned the island so that Cuban revolutionary forces could not traverse the length of the island. Revolutionaries ended up conquering them in 1896 and 1897, however, and invading the western part of Cuba. Mariel is the port from which hundreds of thousands of Cubans desperately fled to freedom in 1980.

The Mambises were greatly underestimated by the Spanish generals at first, but their exploits quickly became the stuff of legend for Cubans and of abject terror for Spanish conscript soldiers.

Chapter Eighteen—Irish Suspicions

The Tacon Theater, now the Gran Teatro de Havana, still holds performances and is still magnificent. Its present Neo-Baroque palatial appearance is the result of enhancements done in the early twentieth century. When Wake was there, the exterior had a simpler design.

Sarah Bernhardt (1844–1923), the female superstar of the late 1800s, performed in Havana and Matanzas several times but didn't like the audiences there. This intriguing lady was known for her sometimes bizarre personal habits, which included periodically sleeping in a coffin. Her marriage to the morphine-addicted Greek actor Ambroise Aristide Damala ended with his death in 1889. Despite losing a leg to gangrene in 1915, she performed right to the end of her life in 1923. She and Martí met in New York in the 1880s.

La Tosca was created by Victorien Sardou with Sarah Bernhardt in mind. She performed it from the opening night in Paris on November 24, 1887, until the early years of the twentieth century. Other actresses who performed the leading role include Fanny Davenport. In 1900, Giacomo Puccini wrote an Italian opera adaptation, which is still popular.

Chapter Twenty—Façades and Candor

The Pension Building in Washington, D.C., is open to the public and is worth a visit. Michelangelo's friend was Cardinal Alessandro Farnese, who became Pope Paul III in 1534.

Chapter Twenty-one—*Le Croix Huguenot*

Charleston has been home to Huguenots since 1687. Built in

1844, the restored French Huguenot church at 136 Church Street still has regular services, including an annual one that celebrates spring and is conducted entirely in French.

Chapter Twenty-two—*Nom de Combat*

The pro-Spanish colonial militia regiments of Cuba (*voluntarios*) engaged in some of the uglier incidents of the long fight for independence and were similar to the pro-British American colonial regiments that fought against American revolutionaries from 1776 to 1781.

Edward Atkins owned many mills in Cuba and had great influence in Washington.

Henry Havermeyer's corporate conglomeration in the 1880s was the beginning of the huge sugar syndicates that controlled Cuba's future in the first half of the twentieth century.

Chapter Twenty-six—*Parque Reina Isabella*

This park is now called Central Park, and a statue of José Martí has replaced the statue of Queen Isabella II. It is a wonderful place to watch people, especially on Friday nights when they argue about baseball.

Chapter Twenty-seven—Anarchy

The Spanish Audiencia is no longer standing, except the small portion of it where Martí was imprisoned, which is now a shrine that's open to the public. There are rumors that some of the original tunnels still exist, but I cannot confirm them.

Billroth's mixture was used for decades in the 1800s as anesthesia, especially in Europe.

Chapter Twenty-eight—Descent into Hell

The Orden Publico units were Spanish colonial police militia.

By 1888, anarchists had spread their terror across the western world and were quite active in Havana.

Chapter Thirty-three—Lost Causes

The Spanish army engineers' barracks were removed in 1902 for construction of the main street that traverses the area, the famous Malecon. It was built by the American occupation government.

Chapter Thirty-seven—Into the Lion's Den

As in other Latin American countries, Freemasonry in Cuba has always been a serious commitment. In the 1880s, there were about eight thousand Cuban Freemasons, which included nearly all of the great Cuban patriot leaders. There are twenty-nine thousand Masons in Cuba today, forming the second largest organization on the island.

The *Grito de Yara* Declaration of Independence by Manuel Céspedes on October 10, 1868, marked the beginning of a thirty-year struggle for Cuba's sovereignty from Spain.

Chapter Thirty-eight—A Scientific Deception

The rail line to Matanzas still operates, but the schedule is very unreliable. The famous Hershey plantation railroad was built in the early 1900s and is a short tourist line today.

Chapter Thirty-nine—Matanzas

The Ensor House was a well-known, American-owned hotel in Matanzas for decades.

Sadly, the Masonic origins and meanings of the flag of Cuba, as well as the relationship between Freemasonry and the Cuban fight for independence, are not well known by Cubans on the island today. It is a story that should be told.

The Sauto Theater, one of the most famous venues in Cuba, still operates.

Chapter Forty-two—The Fastest Bloody Cruiser in the World!

Reina Regente was indeed a formidable warship. She served in the Spanish navy all the way up to the Spanish-American War, during which she was destroyed at the Battle of Santiago.

The Ward Line served ports in Cuba until the 1950s. In the 1880s, it was the primary link between New York and Havana.

Chapter Forty-three—A Double-False Flag

The *City of Washington* served on the Cuban route from 1887 to 1908. In 1898, while anchored near the U.S.S. *Maine*, she was damaged by the explosion aboard the warship, but her crew still saved nearly one hundred sailors' lives. During the ensuing war, she transported troops. In 1917, she wrecked at Elbow Reef in the Florida Keys and is a dive site today.

Chapter Forty-four—Martí

The *New York Sun* (1833–1950) was one of the country's most influential papers. Journalism's famous guideline is attributed to John B. Bogart (1873–1890), the paper's city editor: "When a dog bites a man, that is not news, because it happens so often. But if a man bites a dog, that is news."

Martí worked out of 120 Front Street throughout the 1880s, and it became the well-known center for Cuban revolutionary efforts in the U.S.

Café Paris still exists at that location, but the hotel does not.

Protective tariffs on foreign imports were a major issue in the 1888 presidential election. Republicans wanted them; Democrats didn't.

Charles Anderson Dana (1819–1897) had many connections in government and exerted major political influence through the *Sun*. He was one of Martí's best friends in the U.S.

The Murchison letter to Sackville is well documented and many historians believe it greatly influenced the election.

What started as the Provisional Executive Commission in New York later became widely known as the Cuban Junta. Martí did end up getting Gomez and Maceo on his side in the late 1880s and by 1892 had unified the various Cuban patriot groups in exile under his leadership. He also managed to keep the revolutionaries focused on gathering military, financial, and political strength until they were ready to take on the Spanish in large-scale combat, which began in early 1895.

Spanish agents, who operated throughout the United States, poisoned Martí in Tampa, Florida, in 1892, but he survived.

Acknowledgments

Each novel in the Honor Series is the culmination of three main phases of work: academic research, "eyeball recon" (research on location in the places I write about), and the writing process. I am quite fortunate to have a network of talented people around the world who help me. I call them my Subject Matter Advanced Resource Team (SMART) and am profoundly grateful to them.

Academic Research

It's difficult to find books in English about José Martí. Listed here are some I used to illuminate the man, his work, and his times.

Liberty: The Story of Cuba by Horacio S. Rubens

José Martí, Epic Chronicler of the United States in the Eighties by Manuel Pedro Gonzaléz

Martí, Anti-Imperialist by Emilio Roig de Leuchsenring

José Martí, Cuban Patriot by Richard Butler Gray

Cuba, or The Pursuit of Freedom by Hugh Thomas

José Martí in the United States: The Florida Experience by Louis A. Pérez

Martí, Apostle of Freedom, an outstanding biography by Jorge Mañach

Havana in the 1880s was a swirling nexus of influences. The following works helped me understand the city and its culture during that time.

Bacardi and the Long Fight for Cuba by Tom Gjelten

Fighting Slavery in the Caribbean—The Life and Times of a British Family in 19th Century Havana, Picturesque Cuba and Our Navy by Luis Martínez-Fernández

Due South by Maturin M. Ballou

Diary of My Trip to America and Havana by John Mark

Insurgent Cuba: Race, Nation, and Revolution, 1868–1898 by Ada Ferrer

History of Cuba by Professor José Canton Navarro

Colonial Havana, A Fortress of the Americas by José Manuel Fernández Núñez

Santiago Before the War by Caroline L. Wallace

Cuba Between Empires: 1878–1902 and Slaves, Sugar, and Colonial Society: Travel Accounts of Cuba 1801–1899 by Louis A. Pérez

In addition, Kiko Villalon, Mario Cano, and Chaz Mena, all devoted sons of Cuba, helped me understand the island's captivating history and culture.

Eyeball Recon

Charles Johnson of the Southwest Florida Fencing Academy (www.swfloridafencing.org) was my saber coach. He taught me how to fight with a saber, researched saber fencing in the 1880s, and took time to review that portion of my text. Charles and I actually duplicated Wake's fight against Boreau several times. The experience was fascinating, exhausting, and invaluable. Captain Alfred Hutton's 1889 book, *Cold Steel: The Art of Fencing with the Saber*, was also important in understanding fencing at that time.

Ted Connally and his brother Masons at the Tropical Lodge in Fort Myers, Florida, were crucial to my understanding the pivotal role of Freemasonry in world history and providing the introduction to Cuban Freemasonry today. They are very impressive.

In Havana, Roberto Giraudy facilitated my travel, lodging, and cultural knowledge of that great city. His wife, Ela Lopez Ugarte, one of the world's foremost scholars of José Martí, taught me much about this most famous son of Cuba and his revolutionary compatriots. The dedicated people at the Centro de Estudiantes Martíanos also have my thanks for sharing their outstanding database of information on Martí. The folks at Hotel Inglaterra, Parkview Hotel, Hotel Florida, and the Plaza Hotel are some of the most hospitable people in the world. Many have become my friends, and I can't wait until we have a Havana Reader Rendezvous so the Wakians can meet them in person.

The director of the Museo Nacional Masonico, Justo Orihuela Alvarez, spent two days of his important time to illuminate the astounding role of Freemasons in the independence of Cuba, their perilous lives, their brother Masons among the Spanish, and the great fraternal connections they forged between Cuba and the United States. Every Mason in the world should make the effort to visit the museum, and every Cuban should learn his island's history there. *Un mil gracias, mis amigos.*

Warren McFarland and Don Andrus of the Florida Chapter of the Morse Telegraph Club (www.floridamorse.com) are nineteenth-century telegraphy experts who taught me about the technology. Father Cas Obie helped me understand the sometimes complicated rules and rituals of the Catholic Church in the late nineteenth century.

Writing

And then there are those who helped me actually write the book and work in this difficult profession. Nancy Glickman is well known to my longtime readers as the celestial expert for my novels. She also is my valued critical reader and did yeoman's work on the manuscript. Without her love and help, this story would never have seen the light of day. Shé Hicks is the graphics/format expert for the Honor Series and has produced beautiful imagery for ten novels. Over the last eleven years (and more than a million printed words), the executive editor at Pineapple Press, June Cussen, has taught me far more than she'll ever realize about the writer's craft. She has my lifelong appreciation. Randy Wayne White has been a mentor and friend since the beginning, always ready with sage advice and decent rum. Thanks go to Mike and Renee Maurer for allowing me to hide out and work at their refuge in the Florida Keys.

My Readers

Lastly, but most importantly, I thank my readers around the world. Affectionately known as Wakians, they have provided years of enthusiastic support and have always given me the energy to forge ahead into yet another project.

Thank you all.

Onward and upward,

R.N.M.

For a complete catalog, visit our website at www.pineapplepress.com. Or write to Pineapple Press, P.O. Box 3889, Sarasota, Florida 34230-3889, or call (800) 746-3275.

THE HONOR SERIES

"Sign on early and set sail with Peter Wake for both solid historical context and exciting sea stories."—U.S. Naval Institute Proceedings

At the Edge of Honor. This nationally acclaimed naval Civil War novel, the first in the Honor series of naval fiction, takes the reader into the steamy world of Key West and the Caribbean in 1863 and introduces Peter Wake, the reluctant New England volunteer officer who finds himself battling the enemy on the coasts of Florida, sinister intrigue in Spanish Havana and the British Bahamas, and social taboos in Key West when he falls in love with the daughter of a Confederate zealot.

Point of Honor. Winner of the Florida Historical Society's 2003 Patrick Smith Award for Best Florida Fiction. In this second book in the Honor series, it is 1864 and Lt. Peter Wake, United States Navy, assisted by his indomitable Irish bosun, Sean Rork, commands the naval schooner *St. James.* He searches for army deserters in the Dry Tortugas, finds an old nemesis during a standoff with the French Navy on the coast of Mexico, starts a drunken tavern riot in Key West, and confronts incompetent Federal army officers during an invasion of upper Florida.

Honorable Mention. This third book in the Honor series of naval fiction covers the tumultuous end of the Civil War in Florida and the Caribbean. Lt. Peter Wake is now in command of the steamer USS *Hunt* and quickly plunges into action, chasing a strange vessel during a tropical storm off Cuba, confronting death to liberate an escaping slave ship, and coming face to face with the enemy's most powerful ocean warship in Havana's harbor. Finally, when he tracks down a colony of former Confederates in Puerto Rico, Wake becomes involved in a deadly twist of irony.

A Dishonorable Few. Fourth in the Honor series. It is 1869 and the United States is painfully recovering from the Civil War. Lt. Peter Wake heads to turbulent Central America to deal with a former American naval officer turned renegade mercenary. As the action unfolds in Colombia and Panama, Wake realizes that his most dangerous adversary may be a man on his own ship, forcing Wake to make a decision that will lead to his court-martial in Washington when the mission has finally ended.

An Affair of Honor. Fifth in the Honor series. It's December 1873 and Lt. Peter Wake is the executive officer of the USS *Omaha* on patrol in the West Indies, eager to return home. Fate, however, has other plans. He runs afoul of the Royal Navy in Antigua and then is sent off to Europe, where he finds himself embroiled in a Spanish civil war. But his real test comes when he and Sean Rork are sent on a mission in northern Africa.

A Different Kind of Honor. In this sixth novel in the Honor series, it's 1879 and Lt. Cmdr. Peter Wake, USN, is on assignment as the American naval observer to the War of the Pacific along the west coast of South America. During this mission Wake will witness history's first battle between ocean-going ironclads, ride the world's first deep-diving submarine, face his first machine guns in combat, and run for his life in the Catacombs of the Dead in Lima.

The Honored Dead. Seventh in the series. On what at first appears to be a simple mission for the U.S. president in French Indochina in 1883, naval intelligence officer Lt. Cmdr. Peter Wake encounters opium warlords, Chinese-Malay pirates, and French gangsters.

The Darkest Shade of Honor. Eighth in the series. It's 1886 and Wake, now of the U.S. Navy's Office of Naval Intelligence, meets rising politico Theodore Roosevelt in New York City. Wake is assigned to uncover Cuban revolutionary activities between Florida and Cuba. He meets José Martí, finds himself engulfed in the most catastrophic event in Key West history, and must make a decision involving the very darkest shade of honor.

Honor Bound. Ninth in the series. In 1888 Wake, U.S. Navy intelligence agent, meets a woman from his past who begs him to find her missing son. Wake sets off across Florida, through the Bahamian islands, and deep into the dank jungles of Haiti. Overcoming storms, mutiny, and shipwreck, Wake discovers the hidden lair of an anarchist group planning to wreak havoc around the world—unless he stops it.